THE COURTSHIP of MIRIAM

by
Donna Adee

ACKNOWLEDGMENTS

First I wish to thank God for pushing me to write this book, the sequel to *Miriam's Dilemma*. Also for all those who helped in so many ways to make it all possible.

Ellis, my husband, deserves special thanks for encouraging me to strive towards the goal of finishing the book much sooner than I thought possible. Special thanks also to Ann Gower and Julia Bland, the artists who worked extra hours to finish their art work in time.

Other special people who made the book possible with their editing skills were: Janet Catlin, Erin Bingham, Larissa Barras, Shelly Adee, Wanda Whitesell and Donna Boss. It couldn't have been written without their willingness to find and correct the mistakes.

Carlton and Gladys of the Mitchell County Museum, Peg Luke from Beloit and Jettie from the Ottawa County Museum helped tremendously by providing information on life in 1900-1905.

Also I want to thank Charity of Good Shepherd Publications for all her help with another book. It would not be possible to provide the quality workmanship without her services.

DEDICATION

This book is dedicated to the six sweet Overmiller girls in Beloit, Kansas, who inspired me to write the first book, *Miriam's Dilemma*.

Also I would like to dedicate this book to my 'young' aunt, Florence Coffman Isham who born in 1908. Her memory of details of midwifery and life in the early 1900s is marvelous.

CHAPTER ONE

MRS. POLINSKY— THE TEACHER

MARCHING into Miriam's room, Melody Cramton exclaimed, "You are crazy as a loon to think about going to finishing school back East, Miriam. You know that Mrs. Polinsky said that you were a born nurse and she would teach you to be a midwife." Stomping her foot for emphasis, Melody lifted her long silk skirt and marched out the door.

"Wait, Melody, don't you tell me what to do and walk away without giving me a chance to express my ideas!" Miriam exclaimed as she followed her to the door.

"I can't stay, Jackson is waiting outside to take me to father's office," Melody answered from the door, as she hurried out the door.

Miriam shook her long dark blond hair, trying to force her mind to work after Melody left. *Was Melody right about me having all the makings of a nurse? I know Mrs. Polinsky is getting old and crippled up, but can I travel far out in the country in all kinds of weather and never know when I would be home from delivering a baby? I don't know if I am made of strong enough stuff. At finishing school I could learn music and drama, the finer things in*

1

life. I will talk to Father and Mother tonight and we can pray about this together.

It seemed like years since Miriam Jensen and her family had left their beautiful home in Kansas City and come to Beloit, Mitchell County, Kansas. Her father had left a flourishing business in Kansas City to start a blacksmith shop in the young town of Beloit. Miriam's mother and four sisters had come with her to the home Aaron Jensen had hired built for his family on the edge of town. Elizabeth, her youngest sister had been born in their new home where Lydia, their mother, taught the girls their school lessons and home making.

I remember how I hated leaving Kansas City and all my friends to come to what I thought would be a humdrum dull little town. Was I ever surprised after meeting Melody! On our first day here Mr. Cramton, Melody's father, on his way to work at the Beloit Gazette, almost ran over Anna with his huge black geldings and buggy. Melody was constantly putting me in a dilemma with her rebellious plans. Mother did not like me spending so much time with her because she saw how Melody led me to disobey her and Father. Our whole family did a lot of praying for the Cramton family until one by one they came to know Christ personally. What a change that made in their lives although Melody continues to struggle against trusting her father's care and protection of her. I wonder if she will ever learn? Miriam reminisced.

Sitting down for supper that evening, Miriam looked at her mother and father and said, "Melody was here this afternoon and she shocked me with the statement that I had no business going back East to finishing school since I am a born nurse and should have Mrs. Polinsky train me. Now I don't know what to do. I do love nursing and I know Mrs. Polinsky did say that she would like to train me to deliver babies. Mrs. Polinksy was so patient teaching me how to deliver little Elizabeth should she not be able to arrive in time with the blizzard that was coming. I can't believe that was five years ago; it seems like it was just yesterday that I

2

was holding little Elizabeth as Mrs. Polinsky walked in the door. I remember her saying, 'You have all the makins' of a midwife, young lady.' As much as I love nursing I don't know if I could handle having all that responsibility for a new life alone. What do you both think?"

"Miriam, you have proved yourself an excellent nurse often here in our family. God has gifted you with the ability to care for the sick with gentleness and confidence. Why not talk to Mrs. Polinsky and see if she is still interested in training you. She may have found some other young lady to train by now."

Emma, who was seven, piped up, "You mean you would deliver babies all by yourself, Miriam? That sounds exciting. Could I go with you? I just love new babies."

"Just a minute, Emma," Aaron reminded, "This is more serious than just delivering babies. Miriam needs to be able to drive a buggy to the farms by herself since I can't take her while I am at the shop. Also Miriam, it will mean middle of the night trips and traveling in weather like the blizzard that Elizabeth chose to arrive in. Another thing to consider is that sometimes even your best efforts can not save the life of the mother or the baby. Can you handle that, Miriam? You are a very capable daughter who can do most any household and nursing task that your mother asks, however this is a heavy responsibility. We need to pray about this before we give our approval."

"Oh yes, Father, that is why I asked all of you tonight so you could pray with me. Also I need to talk to Mrs. Polinsky and learn how to drive a buggy. It overwhelms me now. Will you pray with me?"

They prayed around the table. When it was five-year-old Elizabeth's turn she said. "Dear God, don't let Mirry get stuck in no blizzard and help her take care of all the babies."

Later that night, Miriam lay awake, restless as Melody's advice kept playing over and over in her mind. Finally, instead of worrying and fretting all night she decided to lay her concerns in her heavenly Father's hands. *Heavenly Father, show me what You want me to do. There is so much to learn. I've never driven a buggy. I don't know where the farms are located and the only baby I have delivered is little Elizabeth.* Finally she was able to drift off to sleep.

Aaron had gone to the blacksmith shop the next morning before any of the family was out of bed. "I wonder why your father left so early. He ate a cold breakfast unless he found some bacon to fry and I don't see any sign of that. There must be a special reason for him to leave so early," Lydia told the girls around the breakfast table.

The whole day seemed to drag for Miriam, "I wish Father would hurry home. I want to know what he thinks of me learning to be a midwife," she told her mother at noon. However, Aaron didn't come at noon for dinner. "Could I take him some of this fried chicken, Mother? He must be starved."

"You may take him some chicken, although he may have been given some food in trade for some smithing job. This is the apple and grape harvest time so they may have given him some of their produce. You know when he is busy, he sometimes forgets to eat," Lydia reminded.

"I know, Mother, and I am worried about him not eating breakfast or dinner. He can't be that busy. I'll take him a nice lunch and see if I can tempt him to eat," Miriam said as she hurried to take off her apron and brush her hair into a bun. She slipped on her hat and reached for her parasol.

Walking briskly along the dirt street, Miriam met Thomas Cramton in his buggy pulled by beautiful black geldings. He doffed his hat in a friendly fashion and hurried on. *Wonder why he isn't at the Gazette office? The paper will be going to print tonight. Why would he be coming from the blacksmith shop at this time of day?* Miriam mused.

Aaron was hard at work sharpening plow shares and did not hear Miriam come into the stifling heat of the shop. Miriam could see sweat pouring off his brow and that his shirt was soaked with sweat. She walked to where he could see her and said loudly, "Papa, I brought you some dinner. I was afraid that you would not stop to eat since you did not come home."

"Oh, Miriam, I didn't hear you come in. I ate some apples from a bushel a farmer traded me for some work, however I sure could use some of that fried chicken. Let's sit outside where it is a little cooler and I'll tell you what I found out this morning. Then you will know why I left so early. I was going to wait until this evening to tell the whole family, although since it concerns you, you might as well be the first to know."

Miriam anxiously waited to hear the news, but Aaron took his time eating his chicken, "I suppose you saw Thomas leaving as you came."

"Yes, does he have something to do with what you were going to tell me?" Miriam asked excitedly. "He seemed in a hurry. Was there some reason for that?"

"He stopped this morning to talk about the Bible study he is planning to have in his home this fall. I told him about your plans to be a midwife and needing some way to travel to the farms or to Mrs. Polinsky's home," Aaron began.

"What could Mr. Cramton do about that? Does he have an extra horse and buggy I could use?" Miriam interrupted.

"Slow down. Give me time to tell. He said that he had a buggy to which we could harness a gentle mare for you to drive. He assured me that you could drive it, as Melody has driven it some. Before he came, a farmer was here saying that he had a gentle mare that he wanted to sell or trade for work on his wagon. I asked him if we could look at her this evening and he said that would be all right with him."

"Oh, Papa, that is wonderful! I never dreamed my prayer would be answered so quickly," Miriam exclaimed.

"Remember this is only one part of the answer. We haven't talked to Mrs. Polinsky yet," Aaron cautioned.

"She will agree, I just know she will! I can't wait to go talk to her. Can we stop at her farm tonight after we see the mare?" Miriam begged.

"I doubt if there will be time for that tonight as the Johnstons live way out in the country. It will be dark by the time we get back. If this mare is the right one, we can take a practice trip with the buggy tomorrow and visit Mrs. Polinsky."

Miriam wanted to hurry back to tell her mother and sisters. Lifting her long skirt, she ran, calling over her shoulder, "I can't wait to tell Mother. Thank you for telling me, Papa."

Bursting in the door at home, she called to her mother breathlessly, "Papa found me a horse and buggy. We are going to see the horse tonight. I can't believe my prayer was answered so quickly."

Hugging her oldest, Lydia said, "I'm not sure that I'm ready for you to be driving all over the country delivering babies. I'll probably lie awake nights waiting for you to come home."

"And I probably won't get any sleep either with you leaving and coming home at all hours of the day and night," fifteen year old Anna added.

"You sleep so soundly a tornado couldn't wake you. You didn't hear Elizabeth crying with a sore throat last night. The rest of the family was awake. You won't even know when I leave," Miriam chuckled.

Following supper, Aaron and Miriam left in their buggy. On the way to the Johnstons, Miriam asked, "How will I find all these farms? I only know where three or four families live."

"From what I hear from the farmers, most come after Mrs. Polinsky and if she has to come back out again she remembers the way. I'm sure they'll do the same for you. We'll work that out as the time comes."

Miriam fell in love with the gentle little mare at the Johnstons. "Her name is Ginger and she will come to your call. Our grandkids used to ride her until they moved to Iowa, so we don't need her anymore," Mr. Johnston reported.

Traveling home with Ginger tied behind the buggy, Miriam asked, "Can we take Ginger to the Cramton's tonight to bring home the buggy?"

"No, Miriam, it will be dark and Ginger needs to be fed and watered and introduced to her new family. There will be plenty of time for that tomorrow."

"You have to work tomorrow. Will you have time to teach me how to drive after work so we can drive out to Mrs. Polinsky's?" Miriam protested.

"Rome wasn't built in a day, Miriam. One-step-at-a-time. You must have patience."

Aaron was gone the next morning before breakfast again. "Your father left even earlier this morning. I was up early, however he had already gone," Lydia commented with a faint smile.

"Is there something you're not telling me, Mother?" Miriam quizzed.

Anna burst in from feeding the animals and said, "I thought your new horse was in the barn; she isn't there now. Do you suppose she got out?"

"Now I think I know where father is," Miriam exclaimed. "He's over at the Cramton's getting the buggy. He knew I was anxious to learn to drive it. Maybe he wants to give me lessons! I had better get dressed and help with the dishes before he returns," Miriam called as she ran to the bedroom.

She had just finished the dishes and was hanging the dishtowel out to dry when Aaron arrived with Ginger pulling the buggy. "Oh Papa, Ginger looks even better than last night. Can I drive her drive now?"

"I stopped by the shop and told Robert and Matthew what work to start on and that I would be back later," Aaron reported.

"That is wonderful of you, Father. However, I am afraid I will not be able to handle the buggy," Miriam moaned.

"Let me help you into the buggy and we will practice. Did

you tell your mother where we were going?"

"Yes, in fact, she seemed to know you were planning this. She wasn't surprised that you were gone before breakfast this morning."

"Fine, let's get started. Here are the reins. Ginger is a gentle horse and she is used to being out on the road. Mr. Johnston said that she won't spook if we meet one of those noisy Overlands (car). You do not have to hold the reins tightly, give her a little slack. She responds with a gentle tug on either rein. Try it on the next corner," Aaron instructed.

After they had driven around town, Miriam began to relax a little. "I think I am ready to drive out to the Polinsky farm now. Would that be all right with you?" Miriam requested.

"Well, if you think you are ready for driving out in the country, I suppose you can try it."

Once out of town, Ginger seemed to sense that it was time for a little more speed. "Hold her back some, Miriam. That looks like Mr. Thompson coming with his high stepping bays. He thinks he owns the road. Keep close to the side of the road and keep a firm grip on the reins," Aaron instructed.

"Mr. Thompson is taking up the whole road! Where can I go?" Miriam cried.

"Here give me the reins. We may have to take the ditch. Easy there, Ginger," Aaron called. Mr. Thompson's bays were almost on top of them. Aaron jerked on the reins, violently pulling them into the ditch as Mr. Thompson roared by with a huge smile on his face.

"Father, we're tipping over!" Miriam screamed. Miriam fell into the ditch while Aaron held on to the buggy as Ginger came to a stop. The reins and harness were all tangled. Pulling himself loose from the buggy, Aaron helped Miriam to her feet. "Let's see if we can untangle the harness. Ginger doesn't seem to be hurt. I hope that the buggy has not been damaged."

"We could've been killed by that wild man and his horses,

Father. He didn't even stop to see if we'd been hurt," Miriam grumbled as she rubbed the scraped place on her cheek.

"God protected us. Mr. Johnston was correct in saying that Ginger would not spook . If she had, we could have been very badly hurt."

Untangling the harness and checking over the buggy, Aaron announced, "That is a well-made buggy. I've seen some that would be in splinters after an accident like this. It will serve you well as you travel. One thing you must keep in mind is that a buggy will tip over," Aaron instructed.

They, at last, were able to drive on to the Polinsky farm. "Whoa, Ginger," Miriam called as she pulled back on the reins.

Mrs. Polinsky was out in the garden as they drove up. Shuffling her heavy frame over to the buggy she greeted them, "What brings you two out to visit at this time of the mornin? Don't you have a bunch of impatient farmers waitin' in line for some plowshares or something?" Mrs. Polinsky asked, pulling her bonnet back a little.

"My daughter is learning to drive a buggy, however we got more than we bargained for this morning. Mr. Thompson and his bays ran us off the road," Aaron answered.

"Yes, that old coot drives like the devil was after him. Don't know why he can't drive like a sane person. Nearly ran me and the mister off the road last week as we delivered cream to the creamery. He pert made us dump the whole thing. Ifen I had not grabbed it quick, it all would have dumped out," Mrs. Polinsky announced.

Miriam interrupted the story, "A - a - a Mrs. Polinsky, I - I - a - came out to ask if you are still willing to have me work with you and learn to deliver babies. Were you serious when you told me after Elizabeth's birth that you could train me? Are you still looking for someone to help you?" Miriam spoke hesitantly, afraid that Mrs. Polinksy might turn her down.

"I shore do need help, but do you know what you're getting into, young lady? Some nights I don't get home at all. My mister don't like it none havin' me gone overnight but sometimes those babies take their time appearin'. I know you would be good at nursing. Saw that when you delivered your little sister. What do you think, Aaron? Are you really sure you want your daughter taking on this difficult work with the atrocious hours? I love helpin' mothers and babies. Most of them won't hear of having the doc," Mrs. Polinsky chirped forcefully as her bonnet bounced up and down.

Aaron interrupted, "Would it be a problem for her to accompany you on some of your trips? We don't want to impose on your busy schedule."

"Don't worry about that none. This daughter of yours is a worker if I ever saw one. Me and her will get along just fine. Me bones are hurtin' more each year so I shore could use her help. By the way, I need to go to the Larsen farm tomorrow. Miz Larsen is due any day. Want to go along, Miriam?"

"I would love to, Mrs. Polinksy. Do you think I could drive Ginger out to the Larsen place, Father?" Miriam looked at her father eagerly.

"You aren't ready for a trip like that yet, Miriam. I'd rather that you ride with Mrs. Polinsky this time."

"Then could I drive Ginger out here so Mrs. Polinsky wouldn't have to come into town for me?"Miriam begged.

"My old man will be glad that I have someone with me. His rheumatism is bothering him the beatinest. He just hates to get up and down in that buggy any more than necessary. Why don't you come out here about two o'clock."

The ride back to town was uneventful. It was almost noon and Lydia and Anna had just set a large beef roast on the table with bowls of potatoes and carrots from the garden. "I knew you two would be starved since Aaron didn't eat breakfast and you rushed through yours, Miriam," Lydia said cheerfully.

"You won't believe what happened to us on the way to the

Polinsky farm this morning, Mother. After Father prays, we will tell you about. You must have been praying for us 'cause we could have been badly hurt," Miriam said quietly.

"You always have all the excitement, Miriam!" Emma exclaimed after hearing the story of their accident. "Why can't you take me with you?"

"After Miriam becomes more confident in her driving, your mother and I may allow you to ride with her around town," Aaron announced.

"Mother, would you mind if I go with Mrs. Polinsky this afternoon? She said that Mrs. Larsen's baby is due any day and she sent Mr. Larsen in to request that she come out today."

"I was planning on having you bake bread this afternoon, however maybe you can help Anna start it and she can finish after you leave," Lydia answered.

"I thought Anna had planned to do it any way. It is her turn," Miriam reminded.

"She had planned to, but Jesse and Emma were churning butter out on the porch and ended up in an argument and spilled cream all over the porch. Anna had to clean up the mess. I should know better than to put those two working together."

Miriam laughed, "It would probably be safer to put one in the garden and the other in the house. It seems like any time they are together, they start something. Aren't you thankful that Anna and I never were like that?"

"You must have forgotten some of your early childhood. Learning to get along with your siblings is great training for life," Lydia reminded.

Miriam hurried through the bread mixing and had it almost ready for the last rise when Aaron called that he had Ginger harnessed. "Are you ready, Miriam? I have to get to the shop. Matthew and Robert may need help. Remember to be careful. Have Mr. Polinsky unharness Ginger and show you where to put her while you are gone," Aaron said.

11

"Pray that I won't meet Mr. Thompson again, Father. From what I hear, he comes to town quite often."

The trees were showing a touch of fall, the cottonwoods in yellow and oaks dropping acorns while the maples were turning flaming red. Sunflowers lined the road like soldiers standing at attention. "I love this time of year," Miriam said to Ginger as they traveled along. "Even the air smells like pumpkin pies and apple cider."

Farmers in the fields shocking corn, waved to Miriam as she drove along. Crows were cawing loudly from their fence post roosts. "Bet they are arguing over which corn field they will feed on next," Miriam confided to Ginger.

Mrs. Polinsky, in her faded blue dress, was sitting in her rocking chair on the porch. "I always wear this dress to deliver babies. I call it my good luck dress. Don't want nothin' to happen to my babies if I can help it," Mrs. Polinsky said as she came out to help Miriam unharness Ginger. "Here comes the mister with the buggy. He'll take Ginger for you. Just hop in and we'll be off."

"I asked Father to pray for us as we drive out to the Larsen farm. Don't you think God can protect everyone better than a good luck dress?" Miriam asked.

"You may be right about that. I never go to church much. Oh, I believe there is a God, but my old man has no use for church so we never got started goin'. Guess we should, however we're getin' too old and crippled up to drive into town any more than we have to for delivering cream and gettin' a few supplies."

"I'm so sorry that you don't go to church, Mrs. Polinksy. I can't imagine Sunday without going. I love the singing and preaching and seeing friends. There is so much to learn from the Bible," Miriam said gently.

Changing the subject, Mrs. Polinsky said, "The Larsens live two miles south and back west down a long lane. Can't even see their house from the road. Mighty purty place for the house with all those maple and oak trees. This has been a most beautiful fall with all the rain in August. I remember some autumns where the trees never turned from being so dry and the grass so dry that prairie fires would start and burn many acres."

"I hope I never see one of those prairie fires. Father says they roar through so fast that some people don't have time to move their livestock out of danger. That would be terrible."

"Say, how is your friend, Melody Cramton? I saw her in the Gazette office the other day when I renewed my subscription, she was so busy talkin' to that young banker feller. She never even noticed me awaitin' there wanting to pay my bill. She only had eyes for that young feller. One of the other workers came to help me. Wonder if her father knows she isn't tending to business?" Mrs Polinsky announced.

"Was she talking to Charles Evans? Melody usually tends to business better than that. She knows that Mr. Evans never goes to church so I don't know why she'd even show interest in him. She knows her father would not give permission for Mr. Evans to court her. I'll call her after we return. Maybe I can talk some sense into her head."

"Don't tell her that I told you this. I don't want to be known as a gossip. It sure didn't look good to me. Her father should know better than to let a spoiled daughter like her be at the front desk, however I never raised any children so I don't suppose I have any call stickin' my nose into their business," said Mrs. Polinsky.

Once they reached the Larsen place, Miriam immediately noticed how neat and well kept it was. All the buildings were whitewashed and the fence and corrals were sturdy and well built.

"That there is Timothy Larsen in the corral. He is the oldest of their three boys. He's a mighty nice young feller. He helped me the last time I delivered a baby for his mother. This one will be their seventh child."

Tim Larsen hurried to open the gate and was beside the

buggy to help Miriam and Mrs. Polinsky down, "I'll take care of the horses, Mrs. Polinsky. Just go right on in. Ma is waiting for you."

"Timothy, this here young lady is Miss Miriam Jensen. She is one of the Jensen girls and my helper," Mrs. Polinsky said as Timothy helped her down.

"Pleased to meet you, Miss Jensen. I believe I have seen you in church," Timothy responded.

Miriam turned to look into the bluest eyes she had ever seen. Blushing she murmured, "Th-thank you, Mr. Larsen." As Timothy helped her down from the buggy, she noticed how strong he was as well as being very much a gentleman. She hoped he didn't notice her red face. Hurrying to catch up with Mrs. Polinsky, Miriam wished she wouldn't get so flustered.

Entering the kitchen, they found a young girl cooking at the stove. "Hello, Esther, this here is Miriam Jensen. She'll be helping me with delivering your brother or sister. Is your mother in the bedroom?" Mrs. Polinsky said as the shuffled off to a side room. Miriam followed after a quick hello to Esther, who must have been almost twelve.

Greeting Mrs. Larsen, Mrs Polinsky walked to her bedside. "I brung me a helper today, Martha. She wants to learn about this here birthin' process. I want you to meet Miriam Jensen, Aaron and Lydia's oldest."

"Glad to meet you, Miriam. I'm sure that I have seen you at church, although I've never had the pleasure of meeting you. With our large family we always seem to be rushed out after church. You will learn much from Ruth. She is the best midwife around here. This will be the third baby she has delivered for our family," Martha responded sweetly, warming Miriam to her immediately.

"So you think that little one is about to make his appearance, Martha?"

"I'm almost positive. Yesterday I felt like a mother bird

wanting to build my nest. I wanted to clean and wash everything in sight. Just about wore poor Esther out trying to keep up with all my projects. Today I am so limp and tired. That is usually a sign these little ones are ready to arrive unless I miss my guess," Martha said weakly.

"Well, let me have a check and I'll tell you how soon. Hmm-m-m. Yes, you are correct. That little guy should be here about midnight unless he goes to sleep on the job," Mrs. Polinsky reported. "Send Paul or one of the boys after me when you think things are really moving. Do you want to be in on this one, Miriam? If you do we can come for you also."

"I will have to ask Father if he wants me to be gone tonight. This is all so new that we're still working out the details. Father only gave me permission for this afternoon."

"We have a telephone so you could call here after asking your parents, then Paul would know to pick you up also. I know Mrs. Polinsky doesn't have a telephone. The men need to get the poles up so she can be on the party line too. It may not work real well, however it is better than taking the buggy out to contact someone. I hate getting you both out in the middle of the night, but the others were born at night so don't suppose this one will be any different," Martha said quietly.

"Babies and death don't wait for no one. We're not in charge of that timin'. They happens when they happen," Mrs. Polinsky chuckled

"Paul is having neighbors in tomorrow to help finish shocking corn so I hate to keep him up all night. However, as you say, we don't choose when a baby decides to arrive. Would you mind if my Esther helped you tonight? She has shown a real interest in this baby and learning about delivering babies. She is such good help with her little brother and sister," Martha mentioned.

"Wouldn't mind one bit. We might need an extra hand to keep the hot water ready and find the baby clothes. You know

Miriam Jensen and Mrs. Polinsky out to deliver a baby.

these men aren't much help along that line," Mrs. Polinsky answered.

Miriam couldn't wait to arrive home to tell her mother the news. The minute she had Ginger in the barn she came into the kitchen to the smells of supper cooking and announced, "Mrs. Polinsky asked me to go with her to help deliver Mrs. Larsen's baby tonight. This will be her seventh."

"I know Martha Larsen. She is a very sweet Christian and her husband and those sons of hers are such gentlemen," Lydia responded. "How will you get to the Larsens? Your father will not allow you to drive to the Polinsky's after dark."

"I know, Mother. Paul Larsen will come for us as the time gets closer. I am to call the Larsens since they are on the party line. Then they will know to pick me up, too. I'm so excited! I didn't think I would be helping deliver a baby so soon. I won't be able to sleep all night. Melody was correct that I should be a nurse. I guess I've known that ever since I helped Elizabeth to arrive."

After calling the Larsens, Miriam went to bed right after supper. Keeping her clothes on and laying her coat and hat near the door she tried to get some rest. Anna came to bed later and found Miriam still wide awake. "Are you still awake? You are going to be all wrinkled by sleeping in your clothes. A proper nurse should not look like she slept in her clothes," Anna teased.

"Go to sleep before I sit on you. What do you know about being a nurse? Those babies and their mothers aren't going to notice if our dresses are freshly pressed," Miriam chided.

Miriam lay there thinking about what Mrs. Polinsky had told her about Melody. She had almost forgotten in the excitement. *O dear God, be with Melody. Open her eyes to see that Charles is not a Christian. Show me if I should talk to her.* With that prayer Miriam dozed off.

It seemed like she had just drifted off when she heard a sharp knock on the door. Waking with a start, she jumped to her feet and ran to the door. Opening it, she found Mr. Larsen.

"I'll be right out, Mr. Larsen. Give me a minute to put on my shoes and coat and hat."

She quickly grabbed her shoes and quietly went to wake her mother to tell her she was leaving. Slipping out quietly she closed the door to find a beautiful moonlight night. "What a beautiful night to be born, don't you think Mr. Larsen? It is so light you could almost read a book. Is this what the farmers call harvest moon?"

Helping her into the buggy, Mr. Larsen answered, "It is indeed beautiful, Miriam, however I would rather be sleeping so I can be ready for that crew of corn shockers arriving at six in the morning. I never could figure why babies wait to come in the middle of the night so that no one gets a decent night's rest. I wonder if they do that on purpose."

Stopping by the Polinsky farm, Miriam jumped down to knock lightly on the door. She knew that Mrs. Polinsky would be awake and ready. "You look mighty perky for not having much sleep, Miriam. Maybe it's the beautiful moonlight that makes us all look better. Hello, Paul, how is Martha doing?"

"Well, the baby hadn't arrived when she woke me and told me to go for you. She and Esther didn't have time to finish picking the fall apples or bring in all the late garden pumpkins and squash. That means the boys and I will have to do it next week 'cause Esther will be busy helping Martha with the little ones. Don't know why babies can't pick a more opportune time to arrive," Mr. Larsen grumbled.

"Oh, you will forget all about the lack of sleep when you see another boy added to your farm crew," Mrs. Polinsky joked. "There is something about a new baby to soften up any disgruntled father."

"I really do enjoy children, Ruth. It's just that Martha had so many fall jobs to finish up and she isn't going to be able to do them for a few weeks. Winter can arrive early so the crops need to be all in. The good Lord has blessed us with a bountiful crop so we must take care of it both for us and for the livestock."

Mr. Larsen helped Miriam and Mrs. Polinsky down and took the horses to the barn. Through the window, Miriam could see Esther was up and heating water on the stove. Turning around as they came in the door, Esther said, "I'm so glad you are here. Mama keeps asking if you have arrived. I've got three pots of water heated. Is that enough? And I found the baby gowns, blankets, and diapers. Is there anything else you need, Mrs. Polinsky?"

"You've done a great job, Esther. Miriam will help you bring in some hot water and a basin while I check on your mama. That baby may be arrivin' while we're standin' here jawin'." With that she shuffled off towards the bedroom, "I'm a comin', Martha. My crew is bringin' the supples. We'll have that youngin' here in no time."

The girls had just stepped into the room with the water and basin when Mrs Polinsky announced, "Looks like Mr. Larsen has another farmer. He sure was impatient to arrive. Hardly let me get my coat off. Here you go, girls. Clean him up and dress him while I help Martha. That was your easiest delivery yet wasn't it?"

Mr. Larsen called from the kitchen, "Would someone tell me if I have a farmer or a farmer daughter so I can go to bed?"

Esther went to the door and said, "You have a farmer, Papa, and I get to name him."

"Tell me in the morning; I'm going to bed."

Miriam laid the screaming baby on the end of the bed on a blanket and began to wash him with soft cloth and warm water. "There, there little one. We'll soon have you wrapped up and cuddled up with your mother. Look at those tiny perfect fingers, Esther. Do you want to help bathe him?"

"Mama said that I could pick his name since my brothers picked the names of the last two. I want to call him Isaac after my grandpa who died last year," Esther said shyly as she helped

Miriam slip the baby's arms into his gown. Baby Isaac started screaming louder as Esther pulled his gown over his head. "What did I do wrong, Miriam?"

"You didn't do anything wrong. He just misses the warm home that he has been living in the last nine months. It is kind of a shock being thrust suddenly into the cold cruel world. The sooner we get him back to your mother, the happier he will be."

"Bet he wants some warm milk to warm up his tummy. Our little kittens sure like it when the mother cat comes around," Esther said. "You really seem to know how to take care of babies. I'm learning more all the time."

"I've had a lot of practice with my little sisters. Did you know that I delivered my youngest sister during a blizzard because Mrs. Polinsky was late in arriving? Maybe I will have a dozen of my own," Miriam said, blushing slightly at the thought of being married someday.

"After cleaning up the bedroom and kitchen, Miriam and Mrs. Polinsky were surprised to find Timothy sitting at the table, ready to take them home. He explained, "Father woke me up and told me to be ready to take you home. It's wonderful to have another little brother. God has given me so many brothers and sisters and I'm thankful for each one."

"Well, we're ready to go if you are, young man. Morning is going to come much too soon. I'm ready to hit the hay, aren't you, Miriam?"

Miriam glanced over at Timothy and saw those brilliant blue eyes watching her. She looked away quickly. She was sure he could see her blush even in the dim light of the kerosene lamp. She followed Mrs. Polinsky outdoors and Timothy helped them into the buggy that he had waiting at the front gate.

Out on the road, Miriam asked, "Could you take me home first, Mr. Larsen? It wouldn't be proper for us to be riding alone."

"Please call me Timothy. Yes, I can take you home first if

Mrs. Polinsky doesn't mind riding a little further."

"No problem for me young man. It's a beautiful night and I'm still wide awake. We wouldn't want to give any cause for people to talk, would we?" Mrs. Polinsky answered.

Timothy helped Miriam down from the buggy once they were in her yard. "Thank you, Miss Jensen, for helping deliver my baby brother. May you have a good night's rest."

Miriam let herself in quietly and found her mother sitting up at the table. "Mother, you didn't have to stay up for me, however I'm glad you are awake so I can tell you how wonderful it was to deliver Mrs. Larsen's little boy. I feel like a special helper for God by delivering this tiny baby, a new creation of His. It is so miraculous. I don't know if I can sleep after all the excitement."

Once in bed, Miriam felt exhausted. *Thank you, Lord, for your protection of little Isaac.* That was the last thing she remembered until she felt someone shaking her awake.'

"Wake up, Miriam. Melody is here," Anna said.

"What time is it? I feel like I just got to sleep," Miriam answered.

"It is after ten o'clock. What time did you get home?" Anna asked in concern.

"I don't know for sure, I think it was near three o'clock. It was all so exciting. What did you say about Melody being here?" Miriam asked.

"I said that she is in the kitchen asking to see you. Do you want me to tell her to come back later?" Anna asked.

"No, tell her I will be out in a few minutes. Bring me some water for the wash basin so I can wash my face."

"There is some warm water on the back of the stove. I'll get you some. Your breakfast is waiting also in the warming oven," Anna said.

Anna came in with some warm water and poured it in the basin. Do you want me to get out your clothes? You seem more asleep than awake."

"Would you see if you can find something for me to wear? That would help so much, I can't seem to wake up," Miriam said.

"I wish I could go with you sometime, Miriam. It all sounds so exciting," Anna said.

"Maybe you can sometime. Mrs. Polinsky told me that deliveries don't always go so perfectly as they did tonight. Go tell Melody that I am almost dressed so she won't leave."

"She does seem to be in a hurry. She is all dressed up like she has plans to go somewhere," Anna reported.

Miriam hurriedly finished dressing and brushed out her hair. A glance in the mirror showed her that she looked like she had been up all night. She hurried out to find Melody dressed in a beautiful pale green brocade dress with a matching hat and cape. "Are you going somewhere special this morning, Melody? That is an exquisite dress," Miriam asked.

"Father has asked me to work full-time at the front desk at the Gazette. I wanted you to be the first to know. I am so excited, I just love visiting with all those who come into the office. Father said that he could trust me more than anyone take care of things properly," Melody answered with a large smile.

"What about your plans to go on with your music training at the finishing school in Boston? What happened to those plans?"

"I don't have any desire for music training now. I want to learn more about running the office. I might need to run it someday. You know I have always worked with Father part-time, however now it will be full-time. I will get to write some of the news items and take orders from all who come in. I love that kind of work," Melody gushed.

"Do you have any time that I could talk to you in private sometime soon? Would you have an afternoon free sometime?" Miriam asked.

"Maybe after the paper comes out tomorrow, I can take off an extra long noon hour. Why don't you meet me at the Ice

Cream Palace at noon. I must run, Jackson is waiting outside to take me to work. I'll see you tomorrow. Oh, I almost forgot, how did you get along delivering your first baby? Your mother was telling me you were all excited when you came home. I probably would have fainted dead away. I can't stand the sight of blood. You can tell me all about it tomorrow," Melody waved a gloved hand as she eased out the door.

"I think Melody has a new dress every time I see her," Anna stated. "Her father may be rich, but what does she do with all those dresses? Doesn't she ever wear the same one twice?"

"That was an unusually expensive one to work in the Gazette office. It would be so easy to ruin it while working on the paper. She seems to be dressing very elaborately for a working girl. When a girl dresses like that, you wonder if she is dressing for someone special," Lydia commented.

"That is why I plan to talk to her tomorrow. Mrs. Polinsky saw her talking to Charles Evans and she was concerned. Surely Mr. Cramton would not allow her to spend time with him. I'm very worried about her, Mother. I don't know if she will listen to me."

CHAPTER TWO

MELODY'S CHOICE

THE NEXT DAY, Miriam ironed her most attractive blue calico, brushed her hair up, and held it with several combs. "Would you help me, Anna? I must look nice to meet Melody at noon. I am thankful I found this new straw hat to match and that I have this blue parasol. I wouldn't want to embarrass Melody," Miriam said apprehensively.

"You don't need to worry about that, Miriam. Your disposition far outshines Melody's expensive clothes. Did you say that you were eating at the Ice Cream Palace? From what I hear about Melody from my friends, she doesn't eat there anymore."

"All I know is that she said to meet her at the Ice Cream Palace. She has changed so much I don't know what to expect."

Walking out to the kitchen where her mother was baking pies, Miriam spun around and asked, "How do I look? Will Melody approve of my outfit, Mother?"

"You look like the daughter of a rich man. I am so proud of you being able to sew beautiful clothes and to find accessories on sale. Melody won't be ashamed of you I'm sure. Most importantly you have the sweet personality to match," Lydia assured her.

"Did I hear you say that Charles Evans comes to the Gazette office to visit with Melody?" Anna asked.

"All I know is what Mrs. Polinsky told me and she said that Mr. Evans has her full attention when he comes in. That's what I plan to talk to her about if she will allow me to do so. Pray that she will be open to talk about this Mr. Evans and her relationship with him. We never see any of his family in church and from what I hear, they do not attend church anywhere. It worries me so that Melody has become interested in someone who has no use for church," Miriam said.

"Melody has always had trouble in trusting her parents or God to do what is best for her. Do you remember how concerned you were when you heard that she had whooping cough and might not live?" Lydia asked.

"I rushed over to her home hoping there was some way I could help her see that she needed Jesus as her Savior. She was so afraid of dying, that the minute I shared with her about Jesus dying for her sins, she was ready to accept Him. She wanted to be sure she would go to heaven if she died. I was so happy that she prayed to receive Him that I ran all the way home to tell you. I just wish she were that excited to obey God now. I don't think she enjoys being with me anymore. She prefers her new friends from the Opera House."

"She still needs you as a friend, Miriam. Don't forget that, and remember that God will give you just the right words to share with her. I'll be praying as you talk to her. You may be able to stop her from making a serious mistake."

"I know what she needs, Mother. However, anything I share may just aggravate her and she won't speak to me again."

"Jackson's coming, Miriam," Emma called from the front porch where she was snapping the last of the fall green beans from the garden.

Always a gentleman, Jackson was standing beside the carriage. "Let me help you up, Miss Jensen. That sure is a beautiful dress. You look very nice, young lady," he spoke admiringly.

"Thank you, Jackson. It is wonderful of you to say so. You

are used to Melody wearing all those beautiful dresses, so I consider it a real compliment for you to notice my dress."

"I haven't seen much of Melody lately. That young fellow of hers takes her everywhere. She hasn't spoken to me for ages," Jackson said sadly.

"How is your health? It has been such a long time since you've driven me anywhere or that I've heard how you were doing."

"I'm getting older and sure don't like the cold weather driving anymore. My rheumatism makes it so difficult to shovel snow and be out in the cold. Mr. Cramton just hired a young fellow that I recommended, for me to train for the winter work. Now the summer driving and garden work I can do. I love the garden and don't want anyone messing with that."

"I remember those beautiful roses and other flowers you raised. If I ever get married, that would be a wonderful place for a wedding," Miriam stated.

"You planning to marry anytime soon? I hadn't heard that you had anyone courting you," Jackson commented with a smile.

"Oh no, there is no one courting me. I was just saying that your garden at the Cramtons would be a beautiful place for a wedding. You can let me off at the Gazette office. I am a little early so I will just wait for Melody in the lobby. You don't need to come back for me. It is a nice day for a walk home. Thank you, Jackson, for driving me down here to the Gazette office. It has been so good to see you again." The old man smiled at her appreciation for his services.

Miriam walked into the office quietly. There was no one at the front desk so she assumed they were all busy. Finding some back issues of the Gazette on a table in a dark corner of the room, she soon became so engrossed in reading the news of Beloit, that she didn't notice a young man come in and stand at the counter. Melody came hurrying out of the back room. "Oh Charles. I'm so glad to see you."

"How is my favorite girl today?" Mr. Evans said as he

26

reached for her hand.

"I won't be eating lunch with you today, Charles. I'm meeting a friend for lunch," Melody said, blinking her large brown eyes at him.

"You are? And with whom, may I ask, are you eating? You know that we have a standing arrangement for lunch," Mr. Evans insisted.

"Oh, it's just a friend," Melody said secretively.

"Come on and tell me. You know I have a right to know who you spend time with," Charles begged.

"Oh all right, it is Miriam Jensen. She and I have been friends since we were young girls. There, do you feel better?"

"I suppose, but don't forget that you are going with me to the Opera House tonight. Be ready on time because I'll be picking you up right after your parents leave. And I want to arrive early so we will have our choice of seats in the balcony."

"I won't forget. You can pick me up before seven o'clock because my parents are leaving at 6:30."

Charles started to leave just as Miriam felt she should make her presence known. She was almost to the counter before Melody looked up in surprise. Jerking her hand from Charles' grasp she exclaimed, "Miriam, when did you arrive? I didn't know you were here."

"I was a few minutes early and didn't see you, so supposed you were busy. I was so engrossed in reading the Gazette that I lost track of time. Are you going to introduce me to this gentleman?" Miriam asked.

"This is Charles Evans. He is a friend of mine," Melody said nervously.

"How long have you lived here, Mr. Evans?" Miriam asked pleasantly.

"Our family purchased the bank just last year. I am vice president and as soon as my father retires, I will be president. I really must be getting back to work. Pleased to meet you, Miss

Jensen," Charles said as he rushed out the door.

Immediately changing the subject, Melody said, "Let me find my cape and hat. I will tell Father that you are eating lunch with me and that I may be back a little later than usual."

As they walked out together, Melody commented, "That blue dress and hat look wonderful on you, Miriam. You always did look good in blue."

"Thank you, Melody. The dark pink silk looks gorgeous on you. How do you ever find parasols to match exactly?"

"You mean this old thing? I purchased it in Kansas City last year and they always make matching parasols," Melody answered indifferently.

"Are you still planning to eat at the Ice Cream Palace or did you have something else in mind?"

"Let's eat at the hotel dining room. I'm hungry for some good food," Melody answered.

Miriam had never been in the hotel before. It was decorated in rich burgundy drapes and crystal chandeliers. The tables were covered with beautiful linen and matching napkins. She knew this would be an expensive meal.

The headwaiter met them at the door. "Will it be your usual table, Miss Jensen?"

Looking slightly embarrassed, Melody answered quickly, "Yes, that will be fine."

The waiter led them to a corner table behind some large potted plants. "How did the waiter know your name, Melody? Do you come in here often?"

"Mr. Evans brings me here almost every noon," Melody whispered confidentially.

"Melody does your father approve of this Mr. Evans courting you?"

"He isn't courting me. I haven't told my father about Mr. Evans. We are just good friends. He meets me here for lunch, so Father doesn't know about it."

"Why hasn't Mr. Evans asked your father if he can court you? Don't you want your parents' approval and God's blessing? This relationship could end in marriage you know," Miriam reminded.

"Charles is a wonderful man. He treats me like a lady. We have so much fun together and enjoy the same things, however we are just friends," Melody rationalized quickly.

"Is Mr. Evans a Christian, Melody? Remember that is the most important issue when you become friends. You know your parents would be broken-hearted should you choose to marry someone who was not a Christian. Your parent's lives have changed so much since they became Christians and they want the best for you."

"Are you finished lecturing me? I thought we were here to enjoy a good visit and eat together," Melody pouted.

"I'm just concerned about you, Melody. Remember how your father told us when we were thirteen that he and my father had the responsibility to protect us and help us find just the right husbands. You've changed so much," Miriam responded in deep concern.

"You can quit worrying about me. I can take care of myself. Can we get off this subject and enjoy our lunch? You've about ruined the whole time for me. Here is our food, I ordered an expensive lunch just for us today. They had it all ready, however you've made me feel so miserable, I don't know if I can enjoy it," Melody said.

"If you do not wish to discuss it anymore, we will change the subject, Melody. You know I will continue to pray that you will make right choices."

"It's my life, Miriam. I'm not going to stay in this town forever. Charles doesn't really like this town either. He can take over his uncle's bank in Kansas City in a few years, so things may change for both of us."

"So you and Charles are making plans, Melody?" Miriam asked.

"I'm not free to discuss them. Let's eat our lunch and enjoy the last few minutes together before I have to be back at work," Melody said irritably.

The rest of the meal was eaten mostly in silence. As they walked to the door, Melody asked, "Shall I call for Jackson to come for you?"

"No, don't call him. I told him that it was a nice day for a walk home. Thank you for the lunch."

Miriam walked slowly home deep in thought, she wondered, *"Did I fail, Melody? Could I have done more to help her see that without her parents' approval of this relationship with Mr. Evan, it will only bring her grief? She doesn't seem to be open to anything now. All I can do is pray that she will come to her senses before it is too late."*

Lydia was surprised to see Miriam home so early. "Why are you so glum, Miriam? Didn't the time with Melody go well?"

"Oh, Mother, I feel so helpless. She seems determined to pursue this relationship with Mr. Evans even when she knows that her parents would not approve. She knows that Mr. Evans is not a Christian. She told me she didn't want to hear any more from me about what she was doing." Miriam fell into her mother's arms sobbing.

"I know, honey, it is so difficult to see someone you love making mistakes that could cause them unhappiness. I was concerned when Thomas gave her so much freedom to work at the Gazette front desk. Melody is used to having her own way so when he gives her freedom she knows no self control," Lydia consoled.

"Shouldn't we say something to her mother? According to Jackson, Melody has Mr. Evans pick her up after her parents leave for the evening. Maybe they could stop her before it is too late," Miriam stated anxiously.

"I'm afraid it is already too late, however if Mary asks for help, I will talk to her, otherwise I don't feel it is our business to tell her and Thomas. They probably already know what she is doing and feel powerless to do anything."

"If they knew, maybe they could send her back East to that school of music. I feel that Melody is planning to do something drastic, very soon. I don't know what, although she said she was not going to stay in this town forever," Miriam said in concern.

"Yes, it sounds like they are making plans. After supper tonight, when your sisters are in bed, we can talk to your father about this and pray for wisdom on what to do," Lydia suggested.

After supper and talking the problem over, Aaron said, "Thomas evidently is aware of what Melody is doing. He seems so worried, however he doesn't feel free to talk about it. Unless he asks for help, I don't feel there is anything we can do, although we can pray for them and Melody."

Miriam was so busy for the next few weeks that she had no contact with Melody. She had hoped she would see her in church Sunday, however the Cramtons were out of town.

One Sunday early in November, Miriam was singing with the church choir. The special number they were singing required Miriam to sing an unusually difficult soprano solo. It was a relief to get through it and sit down. She didn't feel that she had done very well. Looking out at the congregation, she found a young man looking intently at her. Blushing, she quickly looked away. Timothy Larsen's intense blue eyes made her heart beat faster.

Following church, Miriam made her way to Martha Larsen's side, "Can I hold that little boy I helped to bring into the world, Mrs. Larsen? He seems to be doing very well. I feel very close to him since he was my first delivery with Mrs. Polinsky," she said as she looked fondly at the little bundle Martha put in her arms.

"You did a wonderful job helping Mrs. Polinsky. Are you continuing to help her?" Martha asked.

"Yes, and I love it," Miriam answered and started to make her way back to her parents at the door.

"Oh, Miss Jensen, wait a minute," a voice called from behind her.

Miriam turned to see Timothy Larsen standing there. His blue eyes shinning, he said with a gentle smile, "You sing beautifully, Miss Jensen."

"Thank you, Mr. Larsen," Miriam answered and hurried away before Timothy could see her blushing. *Why do I always have to blush everytime I see him?* she wondered.

Monday morning, Aaron was reading the Gazette, "Listen to this, it says we are going to get a telephone book in January. With so many people installing telephones in their homes, they needed to put out a telephone book. Now, I can keep track of all those numbers I need to call at the shop and won't have to make so many trips downtown to confer with other businesses. Having the telephone at home will help your mother also."

"Will farmers have telephones also?" Miriam asked. "I wish Mrs. Polinsky had a phone so she could call me when she needs me to go with her. That would save both of us a lot of trips."

"Since the Polinsky's live so close to town, if they can get some help putting up poles and wire, they could have a telephone anytime. It would be a party line where everyone on the line could hear. Some people like that so they are the first to hear the latest gossip. Might even put the Gazette or Weekly Courier out of business," Aaron chuckled.

"Oh Father, that's not what a telephone is for," Miriam insisted.

Later that morning, their telephone rang and Lydia answered, "Hello? Oh hello, Mary. What is wrong? You want me to come right away? Melody has gone where? Yes, I will be right over. No, Jackson doesn't need to come. All right, if you insist, I will be ready by the time he arrives. Good bye," Lydia said hanging up the receiver.

"Miriam, that was Mary, you were right about Melody planning something. Her little brother knocked on her door this morning and there was no answer. Mary called to her and opened the door to find that her small trunk was gone, as were several of her dresses and her traveling cape. Mary immediately contacted the train depot agent and was told that Melody had purchased two tickets last week. By the time Mary told me that much, she was sobbing so hard I had difficulty understanding her. Can you stay with the girls so I can be with her?"

"Of course you need to be with Mary, Mother. We all will be praying for Melody that God will make her see the terrible mistake she is making," Miriam answered.

Miriam prepared dinner in her mother's absence and afterwards was quietly knitting and visiting with Anna. Suddenly there was the sound of a buggy coming into the yard and a knock on the door. "That looks like some farmer whose wife is ready to have a baby. I may have to leave," Miriam said.

Opening the door, Miriam was greeted by an anxious Mr. Raston, "Are you Miss Jensen? I am John Raston. Mrs. Polinsky sent me to pick you up first to allow her to finish her butter churning so she can leave when we return. Are you ready to leave, Miss? My misses said to hurry," Mr. Raston said anxiously.

"Yes, let me get my cape and tell my sisters where I am going," Miriam answered. Back inside Miriam picked up her cape and hat. "I will be going with Mrs. Polinsky out to the Raston farm. I may not be home tonight because according to Mrs. Polinsky, this woman usually has long difficult labor. Tell Mother not to worry about me, I will be with Mrs. Polinsky."

Miriam left with a heavy heart. She wished she could be with her mother trying to console Melody's mother. She kept praying over and over silently, *Wherever Melody is, dear God, make her see that marrying a non-Christian is disobeying You.*

Lydia hurried into the house the minute Jackson stopped the carriage. Mary was waiting in the dining room with tears streaming down her face. "Lydia, what are we going to do? I called Thomas at work and he is coming right home. He says he is going after her, although that may just make matters worse if she won't listen to him," Mary sobbed.

"First thing we need to do, Mary, is to ask God for wisdom. You and I both know that she is old enough to marry without your permission. Only God knows if Thomas could find her, and if he did would she even listen to him and come back? It might only make her more determined to elope with this Mr. Evans. Miriam talked to Melody about this a few days ago over lunch and Melody was not open to listen to her at all," Lydia advised.

"Did we do everything wrong is raising her? Since the time you told me about Christ and my need to believe that He died for my sin and I became a child of God, I have tried to undo the mistakes we made in raising her. She has been so stubborn and determined to go her own way. You already know some of what we have gone through. For a while it seemed like she wanted to be obedient to God and seek His plan for her life, although lately she has hardly been civil to us. She is gone at all hours and Thomas has seen her talking to that Mr. Evans numerous times, however we didn't know until lately that she has been going out with him after we would leave in the evening. She evidently has been planning to elope with him for some time."

"Yes, after Miriam talked to her, we both felt that she was planning something drastic because Miriam asked if Mr. Evans was courting her and Melody said she knew that her father would not approve because Mr. Evans was not a Christian. She told Miriam that they were just friends. That night Aaron, Miriam and I prayed about talking to you and we felt it was not our business to interfere," Lydia said gently.

"I had planned to give her a nice wedding after she had been courted by a young man who met our approval and who wanted to be obedient to God. Now she has ruined it all. She never mentioned Mr. Evans' name to us at any time. All that we know about him is that his father owns the bank. They are so new in town, no one knows about their family. Oh, Lydia, my heart is breaking. Has God forgotten us and all the changes we have made to undo the mistakes we made in spoiling Melody before we became Christians?" Mary sobbed.

"No, Mary, God has not forgotten you, nor has He forgotten Melody, however He gives everyone a free choice. We have the choice to accept His Son's death on the cross as payment for our sins and we also have the choice to obey Him each and every day. Melody evidently didn't trust God to give her the kind of husband that would make her happy so she wanted to make that choice on her own. God allows us to go our own way, but we are not free to escape the consequences. Just like King David when he sinned with Bathsheba. God forgave him, however the results of that sin followed him the rest of his life."

"From all I have heard about the Evans family, they don't go to any church. How could Melody even consider someone who has no desire to be with her in church?" Mary asked.

"I almost made the same mistake myself, Mary, when I was Melody's age and almost as head strong. Mother had died when I was young and then my father moved us in with Grandmother. He died when I was sixteen, so all I had left was Grandmother. I didn't think she knew what was best for me so when a young man asked to court me and she refused knowing that he was not a Christian, I would sneak out and meet him without her permission. I came home late one night and found her on her knees beside her bed praying. I remember her words as if it were yesterday, she said, 'Dear God, bring Lydia to her senses even if you have to strike her with some sickness. Make her so miserable that she won't even think of marrying this man who doesn't love You.'"

"What did you do after you heard her prayer?" Mary asked.

"That prayer put fear into my heart. I ran to my bedroom and fell on my knees beside my bed and begged the Lord to forgive me and give me strength to say 'no' to this man I thought

Lydia Jensen on the telephone; Elizabeth holding her apron.

I loved. Although it was a very difficult thing to do, I told him the next day that I couldn't see him anymore. I knew that I had done the right thing, although I also was afraid I might never find someone who would love me like I thought this man did."

"How long was it before you met Aaron?"

"A few months later a young man started coming to our church. His family had moved to Kansas City from Mentor, Iowa and he was working in a blacksmith shop not far from my grandmother's home. After being in church several months and seeing me in the choir and at box suppers, he purchased my box so he could talk to me. It wasn't long before he asked my grandmother if he could court me. She sat him right down and asked, "Young man, where do you stand with the Lord? Once she found that he loved and believed in the Lord, she said, 'Young man, you are welcome at my house anytime to court my granddaughter. I give you my blessing.'"

"That is wonderful how everything worked out for you, but we may never see Melody again. She is so determined to keep us out of every area of her life now," Mary said with a sob catching in her throat.

"I know it may seem that way, Mary. God works when everything seems impossible to us and there isn't any hope. He cares about Melody so much more than even you and Thomas do. I know He is working with Melody right now wherever she is. She is His child even in her rebellion. In the Bible, it says that God chastens us as a loving parent and we can be thankful that He does. Melody just has to learn the hard way."

CHAPTER THREE

CONFRONTATION

THE FRONT DOOR burst open and Thomas came rushing into the parlor. "Mary, did you contact the station agent to see which city Melody purchased tickets for?" Thomas asked impatiently. "I'm leaving on the next train to try to stop Melody from this nonsense. How dare that scalawag sneak her away right from under our noses!"

"The ticket agent said that she purchased two tickets for Kansas City," Mary answered tearfully. "Before you leave, Thomas, please come and pray with Lydia and me. It seems almost impossible that you will be able to find them, much less stop their marriage." Mary wiped her eyes with her tear stained handkerchief.

"You are right, Mary, we need to seek God's wisdom. In my anger at both of them, I keep forgetting that important element. Rev. Stanwick was at the office this morning and reminded me that he had been praying for Melody ever since he had seen her talking to Mr. Evans so often."

"You didn't tell me about her visiting with Mr. Evans. How long has this been going on?" Mary asked sadly.

"You know she visits with everyone, so I didn't think much about it until the last few weeks when she has been gone in the evening without our permission. I trusted her and thought she trusted us enough to allow us to help her find a right husband. I felt sure that she would urge Mr. Evans to ask to court her if this was more than friendly visiting," Thomas answered wearily.

"Thomas, I'm afraid that Melody knew you wouldn't approve of Mr. Evans right from the start," Lydia said gently.

"I must hurry to catch the next train. Let's pray and ask God to guide my trip and show me where to search for Melody," Thomas said. Bowing his head he led in prayer, "Lord, I do not know where we have failed in raising Melody. We wanted your best for her, although it seems that she didn't want your plan for her. Wherever she is right now, convict her of this rebellion and stop her marriage to Mr. Evans. Show me what to do." Thomas pulled out a large linen handkerchief and blew his nose loudly.

"Amen," Mary and Lydia said together.

"Jackson is waiting to take me to the train. Is there anything you need him to bring to you on his return trip?" Thomas asked Mary.

"No, Thomas, I have everything I need. Seth is taking this real hard with his sister gone. Would you talk to him before you leave, Thomas? He is crying in his room. I almost forgot about him in all my worry about Melody."

"Melody has ignored him for the last several months, it is no wonder he feels bad. You'd think that she didn't have a little brother. That is going to change if I find her and she will come home with me," Thomas said as he strode into Seth's bedroom.

"Thomas, if Lydia will have us, Seth and I may visit them this afternoon. We both need someone to talk to and something to do. You can put us to work, can't you, Lydia?" Mary asked eagerly after Thomas had talked to Seth.

"Mary, you know you are always welcome at our home. We are finishing up the fall garden harvest. We could use some help snapping beans. I would enjoy your company as we work, and Seth can entertain Emma and Elizabeth. They always enjoy his company."

Thomas reached for his hat and top coat. "I may not be back for a few days. I will look for her until I have searched in every possible place. Rev. Stanwick is in charge of the paper. He is wonderful to come help on a short notice like he did during my heart attack scare. If I find any news on Melody, I will call you," Thomas said.

Thomas caught the eleven o'clock train and prepared for a lonesome ride. With his head in his hands, Thomas cried out to God, *I've never been so discouraged, Lord. I tried to undo the damage of raising Melody before we became Christians, but it looks like I've failed at everything.*

"Mr. Cramton, is that you? Has there been a death in your family? I almost didn't recognize you," a richly dressed matron spoke to him from across the aisle.

"A, oh, well, no there hasn't been a death. I'm not free to talk about it, although I thank you for your concern. I could use your prayers, if you are a praying woman," Thomas said wearily.

It was almost dark by the time the train pulled into the Kansas City station. Thomas found a carriage driver to take him to his mother's home. Knocking lightly on the door, he let himself in before the butler came. "Hello, Mother, where are you? I just arrived from Beloit," Thomas called from the hall.

"Thomas, what a surprise! Why didn't you tell me you were arriving, so I could have waited to eat with you? I'll call Olive to warm up something for you," Rosie Cramton said.

"No, Mother, I don't feel like eating. Melody has eloped with Mr. Evans from the bank. Has she contacted you anytime today?"

"I haven't heard from her for months, Thomas. You say that she arrived this morning? I doubt if she would have come here. She knows I would not approve of her eloping with someone you did not find acceptable. No, she would stay far away from me. She knows I'd give her a piece of my mind," his mother answered vehemently.

"I'm going to check out all the hotels tonight. I may be able to stop the marriage if I find them in time," Thomas said strongly.

"You could call each of them and save yourself from traveling all over town, Thomas," Mrs. Cramton suggested.

"I have no idea under whose name they would be registered or they may have requested that their name not be given out. No, I have to check out each hotel in hopes that I will see them. Pray for me as I look, Mother."

"I'm afraid you are on a wild goose chase. Knowing Melody, she has probably taken every precaution to not be found. I could just shake her for being so rebellious. She never seems to learn from her mistakes. However, if you are determined to look for her and that whippersnapper of a banker fellow, Morris can take you out in my carriage. I'll leave the door unlocked for your return and may God guide your steps," his mother responded sympathetically.

Thomas directed Morris to stop at every hotel and rooming house that they were aware of in the Kansas City area. At each one, Thomas would go in and inquire, "Do you have a Melody Cramton or Charles Evans registered here?"

At each one the answer was always, "No, we have no one here by that name. Sorry."

Long after midnight, Thomas wearily directed Morris to deliver him back to his mother's home. With shoulders drooping, he trudged upstairs to his bed. He hadn't felt this tired since his heart problems five years ago. Falling into bed without undressing, he fell into a fitful sleep.

The next morning, the sun was high in the sky before Thomas awoke. With a start, he hurried to wash his face and straighten his clothes. Downstairs, he found his mother had waited to eat breakfast with him.

41

"Did you find anything out last night, Thomas?" she asked in concern.

"No, Mother, I checked every hotel and rooming house that I knew about; not one had Melody or Mr. Evans registered there. Do you have any other ideas of where to check?"

"Could she be staying with some of her friends? Last summer she brought several new friends to visit. I didn't really approve of them, however I might be able to recall some of their names. Would you like for me to call their families?"

"Yes, Mother, that might turn up some helpful information. As soon as I finish breakfast, I want Morris to take me to the courthouse to see if they have purchased a marriage license. Also the justice of peace would have record if they were married there yesterday. After that, I don't know where to look. God will have to show me the next step," Thomas said resolutely.

"Take Morris and stay as long as you need to look. I will have Olive fix a lunch for you and if you are not here that will be all right. It might be a good idea to stop to see if I have found out anything from her friends. Although, knowing Melody like I do, it's my guess she wouldn't stay with anyone who knows her."

Thomas had Morris stop at the courthouse and he ran up the steps and down the long hall to the office of the county clerk. "Did a Melody Cramton and Charles Evans come for a marriage license here yesterday or this morning?"

"Who are you, may I ask?" The clerk asked looking over the top of his glasses at Thomas.

"I am Melody's father. I have to find her. Do you have anyone by that name in your book?"

"Let me check." Running his finger down the book, the clerk pushed his spectacles back up on his nose, "No, sir, there's nobody by those names on the book."

"Thank you. Could you direct me to the office of the justice of peace?" Thomas asked.

"Upstairs and the first door on your right. If they didn't

get a license, it won't do you no good to look there," the clerk offered.

"I have to check every possibility. Thank you for your help."

Thomas ran the steps two at a time. He hurried to the desk of the secretary for the justice of peace. "Ma'am, could you help me?"

Looking rather grumpy, she answered, "Is there something you wanted, Mister?"

"Why yes... d-d-did my daughter get married here yesterday or this morning?" Thomas blurted out.

"The judge did perform several marriages yesterday. Tell me your daughter's name and I can check to see if she was one of them," she answered a little more pleasantly.

"Melody Cramton is her name and the man's name is Charles Evans."

Running her finger down the page while Thomas held his breath, she finally said, "No, there's no one by that name, sir. Sorry, I couldn't help you."

"Oh, don't be sorry. That is good news. I mean, oh, it is just good news. Thank you for your help," Thomas said as he hurried back down the stairs. *Now, where do I look, Lord? They didn't get a license so they must not be married yet. Show me where to look next,* Thomas prayed.

"Let's stop at churches, Morris. She may have insisted that a preacher marry them, and be there talking to one even this morning." At a large impressive church on the corner, Thomas thought, *This looks like the kind of church where Melody would like to have her wedding.* He climbed the steps and opened the huge wooden door. Looking inside he found the janitor at work. "Could you tell me where to find the Reverend?" he asked.

"You will find him next door at the manse, sir," the janitor said.

"Thank you," Thomas said as he pushed open the heavy door. Walking over to the manse, he knocked on the door. He was greeted by the maid. "Could I talk with the Reverend a minute?" Thomas requested.

"He doesn't like to be disturbed while he eats his lunch, Mister," she responded.

"I have a quick question for him and then I will be on my way," Thomas insisted.

"Well, all right. However, I want you to know that he won't like it none. Follow me," she answered, walking off at a fast trot.

Leading the way into a formal dining room, she pointed into the room. "He's right in there."

Thomas cleared his throat and walked hesitantly into the room, "Reverend, I'm sorry to bother you, however I am looking for my daughter. She eloped yesterday with a man from our town. Did you happen to marry a Melody Cramton and Charles Evans yesterday or this morning?"

"No, I did not marry anyone by that name. Didn't the maid tell you that I don't let anyone disturb my lunch? And now if you will excuse me, I would like to eat in peace," he answered irritably.

"Thank you, Reverend." Thomas said as he hurried to get away from this unfriendly preacher. *He sure doesn't have much love or concern for anyone but himself. I'm thankful that Rev. Stanwick isn't like that.*

Thomas walked dejectedly back to the carriage. "Let's try another church, Morris." Pulling out his pocket watch, Thomas said, "There is time for another church or two before lunch."

Each time the answer was, "We didn't have anyone here by that name."

Thomas was feeling more hopeless each passing hour. "They could have taken the train to any other city by now. Take me back to Mother's home, Morris," Thomas requested.

Thomas bounded up the steps, hoping that his mother

had some information for him. "Mother, did you find any information from Melody's friends? Had any of them seen or heard from her?" he asked worriedly.

"No, Thomas, none of them had seen her since last summer. I told you that she would probably stay away from anyone who might talk some sense into her. I also called several churches to see if they had married them and not one of them had. Let's have some lunch and talk to the Lord about that rambunctious Melody and Mr. Evans. Just might be that God has some wisdom we don't have," Mrs. Cramton answered.

After lunch, Mrs. Cramton said, "Thomas, maybe we are looking in all the wrong places. Maybe Melody did not come here to get married. They may be out at the racetrack enjoying a day of fun. You know how much Melody enjoyed the races and she wouldn't have me telling her not to gamble."

"I'm going out there right now. If I could find her right away we could catch the five o'clock train back to Beloit," Thomas said.

Morris delivered Thomas to the racetrack. The stadium was crowded and the race was in progress so people were standing and cheering for their horse. "Get your tickets right here, Mister. Did you want to place a bet? There's still time," the ticket taker called.

"No, I do not want to place a bet. I'm looking for my daughter," Thomas muttered as he handed over the money for the ticket. He got through the gate and searched the crowd. After several minutes he thought he saw someone who looked like Melody and headed that way only to be disappointed to find it was someone else. *How can I find anyone in this crowd? One would think the gambling was more important than anything else.* Thomas thought as he struggled to get through the crowd.

Thirty minutes later, Thomas walked back to the carriage. "It's no use, Morris. Melody has just disappeared."

"Would you want me to drive you through the parks, Mr.

Cramton? It's a nice day for a walk. They could be there," Morris suggested.

A tour through the parks proved fruitless. "It's hopeless. I can't find her anywhere. I don't know any more places to look. I might as well go home. Take me back to Mrs. Cramton's. I've got to pick up my valise and get to the station for my trip home," Thomas said dejectedly.

Walking slowly into the house, not wanting to admit to his mother that he hadn't found anything, Thomas found her very excited. "I just thought of something, Thomas! Didn't you say that this young fellow's name was Evans and that he had an uncle here in town? I looked in the telephone book and there are three Evans families in the book. Would you want to call them? They might know something about where Melody and Mr. Evan's are."

"That's a brilliant idea, Mother. This may be just the place we need to look. Tell me the first number and I will call them," Thomas said with excitement in his voice.

Ringing central, Thomas said, "Number 36 please," After hearing a voice on the other end of the line, Thomas said, "This is Thomas Cramton from Beloit. Do you know a Charles Evans? Oh, you are his aunt? Have you seen him in the last few days? My daughter seems to have left town with him. What? You have seen them? Where are they now?" Thomas couldn't think straight. "Oh, you don't know where they are. They might be at Charles's cousin's home? Could you give me that number?" Thomas begged.

Hanging up the telephone, Thomas rang central again, "Please give me number 42." A young man answered. Thomas said, "I'm Thomas Cramton and I am looking for Melody Cramton and Charles Evans. Would you happen to know where they might be?" Thomas asked anxiously.

Hanging up the telephone, Thomas said, "They left separately about an hour ago and he has no idea where they went.

He said Melody called a carriage and being angry with Charles, she told no one where she was going. It doesn't look like we are any closer to finding her. I might as well have Morris take me to the station and catch the five o'clock train. It wouldn't serve any good purpose for me to stay here. Melody may have taken the train to Chicago or Boston for all we know. She had an hour to be on her way," Thomas said wearily as he picked up his valise and gave his mother a quick kiss, "Goodbye, Mother. Keep praying."

"If Melody shows up here, I will do more than pray. That daughter of yours needs to hear some strong talking. She is heading for trouble, if someone doesn't talk some sense into her," Mrs. Cramton said.

"I am sure you will straighten her out, Mother. You've always been good at that. That may be just what she needs. I must hurry and catch my train," Thomas said chuckling in spite of his discouragement.

Out in the carriage, Thomas said, "Off to the station, Morris."

Thomas purchased his ticket and paid for a copy of the Kansas City Star to read while he waited. He was so discouraged that even reading his favorite paper couldn't hold his attention. He gave up and started watching the crowd coming into the lobby to catch the evening train. There were families with small children heading home after a day in the city and businessmen with their heads stuck in newspapers before leaving for their homes in the country. Seeing the families enjoying each other sent a pang of sorrow through Thomas. *Melody could be on a train east by now. I know she found Beloit dull and since she has left Mr. Evans, she would be embarrassed to come back. How will I ever tell Mary that I came so close to finding her only to miss her by an hour?* Thomas pondered in deep sorrow.

Sitting there with his head in his hands for a long time, Thomas felt constrained to look around the lobby. It was mostly filled by this time. He looked in every area in a hope against hope that somehow Melody might be there waiting for a train. Far back in a dark corner, he saw something that caught his eye. Could it be? He had to find out. Without attracting too much attention, Thomas made his way through the lobby crowded with trunks and valises blocking the aisles to a sobbing huddled figure on a bench. "It is Melody!" he whispered. Sitting down quickly beside her, before he collapsed with the overwhelming joy of finding her, he touched her lightly. "Melody, it's me, your father. Are you ready to come home with me?"

Throwing her arms around him and crying even harder, Melody said, "How did you find me? I was so scared and worried. I was afraid to go home, however I didn't know what else to do."

Putting his arm around her and pulling her tight, Thomas said, "I've been looking for you since last night. I had given up and was here to catch the five o'clock train."

"Will you ever forgive me, Father? Why didn't I listen to you?" Melody sobbed.

"I'm here because I love you, Melody and I want to help you if you will allow me to do that. However, what happened to Mr. Evans? Weren't you planning to get married?"

"He was terrible to me. He wanted to get married right away. However, when I said that I wanted to get married by a preacher in a church, he told me that he wanted nothing to do with preachers and churches. When I insisted, he slapped me and told me that if I felt that way, I could just go home to my mother. He said he didn't want any of my religious stuff," Melody cried.

"Oh, honey, I am so thankful that you didn't marry him," Thomas said.

"He wasn't the gentleman that he had been all summer. He had treated me like a lady every time we went someplace, but he changed the minute I mentioned preachers and churches. Do you think that he hates God or something,

Father?" she asked sadly.

"I don't know, Melody, I am so thankful that God stopped you from marrying him. I thought I was too late to stop you, however I see that God stopped you before you made that terrible mistake of marrying someone who does not love God."

Pulling out his watch, Thomas said, "I have a few minutes to call your grandmother, who has been praying all day and helping me search for you. She can call your mother to tell her that I have found you. You don't know how worried we all have been."

"Will God forgive me for my terrible disobedience? I could have wrecked my whole life by my rebellion. How can I get this whole mess straightened out?" Melody wailed.

"Let's don't talk anymore. We are both too worn out to think. Once we get home and rested, we can work it out together. You do remember that God forgives when we admit our sin, don't you?

"Yes, Father, I know that God forgives, however I can't forgive myself. How can you, or Mother or even God trust me ever again?" Melody sobbed.

CHAPTER FOUR

MELODY'S NEW START

FEELING MUCH BETTER after a bath and breakfast, Melody descended the stairs to find her mother waiting near the door. "Melody, you look much better. That dress you were wearing last night looked like you had slept in it for a month."

"Mother, I felt like I had not slept for a week or more. I think it will take me all week to recover from this devastating blow. I'm so sorry for hurting you and Father so."

"Melody, I'm so thankful you are home. I told Lydia before we prayed that I didn't think we would see you again. I was so doubtful that your father could find you. However, we can talk about this later. Go on to see Miriam. I know that she is anxious to see you. Lydia called while you were in the bath to say that she will be leaving in an hour or so to stay with Mrs. Raston. She was so worried about you, I know she will want to see you before she goes."

"Why does Miriam have to go to stay with Mrs. Raston? Didn't the baby arrive yet?" Melody asked.

"I don't know, Melody. She will tell you. I wanted you to know, so you would know that she has a lot on her mind today."

"Since it is a warm day I think I will ride my bicycle, Mother. I need some time to think and the ride will do me good."

"You haven't ridden for such a long time Melody, although I am sure Jackson has kept your bicycle in good shape in the carriage house," Mary said.

Dressed in new olive green bloomers with matching cable-knit stockings, Melody peddled the mile to Miriam's home at the edge of Beloit. Thinking of all that had transpired through the summer and fall with Charles Evans, Melody suddenly realized, *I've ignored all my friends all this time. I wonder if Miriam really wants me for a friend after the way I have treated her?*

Miriam, sitting by the window, looked up in surprise. "Here's Melody on her bicycle! She hasn't ridden that since she was in the riding club with some of the boys in town. Wonder what possessed her to ride today? Would you look at that outfit!"

"A proper young lady wouldn't wear those awful bloomers. I wonder if she realizes what people think of her for wearing them?" Lydia said.

"Don't worry, Mother. You won't find me wearing them. I don't even like them. I was reading in the Kansas City Star that not many girls are wearing them now. They just aren't respectful," Miriam said.

Melody burst in the door without knocking. "I couldn't wait to see you, Miriam. I hope you don't mind me coming in without knocking."

"You know that you are always welcome anytime, Melody. I'm so glad to see you are back. Do you want to sit out here in the kitchen, or go downtown to the Ice Cream Palace? I can drive us down in my buggy if you like," Miriam suggested.

"Let's talk here. I'm too worn out to go anywhere. I really haven't had any sleep for the last two days. You must have been praying for me because something kept me from marrying Charles. I owe you an apology, Miriam. You tried to warn me that Charles wasn't right for me and I wouldn't listen."

"What made you not marry him, Melody? Isn't that why you

took your trunks and left without telling anyone?" Miriam asked.

"It wasn't until Charles slapped me after I asked to be married by a preacher. That slap seemed to be God's reminder that I was making a bad mistake. I finally saw what Charles was really like. I've hurt so many people by going my own way. You and my parents just kept loving me in spite of my rebellion."

"We all make wrong choices, Melody. The important thing is to admit it was wrong and make the choice to get away from the temptation. You did that by leaving Charles in Kansas City and coming back home. God forgives us after we agree with Him that our disobedience was sin."

"I know that, Miriam. I've heard it all in church," Melody responded.

"Then you know He will give you the strength and wisdom to do the right thing even when others are doing the wrong thing."

"Yes, Miriam, I know all that. Let's quit talking about me. Tell me what happened with your delivering Mrs. Raston's baby. Mother said you had had a difficult day."

"Yes, it started out to be a wonderful day. Truly an Indian summer fall day. I was looking forward to riding out to the Raston farm because they live just beyond the Larsen farm."

"Why would you care if you were going by the Larsen farm? Is there something special about the Larsen farm? Is there some reason why you like going by the Larsen farm?" Melody asked with a twinkle in her eye.

"Oh, I like that farm. It is always so neat, and you remember that I helped Mrs. Polinsky deliver Mrs. Larsen's last baby."

"Is that the only reason that you like going by?" Melody teased.

"Well, not exactly. I thought maybe Timothy Larsen might be out working the field and would see us go by. Sure enough he was, and waved real big at us."

"What is so special about Timothy Larsen? He's just one

of those farmer boys."

"You haven't met Timothy, I can see. He has the most beautiful blue eyes. Haven't you seen him at church? Oh! I forgot you haven't been there much lately."

"You don't need to rub it in. I know I haven't been there much, but Charles would always say that if I wanted to take a ride that we needed to go in the morning while it was cool," Melody explained.

"If you had insisted that he come to church with you before you went for a ride, do you think that would have changed anything with your eloping with him?"

"Maybe it would have, however we were talking about your day with Mrs. Raston," Melody insisted.

"As I said, we saw Timothy out shucking corn. It brightened up my whole day just to see him."

"What happened at the Raston farm?"

"Well, the minute we opened the door, we heard Mrs. Raston crying, and their little four year old, Adam, was huddled in the corner whimpering. Mr. Raston told us that she had been in labor all night. Mrs. Polinsky examined her and found that the baby was in breech position (seat first) and he was a big baby. Mrs. Polinsky sent me out to request Mr. Raston to go for Dr. Blackwood. She knew that Mrs. Raston had lost two other babies, and this was going to be a difficult delivery."

"What did you do to help?" Melody asked. "You had never delivered a breech baby before had you?"

"No, although I could see that little Adam was in need of help the most, because he kept crying, "I want a little brother, I want a little brother. I don't want him to die." So I took him outside and we sat down under a large elm tree and talked.

"Adam, why are you crying so hard?" I asked.

"'Cause Mama says I may not get a little brother 'cause he might not live."

"Mrs. Polinsky has delivered a lot of babies. I'm sure she

Paul and Martha Larsen's farm.

54

will know what to do," I told him, even though I wasn't so sure anyone could deliver this baby alive.

"Would you like me to pray for your little brother right now, that God would take care of him and your mama?" I asked.

"Oh, yes. I want a little brother so bad. Can God get me a little brother?"

So I prayed, "Dear God, little Adam here is asking that you give him the little brother he has been wanting so bad and take care of his mama also."

After we prayed, Adam was much happier. "Can you stay out here and play with your doggy while I go help Mrs. Polinsky? You know that I am her special helper, and you can be a special helper right now by playing out here so we can help your mama and that new little brother to arrive safely."

"Did he stay outside like you asked? And what did you do to help Mrs. Polinsky deliver this backward coming baby? Did Dr. Blackwood arrive in time to help?" Melody asked impatiently.

"You're getting ahead of the story. Mrs. Raston was still upset and crying when I came back inside. Mrs. Polinsky called to me to talk to Mrs. Raston while she tried to turn the baby. There was no way he was going to be born unless he was turned. Mrs. Polinsky was more worried than I have ever seen her; she told me to pray hard. At first I didn't know what to say to Mrs. Raston because she knew as well as I did that the baby might not live, after losing the other two. I told her that Mrs. Polinsky needed her help if she was going to deliver the baby. I told her, "You must calm down and relax, Mrs. Raston. Remember that God is in charge of all these difficult problems. Pray with me that Mrs. Polinsky will know just what to do. I talked to your little Adam and prayed with him for a little brother." It was just like a light dawned on her; she prayed with me and a wonderful peace came over her so that Mrs. Polinsky was Abel to turn the baby head down and it wasn't long before we had a big handsome boy delivered."

"Did the doctor ever arrive?" Melody asked.

"Oh, yes, he came in the door just as the baby gave his first lusty cry. Dr. Blackwood came into the room and said, "Looks like you women have done a wonderful job with the delivery of this big boy. I can take care of things with Mrs. Raston if you want to take care of the baby. I can see she will need someone to stay with her for a week or two." Looking at me he asked, "Would you be able to stay with her, Miss? You seem to be very capable in helping Mrs. Polinsky."

"Well, yes, if I can go home for some clothes and to tell my mother where I will be," I answered.

"What did Adam think of his little brother?" Melody questioned.

"He had followed Dr. Blackwood and his father into the house. By then I had the baby cleaned up and wrapped in a blanket. 'Do you want to hold your baby brother, Adam?' I asked. He came shyly over to me and held out his arms, not saying a word. As I laid that baby in his arms he kept saying over and over, 'Thank you, Jesus, for my little brother. I'm going to name him Abel, after the first baby in the Bible that Mama told me about.'"

"When are you to leave to be with Mrs. Raston? Do you know how long you will be staying there with her? Why couldn't her husband do the cooking and washing? I thought farmers knew how to do all those things," Melody asked.

"Probably Mr. Raston knows how to do some cooking and washing, however he has corn shucking to do. He told me that a crew of neighbors are to come to help him tomorrow so I will have to be cooking for about a dozen neighbors, as well as taking care of Mrs. Raston."

"You're going to cook for a dozen men? I don't know if I could cook for one man, let alone a dozen. Maybe I'm not ready for marriage. I never thought about that. About the only thing I know about cooking is what you and your mother have taught me. I've never ever cooked a full meal by myself. I never thought about that when I eloped with Charles. He would have soon learned that I couldn't cook. However, I expected him to find a maid and a cook like we have at home so I could enjoy being a banker's wife and enjoy the theater groups and women's clubs."

"Melody, I'm shocked at you. I thought you really wanted to learn to cook so you could feed a husband and family sometime. What if you marry a man who can't provide a maid and a cook? You might starve him the first week," Miriam laughed. "By the way, what are you going to be doing? Have you thought about being a teacher? Your father would approve of teaching and there are lots of country schools around here looking for teachers."

"You mean be an old maid school teacher? That would be horrible! No, thankyou. I have no interest in teaching a bunch of obnoxious children. My little brother, Seth, gets on my nerves enough, without trying to teach the children of the farmers out in some far off country school. I want more excitement in my life than that," Melody stated emphatically.

Miriam looked at the clock, "Oh, it's getting late. I must harness Ginger to the buggy and be heading out to the Raston farm. I don't want to be out after dark, and it gets dark early this time of the year."

"Why are you taking your knitting? Do you really think you will have time to knit with all the cooking and cleaning you will be doing?" Melody asked.

"I'm sure there will be a few times when I am not busy in the evening. Besides I want to make that little Abel some booties. I need to keep improving my skills. Someday I may have children of my own, and be making booties for them."

"Well, you probably will be married to some farmer with a dozen kids sometime. I want to make a name for myself; and I'm not planning to stay in Beloit all my life."

"Have you asked God what He would have you do or be?

57

Being where and who He wants you to be is exciting and fulfilling."

"You better get your horse harnessed and head out to that farm before it gets dark. I don't want to be responsible for you getting lost after dark. Besides, if you hurry, you might be able to wave at a certain Timothy Larsen on the way."

"Oh pooh, Melody! You are such a tease. Do you want me to call you when I return?"

"Yes, call me. If I haven't left for the school of music back East, I might be stuck in the back room of Father's office where he can keep an eye on me, and I will need rescuing."

Miriam harnessed Ginger and waved to her mother and Melody, where they stood talking on the porch, as she left.

"Melody, I couldn't help overhearing that you want excitement in your life. Why do you have to have excitement?" Lydia questioned.

"I hate being in a monotonous humdrum life. I want to be involved in the rights for women. I think women should be allowed to vote here in Kansas."

"Maybe you would in be interested in this paper of Aaron's grandmother of Minneapolis, Ottawa County, Kansas. She sounds like she would agree with you. I'm happy allowing Aaron to do the voting for our family, as he and I talk about the issues and candidates so his vote is what I would make myself. I'm concerned that when women get involved in politics, all sorts of problems will start. God said back in Genesis that man is to be the head of woman, after they had disobeyed God and eaten from the fruit of the tree of knowledge of good and evil."

"Can I take those copies of *The Woman's Column* home to read? I see that it is published in Boston and it only costs 25 cents a year. Thank you for giving this to me, Mrs. Jensen, you may have just given me a purpose in life," Melody mused as she got back on her bicycle for the ride home.

"Melody, wait a minute. Are you really sure this is something God would want you to be involved in? Show those papers to your father and seek his opinion on your involvement. Remember he loves you very much and is seeking the best for you. He may see some dangers that neither you nor I see. Look on page two of that one paper I gave you quoting an old hymn, 'Satan finds some mischief still for the idle hands to do.' The writer said that is also true of idle brains. Melody I am concerned about you. Do you really fill your mind with quality things and God's word each day or do you only do what Melody wants to do?"

"Sometimes I want to do what God says, but it seems like I keep making wrong choices. It seems like I am so weak and selfish. I think if I helped in women's suffrage, I would be doing something worthwhile," Melody stated.

"It also may bring you lots of grief, Melody. Do ask your father."

"I'll think about it, Mrs. Jensen. I really must be going," Melody called as she peddled off. All the way home, Melody was thinking, *Allowing women to vote really intrigues me. Why should we be stuck at home cooking and cleaning when we could be helping bring about a better country? We could even be in Congress and help start new laws to better the life of women. Maybe I won't have to be stuck in this town all my life after all.*

CHAPTER FIVE

MELODY FINDS
HER CALLING

MELODY PEDDLED her bike home unusually fast for someone who had not ridden for months. Arriving home out of breath, she ran to her room without a word to anyone. Lying on her bed, she spread out the copies of *The Woman's Column* which Lydia had given her. *Woman's suffrage sounds so exciting. I have got to find out more. I wonder whom I could talk to about this. I know, I could talk to Mr. Jensen's grandmother in Minneapolis. Since she takes* The Woman's Column, *she must be very interested in women gaining the right to vote.* With that thought she relaxed and fell asleep.

It was almost noon the next day when she awoke with a start. The sun was shining in her windows, so she knew it was long past breakfast time. Grabbing her clothes, she dressed quickly and ran down the stairs. "Mother, why didn't you call me? I wanted to talk to Father before he left for work," she complained.

Mary, who was sitting quietly at the table, reading her Bible, answered, "You were sleeping so soundly when Father looked in as he came to breakfast that we decided that you needed the sleep."

"But Mother, I needed to talk to Father. Can I have Jackson take me to the office so I can talk to him?" Melody begged.

"You know that you can talk to your father any time, Melody. I know that he has been saving some work for your return. You realize he has become very dependent on you."

"Oh, Mother, all the help can work circles around me. I really do not think I want to work there anymore. Mr. Jensen's grandmother sent him some papers that greatly interest me. That is what I wish to talk to Father about," Melody explained. "Can Annabel set out some lunch for me while I finish dressing? Could she tell Jackson that I will be needing a ride shortly?"

"I will tell her, Melody, although I doubt if Jackson will want to get out in the cold to take you. That is why your father hired Matthew to do the winter driving. Jackson is so crippled up with arthritis in the winter that we allow him to stay inside as much as possible."

"Well, tell Matthew I want a ride. I need to talk to Father right away."

Dressing in beautiful dark blue velvet with matching hat, Melody pulled her dark hair into a loose bun at the back of her neck. Reaching for her heavy cloak, she tripped back down the stairs. Taking a few bites of lunch, she put on her hat and cloak. "Thank you, Annabel, for the lunch."

"Melody, you hardly touched your food. You need to eat if you are going to keep up your strength. Remember you have been through a lot of stress this week. I don't want you coming down with something," Mary stated.

"I am not hungry, Mother. I have so much on my mind. I must talk to Father right away. I may not be home for supper," Melody said as she headed for the door.

"You aren't planning on going somewhere out of town, are you Melody? You just arrived home. Your father and I need to talk to you this evening. Why can't you wait a few days?"

"I will try to be home this evening, Mother. However, this

is something that I must check on right away. Lydia told me that I should check with Father before I did anything," Melody answered as she closed the door.

Matthew was waiting with the carriage. He was young and very attentive to helping Melody. "Where to, Miss Cramton?"

"To the Gazette office, Matthew, and hurry."

Much to Melody's surprise, Matthew loved speed, so they were racing through town like a runaway. They almost ran over a little old lady crossing the street. Several men ran out to try to catch the runaway while Matthew sped right on and pulled to a sudden stop at the front door of the Gazette. Turning to Melody, Matthew grinned, "Was that fast enough Miss Cramton?"

Looking white as a sheet, Melody answered tersely, "Yes, Matthew, that was fast enough. Remind me not to ask you to hurry again. You almost ran over that lady back there. Father won't like that, and you can be sure you will hear from him." Still shaking, she started to step down, although Matthew was at her elbow helping her down.

"I really didn't mean to scare you. Everyone says you like excitement; I thought you would like that type of driving. Do you need help to make it to the door?"

"I can make it now. I am just a little tired from my trip. However, do wait here until I see if I will be needing a ride to the station," she responded weakly.

Standing at the door, trying to gain confidence before facing her fellow workers who knew why she had been away, Melody sucked in her breath and pushed the door open. Harold was at the front desk. Seeing her, he came right over. "Good morning, Miss Cramton. Glad to have you back. We've been saving work especially for you."

"I'm not here to work, Harold. I came to talk to Father. Is he in his office?" she asked curtly.

"Yes, ma'am, he has been there all morning. Not like him

to stay stuck away out of sight that long. Must be somethin' troubling him."

Knocking lightly on the door and hearing a muffled, "Come in" Melody let herself in. She was surprised to see her father looking so worried and discouraged. "What's wrong, Father? Has something terrible happened?" she asked in genuine concern.

"Oh, Melody, it's you. I have been sitting here thinking about you. I am glad you came to the office. I was thinking about your plans for the future. I don't think I can allow you to work the front desk anymore."

"You are right about that, Father. It's just too tempting for me to talk to everyone who comes to the office. I've been doing some thinking also, and I really do not wish to work here anymore. Mrs. Jensen gave me some papers yesterday that interest me very much. I came to ask your permission to visit Mr. Jensen's grandmother in Minneapolis," Melody asked sweetly.

"No, I will not allow you to travel that far unescorted and not at this time. You are in no condition to travel now, and your mother and I wish to spend some time with you working out plans for your future."

"Father, Mr. Jensen's grandmother lives in Minneapolis, Kansas, so I would only be gone a few hours. I told Mrs. Jensen that I would talk to you before I did anything. Would you mind if I went this afternoon? I must see Mrs. Glendinning right away," Melody insisted

"Well, if it is only to this Minneapolis. I don't like the idea of you leaving so soon after just getting you home. However, I suppose that there wouldn't be any problem visiting Aaron's grandmother. Just be home before dark so we can have the evening to talk."

"Yes, Father. I'll make every effort to catch the four o'clock train so I can be here before dark. Then we can talk this evening. Thank you, thank you," Melody said, gently kissing the top of his head.

"Oh, Father, Matthew nearly scared me out of my wits the way he drove down here. He drove so fast that he almost hit a little old lady," Melody complained.

"I will talk to him, Melody. Thank you for telling me. He came highly recommended as a good worker, and Jackson likes him, so maybe he just needs to be reprimanded," Thomas responded.

As Melody walked out the door, Thomas reminded, "Remember that you are to be home in time for the evening meal. I still haven't recovered from the scare you gave me a few days ago, and I don't wish to be worrying about you this evening."

"Yes, Father, I'll be very prompt. I will tell Matthew to be at the station by seven o'clock."

Matthew delivered Melody to the station. Helping her out he asked, "Will you want me here to meet the train on your return?"

"Yes, Matthew, and you won't have to hurry because I won't be back until seven o'clock. Would you tell Mother that I have gone to see Mr. Jensen's grandmother?"

Melody settled into a seat in the back of the train car and pulled out the copies of *The Woman's Column. This is so interesting. I just know this is something God would want me to do. I can help women all across America to gain their rightful place to vote. We women deserve it. We are as intelligent as any man. Here is an article about the first woman senator and the first bill that she helped write. I could do that and I would love every minute of it. Maybe that is where God is leading me. I know Mrs. Glendinning can help me learn more about woman's suffrage.*

She was so engrossed in her reading that she did not notice a bearded man who had boarded the train and was sitting across the aisle from her. She looked up to see him watching her.

"I could not help noticing that you are reading one of my

wife's favorite papers. In fact she speaks often for woman's suffrage. You may meet her sometime. My name is Williams, Robert Williams."

"I would love to meet her. Do you live in Beloit? I did not know anyone in Beloit who was working for woman's suffrage. Could I come visit her sometime?" Melody requested in her usual forward way.

"She has piles of material from Susan B. Anthony and Cady Stanton who put out the *Revolutionary* paper several years ago. We have been to the Boston Suffrage Fair and plan to go this year. Perhaps you would care to join us. It will be the first week in December this year," the stranger announced.

Forgetting that her father had cautioned her not to talk to strangers, Melody answered, "I'd love to go the Fair. How soon do you have to know if I will be going? I will have to convince Father to allow me to attend. He is not very interested in woman's suffrage."

"Who is your father, Miss?" the stranger asked.

"Thomas Cramton, the editor of the *Gazette*. You probably know him."

"I sure do, and he knows me. I'm sure he would not mind if you accompanied us to Boston. Where are you headed this afternoon, unescorted?" Mr. Williams asked.

"I am, a, um. Well, I am going to visit Mr. Jensen's grandmother who gave him these papers. I did not know anyone else who was interested in suffrage, and I want to learn all I can."

Looking out the window, Melody exclaimed, "We are already at Minneapolis. The time has gone so fast while talking to you. I hope we will meet again soon. I must hurry so I can find a ride to Mrs. Glendinning's home right away."

"May you have great success in your search for information. It is a great cause and there is plenty to do before we get that amendment passed."

Melody gathered all her papers and moved to the door as

65

the train came to a stop in Minneapolis. "How am I going to find Mrs. Glendinning's home, and how will I get there?" she muttered to herself. She did not have to wait long before she sighted an older man with a buggy waiting by the station door.

"Do you need a ride young lady? I am waiting here to deliver ladies and gents anyplace in Minneapolis. Just tell me where you wish to go."

"Do you know where Mrs. Richard Glendinning lives? I wish to visit her, however I do not know where her home is," Melody lamented.

"You bet I know where Mrs. Glendinning lives. Her house is on east Second Street. She has company often. I ought to know as I live next door. Mostly her sons and their families visit 'cause most of them live around here so she is a busy woman for being eighty years of age."

Arriving at the door of the two-story house with the wide front porch, Melody suddenly realized she did not know what she was going to tell Mrs. Glendinning. How could she explain the reason for her visit? She knocked lightly on the door. Mrs. Glendinning opened it as if expecting someone. "Oh, I was expecting Jessie. Whom, may I ask, are you?"

"I am Melody Cramton. Aaron Jensen is a friend of ours, and Mrs. Jensen loaned me the copies of the *Woman's Column* that you sent to them. I wanted to talk to you about them. I am so interested in woman's suffrage. Do you have time to talk to me?" Melody rushed through her speech.

"Come right in, Miss Cramton. It is too cold to stand out on the porch and talk about this topic. Here, let me have your cloak. May I get you a cup of tea? I have the tea pot heating on the back the stove," Mrs. Glendinning offered.

"Mrs. Glendinning, how long have you been studying about woman's suffrage? I hadn't heard anything about it until I read your papers."

"I have been studying it for years. We have speakers on the

subject every few weeks at the Opera House. I am sure that you have had the same women speaking in Beloit. I registered to vote for mayor in eighty-seven and did vote, even though not too many other women did. I may not live long enough to vote for the president. I would love to go to the Suffrage Fair in Boston, however I am too old for that kind of traveling. Maybe you could go. You would hear all the great speakers on suffrage."

"Do you think I could attend, Mrs. Glendinning? I want to help other women. Mrs. Jensen didn't think much of the papers and I think she was sorry she showed them to me," Melody said eagerly.

"Yes, Aaron does not agree with woman's suffrage, and Lydia is content to allow him to do the voting for the family. We just don't talk about it when we are together," Mrs. Glendinning said.

"How long have women been working to get the right to vote, Mrs. Glendinning? Why have I not heard more about it?" Melody asked

"Oh, they have been working since the 1850s, and in 1872 Susan B. Anthony took 12 friends to persuade the inspectors to allow her and her friends to vote. They did vote, and two weeks later she, her 12 friends, and the 3 inspectors were arrested. Anthony received a grossly unfair trial during which the judge repeatedly displayed antifeminist, prejudiced treatment. The judge imposed a $100 fine. She refused to pay it, and the judge, who was afraid she might appeal, allowed her to go. The election inspectors received heavy fines which were paid by sympathetic spectators."

"I would have loved to have seen that. Those woman must be strong and determined," Melody said admiringly.

"That they are, Miss Cramton. All the women that I have heard speak are very determined to stop at nothing to push through an amendment. I am sure there are women in Beloit who are working for this also. Check out the WCTU (Women

Christian Temperance Union). They can help you find information.

After visiting for several hours, Melody looked at the clock. "I really must be going. I told Father that I would be on the four o'clock train. Do you know how I could get a ride to the station?"

There was the sound of someone coming up on the porch. "That must be Jessie coming home from school where she teaches. She will take you to the station. She is the oldest child of my son, Richard, whose wife died at the birth of their sixth child. Jessie was only twelve years old at the time, yet with my help, the family is doing fairly well. Richard has never remarried. He is here often to look after my needs since his father died three years ago."

"I am sorry to hear that your husband has died. It must be very lonely for you," Melody sympathized.

"I have someone here most of the time. Jessie lives with me while she is teaching, and usually one of her brothers is here also. Seems like all I do is make quilts for the family and cook for them, while they bring me vegetables and chickens to keep me fed. Jessie even purchased a new cookstove for me which covered a month's rent which she pays me."

Tall slender Jessie came in the door. Melody noticed that she didn't seem to be much older than herself. "You teach school? How long have you been teaching?" Melody asked.

"I have been teaching right out of 8th grade. Many times some of my students have been older than me, for often the boys are needed on the farm and are never able to go to school for more than a few months each year," Jessie answered.

"Jessie, Miss Cramton needs a ride to the station. She has to catch the four o'clock train back to Beloit."

"My buggy is right outside. I was ready to put Bessie away for the evening, however I will deliver you to the station first. Are you ready?" Jessie asked.

"Thank you, Mrs. Glendinning for all your help. I may visit you again if that would be all right with you. And thank you for the tea," Melody graciously stated.

"You are welcome to visit me anytime. I am home most of the time unless Richard or one of my other sons needs some help with cooking or washing chores."

Jessie took Melody to the station and Melody stepped down from the buggy, carefully holding up her long skirt. "Thank you, Jessie, for bringing me back to the station. My father requested that I be on time."

"I do a lot of traveling myself, Miss Cramton, so I know what it is to arrive on time. Sometimes my brothers do not appreciate my need to be delivered on time," Jessie admitted. "My oldest brother, Bennie, was delivering me to a suffrage meeting here in Minneapolis and he was not paying attention and lost the wheel off the buggy. Almost made me lose the debate, since I was so late that I had to grab Mr. Snodgrass to help me defend the rights of women. We won the debate, much to the unhappiness of my good friend."

"You are really interested in the rights of women, aren't you Jesse?"

"Yes, I think my wearing the button about suffrage has caused me to not get several teaching jobs. There are strong opinions about it on both sides."

All the way home, Melody rehearsed what she would say to convince her father to go to Boston. *He talked about me taking more music training when I was younger. That is what I will tell him. I could visit his cousin, Julia, in Boston so that I could check out the school and be there to start in January. He would not mind me staying with his cousin, and while I am there in December I could spend a week at the Suffrage Fair. If Mr. and Mrs. Williams invited me to travel with them, he should have no objections at all.* By the time the train squealed to a stop in Beloit, Melody had her talk all ready for her parents.

True to his word, Matthew was waiting at the station with the buggy. Once seated in the buggy, Melody noticed how tired she was. In her excitement to gain information on suffrage she had kept pushing herself. However, she had to remain strong so she could convince her parents that the Boston School of Music was just where they should send her for training.

CHAPTER SIX

CHALLENGES FOR MIRIAM

Miriam ARRIVED at the Raston farm by mid-afternoon. Adam was so happy to see her that he was jumping up and down, "Mama said you would come back and bake me some cookies. Can I help you? I'm a good helper-boy."

Miriam smiled at his excitement. Taking off her coat, she walked back to the small bedroom where she found baby Abel, sleeping contentedly in his mother's arms. "Mrs. Raston, would you like Adam and me to bake cookies this afternoon? He says he will be my helper."

"O yes, I haven't been able to bake anything for several weeks. We are completely out of bread and Arthur told me at noon that he would be having a dozen neighbors here to help with the corn shocking tomorrow. That is a lot of men for you to cook dinner for. Why don't I sent Arthur over to the Larsens and ask if Esther can come in the morning to help you."

"Would you tell me where I can find the flour and sugar? I expect that Adam can find the eggs and milk," Miriam asked.

"Yes, Adam loves to gather the eggs, and the milk is out in the springhouse behind the house. You will see the big jars of it there on the shelf and also some butter that I made. The flour is in the bin next to the stove, the sugar is in the tin on the shelf." Miriam nodded and went to find Adam.

On the way out, she picked up a bucket and said to Adam, "Let's go gather the eggs. Show me where your hens lay their eggs."

"But they peck me when I reach for them. I don't like to get pecked," Adam complained.

"I've learned that you have to reach in real quick and get the hen off the nest. You carry the bucket and we'll get the eggs for our cookies."

They fed the hens and took the eggs to the springhouse. "Oh, here are the jars of milk and pats of butter. Can you carry the butter and eggs while I carry the milk? We are going to make some nice sugar cookies," Miriam said.

"I know where the sugar is 'cause I sneak some when Mama isn't looking," Adam said impishly.

Smiling to herself, Miriam said, "You find me the bowl and mixing spoon and show me where the cookie pans are while I mix the eggs and sugar. Do you know that my little sisters like to bake cookies also? We made cookies last Christmas to give to friends and we had flour all over the kitchen, however it was lots of fun." They worked together rolling and cutting cookies.

Mr. Raston came into the kitchen carrying two pails of foaming milk. "Smells mighty good in here. What are you cooking there, Adam?"

"Me and Mirry are cookin' some sugar cookies. Do you want some?" Adam answered.

"Can you take this milk and strain it, Miriam? You will find the strainer out in the springhouse. You may have to wash some jars to pour it into since I haven't done much dish washing lately."

"I would be glad to do it Mr. Raston. Want to come help me, Adam? You bring this clean jar and I'll carry the milk pails," Miriam said.

"I'm your helper boy. Just follow me and I will show you that ol' strainer," Adam said as he marched out the back door.

Peeking into the smokehouse, Miriam spotted some bacon hanging on a wire. "Here is something we can have for supper. And here are some potatoes. We could fry those in the bacon grease and add some eggs. How does that sound to you, Adam?"

"Makes my hungry tummy even hungier," he said as they walked back into the house with their arms full.

Adam helped set the table after he cut the cookies that Miriam had rolled out. "While these are baking, I will fry the potatoes. Why don't you tell your mother all that we have cooking and see what she would like to eat."

Mr. Raston arrived with an armload of firewood. "Supper smells mighty good, Miss Jensen."

"Me helped too, Papa. I cut out the cookies and set the table. I'm so hungry I could eat them all," Adam announced as he came running from his mother's room.

Miriam took food in to Mrs. Raston. "Would you have Arthur come here? I don't want to call for fear of waking little Abel, he's sleeping so peacefully."

Arthur came out of the bedroom a few minutes later. "The missus said that feeding the men dinner tomorrow was too much work for one woman. She told me to git right over to the Larsens tonight and see if their girl could help you. I'm gonna go right now so she can be here early to help."

"I could use some help since there will be bread to bake. What about meat for the meal, did she have something in mind? I've only been able to find the bacon out in the smokehouse," Miriam said as Mr. Raston started for the door.

"A big batch of chicken and noodles would feed quite a few hungry farmers. There's a couple of hens that aren't laying much. I'll wring their necks in the morning if you can have some hot water ready to scald them," Mr. Raston said as he took his coat and hat off the hook. "I'll be right back. Wish we were on that party line with the Larsens. Maybe by spring I can get the poles and lines up. Sure would save us a lot of trips back and forth."

Miriam and Adam ate without Mr. Raston. Miriam took food to Mrs. Raston. "That was delicious, Miriam," said Mrs. Raston.

Adam was still eating cookies when his father came home. Miriam gave him his supper that was in the warming oven. After she had finished the dishes she said, "Now Adam, I think we had better put the cookies in the cookie jar."

"The Larsens said that Esther would arrive with the men tomorrow morning to help you, Miss Jensen. Now, Adam, if you are going to work with the men tomorrow you had better get to bed. Here is your storybook, I will read you a story," he said as he gathered the little boy up in his lap.

Later that evening after everyone was in bed, Miriam lay on her cot in the kitchen, *How am I going to feed that many hungry men? Dear Lord, I need your help to get it all done in time. Even with Esther's help, I will have to start the bread very early so we can make the pies. It will probably take at least four for that many men. I've never done a whole meal for that many men before. Lord, give me strength*, Miriam prayed silently.

Miriam had breakfast cooking and bread started before Mr. Raston came in with the pails of milk. "You are up and around early, Miss Jensen. As soon as I eat, I'll catch those two old hens. They're big and heavy so you will have plenty of fat for the noodles. Bring out a pail of hot water and if the guys haven't arrived, I can help you dress and gut them."

Esther arrived with her three older brothers and father as Miriam was outside finishing dressing the two hens. "Good morning, Esther. Help me finish up these hens and we'll put them to cooking while we work on the bread."

"Mother thought you were brave to feed so many men on your first day at work. Mama and I hurry all morning to get a meal for the men when they shock corn and we usually start the day before with the bread and pies."

74

"I am so glad that you could help. We'll do the best that we can. It will hurry us to get the noodles, bread and pies all done at the same time. Are you better at bread or pies? We will do them first to get them done while the chicken is cooking."

"I guess I prefer pies if that is all right with you. Mother usually has me do the pies while she does the bread because she is faster at that. What kind of pies are we going to make?" Esther asked pleasantly.

"I found some apples out in the springhouse. I'll go see if Adam is awake and give him his breakfast. He probably will bring the apples in for us and help us find things in the kitchen, unless his father has promised he can watch the men work."

Adam dressed quickly and came running into the kitchen, "Where is my papa? I wanted to ask him if I could ride on the wagon today."

"The men have already left for the field, although we could use a big helper-boy in here. After you finish your breakfast, you could go to the springhouse and bring us a pail of apples for the pies. That would help us so much."

"I'll eat real fast and get your apples. I can bring in two pails if you want them," Adam said, as he shoveled large spoonfuls of oatmeal into his mouth. "I gotta go see my baby first. Then I will be your helper-boy." He jumped up and walked into the bedroom.

Miriam laughed. "Yes, you must check on that little brother. You can teach him many things when he gets a little bigger."

Following Adam into the room, she picked up Mrs. Raston's breakfast tray. "Is there anything I need to know about dinner, Mrs. Raston? Do you have enough plates for them all? I only saw eight in the cupboard," Miriam asked.

"I have some fancy plates in a box under the bed. I think there are four of those. I feel a little stronger today. I may be able to come out and eat at the table after the men are finished. Might do me good to get out of this bed."

Both girls were flushed with the heat from the stove by the time they had the bread and pies finished and the noodles cooking in a huge pot on the back of the stove. Miriam looked at the clock and saw that she only had thirty minutes before the men would be coming in to eat. "Do we have everything ready, Esther? I'm so nervous, I'm sure I will forget something."

"It all looks good to me. Don't worry about my father and brothers. They will be happy with anything they are served. Timothy would eat anything you served even if he didn't like it," Esther said with a wry smile.

Miriam stared at her, "What do you mean by that, Esther?"

"Can't you see that he is sweet on you? I heard him telling Daniel last night after they went to bed that he couldn't wait to eat your cookin'."

Miriam could feel a blush coming on the minute the men walked in the back door to start washing up for dinner, *Why do I always blush when Timothy comes around? My heart is beating so fast, I may spill something on one of the men. O, Lord, help me to calm down real fast,* she silently prayed.

She chanced a quick glance at the men as they started to sit around the table. Timothy was still waiting to wash up and had his back towards her. She noticed his broad shoulders and shock of blond hair that needed combed. Something about him made her feel comfortable. He wasn't the cold proper man that Charles Evans had been when Melody introduced her to him. She thought, *I'm so thankful that she didn't marry him. It would have been a disaster from the start. I wonder what she will do now? She won't be content to just work in her father's office. Not Melody.* With a start, Miriam brought herself back to the serving of the meal.

"Here, Esther, help me put this bowl of noodles on the table, along with the stewed tomatoes. Let's see," Miriam paused, "we have the bread cut and the butter on. Looks like it's already, Mr. Raston."

Mr. Raston cleared his throat, and looking at Mr. Larsen, he said, "Paul, would you say grace for us?"

As soon as the prayer was said, Adam, who was sitting with the men, looked up at his father and said, "Papa, don't you need a helper-boy this afternoon? I'm tired of being a house-helper."

The men all laughed. "You can ride the wagon for awhile, however I don't want you underfoot 'cause you could get stepped on by the horses. Do you understand?" Mr. Raston said.

Soon, big plates of chicken and noodles were being eaten with vigor, along with large slices of bread. "These are mighty good noodles you ladies cooked up. You would make some lucky men great wives," Mr. Raston said around a mouthful of noodles.

Miriam looked up in embarrassment at the compliment and found Timothy's bright blue eyes on her. "That's right, Miss Jensen. I know you made the noodles 'cause Esther can't make 'em that good," Timothy announced.

"That's not right, Timothy Larsen. I can too make noodles and besides we made them together," Esther responded in mock anger.

When the men were finished devouring the main dish, Miriam and Esther served the apple pie and received even more compliments. Soon chairs were being scooted back. "Let's get back to work, men, so we can get home before dark to do the evening chores. Thank you for the delicious meal, Miss Jensen and Esther," Paul Larsen announced.

Timothy Larsen lingered a little behind and finally said, "That really was good cooking, Miss Jensen." Miriam was glad that all the men had filed out because she could feel her face turning red.

Miriam quickly turned and started picking up the dinner dishes before Esther could see her face. "Esther, we need to wash some plates so we can serve some noodles to Mrs. Raston and sit down to eat ourselves before everything gets too cold."

Esther didn't seem to notice Miriam's blush. "I can wash

the plates while you help Mrs. Raston to the table. I remember Mama being so weak for the first few days," Miriam said as she headed back to the bedroom.

Once Mrs. Raston was seated, Miriam asked, "Mrs. Raston, will Esther and I be expected to serve the men anything this afternoon or evening?"

"Some might come in for cookies and coffee, although most will be trying to get finished so they can be home before dark. I think if you have a pot of coffee on the back of the stove that will be fine with those cookies you and Adam made yesterday. He sure was so proud of those cookies."

Miriam asked, "Do you think you would be strong enough by next week for me to go home, Mrs. Raston?"

"Possibly by the end of the week, if you could have a supply of bread baked up. I can cook a simple meal, however when it comes to baking bread, I can't do the kneading yet. I'm so thankful for you being here today to cook for the men. Otherwise, they would have to go to some other farm to eat and Arthur wants to feed them when they help him."

"Esther and I could bake more bread this afternoon. We went through several loaves for dinner so there is only one loaf left. Would you be willing to do the dishes, Esther, while I do the bread? Or would you like to do the bread for practice?" Miriam asked.

"I'll do the dishes. I don't mind baking pies, while bread baking is hard work. It takes so much muscle to do the kneading, at least the way my mother wants it kneaded. It is hard work."

Much to the girls' surprise, most of the guys were back for some hot coffee and cookies. "Is there any of that delicious pie left?" Mr.Raston asked.

"There is one pie left, however we have cookies also," Miriam answered as she pulled six loaves of bread out of the oven.

"Do you allow us to have a slice of fresh bread, Miss Jensen?" Timothy asked admiringly.

"If you would rather have that than the pie, we could spare a slice or two. Can you get the butter, Esther?"

Mr. Raston stopped in the middle of a bite and asked, "Say are there any of you men who would be available to help me butcher an old sow tomorrow? We are clean out of meat for winter and Old Sharp Ears is getting too heavy."

"Timothy looked quickly at his father, 'Could you spare me and Daniel tomorrow, Pa?"

"Probably could in the mornin', however I need all of you for the corn shocking in the afternoon. You could be done by then wouldn't you, Arthur?" Paul Larsen asked.

"With the speed that your sons work, we probably could be done by noon providin' all goes all right," Mr. Raston answered. "Could you fix another dinner for a couple of extras tomorrow, Miss Jensen?" Mr. Raston asked.

Without hesitation, Miriam answered, "That would be easy after today, and I already have the bread baked. What would you want for meat?" Miriam asked.

"My missus usually cooks the liver when we butcher. Liver and onions usually is what we have that day."

"Do you have any chicken and noodles left? I'm not one for liver much," Timothy asked.

"Yes, there are some noodles and chicken left. But I bet I can make liver and onions in a way that you will like it," Miriam boasted, surprising herself at her boldness.

"Then it's a deal. We'll see you two men in the morning about eight o'clock," Mr. Raston answered.

Following clearing the table, Miriam walked in to talk to Mrs. Raston. "What do you usually do with the meat at butchering time? I've never helped with butchering. We get our meat from the Smith family when they butcher."

"Mostly you need to find my large pans for the liver, heart and tongue, and wash them up for cooking. We usually have the liver for the first meal and I put the heart and tongue on to cook with lots of onion. After cooking them I add a little vinegar for flavor and allow them to cool in the liquid. They make good sandwiches when sliced cold. The rest of the meat has to cure for several days. Usually if it is cold weather, we just cut off chops and roasts as we need them. However, if it turns warm, I have to start canning it. Have you helped your mother can meat?"

"No, I have canned vegetables and fruits, however we have never canned meat. Is it more difficult than vegetables and fruit?" Miriam asked.

"Not too much, although it takes more time to cook. It is worth it though because it is delicious and ready for a quick meal."

Daniel and Timothy arrived early the next morning before Mr. Raston had the block and tackle over the cottonwood tree limb for the scalding of Old Sharp Ears. Knocking on the door of the house, Timothy stuck his head in the door and called, "Miss Jensen, your mother called to tell you that Melody Cramton wanted to see you before she left for Boston Monday. She wanted to know if you would be at church tomorrow so she could talk with you. Ma said you could ride with us if you can leave Mrs. Raston for the day. We have a basket dinner at church this Sunday. You can let me know at noon."

"Thank you for telling me, I will talk to Mrs. Raston and let you know," Miriam answered.

Later in the morning, Miriam walked out to see how the butchering was going. Just as she came around the corner of the house she heard a sharp snap and crackle as the old block and tackle rope broke, and Old Sharp Ears was dumped headlong into the fifty gallon barrel of hot water. Mr. Raston yelled, "We've got to get her out of there. She'll scorch. What in the tarnation happened?"

Timothy hurried over to the barrel and pushed it over. "Look out! Stand back so you don't get burnt," he said, looking at Miriam.

Little Adam was so excited that he was clapping and jumping up and down, "Look at that, Mirry! We've got Old Sharp Ears stuck. She looks like a fat old lady." Soon he was down on his hands and knees making mud pies from the hot mud created by the water dumped out of the barrel.

"What in tarnation do we do now? Quick, help me pull her out of there before she boils!" Mr. Raston exclaimed.

With much tugging and pulling, they finally extracated the pig from the barrel and onto some planks. "Now we can get her scraped and dissected. I'll never let one get this big again. Should have gotten a new block and tackle for Old Sharp Ears and her 500 lbs."

Miriam admired Timothy's calmness in the whole incident. Walking back to the house she was thinking, *He seemed to know what just what to do even when Mr. Raston panicked.*

"Bring the pans for the liver and heart, Miss Jensen," Mr. Raston called to Miriam. "We've just about got her gutted."

Seeing all the bloody liver and heart that Timothy dumped into her pans, Miriam said, "Do you really eat this? It doesn't look appetizing to me. Are you sure you want this for dinner, Mr. Raston?"

"Yep, it won't keep. Slice it and dump on loads of onion and maybe even Timothy will eat it," Mr. Raston said with a wry chuckle.

With much struggle, Miriam finally got the liver sliced and into the skillet for frying and added several chopped onions. "I don't think I can eat this after cutting it up," she told Adam who had followed her into the house.

"I lub liver. Mama said it would make me grow up big and strong," Adam said.

Following the meal of mashed potatoes, fried apples and liver, Timothy announced, "Now that was almost edible liver. Pa always wants it cooked as crisp as a shoe sole and I can't stomach it at all."

"Well, thank you Mr. Larsen. I consider that a real compliment since you said you couldn't stand liver," Miriam smiled.

"Do you want our family to come by for you for church tomorrow, Miss Jensen?" Timothy asked eagerly as he and Daniel prepared to leave.

"Mrs. Raston said she could spare me for the day as long as I cooked breakfast and had meat on cooking for dinner. So yes, I'd be glad for a ride."

Sunday morning appeared cold and clear as Miriam hurried through the breakfast meal and put a roast in the oven for the Rastons' dinner. Humming a little as she worked, she didn't hear Adam come in for breakfast. "What are you hummin' Mirry? Sounds like a church song."

"Oh! You surprised me, Adam. I didn't know you were up yet. I was humming a church song. It is called, *Count Your Many Blessings*. I like the words because they say, 'count your many blessings name them one by one' and I have so many of them to count," Miriam answered.

"What is a blessing, Mirry? Do I have blessings?" Adam asked.

"You have lots of blessings, Adam. You have your mother and father, you have your little brother and you have a warm house and good food. Can you think of others?"

"Sure, I've got warm mud to make mud pies like I did yesterday," Adam answered getting caught up in the game.

"The Larsens are coming after me for church today, Adam. Do you think you can take care of your mama while I am gone? It will be almost supper time by the time we return."

Adam nodded. "Papa can help me. I can set the table and Papa can wash the dishes. I'm a big boy so don't you worry about us. But I wish I could go to Sunday school. Mama and I went sometimes, but we don't go no more. Papa won't take us," Adam said sadly.

"I wish you could go too, Adam. Tell you what, as soon as I dress for church, I will read you a story out of my Bible. How would that be?"

"Oh, goody, goody. Will you tell the story about Daniel and the lions?" Adam asked.

Miriam had just finished reading the story and answering Adam's questions when they heard the dog barking. "Here comes a buggy! Bet Timothy is driving it. I'm going out and ask him if he will give me a ride!" Adam exclaimed and ran out the door without his coat or hat.

Miriam followed, carrying Adam's coat and hat. "Here Adam, if you are going to be outside, you must have these on. Your mama wouldn't want you coming down with consumption."

"I want to ride with my friend, Timothy," Adam insisted as he climbed up onto the driver seat to sit beside Timothy.

Mr. Raston came out of the barn at the sound of the dog barking. "Adam what do you think you are doing up there? Timothy has to leave. Now get right down and come help me in the barn, do you hear?"

"Yes, Papa," Adam answered with disappointment.

"I'll take you for a ride this afternoon when we bring Miss Larsen home. Ask your papa if that would be all right with him," Timothy said.

Helping Miriam into the carriage, Timothy said, "You can sit beside Ma. She has the comforter for her and the baby."

Miriam felt her heart beat faster as Timothy helped her up into the carriage. She could feel all their eyes were on her and knew she couldn't keep from blushing. Sitting down quickly she said, "Good morning, Mrs. Larsen. How is that little one today?"

"He is doing very well. How is Mrs. Raston's baby doing and is she regaining her strength?" Mrs. Larsen asked.

"The baby is doing well for his difficult birth. And Mrs. Raston was up some yesterday to eat her meals. Little Adam really wanted to go to church with us. Does the family go to church anywhere?" Miriam asked.

"I don't think that Mr. Raston goes much at all, although

we have taken Mrs. Raston and Adam several times, and I think they attend the little country church that meets in the school house some Sundays."

Miriam thoroughly enjoyed the ride in the cold fresh air. "I've been inside so much this week that I didn't realize how cold it had become. I enjoy the fresh air."

"The fresh air helps prevent consumption, they tell me," Mrs Larsen responded.

As they pulled into the church yard, Miriam saw Melody and her family pulling in, with Matthew driving their big black geldings. Melody was dressed in a fur trimmed cape with matching hat and muff. Melody waved vigorously.

Miriam waited impatiently until Timothy had helped his mother and sisters from the carriage. He seemed to be leaving her until the last. "May I help you down, Miss Jensen?" he asked with a big bow.

"Yes, you may, Mr. Larsen. And if you do not hurry, I may jump and embarrass us all," Miriam smiled.

Melody was holding up the hem of her long skirt, and hurrying towards her. "Miriam, you got to come! I'm so glad you could. I must talk to you before I leave."

"I thought you didn't want to go to music school when your father wanted to send you several years ago," Miriam stated.

"Church is starting so we had better get seated. Come sit with us. Father doesn't like to be coming in late," Melody said as she reached for Miriam's arm. Miriam had no choice except to sit with the Cramtons without even a chance to talk to her family. She nodded to her mother as she followed Melody to the special front seat where the Cramtons always sat.

Miriam had difficulty concentrating on the sermon. She kept mulling over and over in her mind, *Why would Melody want to leave town in such a rush? She just got back from a near disaster. She needs to be with her parents and people in the church. Does this have something to do with almost eloping with Mr. Evans?*

Following church, Miriam was surrounded by her sisters all talking at once. "What have you been doing out at the Rastons?" Anna asked. "When are you coming home? Are you going to eat with us?"

"One question at a time. I have been cooking, cleaning, and cooking and cleaning at the Rastons. I may come home the end of next week. And yes, I will be eating with you. Now, are you satisfied?" Miriam asked with a smile.

The men were busy moving the pews back against the wall and putting boards across saw horses for holding the food. Melody came over and whispered, "Come over here in the corner where we can talk. I have so much to tell you." Miriam followed reluctantly.

"What did you mean by saying that you were leaving for Boston tomorrow? Why are you going there anyway? I thought you did not wish to go to the school of music," Miriam asked.

"I've changed my mind. Father gave me permission to go and I need to check out places to live and other details before I enroll," Melody said.

"This is November and Christmas will be coming. Aren't you going to stay here until after Christmas? The second session doesn't start until January, does it?" Miriam reasoned.

"If you must know, I'm not going just for music school," Melody gave a sigh of impatience. "I wish to attend the Womans Suffrage Fair in Boston the first week in December. I may be back for Christmas, depending on how involved I am by that time. I have been so excited about womans suffrage ever since your mother gave me the copies of *The Woman's Column* belonging to your grandmother."

"I'm surprised that my mother would give them to you since she doesn't agree with what the women write in that paper," Miriam stated.

"She told me that she didn't agree with them, although

85

thought I would find them interesting. I certainly did find them interesting. I feel that God is calling me to help all women this way. That may be my calling in life just like you help women with babies," Melody announced.

"What convinced you to attend this fair in Boston. Didn't you decide rather suddenly?"

"I rode the train to Minneapolis to visit your grandmother, Mrs. Glendinning. She was so encouraging, and she thought I should go. She told me that if she were younger she would go herself. We agreed that women should be allowed to vote and we may have to fight hard to accomplish that. It is all so interesting. Don't you think so, Miriam?"

Miriam gave her a dubious look. "Not really. From what I have read in the Bible, the men are to handle business like this," Miriam answered.

"Oh pooh! You and your picayune (small) ideas. I am looking for excitement and a challenge in life. I'm not going to stay here in Beloit and wither away. I'm going to do something with my life! You just wait and see."

CHAPTER SEVEN

TIMOTHY

MELODY AND HER FAMILY prepared to leave for home soon after the basket dinner was served. Before leaving, Melody confided to Miriam, "I probably won't be home for Christmas and maybe not until next spring, so I need to hurry home to pack my trunks. I'm not planning on telling Mother and Father that I am not coming home until after I have been there for awhile. They might not allow me to leave if I were to tell them now." Miriam frowned and started to speak. Not allowing Miriam to say a word, Melody gave her a big hug, and waved a gloved hand in goodbye to everyone standing around. Lifting the hem of her Sunday gown, she followed Mary and Thomas out to the carriage where Matthew was waiting.

I wonder if I will ever see her again? Miriam mused. *She seems so discontented living here. I wonder if she would be contented anywhere?* Walking over to where Mrs. Larsen was picking up her pans of food, Miriam asked, "Do you need some help, Mrs. Larsen? Are you ready to leave? I can help you carry these dishes."

"Would you like to hold the little one so I can finish cleaning up our dishes? I know you haven't had time to visit with your family today so why don't you visit with your family until

Paul is ready to leave?" Martha asked as she looked over at Paul standing with Aaron Jensen and some of the farmers.

Miriam sat down beside her mother, who lifted a corner of the blanket of the bundle she was carrying, "Oh! You have the Larsen baby. Isn't he cute? Are they getting ready to return home? I hoped that we would have a few minutes of your time, however Melody kept you busy until she left. Did she say why she is going to Boston?" Lydia asked.

Miriam tucked the blanket snuggly around the baby and answered. "She has convinced her parents that she must go to music school in Boston, although she isn't telling them the real reason and that is to attend the Woman's Suffrage Fair there in early December. She also isn't telling them that she may not return until next spring. I know that will break her mother's heart. Thomas probably would not allow her to leave if they knew. I couldn't seem to make her understand that. She has her mind made up."

"If only I hadn't given her those copies of *The Woman's Column* from your grandmother. I knew I had made a mistake when she became so excited about seeing them. It was too late to take them back," Lydia said remorsefully.

"Mother, Melody is constantly searching for something exciting. She would have found material on woman's suffrage sooner or later. I don't think she heard a word of the sermon this morning from Proverbs 3 about seeking God's plan and not your own. It was just what she needed to hear."

"No, it doesn't seem like she did. Her life seems to be even more leaning on her own understanding and she will direct her own paths. All we can do is to pray that God will protect her from the many temptations she will encounter in Boston," Lydia said. "I need to talk to Mary. She might think I encouraged Melody to be involved in the woman's suffrage movement, although I'm sure she knows I do not agree with women voting."

"You and I both know that if it wasn't woman's suffrage,

Melody would have found some reason to leave Beloit. She wants to be where there is excitement and culture. She seems to think obedience to God and being content where He puts you is so dull. I find each day exciting from the people He brings into my life to working with the challenges of helping Mrs. Polinsky deliver babies," Miriam finished.

"Miriam, here comes Esther Larsen. Looks like they are preparing to leave," Anna commented from her seat across from Miriam. "Will you be coming home this week?"

Miriam stood up. "If Mrs. Raston continues to gain strength, I should be home by the end of the week. She has no relatives to come in to help like most families around here do, so I can't leave until she is strong enough to do the cooking. I may even have to go back and help with the washing, because I know she won't be strong enough for that for several weeks," Miriam answered as she prepared to get in the carriage.

Aaron walked out with her. "Be careful this week, Miriam. Don't do anything foolish," he cautioned. And as the Larsen family climbed into the carriage, he hugged her, calling "Goodbye," as they drove away.

Riding home with the Larsens, Miriam marveled at how much she enjoyed being with this family. She felt so comfortable with them. It seemed like they were family already. She wished the ride would never end. Martha Larsen interrupted her thoughts, "Miriam, does Mrs. Raston have plenty of soap made up for winter? Since they just butchered, you probably should cook out the cracklings for the lard. If you like, Esther can come help. With a new baby, there will be extra clothes and diapers to wash."

"Why yes, Mrs. Larsen, if you can spare Esther tomorrow afternoon, we could make up a big batch and it could be curing when I leave," Miriam answered. "Would you send your recipe? It has been a year or more since I helped mother make soap."

As they drove into the Raston yard, the dog started barking and little Adam came running towards the carriage with his coat and cap on this time. "Can I ride now, Mr. Timmy? Papa says I can."

Laughing at little Adam's eagerness, Timothy helped Miriam down from the carriage. She wished she had been home so she could have worn a nicer dress, although Timothy didn't seem to notice. "Enjoyed having you ride with us, Miss Larsen," he said as he helped her to the ground. Miriam felt her face turning red so she was thankful to hear Mr. Raston call from the barn.

"The missus said to send you right into the house. She overdid this afternoon and needs help," he called.

Miriam hurried to the house, taking off her cloak before going to Mrs. Raston's bedside. "Are you feeling alright, Mrs. Raston?"

"I tried to stay up to spend some time with Adam and Arthur, however I was so weak I almost fainted. They had to help me back to bed. I am afraid I may need you for another week if I don't start gaining strength."

"I will stay as long as you need, Mrs. Raston. I was able to spend some time with my friend and a little time with my family so I am free to stay," Miriam reassured her. "Mrs. Larsen asked if you had plenty of soap made up. She said she would send Esther over to help me make some tomorrow afternoon, if you would like for me to make it."

"That would be wonderful if you would. That was another job I didn't get done. You will need to cook those cracklings down so there will be enough lard. I have some lye crystals saved from last year. Would you be able to do the washing in the morning? The baby is running out of diapers and Arthur said he needed long johns by Wednesday."

"I think if I started early heating the water and had all the clothes sorted we could have them on the lines before noon. It looks like it might be a drying day tomorrow, but maybe a little cool."

By Friday, Miriam had the soap and bread made, and the washing and ironing done up. Mrs. Raston came out to the kitchen and watched as she finished making some apple pies. "Miriam, I am much stronger now, I think you could go home tomorrow if you would like. You have done a wonderful job."

"Really? Adam is good help to me, so if you can keep him inside for awhile perhaps he will help you with some of the trips to the springhouse," Miriam said smiling broadly.

"Keeping him inside will take some convincing. He thinks he is his pa's helper, although he is also excited about a little brother so he might be willing to stay inside and help."

"He loves to have the Bible stories read. I can tell that you have been telling him Bible stories because he knows many of them," Miriam said.

"Yes, I try to make up for not being able to take him to Sunday school, however once the spring weather settles down, Adam, Abel and I will be going to the little meeting at the schoolhouse. I keep praying that Arthur will go with me, however he always says he has work to do on Sunday. Maybe someday he will, but I'm afraid Adam will decide not to go. He is influenced by his father."

"Was Mr. Raston a Christian when you married him, Mrs. Raston?" Miriam asked gently.

Mrs. Raston lowered her eyes, "We never really talked about it. He was working for my father and he asked my father if he could court me. My father has no use for church so it didn't matter to him, and with five daughters he was anxious for me to marry. It wasn't until after we were married that I realized that Arthur wasn't a Christian. We couldn't talk much with my father usually in the room when he came to court. I should have known he wasn't, because he always worked with my father on Sundays just like any other day of the week. Be careful that you marry a Christian, Miriam, because a wife can't change a man once his mind is made up."

Miriam was anxious to return home so after packing up her knitting and clothes, Mrs. Raston came out carrying two beautifully embroidered pillowslips. "I want you to have these for your hope chest, Miriam. Someday God will give you a Christian husband and you will need these. They aren't much, but that is all I have now. Thank you so much for staying to help me get on my feet."

"Those are beautiful, Mrs. Raston," Miriam gasped. "How did you know that I didn't have any in my hope chest? I've been knitting some afghans and dish clothes, however haven't had time to make any pillowslips. Thank you."

Adam came running into the house and saw what was happening. "Mirry, you can't go home. Who will read me stories and help me bake cookies? Tell her to stay, Mama."

Miriam knelt down in front of him. "I will miss you too, Adam, but I need to get home because Mrs. Polinsky may need my help delivering another baby. The next time your papa comes to town, why don't you ask him if he will bring you by our house and you can help me and my sisters bake cookies. Even if I am not there, they will let you help them. They like company. How does that sound to you?"

"Sure, can I come tomorrow? Papa said he was going to town tomorrow," Adam said jumping up and down.

"No, Adam, if your father goes to town tomorrow, I will need you here to help me with the cooking. When I get a little stronger, you can go with him." Adam's face fell. "Who will gather the eggs and feed the chickens if you go to town?" his mother asked.

Miriam hugged him and stood up, "If you are still too weak to do your washing next week, Mrs. Raston, send Arthur to the Larsens to call me. If I am not out with Mrs. Polinsky, I can do your washing and read Adam some stories," she said with a grin. Mrs. Raston nodded and Adam followed Miriam to the bedroom.

"I'll help you harness Ginger. Papa showed me how, and she is so little I can almost reach over her head if I stand on my tip-toes," Adam said.

"I could use some help from a big boy like you. Can you carry my valise while I carry this other bag of clothes? I'll be praying for you, Mrs. Raston," Miriam said as she left. They walked out to the barn with their load.

Mr. Raston came out of the shed where he was feeding the hogs. "Are you leaving, Miss Jensen ? I'm much obliged to you for all the help you have been to the misses. We don't have no relations to come in and help."

"I was glad to do that, Mr. Raston. I told your wife that I would come back out if she needed help with the washing next week. Just give me a call from the Larsens when she needs me."

"Wait for a minute, please. I have something I want to give you," Mr. Raston said as he hurried away. In a few minutes he came back carrying a small ham wrapped in cloth. "I can't pay you much, however this might help out at home."

"Thank you, Mr. Raston. We can always use fresh meat. Another way that you could thank me is to read Bible stories to your son. He was so worried that no one would read to him, once I left. Mrs. Raston will be busy with the little one now so Adam needs some extra care from you. Could you read the Bible to him?" Miriam asked pointedly.

Mr. Raston rubbed the back of his neck uncomfortably. "Well, I guess I could. Never was one to read the Bible much, but guess it wouldn't hurt me none to read a little to Adam."

"Adam would be grateful and so would I, Mr. Raston," Miriam called. "Good bye, Adam. Thank you for helping me harness Ginger," she called as she drove away.

Miriam enjoyed the warm weather driving home. Hearing the blue jays chattering and seeing the pheasants fly across the road to the corn field with their beautiful feathers of rust and green reminded her of God's wonderful creation. *Thank you, heavenly Father, for the beautiful blue sky with the fluffy white clouds and the animals you provided for our food and enjoyment.* Driving slowly past the Larsen farm, she hoped to catch a glance of Timothy, however could see no one working outside. *I wonder where they are on a nice day. They usually are out doing something on a nice day like this,* she pondered.

Driving on she saw other farmers sawing firewood and working on fence lines. Waving to all who looked her way, she kept thinking, *Why aren't the Larsens working today? Maybe there has been a death in the family. I know that Grandpa Larsen was not well.*

Nearing town, she met Timothy Larsen driving his mother on their way home from town. "Hello," they called as they passed. Something about the way Timothy looked at her caught her attention. *Why were those bright blue eyes looking even brighter than usual?* she wondered.

Miriam drove by her father's smithy shop and noticed smoke still coming from the chimney. *He must have had a hard job to finish up,* she reasoned. Pulling on the reins, Miriam called, "Whoa there, Ginger. Let's stop and see why Father is working so late."

Walking into the smoky dark interior, Miriam found Aaron shrinking wagon wheel rims. Feeling fresh air on his back, Aaron turned and exclaimed, "Miriam, I didn't know you were home. How did you know to stop? I have some special news for you."

"I saw smoke still coming from the chimney so thought I would see why you were working so late. Besides I wanted you to know that I was home. What is the news you have for me?" She walked closer.

"This doesn't seem like the proper place for this kind of news, although I had a visitor this afternoon. Someone you know came by to talk to me."

"Who was it, Father? Did it have something to do with Melody?"

"No, it didn't have anything to do with Melody. What would make you think it was about her?"

"Because she is in Boston and something bad could have happened to her," Miriam answered.

"No, this visitor was Timothy Larsen. He didn't have any work for me to do as far as I could see, but he just stood around until everyone else left."

"Yes, Father, what did he want?" Miriam asked anxiously, leaning forward.

"He kind of stood around and acted like he didn't know quite what to say so I asked, 'Timothy, was there something you wanted to talk to me about?'"

"And what did he say?" Miriam asked nervously

"He finally got it out. He asked, 'Mr. Jensen, would you or could I uh, could I come to court your oldest daughter, Miriam?' he said in a sudden rush of words."

"And what did you tell him, Father? Did he really want to court me? I can't believe it. I'm so excited. What did you tell him?" Her face lit up as she talked.

"Well, I told him that I would have to take it into consideration and would need a private talk with him before I gave him an answer," her father answered. He picked up his hammer to finish the work on the rims.

"You mean you didn't tell him 'yes' right off?" Miriam asked incredulously. "You know the Larsen family. You have done work for Mr. Larsen and we go to church with them. Why couldn't you have told him right then?"

"I do know the Larsen family and have done work for Paul and have seen them at church, Miriam, although I do not know where Timothy stands with the Lord. Just because he goes to church doesn't mean that he knows Christ personally. That is

95

something we will talk about when he comes in the next time," Aaron answered.

Miriam ran to her father and gave him a big hug, "I love you, Papa. You are so right; I don't know Timothy's relationship with the Lord. I was getting in such a rush that I couldn't wait for you to find out. I'm sorry."

"You're forgiven, however your mother might not forgive those smudges on your dress from my dirty overalls," Aaron said with a chuckle. "You better get home and tell her I will be there shortly.

"I can't wait to tell everyone the news about Timothy!"

"Miriam, I want to talk to your mother about this before you announce it to your sisters. You understand the reason, don't you?" Aaron asked.

"Yes, Father, but it will be difficult to not tell them. I'm so excited they may guess that something has happened and want to know what has me so happy."

"That may be true, Miriam, although you can say that you will tell them later."

"If you say so, Father, I can wait. Are you going to talk to Mother tonight?"

"Yes, I plan that we will talk as soon as the younger girls are in bed. What do you think of having Anna join us for a time of prayer about the request from Timothy?" Aaron asked.

"Oh yes, Papa, I want Anna there. She already knows that I think a lot about Timothy."

Aaron patted her on the arm, "I'll see you at the house in a little bit."

Miriam felt that she was floating on a happy cloud as she drove Ginger on home. Putting Ginger in the barn and giving her feed and water gave her time to think how she was going to talk to her sisters without them guessing why she was so happy. Opening the door to the kitchen, she found Lydia and Anna cooking supper. "Oh, Miriam, we didn't hear you pull into the yard. What a nice surprise to have you home for supper. It seems like it has been weeks since you have eaten with us," Lydia said cheerfully, while drying her hands and coming up to her.

"Tell us all about your time with the Rastons, Miriam," Emma said as she grabbed her big sister around the waist.

"It must have been fun because you seem so happy," Anna commented.

"I did enjoy working with little Adam and being able to leave Mrs. Raston with homemade bread and pies and having all of her washing done up. Mother, I even made her a batch of soap with Esther's help. I had never done that by myself before and I must say it turned out very well. The one thing I didn't enjoy was helping with the butchering. Cutting up fresh liver for a meal was not fun at all. I don't think I can eat liver ever again after that," Miriam reported. Thankfully Anna didn't pursue anything more on why she was so happy. Miriam got out her knitting and worked while supper cooked.

Elizabeth curled up beside in the chair. "Mirry, did you have fun with the new baby?"

"Yes, Elizabeth, although I didn't have much time to play with him. I was busy cooking and washing clothes."

"I wish I could go with you to help with the babies. I am good with babies." Elizabeth bragged.

"Maybe someday you can come with me, Elizabeth. Here comes Papa for supper. Let's go wash our hands."

Following a supper of fresh ham, sweet potatoes and fried apples, Aaron read a Bible story to the family. "Now, I want Emma, Jessie, Danielle and Elizabeth in bed early. Your mother and I need to talk to Miriam and Anna," Aaron announced.

Lydia looked at Aaron with a question on her face, but without a word she started preparing Elizabeth for bed. Anna and Miriam cleaned off the table and washed the dishes while Aaron read the Beloit Gazette. "Here is a little item in the society news you might be interested in. It says, 'Miss Melody

Cramton has been accepted at the New England Conservatory of Music for the winter semester.'"

"Have her parents heard from her since she left?" Miriam asked.

"If they have, Thomas hasn't said anything. She probably doesn't want them to know what she is doing. Your mother told me she was planning to attend the Woman's suffrage fair. She knows they would not approve of that," Aaron responded.

Lydia came back into the kitchen, "Everyone is in bed, Aaron. Looks like the dishes are almost done. Shall I get some sewing to work on while we are talking?"

"You can work on your sewing, Lydia, it will not distract from our talking. By the way I need some work socks. Would you have time to knit a pair for me this week? My last pair has the toes worn out."

"Why didn't you say so? I should have started them before now. I can repair your old ones until I can get another pair knitted," Lydia answered as she headed for the bedroom for her knitting bag.

Miriam and Anna pulled out chairs and sat around the table. Clearing his throat as if ready to make an important announcement, Aaron said, "I had an unexpected visitor this afternoon and since Miriam stopped by on her way home, I shared the news with her."

"Who was the visitor, Father?" Anna asked. "Was it someone we know?"

"Give him time to tell you what happened, Anna. I could hardly wait to tell you the exciting news," Miriam said joyfully.

"Was it Thomas with some news about Melody?" Lydia asked. "Mary has been so anxious to hear from her."

"No, it was not Thomas. It was Timothy Larsen. He came to ask me if he could court Miriam. I'm not quite ready for our oldest to be courted. I keep forgetting that she is eighteen," Aaron said looking over at Lydia.

"Oh, that is exciting, Miriam! I really like Timothy and his brothers. When will he start courting, Father? You did tell him 'yes' didn't you?" Anna asked.

"Just a minute girls. We have not asked God what He thinks of this relationship of Timothy and Miriam," Aaron reminded.

"I have been praying, Papa, for several years that God would guide you in finding a strong Christian husband for me," Miriam said quietly.

"I also have been praying for you, Miriam, because I know the mistake I almost made before your father started courting me. Thanks to Grannie's prayers, God stopped me in time," Lydia said hesitantly.

"I'm mighty thankful for your grandmother's prayers, Lydia, and for her determination to not allow you to marry an unbeliever," Aaron said. "Now let's pray about Miriam and Timothy. Even though we all like the Larsen family that doesn't mean that Miriam should marry Timothy. Only God can give us that wisdom."

Following the time of prayer, Miriam prepared for bed. Lying in bed beside Anna, she couldn't go to sleep. Anna sensed she wasn't asleep. "Miriam, as much as I like Timothy, I don't want for you to get married and leave home. It won't be the same without you here every day."

"I know, Anna. We've been so close all these years, however if I marry Timothy, we won't be far away. I assume that he will continue to farm with his father or on a nearby farm."

Anna reached over and gave Miriam a hug. "I am so happy for you. It will be wonderful having another man in our family."

Miriam still couldn't sleep. Laying there thinking and praying, *Lord, it this what you want for my life? I don't want to get away from your plan. You know I really do like Timothy.* With that prayer, she was able to relax and fall asleep assured that God would lead her and Timothy in their relationship.

The next morning, Miriam helped her mother do the weeks washing, "Mother, teach me how to get clothes really clean and white especially in the winter when you can not hang them out in the sun to bleach the whites. There is so much I need to learn if I am going to get married."

"Yes, the sun does help whiten the whites. Some of that new soap that I made seems to help with that also. Would you and Anna want to finish the washing today so I can visit Mary? She called me on the telephone to see if I could do a Bible study with her today. I know she is struggling, with Melody not contacting them and being so far away in Boston."

Miriam agreed immediately, "Go on, Mother. Anna can help and Emma can work on dinner. We need the practice. Can we hang the sheets out on the line to freeze dry? There isn't enough room to hang them in here," Miriam asked.

"Yes, hang them out. There is enough wind that they should dry. And they smell so much better after being hung out," Lydia said as she put on her hooded cloak. "I should be home near dinner time. Matthew is coming to pick me up so I won't have to get our buggy out." A few minutes later the Cramton carriage pulled into the drive.

By noon they had the washing all done, hung up and the tubs of water dumped out back where it wouldn't make ice puddles. "Now for finishing up dinner. Emma are the butter beans done so we can feed Papa when he arrives in a few minutes?" Miriam asked. "My back is tired from bending over that washboard all morning. I think I will be a hunchback. Can you cut the bread and set the table?"

That evening after the clothes were folded and ironed, Miriam was sitting at the table reading beside her father, "Father, when are you supposed to have that private visit with Timothy?"

"Why? Are you in a hurry, Miriam?" Aaron asked with a smile.

"Probably not any more than Timothy," Miriam said seriously.

"He told me that he would be in town again early next week so we could talk. However, I can tell you right now that your mother and I are thankful you are willing to seek God's plan on this relationship. That makes it easier for me to talk to Timothy," Aaron announced.

"I can hardly wait until you talk to him. What if you talk to him and feel that it wouldn't be right for him to court me? That would be so difficult for me to accept."

"Miriam, don't worry about the what-if's. Don't you remember that God tells us in Romans chapter eight that He uses everything for the good of those who love the Lord? Trust God to know what is best for you and Timothy."

CHAPTER EIGHT

STRUGGLES

MIRIAM WAS HOME one afternoon sewing on a dress. She heard someone drive hurriedly into the yard. Glancing out the window she saw a farmer coming to the door. Opening the door at his knock, he greeted her with, "Are you Miss Jensen? Mrs. Polinsky is sick and sent me to fetch you since our baby is about to arrive. My name is Johnston and we live out to the west of town."

"Do you want me to come with you now or bring my own buggy?" Miriam asked.

"I would rather you come with me now. I don't like the looks of this weather," he said glancing back over is shoulder at the dark clouds rolling over head.

"Let me pack my valise and tell Mother that I am leaving and I will be with you. Do you want to come inside and wait?"

"Naw, my boots are muddy. I'll wait for you out in the buggy."

Miriam quickly gathered up some clothes, her Bible and some knitting. "Mother, I will be at the Johnston farm. I don't know where they live, perhaps Father does. I should be back in a few days. I will try to get you on the telephone if it turns out to be longer."

"Good bye, Miriam. I will be praying for you as you help Mrs. Johnston without Mrs. Polinsky," Lydia said in concern. The Johnston farm was far out in the country. Miriam had never been in that part of the county before. Driving along toward their farm, Mr. Johnston said, "I have to check my cattle, Miss Jensen. There seems to be a storm brewin' so I will be gone for several hours roundin' 'em all up to be in the shelter of the trees and barn. Is there anything you need before I leave? That storm looks to be arrivin' before dark."

"Is there any neighbor lady who could help me with the baby's delivery? I've always worked with Mrs. Polinsky at the other homes," Miriam asked.

"Go on inside and ask Mrs. Johnston. She might know of a woman who could come. You can try calling her on the telephone. If you can't reach anyone send John out to tell me, then I'll go ride over to ask for help."

Miriam hurried to the house to find two young children seated at the table eating cold cornmeal mush. "Hello, I am Miriam. Can you tell me where to find your mother?"

"The little girl ran to Miriam and reached for her hand. "Mommy's in here. She is crying and I am scared. Can you help her?"

"I hope that I can." Miriam, following the little girl, and found Mrs. Johnston on bed with her face contorted with labor pains. "Mrs. Johnston, I am here to help you. Mrs. Polinsky is sick so she asked me to come alone. Do you know of any neighbor lady who could come help me?"

"You look awfully young. Have you delivered a baby before?" Mrs. Johnston asked.

"Yes, this is my fourth baby, really the fifth because I delivered my little sister five years ago," Miriam answered.

"I think Mrs. Andrews might come. Her children are older and she lives just a mile away. My aunt said she would come as soon as the baby arrives, however I cannot call her since she does not have a telephone yet. She is the only kinfolk that I have near here."

"Please hurry, I think the baby will be arriving real a-a-soon," she stammered as another pain hit.

Miriam rang central. "Could you give me Mrs. Andrews, please?" she yelled. *Oh Lord, please help her to be home. I need help right away.*

A voice on the other end of the line answered. Miriam could not tell if it was man or woman so she yelled, "Please send Mrs. Andrews over to the Johnston home. Her baby is coming."

Turning to the children, she asked, "What are your names?"

"Mine is John and hers is Emily," five-year-old John answered.

"Well, John, can you help me find your mother's big pans to heat some water? I will stoke up the fire if you bring me the pans," Miriam requested.

While cutting up some roast beef for the children to eat with their cold mush, Miriam kept praying that Mrs. Andrews would arrive soon. "Now, John, can you show me where your mother keeps the sheets and towels? Do you know if she has some baby clothes out for this baby?"

"Yes, ma'am, I know where all that stuff is. Come with me and I will show you," John answered importantly.

There was a knock on the door. Little Emily ran to open it. "Come in Mrs. Andrews. Mama needs you and this nice lady needs you."

"Oh thank goodness you are here, "Miriam said. "The baby is arriving and I need help. I've always been Mrs. Polinsky's helper before."

"Just tell me what you need for me to do. I do hope that baby arrives soon as my husband told me not to stay with that storm coming. It looks like a bad one."

"Her pains were five minutes apart the last time I checked, so it won't be long," Miriam answered. "if you can help I think that baby will be here very shortly. Can you children play here quietly while we help your mama?"

"Yes, ma'am. I will see that Emily doesn't cry 'cause I want a little brother," John announced.

"What is your name, Miss? Your face is familiar, although I don't recall your name," Mrs. Andrews asked.

"Miriam. Miriam Jensen is my name. My father is Aaron Jensen from the blacksmith shop. You may have seen me there with Father."

"Of course, I know your father. He has repaired many a wagon wheel for us. Seems like we break so many, living so far out in the country."

"Mrs. Andrews, if you will stand on that side of Mrs. Johnson to help and I will stand on this side, we will help that baby arrive. He seems to be impatient. Are you doing all right, Mrs. Johnston?" Miriam asked.

"Just help me push. I know he is coming," she said gritting her teeth with the pain.

Miriam was correct. Within minutes she exclaimed, "You have a baby boy, Mrs. Johnston. Do you want me to call John and Emily to see their new baby brother?"

"Oh yes, John and Emily have been so good all day not to bother me. They need to see that God answered their prayers. Robert and I picked Isaac for his name."

They had just bathed and dressed the baby when Mr. Johnston burst into the house. "It is starting to sleet. Can you ladies look after this baby calf and warm him up? I found him almost frozen out in the storm." With that, he laid a limp little calf on the floor.

"I know how to take care of baby calves, Miriam, if you want to finish cleaning up Mrs. Johnston," Mrs. Andrews said, "Come Emily and John, find me some old rags and we will rub this little fellow dry and put him behind the stove to warm up."

Miriam handed the baby to his mother. "There, there little one. It is time for your first meal. Is there anything else you need, Mrs. Johnston?"

"No, I just need to rest. God is so good to give us another little boy. You can go help Mrs. Andrews with the calf. There will probably be more before the night is out, by the sound of that sleet hitting the window," she answered with a tired sigh.

"I can take over now, Mrs. Andrews. You better leave for home while there is still some daylight, and before the storm becomes worse."

"Yes, I had better head for home. If the storm is not too bad, I will try to bring over some food for the family. I know they don't have any kinfolk near."

Mr. Johnston came in after she left, "How is the missus doing?"

"You have a healthy son, Mr. Johnston."

"I've got to take a look at that little fella, who chose to arrive in a storm," Coming out of the bedroom, he said, "Were you planning on me taking you home tonight, Miss Jensen?"

"I couldn't ask you to do that, Mr. Johnston. I can wait until the storm stops. Sometime tomorrow would be fine," Miriam answered.

"I really do need your help tonight. I may be up all night with the way these calves are arriving. If I do not get them inside right away, they will freeze. How is that little one I brought in earlier? I best take him out to his mama so she will not forget he belongs to her. Why don't you call your mother to tell her you will be staying here tonight."

Miriam rang central, however all she could hear was loud static. "If anyone can hear me, tell Aaron Jensen that their daughter will be staying with the Johnston family tonight and that the baby and mother are all right," she yelled. She heard the telephone go dead the minute she finished giving the message. *Oh no! The lines have gone down with the ice and wind. They probably will never get my message. O Lord, help all of the farmers tonight*

106

who are out in this storm with baby calves and help me know what to do while Mr. Johnston is out with the livestock, she prayed.

Miriam cooked supper for the children and some broth for Mrs. Johnston. "Would you want me to bake some bread? Where does Mr. Johnston keep the dry wood? Shouldn't I bring some extra inside?" Miriam asked.

"John can help you with the wood. Yes, it would be good if you bake some bread. I did not feel up to doing it before the baby arrived. Has Robert been in from the barn yet? I fell asleep and didn't hear anything while the baby was nursing."

"Yes, he was in to get the little calf and take him to the barn. Do you think he will be in to eat supper? I will put it in the warming oven if he will be back inside," Miriam asked.

"Yes, he should be back because he will have to milk sometime. You may need to wash some crocks for the milk. I felt too bad to do any dishes this morning."

An hour or so later Mr. Johnston came in with two buckets of foaming milk. "It's getting mighty nasty out there. Everything is covered with a sheet of ice. I have most of the cows near the barn, however I will have to stay with them to make sure none of them drop a calf that doesn't get right up. Can you take care of things in here, Miss Jensen?"

"Why don't you take a minute to eat this plate of food? You need to eat to keep up your strength for the hard night ahead. Is there anything else you want me to do?" Miriam asked.

"I see you have already brought in wood. That was good thinking. It does not burn good covered with ice. Thank you for the supper. I didn't realize how hungry I was getting'. Put John and Emily to bed at nine o'clock. They know what they need to do. I need to peek at that little one before I head back out and let Rosetta know how the calving is going."

Miriam read a Bible story to John and Emily and tucked them into bed. "Now, can I pray with you before you go to sleep?" she asked.

John answered importantly, "My papa usually prays with us, but since he is outside I guess it would be all right if you did."

Miriam checked on Mrs. Johnston. "Mrs. Johnston, is there anything you need before I go to bed? I seem to be unusually tired. Where did you plan for me to sleep?"

"There is a big feather tick in the parlor and you can sleep on the sofa. There isn't a stove in there, so you will need to tuck in a hot brick to keep your feet warm."

"If you need me, call. I will take one of the lamps in so I can light it if you call. I have banked up the stove so it should last most of the night, however I will get up early to add more wood. Goodnight."

Miriam found the heavy tick and slipped a towel-wrapped brick in at the foot. Blowing out the lamp, she slipped quickly inside the tick shivering. *Lord, that storm sounds terrible with the sleet and wind. I wonder how the Larsens are doing with all their livestock in this storm? They are probably staying up all night so Timothy will not be able to come to talk to Father for a week or more if this storm continues. Lord, be with all the farmers and especially with Timothy wherever he is right now,* Miriam prayed.

It was still dark when Miriam woke with a start. Had she heard someone call her? "Miriam, Miriam, can you come?" She struggled out from under the warm tick and lit the lamp.

Walking into Mrs. Johnston's room, she asked, "What is it, Mrs. Johnston?"

"It's getting so cold in here. I am concerned about the baby, can you put some wood in the stove and heat me a brick to warm up my feet? I seem to be chilling for some reason."

"Would you like for me to bring you some hot tea? That might help to warm you even more," Miriam asked.

Miriam stoked up the fire and added more logs. Taking a cup of tea and a hot brick to Mrs. Johnston, she sat down beside the bed and waited. "Is that helping, Mrs. Johnston?

Mother sent some hyssop and some feverfew with me. Could I add some to your tea?"

"Yes, that would help." After drinking the herb tea, Mrs. Johnston relaxed and fell asleep. Miriam slipped back into her cold bed with a fresh hot brick.

At the first hint of dawn, Miriam was up. "I must get that fire going strong and start breakfast, although it doesn't seem like I have been in bed long." She had oatmeal cooking and bacon frying when Mr. Johnston came in with the morning milk.

"It's not fit for man or beast out there. I lost two calves last night—couldn't get them all in the barn and they froze before they could get up and suck," he said sadly.

"I'm sorry to hear that Mr. Johnston. Won't you sit down and eat? I'll fry some eggs to go with your bacon. The coffee is ready."

"You seem to know just what to do. You will make some man a wonderful wife," he said smiling. "How is the missus this morning?"

"She called for me during the night. She was suffering from a chill. I made her some herb tea and gave her a heated brick to warm her feet. She drank some warm tea this morning, so I think she is doing much better. I'll take her some breakfast in a few minutes. Should I wake Emily and John or let them sleep?"

"Oh, they'll be out here in a few minutes as soon as they smell that food. The little rascals smell food even in their sleep," Mr. Johnston said fondly. "Tell John to bundle up good and he can help me feed the cows this morning and gather the eggs before they freeze."

"I don't suppose it will be possible for you to take me home today?" Miriam asked wistfully.

"I really need your help today. With the ice storm, tree limbs are all over the yard and road. It is really slick out. If you could stay here for a few days until the wife gets on her feet or her aunt arrives it would be much appreciated. I called her aunt's neighbor yesterday morning to let her know that the baby was on the way so she may come once the roads are passable."

"I can stay. I only hope that Mother got the message before the telephone went out."

Emily and John were overjoyed with Miriam staying. "You can read to us and play jacks," John said.

"Yes, I can do all those things if you will help me bake the bread, do the dishes, cook the food and do the washing," Miriam laughed.

"That's girl's work. I'm going out to help Papa. He always has me help with the morning feeding."

"Yes, your father did say that he wanted you to bundle up real good and come out to help him. Did you know that he has been out in the barn all night?"

"I will help you, Miriam. I can do dishes and help hang up the washing. I help Mama all the time," little Emily said.

Miriam kept busy all day cooking and doing the wash and hanging it inside. At supper she asked, "Mr. Johnston, I am so tired. Do you mind if I go to be bed early? Is there any possibility that I could go home tomorrow?"

"That may be possible by afternoon, especially if the sun comes out so Rosetta's aunt can come from the other side of Beloit. Would you mind staying until she arrives?"

"No, I can stay. It is just with Mrs. Polinsky sick, I may be needed to deliver other babies." She couldn't bring herself to say that the reason she wanted to be home was to know if her father had talked to Timothy.

Wrapped in her feather tick in the cold parlor, Miriam pondered all she and her father had talked about last week, *Lord, I really do want Timothy to court me. I think he is the one that You, Lord, have for me. Why did You send this miserable ice storm to mess up all our plans? Help me to be willing to wait on Your timing,* she prayed just before falling asleep.

The morning sunlight shone in the window, waking

Miriam up to a beautiful scene of ice-covered tress, bushes, and weeds glistening like diamonds. *Thank you, Father, for our sunshine-it makes even the ugly weeds beautiful.* Miriam was about ready to sing from the excitement and possibility of going home. Dressing quickly in the cold room, she tied on an apron and hurried out to the kitchen to start breakfast. Mrs. Johnston was sitting in the rocking chair nursing the baby.

"Good morning, Miriam. Robert was up early and stoked up the fire, so I came out here to feed the baby. You seemed to be sleeping so soundly when he looked in that he didn't wake you."

"He should have, Mrs. Johnston. I'm supposed to be taking care of you."

"I'm feeling quite strong and Robert said that you were wanting to go home today," Mrs. Johnston said.

"I am just too impatient, Mrs. Johnston. I don't really know that Mrs. Polinsky is still sick or that she would need me. I'm just anxious to return home, however if your aunt can't come today, I can stay to help you."

"Thank you so much, Miriam. Robert is so busy with the calving that he hardly takes time to eat, as you may have noticed. If you weren't here, he would try to do my work and his also."

Miriam spent the day baking bread and washing diapers. Her fingers were sore from scrubbing on the wash board. Emily helped as she had said she would. "Now tell me a story, Miriam."

"Yes, although this morning who did I promise to read a story to when we finished our work?" Miriam asked.

Little Emily looked up in all innocence, "God?" Miriam couldn't keep from laughing.

"No, I said that I would read to both of you when we finished our work, and John is still outside helping your father. We have to wait for him."

"No, I want a story now! I don't want to wait for John," Emily said, stomping her foot.

"Now listen here, young lady. You will not talk to Miss

Miriam holding a baby she has delivered.

Jensen like that. Just because she is helping Mother doesn't mean you can order her around," Mrs. Johnston called from the rocking chair. "You go to your room and wait until John comes in."

Emily ran to her room crying, although she soon came out and snuggled up to Miriam and said "I'm sorry. Would you read me a little story until John comes back?"

Miriam had just started to read when John came in with a cold red face from the frosty air. "I'm in for our story, Miriam. You haven't started without me have you?"

"We were just reading one little one for Emily. The big story about Joseph in the Bible is just for you, John. It's a boy's kind of story."

About four o'clock, the dog started barking. Emily and John ran to the window to see who was coming up the lane. "It's Aunt Melinda! Goody, goody she always brings us peppermints."

Robert followed Melinda and her husband into the house. "Are you ready to leave young lady? I need to be home before dark, can't leave the livestock very long with weather like this."

"Where does this young lady live, Robert? If she lives anywhere near Beloit, I can take her as I return home," Melinda's husband said.

"She is right on your way home at the edge of town. That would help so much if you could deliver her home."

Miriam eagerly ran to fetch her valise and heavy cloak. As she was putting on her cloak, Mr. Johnston came over and slipped a silver dollar into her hand. "Thank you for your help Miss Jensen. You are a very capable worker."

"Yes, thank you, Miriam," Mrs. Johnston called from the rocking chair. "You will be a wonderful midwife."

"Thank you, I am just God's servant. He is the One who does it all," Miriam answered.

Out on the road, Miriam was shocked at the sight of all the broken tree limbs on the road and the ice covered bridges. "If it wasn't for the broken limbs, it would be gorgeously beau-

113

tiful—just like a magical world," Miriam exclaimed.

"Yes, you are right, it is purty. However, sure makes taking care of farm animals a lot of extra work. I had to spread ashes on all my paths to the barn and sheds to keep from falling," Melinda's husband responded.

Miriam was so anxious to return home, she barely thanked the man for her ride as she hurried inside. "Mother, Anna, I'm home. Has Timothy come to town to talk to Father yet?"

Lydia looked up from her patching, "Miriam, you surprised me. Now how do you think Timothy would be able to leave their livestock and come to town? All the farmers are having trouble and terrible losses from the storm. Some of them were able to bring the cattle in to shelter. Mrs. Smith said even with their small herd, they had difficulty, although with their large barn, they were able to save all except one calf."

Miriam said, "Why oh why did we have to have a terrible storm like this now? The farmers are all struggling so hard." She was almost in tears.

"Miriam, you are tired from the strain of helping Mrs. Johnston. Why don't you make some feverfew tea and get some rest before supper? The rest of us would like to hear your stories about helping the Johnston family."

"I'm worried about Timothy, Mother. I wish the telephone was working so we could call out to the Larsens to see if everything is all right."

"We probably won't have a telephone until spring with so many lines down," Anna said. "You'll just have to wait until spring to hear from Timothy."

"Anna, why do you tease so when I am tired? It isn't funny now," Miriam said as she drank her tea and went to bed.

At supper, Miriam gave an account of the time with the Johnston family. "Has anyone heard from Mrs. Polinsky? I'm concerned about her. It seems like every year her health becomes worse, just when she is beginning to teach me.

Thankfully, Mrs. Johnston had no trouble, although if she had needed extra help, I might not have known what to do."

The next morning was a little warmer. "Father, do you think I could take Ginger out to see Mrs. Polinsky today?"

"Possibly you could this afternoon when the sun has time to melt some of the ice."

Miriam harnessed Ginger to the buggy after dinner. She was surprised to see many broken limbs were still lying on the road. Some had broken fences and fallen on roofs breaking holes. "This looks almost as bad as the tornado damage." Miriam remembered.

Mrs. Polinsky, looking pale and weak, answered the door. "Come right in and sit a spell, Miriam. Tell me all about birthin' the Johnston baby."

"Are you on the mend, Mrs. Polinsky? I don't want to wear you out by staying too long," Miriam said gently.

"Just had a touch of consumption. I should have knowed to air out the house and the feather bedding this fall, but I got so busy deliverin' babies and finishin' up the fall garden that I plum forgot all about it," Mrs. Polinsky explained.

"Why didn't you call? I would have been glad to help you. However, why do you have your arm in a sling? Did you break it or something?"

"I fell on the ice and put my shoulder out. The mister took me to that doctor and he about killed me putting it back. Told me not to use it for two weeks. How does he expect me to do the cookin' with only one hand? I've been using it and putting some of my special salve I make on it and every day it is a little better. I'm not going to lay around having Pa wait on me. Besides he can't cook worth a darn anyway."

"Do you know about any more babies that are due this month, Mrs. Polinsky? I hope that you are able to go with me the next time. There is so much I do not know yet."

"Seems like I've heard about a few, although nothing definite. Usually they let me know the day that they need help with the weather like it is."

Driving back to town, Miriam drove by her father's shop. There, tied to the hitching post, was one of the Larsens' horses. "Oh, maybe Timothy is there talking to Father," Miriam whispered to herself. She wanted so badly to stop, although she knew it wasn't the right thing to do. *Oh God, be with Father and Timothy as they talk,* she prayed.

Hurrying on home, Miriam put Ginger away and fed and watered her. Walking into the house she called, although no one seemed to be home. "That's funny, Mother didn't tell me they were going anywhere. Wonder where they could have gone with supper time so close?"

Miriam was peeling potatoes and started to cook the sliced ham before her mother and sisters returned. "I'm so thankful you started supper, Miriam," Lydia said as she came into the kitchen tying on her apron. "Jackson came by with a note from Mary asking that we come over for tea and a visit. He waited until we were ready, to deliver us to the Cramton home. I knew it must have been important, or Mary would not have sent Jackson over to get us."

"Has Mary heard from Melody?" Miriam asked. "It has been over a month since she left."

"Yes, that was one of the reasons that she wanted me to come. Melody wrote to inform them that she would not be home for Christmas and probably not return until Easter. Mary was very distraught over not having the family together for Christmas. She said that little Seth keeps asking why Melody doesn't come back."

Did Melody tell them why she was not coming and that the New England Conservatory of Music doesn't start the January session until mid January?" Miriam asked.

"She just told them that she was terribly busy and enjoying every minute. She is living with Thomas's sister who is very much involved in the Boston Society. She isn't a good influence on Melody."

"Did she give you the address so I could write to Melody?" Miriam asked.

"Yes, I have it here. It might do some good for you to write. She didn't even ask for her mother to write."

"Mother, I almost forgot to tell you the exciting news. Timothy's horse was tied to Father's hitching post when I came home," Miriam shared excitedly.

"You probably won't allow Father to eat supper until he tells you every word that Timothy shared," Anna teased.

"Now, you know that I will let him eat supper and besides he can't talk until the younger girls are in bed. So there!"

"Now girls, if we are going to have supper ready by the time your father arrives, we must hasten," Lydia reminded.

Aaron came a few minutes later with a large smile on his face. "You would never guess who visited me this afternoon."

"It was Timothy," Anna injected.

"How did you know that, Anna?" Aaron asked.

"Miriam saw Timothy's horse tied to the hitching post on her way from Mrs. Polinsky's farm."

"So you know already. After supper, I will share with you some of our conversation. I think you will be pleased with it."

Supper seemed to drag, and their Bible study time seem to go on forever to Miriam. The minute it was over, Miriam said, "I will wash the dishes if you will dry, Anna. Do you suppose the younger girls could go to bed a little early?"

"I don't want to go to bed early!" Emma complained.

"Yes, we have some things to talk over, Emma. You may take a lamp and read for a while if you like," Lydia suggested.

The younger girls were in bed at last, the dishes done and Miriam was hanging the dishtowel to dry when her father cleared his throat as he always did for important announcements. "Well, are you ready for the news from Mr. Larsen?"

Aaron asked half in jest.

"Yes, Papa, please don't make me wait any longer. I'm bursting at the seams to know what happened," Miriam said anxiously.

"Well, you might not have recognized Timothy, if you had seem him," Aaron reported.

"Why, Father, what has happened to him? Was he hurt? Did he break something?" Miriam asked

"Give me a minute to answer each question. Nothing major happened that won't heal with time, however he sure looks colorful with a huge black eye where a cow butted him in the head as he stooped to pick up her calf."

"Oh, Father, he could have been killed. What night was that? I was praying for him especially during the ice storm," Miriam exclaimed.

"He said that it about knocked him out so his ma applied ice packs and some special salve she makes. He says he doesn't have much pain now."

"I wish I could have taken care of him," Miriam lamented.

"Now, you can't be nurse to every one, Miriam," Anna said.

"Back to Timothy. What did you and he talk about, Father?" Miriam asked

"Well, I started right off and asked him what his relationship was with the Lord, Jesus. Moreover, he didn't hesitate a minute. He answered, 'I accepted the Lord as my Savior as a young boy at my mother's knee.'"

"What else did you ask?" Miriam asked.

"I asked if he was ready to support a wife," Aaron answered

"Father, wasn't that a little presumptuous ? You don't know absolutely that we will marry," Miriam asked in surprise.

"Any young man who has asked to start courting must have plans for marriage. You will be pleased that Timothy has purchased a neighboring farm and will be starting to fix up the house this spring."

118

"That's wonderful, Papa. Is there anything else?"

"Yes, he asked if he could call next Sunday afternoon if the weather would allow him to come. And I told him that I would think about it, and let him know in a week or two," Aaron teased.

"Father, what did you really tell him?" Miriam begged.

"I invited him to dinner following church. Was that all right?"

"Oh yes, Papa. I love you so much," Miriam exclaimed, running to give her father a big hug.

"There is one thing I forgot to tell you. Do you remember the Sunday that you rode in to church with the Larsens? Paul Larsen came over to me after the dinner and said, "That oldest daughter of yours is my choice for a wife for my oldest son. What do you think of that?" Aaron asked with a large smile.

CHAPTER NINE

THE CALLING

MIRIAM COULD NOT WAIT until Sunday. The week went too slow. Lydia found her scrubbing the kitchen for the second time. "Miriam, do you think that Timothy is going to look into every corner of the house? He is coming to see you, not the house."

"Cleaning and cooking keeps me from stewing so much. I want to make a good impression on Timothy, although I am worried about what the rest of you are going to do while Timothy and I visit," Miriam said anxiously.

"We are going to sit and listen to every word," Emma said, as she slaved away cleaning the stove as Miriam had requested that she do.

"Anna, can't you find something for the girls to do so they won't just sit and listen?" Miriam begged.

"I suppose we could all go out to the barn and play in the hay loft," Anna joked as she cleaned the kerosene glass chimneys. "You remember that Timothy is used to having younger brothers and sisters and he probably won't mind if we are in the room."

Lydia came in from the bedroom carrying an armload of clothes to be ironed. "Anna would you restart the stove now that Emma has it cleaned? I need to heat this flat iron for ironing our Sunday clothes."

"Mother, can I pick what we are going to serve for dinner Sunday?" Miriam asked. "I would like to bake the apple pies, if Anna would be willing to bake the bread. Also, I would like to serve ham and sweet potatoes."

Elizabeth said, "I want to give Timothy some of that strawberry jam we made last summer. Can I, Miriam?"

"I want to give him something too, Miriam. Can I give him some watermelon pickles?" Tabitha asked.

"Yes, you all can help with the meal, especially if you will not disturb Timothy and me when we talk after dinner," Miriam requested.

"We promise to be as quiet as church mice don't we?" Emma said, looking at Tabitha and Elizabeth.

Sunday morning, Miriam looked out the window to a dreary cold day with a hint of snow. *Oh, I hope there isn't a storm coming. Lord, couldn't you give us a sunny day for Timothy to come calling?* Miriam complained to God.

Dressing in her most beautiful blue silk which she and her mother had made that fall, she was brushing her long dark blond hair when Anna walked in from cleaning up the breakfast dishes.

"Are you wearing your best dress when it looks like it might rain? Do you need help with your hair? I have this new comb that might hold it better."

"I wish I had a parasol that matched my dress, however black is all that I own," Miriam moaned.

"Miriam, you aren't going to tea at the mayor's house. I know that Timothy's mother doesn't wear expensive dresses. Timothy would probably be more comfortable if you weren't so dressed up."

"I wanted to wear blue because everyone tells me that I look good in blue," Miriam answered. "I will change it after church."

"Yes, you do look good in blue, however you should remember Timothy is a farm boy, not the banker's son, so you don't have to dress like the banker's daughter."

"I know, Anna, however I am singing in the choir this morning and all the ladies dress extra nice for that."

"All those riding in the Jensen carriage to church be on the front porch in ten minutes," Aaron interrupted their conversation.

Miriam quickly pushed a few more pins in her hair and put on her matching hat. Wrapping herself with her navy cape, she went to the kitchen where Aaron was waiting patiently on his seven women. "How do I look, Father?" she asked as she twirled around.

"Well, if I was a young man looking for a wife, I would marry you if you could cook," Aaron answered with a huge smile.

"Father, for that comment, I may not make you any more apple pie. You have to settle for Anna's pies," Miriam laughed.

"The carriage is ready to leave. Come on ladies or the Jensen family will be late arriving for the singing of Miriam." Aaron called from the porch.

"Father, you are so funny today. We are not going to church today just to hear me sing."

Pulling into the church yard, Miriam searched for the Larsen carriage, even though they had not arrived yet. "They aren't here yet. Maybe they are all sick," Anna said when she saw Miriam searching so intently.

"Who's not here?" Aaron called from the driver's seat.

"You know, Father. Timothy Larsen and his family," Emma explained.

"Oh, yes, they are the only people who come to church," Aaron teased.

"Father, you are such a tease today! You act like you are the one who is coming to dinner to visit Miriam," Anna commented.

"Well, your father remembers when my grandmother allowed him to come calling on me. Grandmother would cook up the most scrumptious dinner. She would never let me cook because she said, 'The way to a man's heart is through his stomach. He will have plenty of time to eat your cooking after you are married,'" Lydia said.

Aaron had just finished helping all the girls from the carriage when the Larsen carriage pulled in.

Miriam whispered to Anna, "There's the Larsen family. I am getting so flustered. Does my hair look all right? Is my hat on straight?"

"Why would you be flustered when you have talked to and cooked for Timothy before?" Anna asked.

"I know that and I am so nervous. I am afraid I will blush or drop my song book," Miriam muttered.

"Just look at me when you are singing and not at Timothy. That should keep you calm. You know that I never get flustered."

Miriam made it through her solo part of the choir number and sat down with relief, however she could not keep her mind on Rev. Stanwick's message. *I wonder if the food will be cooked enough and not overcooked. I don't even remember if Timothy likes apple pie.*

Her thoughts were interrupted with "Let us all turn to hymn 35, *Rock of Ages*," the song leader called.

Following church, Miriam whispered to Aaron, "Can we leave right away so I can change my dress and put dinner on the table before Timothy arrives?"

"Your mother is talking with some ladies over there. She is probably getting the latest news on the new babies and wedding plans. As soon as she is finished we can leave."

Miriam tried to visit with those who came to compliment her on her solo. "Yes, thank you," she kept saying while watching Timothy, who was standing beside her mother. He said something and nodded his head in agreement.

Miriam walked over and touched Lydia on the arm, "Mother, can we leave now? We need to check on dinner."

"Yes, Miriam, can you find Tabitha and Elizabeth? They were here a minute ago, although I don't see them now."

Miriam found the girls and met her father at the door as Lydia came with Jesse and Emma. "Now we can leave, Miriam."

"Hurry, Father," Miriam called anxiously. "I need to change my dress."

"It wouldn't look right for us to race through town as if we were going to a fire. All the neighbors would start asking why the Jensen family is racing home from church and start saying things like, 'they must be serving the preacher for dinner today,'" Aaron teased.

"Father, you are such a tease today. Can't you see that I want to have everything just right for Timothy?" Miriam begged.

"I know, Miriam, I'm sorry. I want Timothy to enjoy being in our home just as much as you do."

The food was cooked just right and with all the girls helping, they had it on the table before Miriam had her dress changed. Timothy knocked on the door as they set the last dish on the table. Aaron went to the door, "Come right in, Timothy. May I take your coat and hat?" Aaron asked.

Miriam was impressed with her father's gracious greeting for Timothy. He seemed to be as eager as she was to help Timothy enjoy the time. Aaron seated Lydia and each of the girls. "You can sit here beside me, Timothy, so we can get a word in edgewise with all these women."

"Shall we thank the Lord for this bountiful food," Aaron announced.

Timothy said, "Amen," following the prayer.

Aaron reached for the plate of ham and handed it to Timothy, "As our guest, you get first choice of the meat."

Elizabeth piped up, "Mr. Larsen, I put out the strawberry jam, you must eat some."

Timothy smiled at Elizabeth, "I will be sure to eat the watermelon pickles, too, Elizabeth. My sisters always insist that I eat their cooking and tell them how I like it."

"Timothy, how is the calving going by now?" Aaron asked.

"Better than usual at this time of year, and even with the storm we have only lost 3 and have 25 new calves so far. God has blessed us to be able to find each cow in time and bring her into the barn or next to the shelter-belt for protection from the weather."

"Do you have a pet calf, Mr. Larsen?" Tabitha asked.

"No I don't, although my little brothers and sister have several they feed from a bottle when a cow has twins or something happens to the mother."

They finished the main part of the meal. "How many of you wish to have a piece of apple pie?" Miriam asked.

"Count me in for that," Timothy answered immediately, "I remember how good your apple pie was when you cooked for us at the Raston home."

"She made it all by herself. She would not allow any of us to touch it," Tabitha said laughing.

Blushing beet red, Miriam quickly turned around to find dishes to serve the pie. After the table was cleared, Timothy said, "Can I help with the dishes? I am an expert at drying."

"I think the women would rather we would retire to the parlor, Timothy. I get the feeling that I am in the way when I help with dishes," Aaron said.

"Miriam, we can do the dishes. You go in and visit with Timothy," Lydia said.

Aaron stoked up the parlor stove and added more wood. "Need to keep it comfortable in here if we are going to visit." He sat down by the window and picked up the Saturday copy of the Gazette and commenced to read.

125

Miriam and Timothy sat across from each other, feeling a little uncomfortable. Finally, Timothy broke the silence. "Miriam, that was the most delicious apple pie I have ever eaten. Even better than the one you made for the men working at the Rastons."

"Thank you, Timothy. I guess pies are my specialty and Anna specializes in bread. You sister, Esther is a good pie baker also."

"Her pies are not anything like yours. You do something to make the apples taste extra good. Is there some spice that you use?" Timothy asked.

"Well, I use nutmeg along with the cinnamon."

"I will tell Esther to try that. Maybe you could tell her how much sometime."

"I would be glad to tell her. I enjoyed working with her at the Rastons. I would never have been able to cook for that many men if she had not helped me. By the way, how is your little brother, Isaac, doing? Since he was the first baby I helped deliver, he seems extra special to me."

"Oh, he is growing like a weed. He smiles all the time now when we talk to him. I love to hold him in the evening. He seems more like a son to me than a brother since he is 20 years younger. I really enjoy children and hope when I get married to have a large family. There is something wonderful about a large family, don't you think?"

"Yes, I love having five sisters, however I would have loved having some brothers also like you have in your family," Miriam answered. It seemed so easy to talk to Timothy because he was very interested in how she felt about important issues.

"Yes, a man with a lot of sons does have an advantage even today and especially in Bible times, it said that a man with many sons was truly blessed. He was listened to at the city gates because there was strength in his family with so many men."

"Suppose you only had daughters like our family?" Miriam asked hesitantly.

"If God gave only daughters then He would provide the help they needed in the fields by hired labor or servants in Bible times. There are no mistakes in God's planning and all children are designed by God before the creation of the world."

"You really mean, God knew about everyone who was or will be born before the creation of the world?" Miriam asked incredulously.

"According to the Bible in I Corinthians and other places it says that. It does seem a little unbelievable, however remember God is all knowing. The more I read the Bible the more I learn. It never ceases to amaze me all that God does for His creation and the people who will obey His principles."

"Do you study the Bible a lot, Timothy? I think that is so important for a man to know the Bible so he can lead the family. God has given the man a big responsibility by having him be the head of the family."

"You are right about that. Right early, there in the book of Genesis, he told Adam and Eve after they had sinned that the man would rule over the woman. What do you think of the man being the leader in the family, Miriam?" Timothy asked seriously.

"I know a lot of women think God was unfair to put men in the place of leadership of the family, however I think God, being all knowing, knew we women couldn't do a good job of leadership. I think being accountable to God put a lot of responsibility on the husband. I wouldn't want that responsibility," Miriam answered.

"I am glad you see that also. I do not think your friend, Melody, would feel that way. Do you think she would?" Timothy asked.

"You seem to understand Melody quite well. Melody has accepted Christ, although she questions anything that might prevent her from doing what Melody wants to do. I am very concerned about her because she has met a man in Boston whom she thinks she might marry. She does not even say if he is a Christian let alone if he is one she would want to be head of their family. Melody decides more on how someone looks or if she would enjoy being with them. I think that God knows what is best for us and if He said the man is to be leader of the family, He does that because He loves us, not as punishment."

"You and I seem to agree on that, Miriam. I am so thankful that you see that also," Timothy said, while glancing up at the clock. "Oh, I didn't realize how late it had gotten. I must head for home. It looks more like snow out there and Father needs each of us boys when the weather gets bad. I have really enjoyed talking with you, Miriam. I see that God has taught you many things also. I hope we can talk again soon if that is all right with you, Mr. Jensen."

Aaron laid down the paper. "You are welcome to come anytime, Timothy. Here, let me get your coat. I have been watching those clouds. It looks like we could be getting a big snow. There are already a few flakes coming down."

By Monday morning a full-blown blizzard hit. No one went anywhere. The snow and wind blew all day. Miriam asked Lydia, "Could I spin that wool that I dyed with the walnut shells last spring? The dark brown would go well with my wool skirt. There might even be enough to make a sweater for Anna also."

"That would make a wonderful Christmas gift. Do you think you could knit two sweaters before Christmas, Miriam? That would take some late night hours," Lydia answered.

"If I don't get called out to deliver a baby, I could get a lot done each day once I get this spun."

"Talking about Christmas, Mary asked me at church if we could spend Christmas day with them since Melody is not coming home. Did you get a letter written to Melody?"

"Yes, she is probably too busy to write. She does not seem

128

to have time for old friends or family. Probably the only way that Mary and Thomas will see her is to go to Boston," Miriam lamented.

The next day, Aaron went out with his team and wagon to help the neighbors open up some of the streets. With drifts several feet high, it was difficult work.

Miriam worked hard at her spinning and knitting. She spent the time also in talking to the Lord, *Most heavenly Father, I am worried about Timothy in this storm.* She was so deep in her prayer that she did not hear Anna come into the parlor.

"Miriam, you've been slaving away at that knitting all morning and afternoon. Why don't we take the younger girls for a sled ride? They are driving Mother into a conniption fit with their running and playing."

"Let me finish this row so I don't lose my place and I will go. Have you asked Mother if she needs help with supper?" Miriam answered, although she would rather have continued to work.

"Yes, she said supper was in the oven and that she would enjoy some peace and quiet."

Miriam put on her father's overalls and heavy jacket to keep warm in the deep snow. Pulling on her boots and mittens, she joined the younger girls who had the sled ready and waiting. "Come pull us, Miriam. You give us such good rides. Anna is too slow," Jessie called.

"The drifts are so high that it is difficult to pull. I will see if I can find a place where I can pull you down a drift."

"Hurry, Mirry," Elizabeth called. "It is so pretty out here. Like a magic land."

Miriam stepped inside the rope and held it to her waist as she pulled the other five around the yard, missing most of the largest drifts. They met Aaron coming back from helping open up the streets. "Papa can we hitch Ginger to the sled and have her pull us?" Emma called.

"No, she isn't used to pulling a sled full of giggling girls.

129

She might bolt and pull you all into a tree or some other hard object. No, don't try that. Besides its about time you came in for supper."

"Let's go, Miriam," Elizabeth squealed. "Go real fast."

Miriam pulled faster and faster and something under the snow caused her to stumble. Falling on her face down in the snow, she felt a sharp pain in her shoulder. "Oh, help me Anna, I've hurt my shoulder, I can't get up. Hurry, get Father."

Jessie ran yelling all the way, "Papa, Papa come quickly. Miriam is hurt."

Aaron came running out of the house without hat or coat. "What happened? Here, help me lift her, Anna."

"Oh, Papa, my shoulder hurts so badly. I must have landed on a rock."

"Lean on Anna and me and we will help you into the house. Open the door, Jessie," Aaron commanded.

Miriam collapsed into the nearest chair, holding her left arm tightly against her. "Oh, it hurts to move it even a tiny bit. How can I get these wet clothes off?" Miriam sobbed.

Lydia carefully pulled the coat off one side, "Here let me hold your arm while Father slides off the coat." Miriam could not keep back the tears from the pain.

"Do you want me to make you a sling out of a dishtowel, Miriam?" Aaron asked.

"I think that would help me to hold it still. Any movement almost makes me faint. What if someone comes needing me to help deliver a baby?"

"With the roads still blocked, you won't need to worry about that for several days. Right now, we need to take care of that shoulder. Mother, do you have some of that willow bark for pain that she can chew?"

"Yes, Aaron, there is some in the sideboard and also some mullein to put on the shoulder to take away some of the pain," Lydia answered.

"How long will it take before I can use it again? I can't even help dress myself," Miriam sighed sadly.

"Time will tell, Miriam. If you are not doing better in the next few days, and I can get to Dr. Blackwood's office, I will see if he can come look at it."

"Girls, you need to put supper on the table while I help Miriam. Do you feel like you could eat, Miriam, or would you rather lie down?"

"I don't think I can lie down. Anytime I try to move the arm the pain is so bad. I might be comfortable to sit in the over-stuffed chair in the parlor. Yes, I do want some supper."

"While you girls are getting supper on, I need to check on the animals. They need extra care with this cold weather," Aaron said as he put on his coat and hat.

Miriam slept fitfully all night sitting in the chair. Every time she woke up, she kept thinking, *Why Lord, did you let me get hurt like this? I did not even want to go outside. Now I can not make Christmas presents, I can't even dress myself and I definitely couldn't help deliver a baby if someone came for me.*

The next morning at breakfast, Aaron asked, "Can you use your arm, Miriam?"

"No, Papa, it is worse. I can barely grip anything, not even a piece of paper."

"We should have the street near Dr. Blackwood's home open today, so I will stop and see if he can come by to look at your shoulder."

"Would you also stop by the post office to see if we received any mail before the trains were stopped by the storm?" Lydia requested.

The morning went by slowly for Miriam. "I feel so help-less. The only thing I do is read or write. I guess I should be thankful it wasn't my right arm."

"Would you listen to Elizabeth read her lesson, Miriam?" Lydia asked.

"I want you to listen to me, Mama," Elizabeth balked.

"Miriam can listen to you as well as I can. I am working on the bread so Anna can do the cooking. We need everyone's help while Miriam is getting well."

"Can you give me my spelling words, Miriam? I need practice," Jessie asked.

"Yes, as soon as I listen to Elizabeth."

Aaron came in at noon waving a letter. "Here is a letter for you, Miriam. It is post marked Boston."

Reaching for the letter, Miriam held it and said, "Anna, you will have to open it for me."

"Looks like Melody has answered my letter at last. Wouldn't it be wonderful if she said that she would be home for Christmas," Miriam mused.

Reading silently to herself, Miriam exclaimed, "Melody has met a man who agrees with her woman's suffrage! She says that she thinks he may be the one God has for her to marry. She says that she plans to bring him to meet her parents at Easter time. She also said that he has an excellent singing voice and will be taking a few college classes at the New England Conservatory of Music. He is very busy as director of music at the First Presbyterian Church in Boston. She says he is very handsome with a goatee and moustache."

"And probably a long-tailed coat and top hat. Even Thomas will be uncomfortable around a stuffed shirt like that," Anna added.

"Now wait a minute you two. You haven't even seen the man so, how do you know exactly what he is like?" Aaron questioned.

"He must be very talented to agree with her on woman's suffrage and still be a music director." Anna said.

"Knowing Melody like we do, it is almost without question that this man will be a little unusual and probably not one her father would chose to court her. Did you notice, Father, that she did not say she was bringing him here for her father's approval, although just to meet him. Sounds like she has decided what Melody wants to do and God and her father will not be asked. Poor Melody, she just continues to make wrong choices. Will she ever learn to wait on God and His plan for her life?" Miriam questioned.

"I would guess that she will choose to get married in a big church in Boston," Anna stated. "The churches in Beloit would not be good enough for her."

"Now, we don't know that. She might wish to show off her beau to the community and choose to be married here. It would hurt Mary and Thomas even more if she chose to be married in Boston." Aaron stated.

"Do you think that the trains will be running tomorrow, Father?" Miriam asked.

"They might be. The telegrapher said they had gotten word that the track as far as Topeka was open. Maybe by tomorrow they will have it open this far. Why did you ask?"

"I would like to answer Melody's letter. It will take a lot of prayer and thought. Although, since I can't do much else, that will give me a project to work on while I am recovering."

Miriam spent the afternoon composing a letter to Melody. *Oh, I do not know what to write to her. It is like writing to a stranger in another world. Lord, show me what to write to her. I feel like she would not be interested in what You have been teaching me*, she prayed.

"Dear Melody," she began, "*Your letter arrived before the blizzard, however Father couldn't get to the post office for two days. I injured my shoulder while pulling the little girls on the sled so I am just sitting around watching the rest of the family work. I am glad to hear from you, although I am concerned about the man you have met. You did not say that he was a Christian. Have you even talked to him about your love for God? Is this man someone your father would approve? Seems like I have asked you these same questions before,*

133

Melody. You know what you should do. You can be sure that I will be praying for you. I want you to have God's best. Father has given Timothy permission to court me and he came to dinner last Sunday. Timothy told father that he was a Christian and desired to be obedient to Him. I may not see him for another week with all the snow and the roads blocked. Write again soon. Your injured friend, Miriam."

Dr. Blackwood dropped by to look at Miriam's shoulder. "What is this about the town's best midwife being crippled up? After this storm, you may be very busy. Let me take a look at that arm. Ahem-m-m....," he said as he felt along her shoulder. "You have put it partially out of place. This is going to hurt, however we are going to have to put it back in place so it can recover." With that he gave her arm a quick twist and shove. Miriam turned white as a sheet from the pain. "Here take a sniff of this smelling salts, young lady. Keep up the willow bark and mullein. Within a week, you should be seeing improvement, unless you have a fracture. If you are a praying woman, you had better pray that it is not fractured. Have your father come for me, if you do not see improvement by next week. Try to keep using it to keep it from getting stiff."

"Do you think I will be able to use it next week?" Miriam asked anxiously. "Mrs. Polinsky is not well, so if I cannot go out, that leaves it up to her."

"Well, young lady, I can deliver babies even if the women prefer you two ladies. The most important thing is for you to regain the use of your arm."

That evening at supper, Miriam requested, "Could you all pray that my arm will recover quickly? It hurts worse now than it did at first, although Dr. Blackwood says I need to keep using it some."

Aaron prayed, "Lord, you know that Miriam needs the use of both arms so we are asking that you heal her arm." The rest of the family also prayed. None of them wanted their older sister suffering like she was.

The next day, Miriam could tell that she had less pain and could use her hand to grip some things. "It is still swollen and so painful that I can't tell if I am going to drop something I pick up, but at least I can pick up a few things. I would like to be able to dress myself again."

"Oh, helping you dress is like helping Elizabeth when she was little," Anna joked.

"I was not hard to dress, Anna. I can dress myself," Elizabeth argued.

Just at that moment, there was a loud knock at the door. Aaron hurried to the door to find a very cold farmer standing there. "I've ridden all the way to town to get Miss Jensen to come help my wife with her baby. They said that she lived here. Can she come right now?" the man said anxiously. "This is our first baby."

"My daughter has injured her shoulder. She will not be able to deliver babies for another week. Do you think that Mrs. Polinsky could go with him, Miriam?" Aaron asked turning to Miriam, who had come up behind him.

"Yes, I think she should be able to come if you have a warm buggy. She cannot stand the cold very well. You also could ask Dr. Blackwood who lives down the road here."

"My wife said she don't want no man helping her. She is mighty frightened this being our first. Where did you say this Mrs. Polinsky lives?"

"She lives 1 mile west of town on this road. We will be praying for you and your wife that both will get along well," Aaron answered.

"Thank you. I could use some prayers. Had to go across the top of the hills to get here 'cause our road is not opened yet. Old Bobbin kept fallin' in the drifts and tangling the harness. Took me forever to get here, however now that I know which way to go, I can go back faster. Thank you, I must hurry back."

After Aaron shut the door, Miriam burst into tears. "I feel

so helpless. This is no weather for Mrs. Polinsky to be out. I know the cold makes her arthritis worse."

"Miriam, there are no accidents with God. He has allowed you to injure your shoulder for a reason. He is teaching you to trust Him when the going is rough."

"Will I ever get the use of my arm again? It has been almost a week and I still cannot use it much. Maybe it is fractured like Dr. Blackwood thought that it might be."

CHAPTER TEN

THE HOMEGOING

MIRIAM'S SHOULDER healed slowly. She was able to have almost full use by the time the roads were opened a week after the storm. "I wonder if the Larsens will be coming for church tomorrow?" Miriam asked her father.

"Since they are on a main road, it probably is opened, however they have a long lane. If they were able to open that, it is my guess they will be there. With those three strong sons, Paul has lots of help with problems such as this," Aaron said while eating dinner with the family.

"Oh, I hope so—it's been two weeks since I've seen Timothy."

"You don't have to see him every week, Miriam. You wouldn't want him to get tired of you," Anna teased.

"How can he get tired of me, when he has only been here once? Mother do you think we could prepare dinner for extras and invite the Larsens if they are at church?" Miriam asked.

"That would take a lot of extra with nine of them and three of them hungry young men. We do have enough meat on hand. If you girls want to bake bread and pies, I could fix sweet potatoes and mashed potatoes," Lydia suggested.

"What if we get all the extra food fixed and the Larsens

don't come to church?" Anna asked.

"We could invite the pastor and his family. They have several children so we would have about the right amount of hungry mouths to feed," Lydia contemplated out loud.

Elizabeth, who had been listening to the plans, said excitedly, "Oh, goody goody, Ruth Larsen is coming to eat with us. I hope she brings her dolly with her."

The girls spent all morning baking pies, bread and cakes. "I want to make a sour cream chocolate cake, Mother," Miriam said, "Is there enough sour cream left after the churning you did earlier this week?"

"I think there is enough for one cake. Why are you baking a chocolate cake? Does someone in the Larsen family like chocolate cake?" Lydia asked with a smile.

"Timothy would think anything that Miriam cooks tastes just like angel food. Just you wait and see," Anna joked.

Aaron came in with a load of wood for both of the stoves. "While I am bundled up, do you need me to take the wagon over to the Smiths to borrow some chairs for tomorrow?"

"Why yes, we will need five or six more chairs. Guess we have never had that many at our table before," Lydia said.

After a long day of cooking and cleaning, Miriam fell into bed beside Anna. *Lord,* she prayed silently. *Please, help the Larsens to be able to come to church tomorrow and that they will stay for dinner.*

Miriam was the first one up to start breakfast while it was still dark. She couldn't sleep thinking about the Larsens coming. She shoved some wood into the stove and went to the lean-to for some bacon. Coming back inside she was met with billows of smoke, "Oh no! What happened to the stove? I must have forgot to open the damper. The smoke is so bad I can't find the stove. Oh, here it is. There, I have the damper open. Now I will have to open all the doors to let out this smoke. "Why did I forget to open the damper? I wanted everything to be perfect for the Larsens. Now the house will smell like smoke," she muttered to herself.

Stumbling out into the smoke-filled room, Aaron said, "What is going on? Is the house on fire or is this breakfast I smell?"

"It isn't funny, Father. I forgot to open the damper. Now how are we going to get the smoke out of the house?"

"Once the chimney gets hot it will clear out. With the doors open, we may freeze, although that will speed up the clearing out."

The rest of the family was soon in the kitchen. "Why do we have such a cold smoky kitchen today?" Elizabeth said shivering in her nightgown.

Lydia came to help Miriam with the cooking. "The kitchen is warming up and the smoke is almost gone," she consoled Miriam, who was almost in tears.

"I know, although I was just trying to get an early start so we could have the table all set and ready for when we return home. In my rush I forgot about the damper," Miriam moaned.

"If that is the worst you do when you are hurrying to prepare for company, be thankful. I remember feeding your father's family and I forgot to put the meat on to cook so we had a vegetable dinner and pie. We had a nice visit and my new mother-in-law was kind enough to never remind me of it again."

Miriam found the only large tablecloth they owned. "Could we use your wedding plates today, Mother? We only have 12 plates without them."

"Why yes, we can use them. My grandma always said to use your good dishes and linens or the next wife would. I thought she was a little funny to say that, although I see many women never use their nice dishes unless they are serving someone very important like the mayor and his wife. I believe in using them," Lydia said.

"Do we have to put all four leaves in the table?" Anna

complained. "If they won't come we will have more table than we have food or room to move around."

"I'm not going to worry about that. God will work out who will eat with us. We have to have everything ready," Lydia said.

The carriages and cutters around the church were few in number that morning, however the Larsen's cutter was there when the Jensens pulled in. "Look, Miriam, your prayers are answered," Emma shouted from the front seat.

"Sh-h-h, Emma, you don't have to tell everyone in church," Miriam reminded.

"We don't know if they will stay," Jesse said.

Miriam was anxious to be inside, however she waited patiently while her father helped her mother down and then her sisters. "Thank you for waiting patiently, Miriam. I know you are anxious to be inside, however I need you to keep the younger girls with their mother while I put the horse in the shed."

The minute the Jensens walked in the door, Timothy Larsen waved and smiled widely. Since church hadn't started, people were standing around in small groups close to the stove to keep warm. Lydia walked over to Martha Larsen and asked quietly, "Could your family join us for dinner today? We made extra so that we could invite you."

"I wouldn't want to impose on you with our nine," Martha Larsen replied.

"We are all prepared. Remember I have all girls and each one can cook some so we have it all prepared. We knew it would be difficult for you to get into church and then to get back before late so we prepared for you."

"Let me talk to my husband and see how soon he thinks we need to get back. He doesn't like to be gone too long from the livestock in the winter. If he says that it's all right, we can stay. It is very nice of you to ask."

Lydia came and took her seat beside Miriam. "Did she say that they could stay?" Miriam whispered.

"She is going to ask Paul and let us know after church. I think they will stay."

Miriam was so excited. She kept praying all through the service. *Dear Lord, Help Mr. Larsen see that they can stay and eat and help them all to enjoy the time.*

As soon as church was over, Esther Larsen came over to Lydia and said, "Mrs. Jensen, Father said that we can eat with you. I'm so glad because I usually have to cook Sunday dinner."

"Thank you, Lord," Miriam prayed in gratefulness.

It was crowded in the large kitchen with the eight Jensens and nine Larsens. Paul Larsen said, "I wager that this is the largest crowd you have served at your table, Lydia. It was a mighty good spread."

"It sure was, especially the chocolate cake that Miriam baked. And while we are here, will you tell Esther what you do to apple pies to make them so delicious?" Timothy bragged.

Aaron asked, "Have you seen a copy of the latest Beloit Gazette, Paul? They must be desperate for new subscribers. They are offering a new piano to any Mitchell county young lady who gets the most votes. For every one-year subscription of a $1, people can vote 100 votes for a lady of their choice and for half-a-year subscription, they can vote 50 votes. The weekly winners will be announced, although the final vote will be at the end of May."

"We could tell all our friends to subscribe and vote for Miriam," Daniel Larsen suggested, with a huge smile at Miriam.

"We already have a piano," Miriam quickly explained, realizing too late that he meant it for her and Timothy's home. Blushing a deep red, she turned away and started clearing the table.

"I think it is time for you men folks to move to the parlor, and allow us women to clean up the dishes before a certain head of our family decides it is time to return home," Martha interrupted Daniel's teasing.

The men moved to the parlor and the women visited

while clearing the table and washing dishes. The smaller children played on the floor by the parlor and kitchen stoves and it seemed like they had always known each other.

"You girls did a wonderful job of helping your mother prepare for this large group," Martha said. "Since Esther and I have all the cooking responsibilities, it must be nice to have all the help you have, Lydia."

"Yes, and I enjoy having some girls my age to talk to," Esther agreed.

"I think having a brother would be fun. He could take us on a sled ride and wouldn't fall down and break an arm like Miriam did," Elizabeth exclaimed from her playgroup on the floor.

"I did not break my arm, Elizabeth."

"What happened, Miriam?" Martha asked in concern. "I didn't know that you had injured your arm."

"I put my shoulder partially out of place when I fell, however it is almost back to normal. It is still weak. I especially hated it that I couldn't help the farmer who came for me to help with the delivery of their baby. I had to send him to Mrs. Polinsky and I know that the cold is so hard on her arthritis."

"Do you know whose baby it was?" Martha asked.

"I didn't know the man and he didn't give his name. Possibly, Father would know who he was."

Miriam went to the parlor and waited until Aaron came to a stop in a story he was telling Paul. "Father, do you know the name of the farmer who came to ask me to come deliver their baby after the storm?"

"Yes, I've seen him a few times at the shop. I think his name is Williams. Do you know him, Paul?"

"Yes, they bought that place out west of town. They are a young couple just starting out," Paul answered.

Going back into the kitchen, Miriam said, "The man's name was Williams."

"So that is the family the women at church were talking

about. They said that their little boy was born crippled and since it was their first, Mrs. Williams is taking it real hard. Mrs. Johnson, who lives next door, was asked by Mr. Williams to come talk to his wife because none of their family could get to them because of the storm. They had Dr. Blackwood look at the baby after Mrs. Polinsky delivered it. He agreed with Mrs. Polinsky that the boy would never walk."

"Oh, I wish I could talk to Mrs. Polinsky and find out what happened. I would have felt terrible if I had delivered it. Maybe I can go out to talk to Mrs. Williams also," Miriam said.

"You have such a caring heart, Miriam. It would have been difficult for you to deliver the William's baby and to find that he was crippled. You might be able to encourage Mrs. Williams and share some of what David wrote in Psalms about all of us being designed by God in our mother's womb. God knew that little baby would be crippled, because He designed him and has a special purpose for him. I know it is hard for a parent to see that, however I think of Mary Cramton's accident. Once she understood that Christ died for her sin, she accepted her accident and has been a real blessing to others even though she will never walk again," Martha said.

"I know that my arm isn't strong enough to drive Ginger yet, although maybe Father will have time to take me out tomorrow."

Mr. Larsen came out into the kitchen and announced, "All the gossip must stop now because the Larsen cutter is leaving in five minutes."

"Paul, we were not gossiping. We were talking of how we could help poor Mrs. Williams with her little crippled son," Martha reported.

After the Larsens left, Emma said, "Wish you and Timothy would hurry up and get married so the Larsens could come every Sunday. We had such a good time together."

"Emma, who said anything about Timothy marrying Miriam?" Lydia asked.

"I can see by the way he looks at her that he plans to marry her. He watches everything she does and thinks it is wonderful. Those big blue eyes of his just glow with 'Miriam-shine,'" Emma replied with a huge smile.

Miriam chose to ignore that comment. "I think I am going to work on my knitting now that my arm isn't so weak. If you would care to help me Emma, you could roll up this yarn that I have spun."

As she worked, Miriam mulled over the afternoon. *Thank you, God for bringing Timothy into my life. Continue to show our parents and Timothy and me if this is your plan for us.*

Monday showed a little improvement in the weather. The sun was shining and more cutters and carriages were moving on the street by the Jensen home. "Father, would you have time to take me out to see Mrs. Polinsky? I am concerned about her health since she had to go out during the bitter cold."

"I can take you this afternoon, however I must check the shop this morning. There may be someone waiting to have some repair work done. Since I haven't been there all week, I should check," Aaron said as he put on his heavy coat.

After dinner, Miriam brought out her heaviest cloak and muff. "I'm ready, Father. Are you going to visit with Mr. Polinsky while I visit with her or will you leave me and come back?"

"I suppose I could visit with Mr. Polinsky, although he is so deaf that it wears me out talking to him."

"Well, I won't be too long. I mainly want to tell Mrs. Polinsky that my arm is recovered and I can go with her or alone for the next birthing."

Aaron got out the cutter and soon they were whizzing over the snow packed road. "It's good to get out of the house. I feel like I have been cooped up for a month," Miriam said.

"Yes, the snow is pretty, however it sure makes doing business and farm work difficult," Aaron said as they passed the smithy. "Matthew came by so I put him to work repairing a sled runner."

There were no tracks out of the Polinsky's barn. "Looks like they haven't been anywhere since the storm. They may need me to pick up some supplies for them."

Knocking on the door, Miriam was surprised to find Mr. Polinsky answer. "Come in, the missus has been asking for me to go for you. She is sick with consumption agin."

Miriam hurried to Mrs. Polinsky's bedside. "Mrs. Polinsky, how are you? I didn't know you were sick. How long have you been sick?"

"I think about a week. I wanted Pa to go for Dr. Blackwood, however he said he couldn't get the cutter out of the barn. I kept prayin' that someone would come and you know I am not much for prayin'. I was gittin' desperate. I'm sicker this time. And you have come."

"What can I do for you? I feel so bad that you are sick. Father can go for Dr. Blackwood. Is there something you need in food or supplies?"

"Pa can give him a list of things we need. I suppose the doctor will bring out something for my cough. It is wearing me out."

"Mother makes the best cough medicine. I'll have Father stop by for some of that."

After Aaron left, Miriam pulled up a chair beside the bed. "Mrs. Polinsky, were you sick when you delivered the William's baby? I felt so sad to not be able to help because I knew you didn't like getting out in the cold."

"No, I wasn't sick then and Mr. Williams had the cutter well supplied to keep me warm, although after that I got sick, I just keep getting' sicker. I keep thinkin' that I need to talk to a preacher or someone about makin' my peace with the Lord 'cause I don't think I'm a goin' a make it."

"Oh, don't talk like that. Of course, you are going to get well. I will stay here and take care of you until you are able to take care of yourself. If anyone needs help with birthing, they know to come here so they can find me."

Aaron returned after an hour or two with Dr. Blackwood. Coming in from the cold, Dr. Blackwood removed his coat and walking over to the bedside, he said. "Young lady, what have you done to yourself to be this sick? The air in the place is so stale, it is no wonder you are down with consumption. I have a list of orders for this young lady to use in caring for you. First off, we need to air this place out without chilling you. Then I want you to fill your lungs to capacity several times in succession, every hour of the day and practice deep breathing. In addition, Miss Jensen will need to cook you some nourishing food to build up your strength. In addition, we want you to take a tepid sponge bath 3 times a week. I see that you do have on your flannel gown. Wear that the year around and stay away from every form of cough syrup, balsam, and cough mixtures. Will you obey these orders that I leave with Miss Jensen?"

"It won't any do any good. It's too late. I just keep a gettin' sicker each day," Mrs. Polinsky said weakly.

"Let's not hear any of that. You need to trust in the laws of nature and God," Dr. Blackwood said as he put on his coat. "I'll be back out here tomorrow."

Miriam followed Dr. Blackwood to the door and outside. Shutting the door behind her she asked, "Dr. Blackwood, is there a chance that Mrs. Polinsky might die? I feel responsible for her getting sick since I wasn't able to go deliver the William's baby."

"She is very sick. The next few days will tell. Try to get her to eat good food each day and breathe deeply every hour. Only God knows if she is going to make it."

Aaron came up carrying in flour and potatoes. "Father, I must stay with Mrs. Polinsky. She says she isn't going to live, and the doctor says she is very sick."

After Aaron and Dr. Blackwood left, Miriam cooked up a good broth soup for their supper and took some to feed Mrs. Polinsky. "Have you been eating anything since you were sick?"

"Not much. Pa can't cook much except some cornmeal mush

and that just wouldn't go down. That broth does taste good."

After supper, Miriam filled the stove with wood to heat up the room and also heat some water to bathe Mrs. Polinsky as the doctor ordered. "I don't want a bath. I just want to lay here and rest."

"No, he told you to follow orders and one is to have a sponge bath. So I am going to bathe you just like I did my little sister when she was younger," Miriam said laughing.

"Oh, if you must and then I suppose you will make me breathe deep. You are a hard taskmaster."

"I'm just want to do everything possible to help you recover."

Miriam and Mrs. Polinsky were both worn out by the time the bath was finished. "Just let me sleep, Miriam. That bath done tuckered me all out."

Miriam lay down on the sofa to sleep for the night. She didn't even have a nightgown, however she was so tired she didn't care. Just before falling asleep, she prayed. *Lord, you look after Mrs. Polinsky tonight. Please don't let her die. She has so much to teach me yet and she isn't ready to meet you.*

Miriam was sleeping soundly when she heard Mrs. Polinsky coughing and gasping for breath. Hurrying to her side, she asked. "Mrs. Polinsky, can I get you something?"

"I can't get my breath. Pray for me, Miriam. I'm not ready to die."

With tears running down her cheeks, Miriam prayed. "Oh, Lord help Mrs. Polinsky get so she can breath again." In a few minutes, the coughing stopped and Mrs. Polinsky was breathing more peacefully.

"Thank you, Miriam. While you are here, would you tell me how to have peace with God? God knows I ain't never had much time for Him and He knows how ornery I have been."

"All you need to do Mrs. Polinsky, is believe that Jesus died for your sins. Do you believe that?"

"I sure do. My mother taught me that when I was a child, although I didn't want her to pray for me. I didn't have time for God. I wanted to do what I wanted to do,"

"Do you want me to pray for you now, Mrs. Polinsky?"

"Would you? Just tell the good Lord that I'm sorry for being a miserable sinner all these years and for not givin' Him the time of day when He sent His only Son to die for my sins."

While Miriam prayed, tears of joy came to Mrs. Polinsky's eyes. "Thank you, thank you for telling me how to have peace with God, Miriam. Now, I'm not afraid to meet Him." With that, she fell into a peaceful sleep.

Miriam slipped back into bed with a grateful heart in knowing that her friend now was prepared to meet the Lord and that she had assurance of going to heaven with God. She couldn't sleep very sound for listening to Mrs. Polinsky's breathing, even though there were no more coughing spells.

The next morning, Miriam was awakened roughly by Mr. Polinsky. "Miss Jensen, come quickly. Somethin's wrong with the missus. I can't feel her breathing. She is just lying there so peacefully with a little smile on her lips. Is she dead?"

Miriam was almost afraid to check, however seeing Mrs. Polinsky's peaceful look, she felt almost relieved. Her good friend was with her heavenly Father and no longer in pain and suffering. Now her job would be to help Mr. Polinsky. "Yes, Mr. Polinsky, your wife has gone to her heavenly home. We will need to prepare her body for burial. When Father and Dr. Blackwood comes, they will help you prepare for the funeral. Would you eat some breakfast while we wait? We need to keep up our strength."

"How can I eat when my best friend and wife is dead? How can I stay here by myself? I can't cook or wash clothes. I just wish it was me who had died."

Praying for wisdom, Miriam said. "God chooses our time to be born and our time to die, Mr. Polinsky. You can stay with my family until we can find a place for you to stay.

CHAPTER ELEVEN

MIRIAM'S NEW FRIEND

MR. POLINSKY came to stay with the Jensen family before the funeral of his wife. Miriam had talked to her father when he and Dr. Blackwood came out to the house. "Do you think Mr. Polinsky could come stay with us, Father, until we can find a place for him? He told me that he couldn't cook nor do any washing. He seems frightened of staying here for even one night."

"That will be up to your mother to decide. I am sure she wouldn't mind if he came for a few days," Aaron answered.

It was a difficult funeral for Miriam. *Dear God, if I was at fault for Mrs. Polinsky getting sick and dying, please forgive me. If only my shoulder hadn't been injured,* she thought in deep sorrow.

Later, while talking it over with her mother, Lydia reminded her, "Miriam, you didn't purposely injure your shoulder and because you were with Mrs. Polinsky before she died, you were able to show her how to have peace with God. God doesn't make mistakes. We can be thankful that we will see Mrs. Polinsky in heaven."

"I still feel guilty for not trying harder to help her."

"I suppose any of us would feel that we could have done more to save the life of a friend. However, right now we have

149

Mr. Polinsky, who needs to find peace with God and help with his daily needs. We should be praying for a place he can stay where he has more privacy and doesn't have the constant noise of your sisters."

"He can be thankful that his hearing is so bad. It doesn't seem to bother him too much that the girls are noisy," Miriam chuckled. "Do you think that I could take Ginger out with the buggy to visit Mrs. Williams and her new baby?"

"Ask your father when he comes home for dinner. Since the temperature is fairly warm and the roads open, I don't see why you couldn't. She probably would appreciate your visit."

Miriam was thankful that Aaron said, "Yes, since they don't live far from town." She left right after dinner.

Knocking at the door, she kept wondering, *Lord, what can I say to Mrs. Williams to help her with her crippled little boy?*

The woman who came to the door surprised Miriam by being so young, "Hello, won't you come inside?" Mrs. William asked almost eagerly.

"Hello, I am Miriam Jensen, I was the one your husband came to first for help with the delivery of your baby. I wondered if you would like a visit?" Miriam asked cautiously.

"Please do come in, I haven't had any visitors for so long. My husband works at the saw mill, so I am alone all day."

"I have been wanting to visit you ever since Mrs. Polinsky told me about delivering your little boy," Miriam said with concern in her voice.

"Please call me Sarah. Oh, you are the one Mrs. Polinsky told me about. She spoke highly of you and said that you had injured your shoulder," Sarah responded.

"Mrs. Polinsky died last week after a severe case of consumption, she hasn't been well all winter.

"Oh no, did coming out to deliver my baby make her sick? She was such a nice lady. She knew I was so scared, however she told me to pray and trust God to help me."

"She told you to pray? She always told me she wasn't a praying person. I am so thankful that I was able to be with her before she died. She called herself an ornery sinner, although she believed Christ died for her sins and she died very peacefully in her sleep."

"How long have your known her?" Sarah asked.

"About five years ago she helped my mother with the birth of my little sister and at that time she told me that I had the talent for delivering babies. She told me that she would train me, if I wanted to work with her. I had started working with her this fall and there was so much more I wanted her to teach me," Miriam said sadly.

"Will you continue delivering babies? Mrs. Polinsky told me you were wonderful help."

"If women ask for me, I will do what I can," Miriam assured her.

"Would you like to see my little Charles?" Sarah asked. "I've grown to love him so much. It was difficult for me and my husband to accept the fact that Charles would never walk. Our neighbor, Mrs. Johnson, came over to talk to me and show me in the Bible what God says about God designing each of us. That helped me so much. I thought I had done something to cause him to be crippled or that God was punishing me."

"She is right about that. I am sure it would be very difficult to understand why your baby will never walk," Miriam said.

"Yes, I still struggle, however I am growing to love him more every day. I see what a joy he is even now. Mrs. Johnson told me that God has a special plan for little Charles and that He has given him to us to train and teach him. She told me that it is an honor to be chosen by God to raise little Charles with him being so crippled. I would have never thought of that."

"You must love the Lord, Sarah, to be able to accept that Charles will never walk," Miriam said.

"Oh, I grew up in a Christian home, and accepted Jesus

151

when I was little, although I have never had to face anything this difficult before. Mrs. Johnson said that God promises not to give us more trials than we can endure and will give us the resources to go through them. In addition, He has helped me so much. I thank God every day for His help, and He has even shown me ways to exercise little Charles' legs. Dr. Blackwood didn't tell me anything to do. I thought there must be something that would help so I asked God, and He showed me to move his legs every day when I changed his diaper," Sarah said with a happy smile. "I think it is helping some already."

Miriam looked at the clock on the mantle, "Oh, it is getting late, I really must be heading home. Father grows concerned about me since my shoulder is still weak and the winter weather can cause problems."

"Please come again. You have made my day so much happier. It is so lonesome here alone all day," Sarah said appreciatively.

"I would like to visit again, Sarah. I think we are almost the same age. I turned eighteen last summer," Miriam said.

"Yes, we are close in age, I will be nineteen this spring. I thought I was very grownup, however having a new baby has shown me there is so much I need to learn."

"If your husband would like to bring you by our home as he goes to work, I could take you home after we visited. We live right on the road in the two-story farmhouse as he turns to the mill."

"If he thinks it would be alright to take little Charles out, I would love to do that. We haven't taken him anywhere since he was born. He was so afraid he might get sick so we haven't been to church for two months and I miss it so much," Sarah lamented.

"Do you have family living around Beloit, Sarah?"

"No, my kinfolks live in Abilene, so in the winter I don't see them much. Mother came for a few days once they got the train through, however she was afraid to stay too long with the drifts so deep."

Miriam drove home slowly, contemplating the conversation with Sarah. *Lord, how marvelous You are. I didn't know how to encourage her and she ended up being a blessing to me. Thank You for my new friend.*

With Christmas arriving in a week, Miriam spent every possible moment working on the sweaters and wool hosiery she was making for gifts. Mr. Polinsky required extra time from each member of the family. He especially adored Elizabeth, although some days even she couldn't bring him out of his tears of mourning. Miriam almost chuckled at Elizabeth's methods to cheer him up. Climbing into his lap she said, "Mr. Polsky. You just quit your crying. You're getting tears on my dolly."

"I am so sad. Mrs. Polinsky left me all alone," he cried.

"Jesus is with you. He goes everywhere with me and He can be with you too if you ask Him to come be with you."

"Will you pray for me, Elizabeth?"

"Dear Jesus, Mr. Polsky is so sad. Show him that You love him and that we all love him and that Mrs. Polsky is with you," Elizabeth prayed.

"Thank you, Elizabeth. I never thought about Jesus loving an old guy like me."

The next few days were busy as everyone prepared their gifts for Christmas. Miriam hadn't heard from Sarah since her visit. "Mother, could I take Mr. Polinsky for a ride? It is a nicer day than it has been all week and I would like to see how Sarah Williams is doing."

"It would probably be good for him to get out. After farming all his life, I don't think he likes being cooped up in the house all the time."

"Mr. Polinsky, would you like to ride with me out to see Sarah Williams? I need some fresh air and would enjoy taking you with me," Miriam said loudly.

"Guess I could. Yup, I guess twernt hurt me none to go with you. Where is it you said you were a goin'?"

" I'm going out to see Mrs. Williams and her baby. Do you

remember that she was the lady that Mrs. Polinsky helped with her baby?"

"Yes, that name does sound familiar. Where did you say she lives?"

"She lives only a mile west of town. I would like for you to meet her," Miriam said as she helped him into his threadbare coat.

As they drove along, Mr. Polinsky said, "Say it is kind of pretty out here. Looks like a Christmas card we got last year. You are a good buggy driver, young lady."

"Well, thank you, Mr. Polinsky. I consider that a real compliment," Miriam said.

"What was that you said? Can't hear good out here in the wind."

"I said that you gave me a real compliment because you are a good buggy driver."

"I've driven many a buggy in my eighty years. And I know a good horse when I see one and this one is a good one."

At Sarah's house, Miriam helped Mr. Polinsky down from the buggy. "I should be helping you, young lady. When I was a young man I always helped the ladies, now my old bones keep me from doing much of anything like a gentleman anymore. My missus was helping me as much as I was helping her. Just wish she was here now."

"Come in and see little Charles, Mr. Polinsky." Miriam said as she led him to the door. Her light knock brought Sarah to the door immediately.

"Oh, Miriam, I am so glad you came. Today, I have been so lonesome. Little Charles has a little cough and Mr. Williams wouldn't allow me to take him out to visit you. Who do you have with you today? Is this your grandfather?"

"No, this is Mr. Polinsky, Sarah. I thought he would like to meet little Charles," Miriam answered.

Going to the cradle, Sarah picked up Charles and laid him

in Mr. Polinsky's arms. "What a wonderful little fellow. I never had a son, never had any children. Your mister must be awful proud to have a son. My missus always said that all babies were beautiful. To hear her talk, you would think they all belonged to her. In a way, I guess they did. She delivered so many babies that she lost count. She would have loved this little fellow."

"Did you know that Charles was crippled, Mr. Polinsky?" Sarah asked.

"He's what did you say? Crippled? Oh yes, my missus was so upset when she returned home from delivering him. Said she wished she was God and could fix those legs. I sure miss her, yes I do," he said with tears sliding down his cheeks.

"I know you miss her, Mr. Polinsky. We all miss her. She was a wonderful lady," Sarah said gently.

Christmas day dawned cold and crisp. Aaron had the cutter out long before Lydia was ready to leave for the Cramton home. "I don't know why your father is in such a hurry. Mary didn't want us there before eleven. Help me, Anna, to put all our food in the basket. I need to finish dressing and fixing Elizabeth's hair. Emma do you have all the gifts ready for your father to load into the cutter?"

"Yes, Mother, they are all ready and so is the one for Mr. Polinsky. I hope he likes the new coat we found for him at the New York Mercantile's sale. He probably hasn't had a new coat in years," Emma answered

"No, I am sure he does not have the money to buy a coat. Mrs. Polinsky mostly got paid with chickens, pork, fruit and vegetables."

As they drove to the Cramton home, Jesse said, "I wish Timothy could have come for Christmas with us. He makes everything so much fun."

"He is having Christmas with his family today, however he said he would eat with us Sunday," Miriam said. "I also wish he could come with us."

Each of the girls had made a small gift for Mr. Polinsky. "You should not have done this," he said as he opened each one. " I don't have nothin' for you girls."

"That's alright, Mr. Polinsky. We had fun making these for you," Emma said.

Mary and Annabel had prepared a wonderful meal for the Jensen family. "You help take away the loneliness that we feel for Melody. Seth continues to ask for her every day. She did send him a toy which came in yesterday on the train, however that's not the same as having her with us," Mary said sadly.

"Is she coming for Easter, Mrs. Cramton?" Miriam asked.

"Yes, and bringing that Walter, whom she has consented to marry. She says that we all will love him and that she thinks he is a Christian, because he goes to church with her."

"We continue to pray for her, Mrs. Cramton. I know it must break your heart that she doesn't consider you and Thomas in her plans. Do you think she even considers God in her plans?" Miriam said lovingly.

"No, she doesn't mention in her letters anything about God or even that she reads her Bible."

Aren't you glad that she isn't getting married in Boston?" Anna asked.

"If he isn't a Christian, I have no joy in her marriage. I know how miserable I was until I came to Christ. I wouldn't want to go back to living like that for anything. However, Melody is determined to go her own way. Sometimes I wonder if she ever accepted Christ when she almost died with the whooping cough," Mary answered with a sigh.

"She did pray to accept Him, Mrs. Cramton. However, we all have to make choices on obeying Him. Sometimes I struggle with wanting to do things my own way. At times I forget that God knows everything about me and wants the best for me," Miriam assured her.

Sunday following church, Timothy came for dinner. When Mr. Polinsky saw the package under his arm, he said, "Young man, you must have brought somethin' for your lady love."

It was Timothy's turn to get embarrassed. "Oh - I - Oh I - yes, I did bring something for Miss Jensen," he stammered.

Following dinner, the rest of the family moved into the parlor leaving Lydia to finish the dishes. Miriam and Timothy sat at the table talking, "I brought you a little something, Miriam. I hope that you like it."

Miriam carefully pulled off the string and wrapper. "Oh, Timothy, a book of Robert Frost's poetry. How did you know that I liked poetry? His poems are so good. They are stories in poem. Thank you so much. Now you have to open my present. It isn't much."

Unwrapping the two pairs of wool hosiery, Timothy exclaimed, "Just what I needed for the winter weather. Mother hasn't had time to knit any for me this winter. The baby has taken so much of her time. Usually she knits each of us several pairs. She is teaching Esther, although Esther can't do hosiery yet. Thank you so much."

They continued to visit while Lydia worked at her knitting by the window.

"Did you know that I purchased the little farm adjoining Father's property? There is a one and a half story stone house there, however it needs some work."

"That's nice to have your property so close to your father, since you all work together," Miriam said.

"Yes, I don't own much machinery yet. However, I plan to go to the horse sale in the spring and get me a team so I won't have to use Father's teams when he needs them. With an extra fifty-five acres to farm, we will need another team. Father helped me purchase the farm and I will start paying him back the money that it cost when I get my first wheat and corn crops. We saw it listed in the Gazette," Timothy announced proudly.

"Is it near the river? Doesn't the Solomon River come close to your parent's farm?" Miriam asked.

"Yes, in fact the river runs through the south edge of the farm."

"Has it ever flooded there? I wouldn't want to live on a place, or I mean, you wouldn't want to buy a place that flooded," Miriam asked in concern.

"From all the old time farmers around that I talked to, they said that it had never flooded the farm ground since it is higher than the river," Timothy smiled at her saying she wouldn't want to live on a place that flooded.

"I don't know much about farming. Since we lived in Kansas City until I was thirteen, the only part of farming I understand is watching Papa fix plow shares and wagon wheels. I don't know when you plant corn or maize. I have seen the farmers out planting when I drove Mrs. Polinsky to the different farms. That much I know about."

"Talking about Mrs. Polinsky, are you planning to continue in her stead of delivering babies?"

"If the women ask for me and trust that I know enough to help them, then I will go. I do wish Mrs. Polinsky had taught me more about difficult birthing. I guess if I have problems, they will just have to ask Dr. Blackwood or one of the other doctors."

"Would you read one of Robert Frost's poems to me? Most poetry doesn't make much sense to me, although I would love to hear you read one before I leave for home," Timothy asked.

"Yes, I will pick one of my favorites, *The Tuft of Flowers*,"

"That was beautiful, Miriam. I've never really cared for

poetry, however his story poems about farming are very good. I noticed the same thing when out raking hay, that the butterflies are all over the fresh cut hay. You can tell that he was a farmer," Timothy said after she finished reading.

Timothy was putting on his coat and Lydia looked up to ask, "Timothy would you like to join us at the poverty social in Solomon Rapids January 14th? Mary Cramton told me that the Epworth League was putting it on and everyone is to wear their old clothing and no jewelry. If you wear good clothing, you have to pay double for your supper. In addition, they fine you 3 cents for wearing a mustache and 2 cents for not wearing one. They are giving a prize for the most ridiculous dressed lady and gentleman."

"If the weather permits, I would like to join you. You know that Father will not let us boys off the farm if snow is coming. I wouldn't have to change clothes for that social, my workin' clothes would fit the bill for that," Timothy laughed.

🌾 🌾 🌾

Early in January, Aaron came home with a letter with a Boston address. "You have a letter from the city, Miriam. And it smells like Melody's perfume."

Miriam tore open the letter and began to read, *"Dear Miriam, Walter and I have chosen the first of June to get married. We will be coming to Beloit Easter weekend in March. I know you will love him. He is such a good soloist and a dream of a dancer. Cousin Julia put on a dance for our friends in her upstairs ballroom. That was when Walter announced our wedding plans. I am so deliriously happy. See you in March. Love Melody."*

"Oh, Melody, Melody," Miriam moaned. "You didn't even let your parents meet Walter before you agreed to marry him. How could you leave your parents out of the very important decision?"

"What's wrong, Miriam? Did you receive sad news from Melody?" Lydia asked.

"Well, Melody would say it is wonderful news, however I think it is tragic. She told Walter that she would marry him and she is bringing him to meet her parents on Easter, as she told her mother."

"Mary told me that she thought that Melody would not want to know how they felt about Walter, especially if he weren't a Christian. She probably isn't going to ask their opinion."

"What surprises me is that she is planning on coming here in June to get married at the church. I thought she would want to have the big church wedding in Boston where Walter directs music."

"Oh, she wants to show off this wonderful man she has caught," Anna said as she came into the kitchen and heard the last part of the conversation.

"Yes, I suppose that is true, although our church won't hold the whole town and she will want everyone invited," Miriam said sadly.

January 14th turned out to be unusually nice, so Timothy arrived at five o'clock to join the Jensen and Cramton families traveling to Solomon Rapids for the social. Miriam was grateful to have Timothy with them. She knew he would sit beside her at the supper.

"Look at Mr. and Mrs. Cramton's outfits!" Anna exclaimed when they stopped at the Cramton home. "I wouldn't have known them, if I didn't know they live here."

Thomas, who always dressed in the most expensive suits and top hat was dressed in some of Jackson's old work overalls, had shaved off his mustache and Mary had borrowed one of Annabel's very large dresses and wore her hair down. "I can't believe you two would get so excited about a party like this," Aaron commented.

"We decided we had had a reputation of being rich stuffed shirts so we wanted to prove to people we could have a good time also," Thomas answered.

They had a wonderful meal and votes were taken on those wearing the most ridiculous outfits. Thomas and Mary won hands down; no one even came close to wearing their unusual clothing.

On the ride home, Timothy confided to Miriam, "That was really fun. I hope I can join your family again for times like this. If this Melody Cramton had any sense, she would forget about that Boston fellow and come back and enjoy her family. However, I suppose seeing her parents dressed as they were tonight would have embarrassed her. Do you think she will ever listen to what you have shared with her?"

"I don't know, Timothy, I just don't know. She has to decide which way she is going to go," Miriam answered seriously.

"Have you decided where God is leading you, Miriam, on our relationship?"

"I enjoy being with you a lot, Timothy. I am waiting on Father's and Mother's final approval before I say anymore," Miriam answered earnestly.

"I want you to do that, Miriam," Timothy said in sincere appreciation.

CHAPTER TWELVE

THE ACCIDENT

JANUARY AND FEBRUARY seemed to fly by with Timothy coming to visit almost every Sunday. Miriam was thankful that she had not been asked to deliver any babies during the winter storms. Lydia found a home for Mr. Polinsky with an older couple, so she and Aaron moved him on a warm day in January. "Now he won't have to put up with you girls chattering at him all day," Lydia laughed.

Late in February Miriam was talking to Lydia, "Mother, it looks like I am not going to be called to deliver babies. People probably think that I am too young."

"Just be patient, Miriam. Babies have a way of arriving when you least expect them. You might receive a call any time. Remember, Dr. Blackwood said that people appreciated the care you had given them."

That same night after the family had eaten supper, read the Bible together and had been in bed for several hours, there was a loud knocking at the door. Aaron groggily went to the door to find an almost hysterical young man. "My wife is having a baby and is begging that I bring Miss Jensen to help. Can she come?"

"Wait a minute, young man. Where do you live? I will not

allow Miriam to go alone out into the country during the winter months," Aaron answered

"Oh, we live on the other end of town. Please would you wake your daughter so we can leave? My wife told me to hurry."

"Come inside and wait while I wake her and see if she will go with you." Aaron went to waken Miriam, shaking her gently he whispered, "There is a young father out in the kitchen asking that you come immediately to deliver their baby. Can you go with him?"

"He what? A baby! Where are my clothes? Tell him that I will be out in a few minutes," Miriam said excitedly as she pulled on her clothes and buttoned her dress so fast she wasn't sure she had it completely buttoned before she grabbed her heavy cloak and rushed into the kitchen.

"Miriam, this is Mr. Mason. He tells me this is their first baby. Do you think you might need Dr. Blackwood to help you?" Aaron asked.

"I won't know until I see her, Father. There will be time to call Dr. Blackwood if we need him. I am ready to go, Mr. Mason." Miriam said as she followed him out the door.

The frosty night air woke Miriam up with a shock. "How long has your wife been in labor, Mr. Mason?"

"Oh, I think about three hours. I hated to come for you so late, however she insisted that the baby would not wait until morning."

The town was silent under the sliver of a moon. It seemed so peaceful with the only noise being the clop-clop of the horse's hooves on the frozen ground. Any other time, Miriam would have enjoyed the almost magical look about the town as the smoke from the wood stoves curled slowly upwards.

Stopping near their tiny house, Mr. Mason said, "Go right in, Miss Jensen, she is waiting for you."

Miriam was not prepared for the sight she saw as she opened the door. Mrs. Mason was huddled in a corner of the room crying hysterically, "My baby, my baby!"

Throwing off her cloak, Miriam hurried to the side of the young mother and touched her gently. "Mrs. Mason, I am here now. We need to get you back to bed so I can help you and the baby." Leading her by the arm, Miriam guided her gently to the bedroom while Mrs. Mason continued to cry uncontrollably.

Mr. Mason came in from putting the horse away, "Could you fill your largest pot full of water and put on to heat, Mr. Mason, and bring me some old sheets. I may need your help in a few minutes."

Praying for wisdom, Miriam got Mrs. Mason into bed. "What is your first name, Mrs. Mason? Mine is Miriam."

"Mable Ann," she answered through clenched teeth as another pain hit.

"Mable Ann, may I pray with you? We are going to have to work together to deliver this baby. Would you allow your husband to help since I don't have Mrs. Polinsky to help me now?" Miriam asked.

"Yes, please pray for me and the baby. I am so scared. Marvin can come in to help if you can convince him to come. He says that having babies is woman's work."

Mr. Mason came to the door. "The water is heating, Miss Jensen. Now what else did you tell me that you needed?"

"Please bring me some old sheets and find the baby clothes while you are looking. I am going to pray with your wife right now. 'Dear Lord, Mable Ann and I need your help to deliver this baby that You are giving them. Help us to trust you and be calm. Amen.'"

Coming back with the sheets Mr. Mason said, "Here are the sheets and baby clothes Mable Ann had laid out. I think I may try to fix me a cup of coffee."

"Could you come help me, Mr. Mason? Your wife would like you to help and I really do need help."

"This is woman's work, however if you need me, I guess I

could help. What do you want me to do?" Mr. Mason asked.

"Would you stand at the head of the bed, hold her hand and talk quietly to her to keep her calm and encourage her to follow the instructions I give?" Miriam asked.

Miriam guided Mable Ann through the long delivery with Mr. Mason's help. Towards morning, she announced, "You have a baby girl. Mr. Mason, can you take her and bathe and dress her while I finish with your wife?"

"Guess I can, however I don't know much about bathing babies," Mr. Mason answered.

"Sure you can do it. Just wash her very gently and keep her covered so she will not get cold. Slip the little gown over her head and put on her diaper. Bring her back in here when you finish."

"What are we going to name our little girl, Marvin?" Mable Ann asked as Marvin gingerly carried his little daughter to the kitchen. "If we had a boy, I wanted to name him Christopher. What do you think of Christina Ann for her name, Marvin?" Mable Ann asked sleepily.

"Yes, sounds good, I'm so thankful she is alive and you are all right. Little Christina, you and I need to get this job finished so we both can get some breakfast and sleep." Turning to Miriam he asked, "What about you, Miss Jensen, do you want me to take you home right away?"

"If you have something ready to cook for breakfast, I can fix it and then you can take me home. Is there someone in your family who can come take care of her for a few days or should I come back after I get some rest?"

"As soon as I can get word to her mother, she will come and stay. Would you be able to come Monday and stay with her while I am at work? Her mother should be here by Tuesday," Marvin answered.

"Yes, that will be all right," she called as she finished cleaning up and walked out to the kitchen to see how Marvin was doing with the bathing and dressing.

"Can't get the confounded pins in the diaper. Can you take care of that, Miss Jensen?" he said in exasperation.

Miriam finished the diaper and said, "You did a good job, Mr. Mason. See you are already learning to take care of this little one."

"She is kind of cute for a baby. My very own little girl!" he said proudly.

"Yes, she was created by God just for you and Mable Ann. Now I had better take her to her mother so she can start her first meal. I'll be back in a minute to fix your breakfast."

Miriam fixed breakfast and sat down to eat with Mr. Mason. "I am mighty glad that you helped last night. Mable Ann was so scared and she would not listen to me. How did you get her to calm down?"

"First I prayed for wisdom, for God to show me what to do. However, it might be that because I am a woman she thought I would understand what she was going through. Every woman is different and this being her first baby, it was frightening for her. She will need your help getting around the next few days because she is very weak. I can drive my own buggy here Monday morning, but could you take me home now? I am so tired."

"I sure will. It will take me just a few minutes to harness old Joe, then I will be at the door to take you home."

Miriam walked back into the bedroom to check on Mable Ann. "I am leaving, Mable Ann, is there anything you need before I go?"

"No, I don't need anything except rest, however I want you to take that afghan on the back of the rocking chair. I hope that you like the color. I wish we had something more to give you," Mable Ann said happily.

Miriam picked up the beautiful blue afghan. "It is beautiful, Mable Ann! I have never seen a pattern like that. It will be wonderful to add to my hope chest. Thank you so much, I will see you Monday morning."

Timothy on his horse looking for cows.

167

"I am glad that you like it, and thank you again for all you did," Mable Ann said strongly.

Riding home, Miriam heard the church bells on the other side of town calling people to church. "Oh, I forgot today is Sunday. Probably all the family has left for church."

"What did you say, Miss Jensen?" Mr. Mason asked.

"The church bells just reminded me that it was Sunday. Your little girl was born on the Lord's Day."

"That's right she was. I hadn't thought about that. Well, here we are at your house. May I help you down?" Mr. Mason said as he gave her a hand as she stepped down.

"Thank you again for all you did," he called after her.

Miriam walked into the house to find the family almost ready to leave for church. "Miriam you are home!" squealed Elizabeth. "Did you get a baby last night?"

"Yes, Elizabeth, the Masons have a little baby girl. Now I am going to bed; I can hardly keep my eyes open."

"What shall we tell Timothy? He was coming for dinner today." Anna asked.

"Maybe if I sleep until noon that will be enough. Wake me up as soon as you arrive home so I can dress and fix my hair before Timothy arrives."

"Don't you want Timothy to see you like we see you every morning?" Emma asked.

"Emma, that isn't nice to tease your sister when she has been up all night," Lydia scolded.

"I'll call you as soon as we come home, Miriam," Anna called as Miriam closed the door behind her.

Just before falling asleep, Miriam prayed, *Lord, thank you for giving me the wisdom to deliver little Christina and that she was healthy.* It seemed like she had just fallen asleep when Anna was shaking her awake.

"Wake up, Miriam! Timothy wasn't at church today. His father said that he had broken his leg when his horse fell on him."

"Oh no! When did it happen?" Miriam was awake instantly.

"He didn't say much except that Dr. Blackwood said that it was a bad break and that he would be bandaged for at least eight weeks. Mr. Larsen said that it wasn't a good time to break a leg because he needed the help of all the boys with the livestock."

"I wish I could see him," Miriam moaned.

Miriam came out to dinner with the family and asked. "Father, could I go to see Timothy today?"

"You know that it wouldn't be proper for you to drive out there alone," Aaron answered.

"I know that, however would you drive me out there after dinner?" Miriam asked seriously.

"Don't you need more rest? You have been up all night," Aaron asked in concern.

"I feel rested and besides I could not sleep with worrying about Timothy. Would you mind taking me out as soon as we finish the dishes?" Miriam requested.

"You go on, Miriam. The girls and I can do the dishes. If you can't rest until you talk to Timothy, then you should go now and come back to retire early tonight," Lydia suggested.

Miriam changed to a more attractive dress in blue and put in her blue hair combs. "Now I am ready, Father. Are we going to take my buggy and Ginger?"

"No, I will take the bigger buggy as it is more comfortable riding."

Riding out in the country which was showing signs that winter was losing its hold, Miriam stated, "I will be so thankful when spring arrives. Then I can take Ginger out on the roads myself and not have to bother you."

"I happen to enjoy taking my oldest daughter for a ride in the country," Aaron answered. "We haven't gotten to do that much since I took you out to train you how to drive and had that accident."

169

"How well I remember. That almost convinced me never to learn to drive a buggy. Father, would there be a possibility that Timothy might never walk again?"

"I don't know, Miriam. That is always a possibility when you break both bones like Timothy did, however Dr. Blackwood is a good doctor. I am confident that he did all that he could. We will have to continue to pray that God will heal it."

"I am so worried about Timothy and that I may not see him for eight weeks unless you bring me out here again."

"He may be able to get around with crutches before long and can ride in the carriage. Don't start gathering up extra worries before they happen. Only time will tell the extent of Timothy's injuries. He doesn't need you all flustered and frettin'," Aaron warned.

"I know, Pa, but I can't help it. I really think a lot of Timothy. Why did God allow this to happen when we were just beginning to understand each other with his visits on Sundays?"

"God's doesn't make mistakes, nor does anything get past His control. He has reasons we don't understand, however He promises to work good out of everything that happens to us."

"How can good come out of a broken leg? It just doesn't seem fair. Timothy was only doing the work his father asked him to do. He wasn't out drinking or running with a rowdy bunch of men."

"God knew about this accident even before Timothy was born or even before He created the world," Aaron assured her.

"Really? How could He know about Timothy before He created the world?" Miriam asked incredulously.

"Because God is all knowing. There is no way that He wouldn't know. Moreover, He has it all under His control. I think that is marvelous. That means we can trust His choice of trials to shape and change us to be like Him."

"You mean that God is using this to shape Timothy to be like Christ?" Miriam asked in surprise.

"And all the rest of us as we allow God to work in the problem," Aaron answered.

"It helps to understand that God knows everything about us and uses all these troubles for our good," Miriam declared.

"Well, here we are at the Larsen farm. Looks like they may have some other company. I don't recognize the horse and buggy. Maybe it is some relative." Aaron said. Knocking on the door, Aaron stood back to allow Miriam to enter first. Esther opened the door.

"Oh Miriam, I am so glad to see you. Timothy was feeling so disappointed that he missed dinner with you today."

"Do you have company?" Aaron asked. "We don't want to intrude."

"Oh, it is just Uncle John and Aunt Rose. They came over after they heard about Timothy. Come in and meet them, they have been wanting to meet you ever since they heard about you and Timothy."

Miriam blushed and said, "I wonder what he told them about me."

"Oh, it was only good things," Esther said eagerly.

Timothy was sitting in an upholstered chair in the parlor. His younger brothers and sister were sitting around him, listening to his every word. It was easy to see that they loved their older brother very much.

"Oh, Miriam, I am so glad you came," Timothy greeted them as they came in the door. "Jonathan, go get Miss Jensen and her father some chairs from the kitchen. You are just in time to hear the story of my accident. That way I won't have to tell it again, although it gets better each time that I tell it," Timothy laughed heartily.

Miriam was relieved to hear his laugh. He seemed to be accepting the accident unusually well.

"I was out checking the cattle since we had had several calves born before we could get them to the barn," Timothy started. "I was on my faithful horse, Stormy, and Buster, our cattle dog, came along. I rode around the pasture checking gullies and thickets for cattle. I had almost given up finding any more until I spotted a cow in a thicket far away from the rest of the herd so headed that way, however what I didn't see was that wild dogs had surrounded her calf and killed it. When I rode up, Buster waded into the wild dogs ready for a fight before I could stop him. They started after Buster who ran back to me with the dogs after him. With the dogs fighting and growling all around her, the horse reared, and I slid off and she fell over on my leg. She struggled and finally stood up, I knew my leg was broken so while Buster fought with the dogs, I used a tree branch to pull myself into a standing position. Calling Stormy to come close, I threw myself across the saddle and told her to go home."

"What happened to the wild dogs?" Uncle John asked.

"I knew Buster would get killed if he stayed so I called him and he obediently came. They were so busy eating the dead calf that they didn't give chase."

"Did you make it back to the house without sliding off the horse, Timothy?" Aaron asked in concern.

"I was praying all the way. As soon as I was in the yard, I yelled for help and Daniel came running to help me into the house. The minute he had me sitting in a chair, I told him to get a rifle and go after those dogs. Joseph took our fastest horse and rode into town for Dr. Blackwood who just happened to be in his office. He came right out. He said that I had broken both bones so it was bad break, and didn't know how well I will be able to walk after the bandages come off.

"Oh, Timothy, I am so sorry you were hurt. It will be difficult staying inside all day with your brothers and father outside working," Miriam sympathized.

"Ma offered to teach me to knit or piece quilts, however I told her I would catch up on my Bible study and do some other

172

reading that I have been wanting to do for a long time."

"Would you like for me to bring you some books from the library in town?" Miriam asked.

"If I run out of reading, I will let you know. I do hope to be able to walk with crutches before long, once the swelling and pain lets up."

Martha called from the kitchen, "I have some apple pie served here at the table. Why don't all of you except Miriam and Timothy come out? Esther will bring some for you two to eat in there."

Once everyone had moved to the kitchen, Timothy said, "Ever since this happened, I felt I should talk to you, Miriam. I was unable to sleep last night so I lay there praying and trying to decide what to tell you. You realize that I may not be able to walk or do farming like I did before. Earlier I was sure that God had chosen you to be my wife, however I don't want to encourage you to marry a crippled man who may not be able to make a living for you. I couldn't sleep last night thinking how unfair that would be to you. I want you to be free to marry someone who could make a good living for you, and I don't know if I will be able to do that."

"Timothy, this accident doesn't change anything. Why are you worrying about what I will think or what you will be able to do? It is too early to know, and even if you can't walk, it would not change what I think of you," Miriam said tearfully.

"I don't want you to answer now. Pray about it for a couple of weeks. By then I should have mastered the use of crutches so I can get into the carriage and come for Sunday dinner if your mother will have me. However, I want you to know that you are to be free to discontinue the courting. Whatever you decide, I - I - will feel it is what God has planned for me," Timothy said hesitantly.

"Oh Timothy, you are still the same person. Can't we go on like we were?"

173

"I do not want you to marry me just because you feel sorry for me or want to take care of me. I want you to be convinced that this is what God wants you to do."

Miriam was crying softly and didn't trust herself to speak. At last, she got herself under control. "Timothy, I wish this terrible accident had never happened, and even more, I wish you wouldn't think it would change anything about our relationship."

"You go home and pray for a couple of weeks and then we will talk again. Thank you for coming out to see me, I feel better already," Timothy said gently.

Aaron called from the kitchen door, "Are you ready to return home, Miriam? I think we should be heading back into town. You need to get some more rest if you are going to help Mrs. Mason tomorrow."

"Were you up helping the Masons last night, Miriam?

"Yes, I arrived home at nine o'clock and slept until twelve when Anna woke me to tell me about your accident."

"You do need to get some more rest. Now I appreciate even more that you came out today. I will be praying for you," Timothy said.

"Thank you, it is good to know that you will be praying for me. Can I plan on seeing you in two weeks?"

"Lord willing, I will be at church and at your home for that delicious dinner you and your mother cook," Timothy answered.

CHAPTER THIRTEEN

THE INVITATION

MIRIAM COULD NOT SHAKE the sad feeling she felt from Timothy's suggestion that she pray about continuing their courtship. She could not bring herself to talk to anyone about it for several days. One morning she and Lydia were alone while the other girls were visiting Mary Cramton. "Mother, I need to talk to you, I am so troubled. Timothy told me that because of the accident that he may not be able to walk or farm as he did before. He wanted me to be free to discontinue the courtship. He wanted me to pray about it for two weeks and then he would come for Sunday dinner so we could talk."

"Oh, Miriam, I am sorry to hear that, I knew that something was bothering you. You have not been yourself for several days. Your father and I have been praying for you. Why didn't you talk to him about it on the way home from the Larsens?"

"I couldn't talk about it without breaking down and crying. I just wish Timothy had not asked me to decide now. I was distressed enough with his accident and now he wants me to make this important decision," Miriam said tearfully.

"What did you tell Timothy when he told you this?" Lydia asked.

"I told him that nothing was changed between us because

of the accident. And that he was still the same Timothy, nevertheless he said that he did not want me to decide anything at that time, however I was to pray about it for two weeks. He did not want me to marry him because I felt sorry for him. Oh, Mother, I do not want to make that decision now. I had already decided that Timothy was the one God had chosen for me. Why would he think the accident would change anything?"

"After we put your sisters to bed tonight, your father and I will talk and pray with you about this. I think that the accident has Timothy scared and it could be that he really has no reason to be scared. He is trying to be fair to you and that is truly unselfish of him," Lydia said gently.

After discussing the problem with her parents that evening, Miriam felt more at peace than she had for days. She felt she could still sing the special solo part of the choir number at church. Following Timothy's accident and his request, she had felt that she could not sing, however Aaron had reminded her, "There is nothing that God can not work out. He will show you and Timothy just what to do and your relationship will be stronger as a result of this test."

Sunday morning she dressed in her favorite blue velvet and worked at her fine hair to keep it all in place before she put on the matching blue hat. "My! You look radiant this morning, Miriam," Aaron said as he came into the kitchen where the family was gathering to leave for church. "Wish that Timothy could see you in that dress."

"Oh, he has seen this dress and he says it is definitely my color," Miriam responded.

There were several new people at church. One man especially drew a lot of attention with his carefully manicured moustache, goatee and expensive suit. Miriam kept wondering as she saw him from the choir loft, *I wonder who that man is? I've never seen him in town before*, she wondered pensively.

The choir started their special number and Miriam felt

like she could sing with great joy, *Holy Ghost With Love Divine*, from her heart. "Holy Ghost, with light divine, shine upon this heart of mine, chase the shades of night away, turn my darkness into day…dwell within this heart of mine; cast down ev'ry idol throne, reign supreme and reign alone." It became her prayer as she sang. The choir joined in and finished the magnificent song with great volume and meaning. Miriam sat down and noticed the eyes of the stranger were on her. She blushed and looked away quickly.

Following the service, the stranger struggled through the crowd to stand at her side. Taking her hand, he held it gently and said, "Miss a- a-."

"Jensen," Miriam responded sweetly.

"Miss Jensen, your solo was extraordinary and so inspiring. I did not hear singing of that quality back East in all the four years I was in law school," he spoke expressively.

"Thank you, I don't believe that I know your name." Miriam said as she carefully pulled her hand from his grasp. She felt her heart beat faster as he continued.

"Marshall Tompkins is my name. I just opened an attorney's office across the street from the New York Mercantile," he spoke in very proper English.

Aaron noticed that the stranger was detaining Miriam so he came to her side, "Excuse me, young man, my family is waiting in the carriage for our daughter. I don't believe that I have met you," he said, rather pointedly.

"No, we probably had not met since this is my first Sunday in town. I recently opened an attorney's office in town. My name is Marshall Tompkins. If you ever have a need of legal advice, you can find my office across from the New York Mercantile. I was telling your daughter how inspiring her singing was to me. I hope that I will hear more of it," Marshall answered still in his proper cultured style.

Aaron took Miriam by the arm, "Come, Miriam. Your

mother is impatient to check on the dinner at home." Miriam allowed herself to be led away, although she wished to learn more about this interesting stranger. Something about him intrigued her.

"He certainly is a fascinating man. He told me that he had not heard singing of my quality at the opera houses back East. Do you think that he was being honest or just flattering me, Father?" Miriam asked in surprise.

"I am inclined to think that he is a great flatterer, Miriam. You do sing well, although it is God who gave you the talent. Remember we have learned the verse "Let him who boasts boast in the Lord."

"I know that, Father, but why would he single me out to compliment? There are several other soloists in choir, who are just as good. Take Julia Watson, she has a beautiful voice."

"That she does, however you have the good looks also which attract men, Miriam," Aaron emphasized.

"There are other young ladies in the church who are very attractive. Why would he choose to talk to me?" she asked in curiosity.

"He must be attracted to you. Wonder why he chose Beloit to set up his office? I've never heard the name of Tompkins before so he must not have kinfolk here," Aaron mused.

Miriam could not get the friendly stranger out of her mind all afternoon. She rehearsed his compliment over and over again. She thought, *Not even Timothy has given me a compliment like that.*

Anna and she were talking that night after going to bed. "What did that handsome stranger say to you this morning, Miriam? He certainly seemed to concentrate all his attention on you. Other people were trying to meet him, yet he ignored them all until Father came to rescue you from his grip," Anna commented.

"He didn't have me in his grip. He was just visiting with me and telling me about his new office. I don't see anything wrong with that," Miriam rationalized.

"He seemed so forward. I don't think Timothy would hold your hand like that and he is courting you," Anna reminded gently.

"Well, he may not be courting me anymore."

"What! Has he decided to stop the courtship?" Anna asked incredulously.

"Not exactly. He told me to decide if I wanted to marry a crippled man. He did not want me to marry him because I felt sorry for him. Maybe he really just wanted to stop the courtship because he wasn't satisfied with me," Miriam countered.

"Miriam, how can you say that? Anyone can tell you that he worships the ground on which you walk. You can see in his eyes how much he loves being with you," Anna responded.

"Well, I don't know. I don't know why he is asking me to decide now."

"Have you prayed about it?" Anna asked searchingly.

"Yes, and Father and Mother prayed with me the other night. However, I-I still don't know how to answer him when he comes next week," Miriam answered hesitantly.

Miriam lay awake after Anna and she had prayed together. She could not get the intriguing stranger out of her mind. Just the thought of him made her heart beat faster. *He makes me feel so eloquent. Timothy has never made me feel that way. Maybe Timothy is right, we should end the courtship now. Why else would God bring this stranger into my life at this time,* she mulled over in her mind just before falling into a troubled sleep.

For the first time in her life, she did not feel like asking God what to do. The next morning, she continued to feel torn two different directions. She liked Timothy, although he was so ordinary—just a hard working farmer, while Marshall

179

Tompkins was an up-and-coming lawyer. *I want to learn more about this Mr. Tompkins,* she decided almost eagerly.

❀ ❀ ❀

A few days later, Aaron came home with the mail from the post office. 'Miriam, here is letter for you in a fancy envelope," he said, waving it in the air.

"It is probably more news from Melody since she will be coming soon," Miriam guessed.

"No, I don't think so. There is no perfume smell on this letter," Aaron said with a chuckle.

Miriam carefully opened the letter. Looking at the signature, she gasped, "This is from Marshall Tompkins! Why would he be writing to me?" She read quickly. "Mother, he is inviting me to the band concert of the Manifold Military Band at the opera house Friday evening. He says there is to be a reception following the concert for all the new business people in town. Could I go with him, Mother? It would give me opportunity to meet some new people. All I ever do is go to church and deliver babies."

"Your father and I will have to talk about it, Miriam. You know that we really don't know anything about this Mr. Tompkins except that he has opened a law office in town," her mother answered guardedly.

That evening following supper, Miriam talked with Aaron and her mother, "Father, I would like to accept Mr. Tompkin's invitation. Would you allow me to go with him to the concert?" Miriam asked, with bated breath.

"Miriam, I do not feel good about you going. You are still being courted by Timothy and we will not allow you to go unescorted with this stranger," Aaron responded.

"Mr. Tompkins said he would come with his carriage to take me to the Cooper Opera House. What could go wrong in that short trip?" Miriam begged.

"Miriam, you know that it would not be proper. It is not like you to request something that you know we would not approve. If you must go to the concert, perhaps your mother and I could accept our invitation."

"Your invitation! You didn't tell me that you were invited!" Miriam said in surprise.

"I didn't tell you, because we had decided to not attend, however if you are determined to go, we will take you. You can answer Mr. Tompkins that you will be attending with your parents."

"I want to ride with him and sit with him. I am almost nineteen, you know," Miriam complained.

"Miriam, the answer is the same. Write back to Mr. Tompkins and tell him what I told you to write. You are still being courted by Timothy and I am not willing to jeopardize that and even if you were not, Mr. Tompkins would still have to ask our permission and have a chaperone," Aaron answered strongly.

"All right, Father, I will do as you say, although sometimes I would like a little freedom," Miriam mumbled as she walked away to find her pen and paper.

"Stop for a minute, Miriam. Are you prepared to tell Timothy when he comes in a week that you wish to discontinue the courtship?" Aaron asked seriously.

"I don't know, Father, I am so mixed up that I can't think straight on anything. Why did the accident have to come when Timothy and I were building such a close relationship?" Miriam answered unhappily.

"Remember I told you that God makes no mistakes. He is teaching you to trust Him and His plans. This is a difficult lesson. You know that your mother and I have been praying for you and Timothy and we will continue to do so."

"I know, Father, and I appreciate your help through this time. I only wish that Timothy had not asked me to make a decision now," Miriam said sadly as she walked away.

❀　❀　❀

Miriam unwillingly sent the note as her father had requested, "Mr. Tompkins, Thank you for your kind invitation. I will be attending the concert with my parents. Sincerely yours, Miriam Jensen." All the time she was writing, she kept thinking, *I want to ride with him. He is so interesting; I could learn more about the world and people by spending time with him. He is so cultured and gentlemanly. Riding with Father and Mother will be so confining. They are restricting my enjoyment of life.*

Friday evening, Miriam dressed in the new wool-silk black dress that she and Lydia had made after Christmas. With the white lace trimmed collar and cuffs, she looked stunning.

"Miriam, you look just like the ladies in the magazines from back East. That dress looks even more expensive than the ones that Melody purchased from Kansas City," Anna reported enthusiastically.

"It does? Thank you, Anna."

"I wish Timothy could see you. His bright blue eyes would really glow with the excitement of being with you. Are you going to wear it so he can see it next Sunday?"

Miriam winced at the mention of Timothy's name. "I don't know, Anna. I might wear it," she answered vaguely. Somehow, she did not think that Timothy would appreciate expensive looking dresses that made her look like a fashion lady from back East.

Aaron came out of the bedroom with his suit and top hat on. Seeing Miriam putting on her black matching hat with the black feather plume, he exclaimed. "Miriam, you look very nice. Timothy would like that dress on you."

There it was again. Everyone reminds me of what Timothy would like and think. Why do they have to continue to remind me?

182

Miriam fumed inwardly.

While Aaron brought the carriage to the door, Miriam pulled on her long white gloves and white stole to match. Lydia came out of the bedroom. "Mother, you look so nice. I have not seen you dress up like that for ages. Where did you find the matching earrings and broach?" Miriam asked.

"I've had it for years, it was a gift from your father on our first anniversary, however in the hurry to get dinner in the oven and make sure that everyone else is ready for church on Sunday, I don't have time to work on dressing extra nice. That takes time as you will find out when you have a dozen children," Lydia said laughing.

"Mother, I don't plan on having a dozen children. Half a dozen like our family would be the right amount," Miriam responded rather sharply.

"Have you talked to Timothy about that, Miriam."

"We did talk a little about it as if that matters anymore. We don't even know if we are getting married," Miriam answered irritably.

"Well yes, I suppose you are right about that, although, if you are getting married, it is a subject that should be discussed," Lydia answered.

"Please, let's not talk about Timothy tonight. I feel so miserable everytime I think about the decision I have to make, that I will not enjoy the evening if we keep talking about it," Miriam said mournfully.

"All right, Miriam, I won't bring it up again, if that is your wish."

Aaron helped the ladies into the carriage. "My! I feel very honored to have two lovely ladies to escort to the Opera House. That old stone building has had many important speakers and events; if it could talk, it probably hasn't had two such attractive women as my women."

"Father, you are so flattering," Miriam said eagerly in an

effort to forget the conversation with her mother.

"Well, I am sure that you two are more attractive than Senator John Ingalls who drew such a large crowd that he had to meet in front of the Cooper House because it was too small for the crowd."

"According to the *Beloit Gazette*, the Fireman's Ball is the best attended event of the year in the Opera House," Lydia added. "Guess we missed out on the excitement."

"I don't care much for social events. Seems like there always has to be some liquor consumed for people to enjoy the time," Aaron said. "Well, here we are ladies, right at the front door. There must be a crowd already because I do not see any place close to tie up the team. Let me help you down and I will find a place and meet you inside."

The Opera House was a buzz as people gathered around in small groups visiting before the concert. Miriam had not been to a performance there before. The Manifold Band did play for the July 4th celebrations in the park and she had always enjoyed their music. Seemed like they played for every major event in town. Arnie Manifold knew what he was doing when he started the band even though it kept him busy with his jewelry store business. Miriam was standing with her mother, taking in all the gas chandeliers and burgundy drapes around the raised stage. She did not see Marshall Tompkins squeezing through the crowd coming towards her.

"Oh, Miss Jensen, I have been watching for you. Come, let me introduce you to my new friends." Taking her arm, he led her away without even stopping to speak to Lydia, who stood there dumbfounded at the way he completely ignored her.

Miriam's heart beat furiously and she felt a blush coming on as Marshall led her to a group of people gathered around visiting. "I want you all to meet Miriam Jensen, she has the most beautiful singing voice in all Beloit and probably should be in opera," he boasted.

"I am so pleased to meet you, Miss Jensen. I have heard nothing else since Marshall heard you sing. I am his partner, Robert Jackson," he said taking her hand.

Finding her voice at last, Miriam asked, "Could I ask you a question, Mr. Jackson?"

"Why, yes, Miss Jensen. What can I tell you?" Mr. Jackson was so attentive.

"Why did you and Mr. Tompkins choose Beloit to open your law office when you went to school back East?" Miriam asked abruptly.

"That's not hard to answer, I grew up near Beloit and we heard from my family that there was an office open for us to purchase. Marshall was willing to try most anything new. He was rather tired of the stuffy people back East. He is very talented in acting and I told him that he could use his talent here at the Opera House."

The Manifold Band was beginning to tune their instruments. "Let's find a front row seat, Miss Jensen. I like to sit up near the front, don't you?" Marshall said as he guided her to a seat.

Aaron came hurrying to Miriam's side. With a worried frown, he said, "Miriam, I have been looking all over the building for you. Mr. Tompkins, would you care to sit with Miriam, my wife and me?"

Mr. Tompkins, looking crestfallen, said, "Yes, I guess I could. The band is starting the opening song so we had better find seats."

Aaron allowed Miriam to sit beside Marshall, however he sat on her other side. Marshall kept up a whispered conversation with her through the entire concert. "Miss Jensen, I wish we could talk alone, however I guess this will have to do. Did you know that Agnes Flannery started her singing career right in this very building? I know you could do the same. I saw your picture in the *Beloit Gazette* today as one of the top women in the Gazette subscription contest. Now that I know you are one of the top women, I will ask all my friends to subscribe. We want you to win that piano. Did you know that I was in Pittsfield, Massachusetts when President Roosevelt was in a collision with his carriage and a trolley? His secret agent, Craig was killed. The President didn't finish his trip because he had to have surgery."

Miriam was impressed. "You seem to do so many important things Mr. Tompkins."

"Call me, Marshall, Miss Jensen. There are so many things I wish to share with you and places we can visit together. Your talent may be just what is needed in the operas they put on here at the Cooper's House. Did you know that I had the lead in a play back East?" Marshall bragged.

"Mr. Jackson said that you had been involved with acting back East. I wasn't aware that you had the lead," Miriam said enviously.

"Oh yes, they wanted me to stay, however I told them that my job must come first," Mr. Tompkins responded.

Following the concert, Mr. Tompkins asked eagerly, "Would you like to sit with me while we enjoy the refreshments for the new businesses in town?"

Miriam looked at her father, "Father could I go with Mr. Tompkins for the refreshments?"

"No, I think we will be leaving before too long. I would like for you to stay with your mother and me," Aaron answered firmly with a frown.

Mr. Tompkins looked exasperated and hurried off. Miriam watched in surprise as he hurried up to a very attractive young lady, took her hand and kissed it and led her to the refreshment table.

Aaron saw what had happened, "Miriam, is that the kind of gentleman you wish to be spending time with in the future?"

"Take me home, Father," Miriam requested and took her father by the arm. It was a silent ride home. Miriam could not say anything, she was so stunned. Aaron helped her and Lydia down from the carriage at the house. "I need to talk to you, Father," she said with tears running down her cheeks.

"I'll be right in as soon as I put the team away. Help your mother put your sisters to bed so we can talk. You might wish to change into something more comfortable before we talk," Aaron answered.

Lydia put her arm around Miriam as they walked into the house. "Oh, Mother, how could I have been so stupid?"

"Go change your dress and we will talk as soon as I check on your sisters."

Jesse and Anna were the only ones still up. Anna saw Miriam's tears and knew that the evening had not gone well. She did not ask any questions; she left to help Lydia with the other girls.

Aaron came inside quickly. Not seeing Miriam, he called. "Are you still up, Miriam? I am inside now," he asked pleasantly.

"I'm changing my dress, Father, before I get any more tears on it. I will be right out."

Lydia changed her dress after she had prayed with the other girls and told them goodnight. Sitting down at the table with Aaron and Miriam, she poured each of them a cup of hot chocolate that she had put on the stove to heat.

Aaron started, "Miriam, I do not have to tell you, 'I told you so' because you already know that Mr. Marshall Tompkins is not what he pretended to be."

"I am so angry with myself for being won over by his charms so easily and that I didn't listen to you when you warned me and tried to protect me," Miriam responded with heartbroken tears.

"Sometimes we all have to learn the hard way. Your mother may not have told you about the man that she was planning to marry before she met me. Her grandmother had warned her that he was not the right one for her because he had no interest in

God, however she continued to see him without her grandmother's permission until she heard her grandmother praying."

"Yes, Miriam, I wouldn't listen to grandmother's advice, although her prayers scared me so bad that I ran to my room and begged God to forgive me. I knew that this man was not a Christian, however I thought he would become one after I married him," Lydia confessed sadly.

"You had never told me about that, Mother. How long was that before you met Father?" Miriam asked.

"I was convinced that I would never marry after I stopped seeing the man I thought I loved, however within a month, your father moved to town and started coming to our church. You know the rest of the story from there," Lydia answered.

"You probably both see that my situation is sort of the opposite of what happened to you. God has brought Timothy into my life and I haven't been content with God's plan. I wanted someone more cultured and exciting," Miriam began to cry softly.

"We all go through times when we think we know more than God, Miriam, and He allows us to go our own way until we finally see that His plan is best. It is not too late for you. Timothy doesn't need to know about Marshall Tompkins and I will not tell him," Aaron said.

"You mean I don't need to tell him how I almost discontinued the courtship?" Miriam asked.

"No, Miriam, there is no reason to tell him unless you feel that God would have you tell him after you are married; I see no need or good coming from telling him."

Pulling out her chair, Miriam stood behind her father and gave him a big hug. Pulling her into his lap, Aaron said, "Now, my oldest, I am thankful that God answered your mother's and my prayer. We knew you were being tempted by the intriguing stranger's charming ways and were being led away from God's plan. Let's pray and thank Him for His protection."

They each prayed and Aaron said, "Miriam, you have a busy day coming up tomorrow, so you had better get some rest."

"I do, Father? I didn't know that I had anything planned."

"You have a big meal to cook for a certain young man who is going to be my son-in-law and I want him well fed," Aaron answered with a chuckle.

"Oh Father, you are wonderful. Thank you for reminding me to prepare for Timothy's coming Sunday."

"Remember I am gaining a son-in-law and after six girls, it is about time we had more men around here," Aaron responded with a happy chuckle.

CHAPTER FOURTEEN

MELODY'S RETURN

MIRIAM SPENT ALL SATURDAY cooking pies and fresh bread for the dinner with Timothy. Hearing singing coming from the kitchen, Anna came to ask, "Why all the happy sounds from the kitchen? Looks like you are cooking for a king or something."

"I am happy because I will be seeing Timothy again. And happy that God finally brought me to my senses," Miriam answered.

"Do these senses have anything to do with Marshall Tompkins or Timothy?"

"Maybe your question should be, does it have anything to do with obeying God by one Miriam Jensen?" Miriam suggested.

"In what way?" Anna asked with empathy.

"I had prayed that God would show me if Timothy was the one God had for me, and I knew that Father felt Timothy had all the Biblical qualifications for a husband, yet I thought I had a better plan. I knew all that, however when Mr. Marshall Tompkins marched into my life with his flattery and cultured ways, I - I - was…"

"You were swept off your feet!" Anna finished.

"Yes, I guess you could say it that way," she admitted slowly.

"Well, I am saying it. I didn't like the looks of him from the minute I laid eyes on him. He looked like trouble, reminded me of those smooth talking men at the carnival at the Wichita State Fair."

"You never said anything to me about your concern about him. Why didn't you warn me that I was making a big mistake?" Miriam asked in surprise.

"Would you have listened if I had?" Anna asked seriously.

"I suppose not. He was so intriguing and interesting."

❧ ❧ ❧

Sunday morning brought forth a warm spring-like day. Miriam dressed in the black wool/silk dress with the white lace trimmed collar. "So you are going to wear that for Timothy?" Anna teased. "Would you like to borrow my black lace parasol to match?"

"Oh, could I? I want to look extra nice today," Miriam said wistfully.

"Do you suppose that Mr. Tompkins will come back to church?" Anna mused.

"It doesn't make any difference to me if he does or doesn't. If he wants to come hear the word of God taught, that might make him a better person, however he certainly will receive no attention from me," Miriam said strongly.

When they pulled into the churchyard, the Larsen carriage was not there. "I wonder if they are coming? Maybe Timothy isn't able to get into the carriage just yet," Aaron commented.

"I hope nothing will keep him from coming today," Miriam said anxiously. She followed the family inside, although she wished to wait outside for Timothy to come, however that would not be proper.

"Come on, Miriam," Elizabeth whispered, pulling on her hand. "They are starting the first song and it is one of my favorites."

Miriam couldn't concentrate on the words of the song. She kept thinking, *What if Timothy doesn't come and I won't be able to talk to him for another whole week?*

They were singing the last verse of *What a Friend We Have in Jesus* when the door opened and Timothy, walking with crutches, led the Larsen family to sit behind the Jensens. He had caught Miriam's eye the minute he stepped into the room and smiled joyfully at her.

Miriam heaved a sigh of relief. Anna poked her in the ribs, "Now you can relax and concentrate on your singing." Miriam gave her an embarrassed grin.

Following church, Aaron turned around to greet the Larsen family. "It's good to see Timothy among us again."

"Yes, he was getting cabin-fever from being stuck in the house for two weeks," Paul Larsen responded.

"That is for sure! I even threatened to take up knitting if they didn't let me out of the house soon. Esther told me I was a difficult patient, as I kept her running for more Bible study books and pen and paper," Timothy laughed.

"He had his chair completely surrounded with books. I couldn't even clean the parlor with all his mess," Esther complained.

"Now, Esther, it was not a mess. I did some excellent studying on the book of Ephesians," Timothy insisted.

"Maybe you can teach our family some of what you learned, Timothy," Aaron said.

"I would like to do that. Is my invitation still open for dinner today?"

"It sure is. Miriam has cooked up enough food for an army," Aaron laughed.

"I'm ready for it. Would you be able to take me home this

afternoon, Mr. Jensen?" Timothy asked hesitantly.

"Why yes, I can do that. I forgot that you can not ride your horse yet."

"It is difficult enough getting into the carriage. It took Daniel and Pa to help me."

After arriving home from church, the visiting during the meal flowed easily as the whole family enjoyed having Timothy back with them. Miriam noticed that Timothy's eyes were on her constantly as she served the meal. "You did bake my favorite apple pie! I dreamed about it last night, and now my dream has come true," Timothy said eagerly.

The rest of the family moved to the parlor following the cleaning up of the dinner dishes. Timothy and Miriam sat at the table visiting quietly.

"Miriam, you look beautiful today. I thought blue was your color, although the black makes you look so mature and elegant," Timothy said cheerfully.

"Thank you, Timothy. Anna told me that you would like it."

"Do you know what I was studying while I was home these two weeks? I learned so much from Ephesians and especially chapter five on marriage. Would you like to hear a little of what I learned?"

"Yes, I have much to learn on that subject," Miriam answered in eager anticipation.

"The apostle Paul placed a bunch of responsibility on us men. Could you bring me a Bible and I will show you," Timothy requested.

They read through the verses together and looking intently into Miriam's eyes, Timothy asked, "Could we pray about God's plan for us, Miriam?"

"Yes, I would like for you to pray."

"Lord, you know that Miriam and I care very much for each other so we need to know what Your plan is for us. Give us a peace in knowing that we are in Your will. Amen."

Hesitating briefly before continuing, Timothy asked, "Miriam, have you had time to pray about our relationship? I will not know for several weeks the outcome of my injuries. After your visit two weeks ago, I felt that I had been too hasty asking you to decide on continuing our courtship. I talked it over with Pa and he agreed that I had been in too confounded a hurry asking you to decide now. I am sorry that I did. Do you have any thoughts on our courtship?" Timothy said in genuine sorrow.

Fearing that she might cry, Miriam looked down at the table a few minutes. "Yes, Timothy, I have prayed about it and I am confident that you are the one that God has chosen for me, and it is not because I feel sorry for you. It will not change our relationship no matter how your leg heals," she answered in almost a whisper.

"Oh, Miriam, I am so glad to hear you say that. God has shown you the same confidence of His plan. Until I know how this leg comes out, I can't make any preparation for our future, because I can't work on the house or do my own farm work. Pa is going to put me to work mending harness this week because I can sit to do that."

"Did Dr. Blackwood say that you would need to be careful with your leg after the cast comes off?"

"I have not seen him since he put the bandages on. He said that if I wasn't in any pain that he would not need to see me for six weeks. Now that the weather has warmed up and I can be outside, hear the birds and see things green up, my disposition will be improving. I don't see how women can stand being stuck in a house all day cooking and sewing. Do you know what I would like to do before your father takes me home?"

"No, what?" she asked eagerly.

"I would like to sing with your family," Timothy answered.

"You would? Can you walk to the parlor so we can use the piano?"

"I can go about anywhere on the crutches if you are not in

a hurry. Just lead the way," Timothy said laughing.

Miriam sat down on the piano stool and Timothy sat in an overstuffed chair beside the piano. "What would you like to sing?"

"I would like to sing, *It Is Well With My Soul.* The words of that song have been going over and over in my head since my accident."

They sang with Aaron and Timothy doing tenor and bass, the girls singing the high parts and Lydia singing alto. "When peace like a river attended my way, when sorrows like sea billows roll, whatever my lot, Thou has taught me to say, it is well with my soul."

"Timothy, you have a wonderful singing voice. I noticed that in church this morning. Why aren't you singing in the choir?" Lydia asked.

"Oh, Mrs. Jensen, I do love singing, however I couldn't make it to choir practice. Our family sings together on Sunday evenings if we can't come to church. You know, if we put both families together, we would almost have our own choir," Timothy said laughing.

"Do you want to sing any more songs, Timothy? Our family loves to sing also," Miriam asked enthusiastically.

"Maybe just one more and then, Mr. Jensen, could you take me home? It tires me out walking with the crutches and heavy bandage."

🌿 🌿 🌿

Monday noon, Aaron brought the mail. "Here is a perfumed letter. Must be a letter from Melody."

"Give it to me and quit sniffing it," Miriam said with a chuckle.

Opening it Miriam read: *"Dear Miriam, Walter and I will be arriving on the train the last week of the month. I've told Mother to plan an engagement party and I want you and Timothy to come.*

That is if you are still friends with him. Mother wrote that she saw you sitting with the new lawyer in town at the band concert. We will be visiting through the Easter break from classes. I know that you will just love Walter. He is so cultured and intelligent. Your friend, Melody."

"Mother, I'm going to have to tell Timothy about Mr. Tompkins because Melody knows it from her mother. If I don't tell him, someone else might tell him and that would ruin everything," Miriam said anxiously.

"Yes, Miriam, it would be wise to tell him the next time you see him. I didn't realize the news would get around so fast."

Once the spring weather allowed the men to repair the telephone lines, Lydia started receiving calls from Mary Cramton. One morning came a desperate call on the telephone. "Oh Lydia! I need your help with Melody's engagement party," she said almost in panic. "She has given me a list of names that seems to include half the town. What am I going to do? Could you and Miriam come this afternoon to help me decide?"

"Where do you plan to have this party, Mary? Oh, Melody has asked that you have it at home? Yes, I think that Miriam and I can come this afternoon to help you plan."

After a couple more words, Lydia hung up the telephone, "Miriam, are you free this afternoon? Mary is desperate for some wisdom on this huge engagement party that Melody has requested that she provide."

"Yes, Mother, I am free and I have missed visiting with Mrs. Cramton. Seems like there is never any time to visit after church, and we haven't been in their home since Christmas. Would it be possible for me to take Ginger and the buggy so I could go out to visit Sarah Williams? I haven't been to see her since the baby was a few weeks old."

"Why yes, you can take the buggy and leave me at Mary's so we can have some time to visit and maybe do a Bible study which we haven't done together in ages. I really miss that time together. Another person that we need to visit is Mr. Polinsky. I was wondering the other day how he was faring with the older couple from church who took him into their home. He may want to be moving back to his own farm now that it is spring."

Putting on their light spring capes and hats, Miriam went to get Ginger and the buggy. Lydia said to Anna, "Miriam and I will be back in a couple of hours, Anna. Could you and Elizabeth start supper while Emma and Jesse work on their reading lessons?"

"Yes, Mother, if you will tell Elizabeth to help, and not to argue with me about what we are going to cook and how the table is going to be set," Anna answered agreeably.

"Elizabeth, you mind your older sister while we are gone and I might have a treat for you when I return."

"Oh what is it? Tell me now," Elizabeth squealed.

"No, it will be a surprise. I must go, Miriam is out in the buggy waiting for me."

Almost before they knocked at the Cramton home, Jackson had the door open and Mary was waiting in her wheel chair just inside the door, "Come right in, ladies," Jackson said in his most proper style.

"Jackson, it is so good to see you still active and strong," Miriam said admiringly.

"I'm still the best butler, gardener and buggy driver around," Jackson joked.

"You are right about that, Jackson. I don't think you will ever slow down and take a life of ease," Mary said joyfully.

They sat around the dining room table and Annabel served them hot tea and cookies. "Thank you both for coming. I need your wisdom and especially help from you, Miriam because you know Melody so well. What kind of party do you think we should have?" Mary asked.

"I would suggest inviting a few close friends and a simple dinner party," Miriam suggested.

"She has sent me a list a mile long," Mary moaned.

"You are her parents and paying for this party. You have a right to decide what would be fitting,"

"You know that if I don't do it exactly as she requests she will make a big scene. If I had my choice, there would be no party because from all she has told us about Walter, I doubt that he is a Christian. How can I be proud to announce her engagement when she knows she is going against our wishes and God's teaching of not being unequally yoked with someone who is not a Christian?" Mary said tearfully.

Going around behind Mary, Lydia gave her a hug. "Mary, we will continue to pray that Melody will see this before the wedding. You have told her you are concerned about Walter not being a Christian. If you refuse to have anything to do with her wedding, she may stay in Boston and have the wedding without you. This way you will have some input in her life while she and Walter are here."

"Thank you, Lydia, for helping me to see that. Since she is not arriving until one day before the party, I think Thomas and I will decide what would be appropriate and plan accordingly."

"Yes, that would be a wise decision, Mrs. Cramton. No matter what you do, Melody will find fault with it so do what works best for you and Thomas," Miriam added.

"You have raised a very practical daughter, Lydia. I only wish we had come to know Christ when Melody was younger so we could have trained her like you have trained your children."

"You did the best that you could, Mary. Melody is making her own choices now and she will have to suffer the consequences of those choices. She has been taught what the Bible says on marriage and what God says about choosing a mate. All we can do now is pray that she will make wise choices," Lydia reminded her. "Do you have any more questions for Miriam? She would like to visit Sarah Williams while I visit with you, if you are not busy."

Miriam drove out to the Williams home; she rejoiced to see that they had some fruit trees planted and a space for a little garden. "Timothy and I plan to have fruit trees and a garden at our farm also. I am so anxious to start planning with him," she said as she was met at the door by an eager Sarah.

"Oh, Miriam! I am so glad to see you. All day I kept wishing I could visit you and now you arrive. Isn't God good to answer my prayer?" she said giving Miriam a big hug. "Come see little Charles. You will be surprised at what you see."

Miriam followed her into a little side room. Baby Charles was lying there waving his arms and kicking his legs a little. "What did you do, Sarah? I can't believe his legs are actually moving."

"You remember that I asked God to show me what to do to help his legs so each day several times I would exercise him and slowly he began to move them with me. He seemed as excited as I was when he could actually move them himself. Wouldn't Mrs. Polinksy be happy to know that he might not be crippled after all," she said excitedly.

"You know, Sarah, I feel that she might just know about that up in heaven. There really isn't anything in the Bible that says we will know things happening on earth, although I personally think that God might give us that special gift of knowing," Miriam said.

"What brings you out this way, Miriam? I have wanted to come visit you for so long, however we thought it would be better if I didn't take Charles out until he was older."

"The reason that I am out today is because Melody Cramton, my friend, is coming from Boston next week. She is bringing her fiancée to meet all of us and has requested that her mother put on a large engagement party."

"What do you think of it, Miriam?" Sarah asked cautiously.

"I told Melody in my letters that if Walter was not a Christian, she should not marry him. And I told her mother that she doesn't have to invite half the town just because Melody told her to invite them."

"My! Aren't you are outspoken. Does this Melody listen to you?" Sarah asked incredulously.

"She used to when we were young girls. Since she became involved with the Woman's Suffrage movement and moved back East, she is showing less and less interest in what I have to share about God's plan for her life," Miriam said with a sigh.

"What are your plans for the future, Miriam? You mentioned Timothy and you planting fruit trees and a garden. Is this something serious? It must be if you are planting gardens together," she said with a laugh.

"I guess I have not told you about Timothy Larsen, who is courting me."

"No you haven't. Tell me about him," Sarah requested excitedly.

"He is the oldest son from a large farm family. He is a strong Christian and encourages me to follow God. I helped Mrs. Polinsky deliver his little brother last fall. That was my first time to work with her and also my first meeting of Timothy."

"Have you and Timothy made any plans yet?" Sarah asked.

"We have not discussed too many yet. He purchased a small farm next to his father's farm and was fixing up the property when he broke his leg," Miriam answered seriously.

"Oh how terrible! How is he doing now? That could be serious."

"It is serious in more ways than one; it almost prevented us from continuing our courtship," Miriam admitted.

"In what way?" Sarah asked in surprise.

"Timothy told me that since he didn't know if he would be able to walk or farm after the bandages came off, that he didn't want me to marry him because I felt sorry for him. He wanted me to pray about it and give him an answer in two weeks. The rest of the story is rather sad and complicated, I'm not sure that you want to hear it all," Miriam hesitated and waited for Sarah to respond.

Deep in thought, Sarah said, "Let me get baby Charles so I can feed him while we talk. I think you need to talk to someone," Sarah hurried to the bedroom and brought Charles and sat him on her lap. "Now go on with your story."

Miriam spent the next hour explaining the whole story. Sarah sat very quiet, even little Charles was quiet as if listening with her. "Miriam, I feel honored that you trust me with this. Your mother was correct in telling you to share it with Timothy because someone else might. He needs to hear it from you."

"Sarah, you were right, I did need to talk to someone to help me see what I should do. Would you pray with me that I would know how to tell him. I don't want to hurt him. I love him too much and he has been so unselfish with me. I fear this may give him reason to not trust me," Miriam said seriously.

They prayed and Sarah said, "Miriam, I have been asking God ever since we moved here, to give me a friend like you. I asked for someone who really wanted to be the kind of woman God wants. So many of the women my age aren't interested in obeying what the Bible says for wives."

"Wait until you meet Melody and hear about the Woman's Suffrage idea. Mother and I don't think women should vote, because we feel that it will lead to women taking more and more of the men's role. They probably will desire to be in congress right with the men. I read in a copy of *Woman's Column,* that grandmother sends to us, that they are already demanding this," Miriam stated soberly.

"I am afraid it will not be good for our country even though a lot of Christian women think so," Sarah said in deep concern. "I trust my husband to know how to vote for our family. He studies the issues and the candidates and we talk it over before he votes. That is more than I have time to do."

"I agree, Sarah. Melody thinks that I am afraid to get involved, however that is not the reason. I see from the Bible that men are to be the head of the home. Melody doesn't agree with this. Oh! look at the time. I must pick up Mother so we can be home for supper. Thank you, Sarah, you are a wonderful friend." Walking over to Sarah's chair she gave her a big hug.

※　※　※

A few days later, a formal invitation arrived in the mail inviting Lydia, Aaron and Miriam to the engagement supper for Melody and Walter. *"Bring Timothy Larsen with you,"* was added in handwriting.

"Mother, is there some way that I can talk to Timothy without my little sisters listening when he comes for dinner Sunday? I want to tell him about Mr. Tompkins before we attend the engagement supper," Miriam asked anxiously.

"I think it would be all right for you and Timothy to sit in the porch swing and talk. Your sisters can stay inside with us. I know you are very concerned about talking to Timothy," Lydia said gently.

" Thank you, Mother. I need your prayers that I will use just the right words so that Timothy will understand."

Sunday morning brought the sound of rain and a day of clouds. "Oh, Mother, that will ruin everything. How can I talk seriously with Timothy with little sisters coming and going through the room?"

Waving her hands at the clouds, Lydia said, "Really, the rain might be a blessing in disguise. The girls will not be able to hear your conversation on the porch while it is raining. God can make good come out of what we think is bad."

Miriam was so nervous through dinner that Timothy kept watching her with a curious frown. She was thinking, *If I tell him about Mr. Tompkins, he may think that I will be attracted to any*

man who comes into church. He may even want to stop courting me.
She just played around with her food; she didn't feel like eating.

Following dinner, Lydia said, "Timothy, why don't you take Miriam out to the porch swing so you can talk without us disturbing you."

Timothy sensed it was serious, "Come on, Miriam. Your mother wants us on the porch." He picked up his crutches and slowly made his way to the porch while Aaron held the door for him.

"Now, Miriam, what has you so upset? You hardly ate any dinner and you look so worried. What has happened?" Timothy asked earnestly.

The rain had slowed to a gentle shower and the tulips were sticking their heads through the ground, however Miriam didn't notice anything except Timothy's eyes which showed a worried look.

"I don't know where to start, Timothy. There is something that I must tell you, however I feel so terrible about it that it is difficult to talk about," Miriam said tearfully.

"Why don't you start at the beginning? You are getting me confused," Timothy said gently.

Miriam hesitantly started telling of her meeting with Mr. Tompkins and finished with, "Timothy, I am so sorry to hurt you and that I didn't trust God's plan for me. Will you forgive me?" Miriam said with tears running down her cheeks.

Timothy wanted to give her a big hug although he knew it would not be proper. Instead, he said, "Miriam, thank you for being honest with me. I love you even more because of your truthfulness even when you thought it might cause me to stop courting you. I admire you even more now," he said sincerely with love.

Heaving a big sigh of relief, Miriam said, "Oh, thank you, Timothy, for being so forgiving. This has hung like a heavy load on me for weeks."

"Well, now that you have told me, let's get onto something more pleasant," Timothy requested. "I for one, enjoy the smell of the rain. Have you noticed how clean everything smells after the rain?"

"Well, I guess I have noticed things smell different. Probably as a farmer you would notice things like that. I don't know if you will think this is more pleasant, however you are invited to the engagement supper of Melody Cramton and Walter Van Squoit III next Saturday evening."

"I don't know Melody very well, except from church so why would I be invited?" Timothy questioned.

"Melody was my best friend for several years when we first moved here. We became even closer when she and her parents accepted Christ as Savior. Melody still struggles with being obedient to God," Miriam continued.

"What did you say his name was? Something about that name is familiar, although I am not sure why," Timothy responded in deep thought.

Miriam answered, "Maybe you heard me mention it when I received Melody's letter."

"That may be where I heard it but I am not sure. It puzzles me where I could have heard or seen that name before. Maybe it will come to me before long. Now, when and where is this supper? You realize that I will still be walking with crutches, don't you?"

"I know, Timothy, however I do want you to come," Miriam answered quickly.

"If you want me to come, I will make every effort to be there. However, I doubt that Walter Van Squoit and I will have much in common. What did you say that he does for a living?"

"He is music director for a large church in Boston. In addition, he sings opera and I think that he and Melody sing together. You knew that she was in music school, didn't you?"

"Seems like you did mention this Walter Van Squirt or whatever he is named."

"The name is Van Squoit. Don't mix that up or we both will be in trouble" Miriam laughed.

"What am I to wear to this shindig? You realize that I can not get into my suit with the bandages. In fact, the only trousers I can wear are these large overalls," he reminded her.

"They will be all right. You can wear a white shirt and tie and put your suit jacket on over them."

"Now tell me what I am supposed to talk about with Mr. Van Squoit. He probably doesn't know a thing about the music that I like such as, *It is Well With My Soul,* nor would he know anything about farming or taking care of cows. Am I supposed to make up something about my great love of opera music or that I am a famous author?" Timothy said in mock seriousness.

"Oh, Timothy, you are so funny," she gasped. "Don't make up something. Just be yourself; that is what I love about you."

"I am not convinced that Mr. Walter Van Squoit III will be impressed, however if you say so I will do it. I have a feeling that I will not enjoy the evening," Timothy groaned.

"You are not the only one. The main reason that I am going is because Mr. and Mrs. Cramton asked us to come. They won't have anything in common with Mr. Van Squoit either. They have reserved him a room in the Anderson House. The hotel has some expensively decorated rooms and a nice dining room so he should feel at home."

"You know, Miriam, we really should pray for Miss Cramton and Mr. Van Squoit that God would give us opportunity to talk to them about their relationship to Christ," Timothy admonished.

"You are correct about that, Timothy. I was so upset at Melody's decision to marry a non-Christian that I had forgotten to pray that God would use us to help them."

"Let's do that right now."

"Would you pray, Timothy?" Miriam encouraged.

The following Friday afternoon the telephone rang. Miriam answered, "Hello, Oh, is that you Melody? I didn't know that you had arrived. You want me to come over to meet Walter this afternoon? I will have to clean up and change my dress so it will be an hour before I can come. Shall I bring my own buggy? Are you saying that you want Jackson to pick me up? All right, I will be ready when he comes in an hour. Goodbye."

Hanging up the telephone, Miriam said, "Mother, what should I wear to meet Mr. Van Squoit? I feel so unprepared and inadequate to meet someone who obviously is very cultured and sophisticated."

"Miriam, God will show you what to talk about and also don't worry about your clothes. Your pleasant smile and personality is more important. I would suggest that you wear that light blue silk that we made last year, it is very flattering to you."

Miriam bathed and dressed quickly. She had just finished putting up her hair and pinning on her flowered hat, when Elizabeth called from the front porch. "Here comes Jackson. Why is he coming to visit us?"

"He is picking me up to visit Melody and Mr. Van Squoit, Elizabeth."

"Can't I go with you and play with Seth?" Elizabeth asked eagerly.

"Not this time, Elizabeth. Someday soon, I will take you to play with Seth. He probably does get lonesome for someone his age in that big house."

Greeting Jackson as he helped her into the carriage, Miriam said, "Will your rose garden be ready for a wedding this fall, Jackson?"

"A-a-I thought Mrs. Cramton said that Melody was getting married in June at the church."

"I'm not talking about Melody. I am talking about

Timothy and me. Of course I haven't talked to Timothy about this so don't tell anyone, please," Miriam begged.

"You don't have to worry about me. Annabel and the roses are about the only ones I see each day. So you're being courted by that Larsen boy? He is a mighty nice boy. Several times, I have been downtown and struggling with some large bags of groceries and if he sees me, he will come right up and carry everything to the carriage for me. Mighty nice boy, if I do say so. And you want to get married in the Cramton's rose garden. Well, I will have to really go all out to keep those roses blooming their best for my favorite lady," Jackson said with a smile.

Jackson let Miriam off at the door. "There you are, Miss Jensen. Go and meet Melody's intended. Can't say that I think much of him. He wouldn't give me the time of day when I picked them up at the depot. You would have thought I was a beggar the way he treated me."

Timidly, Miriam raised the knocker. Annabel opened the door while Jackson put away the carriage. "Come in, Miss Jensen. Miss Cramton and Mr. Van Squoit are in the parlor." Miriam noticed that Annabel was trying to act very proper. It almost made her chuckle because she knew Annabel probably felt like Jackson about Mr. Van Squoit.

Miriam walked to the door and waited until Melody spotted her, "Oh Miriam, come meet Walter."

Walter hesitated a minute and then got to his feet and walked to face Miriam and took her hand and kissed it lightly. "Pleased to meet you, Miss Jensen. Melody has told me so much about you," he said in a clipped, almost British, accent.

"I am glad you have come to meet Melody's parents and friends," Miriam responded with a large smile.

"Sit here by me, Miriam," Melody requested. Miriam noticed how different Melody looked; she was dressed in a very fashionable low-cut black silk and had a new type hair cut. Even her accent was more Eastern. It was Mr. Van Squoit who made

Miriam a little uncomfortable. He was dressed in the latest style of suit and his goatee and mustache were trimmed very properly. He kept watching Miriam so intently that she had difficulty concentrating on Melody's constant chatter.

"Miriam, Walter and I have decided on June 10th for our wedding at the Christian church. Since I don't have a sister, would you stand up with me? Mother and I will provide your dress, shoes and hat," Melody stated matter-of-factly.

"This is all sort of sudden. Could you give me a day or two to think about it?" Miriam answered rather vaguely.

"You mean you don't know if you could stand up at the wedding of your best friend?" Walter asked, looking a little shocked.

"I meant that I needed to think about it and see what my parents think, and Timothy," Miriam answered quickly.

"Oh, are you and Timothy still friends? I wasn't sure that you were after what Mother told me," Melody said teasingly.

"Melody, that was a bad mistake on my part and Timothy knows all about it. It is over with and forgotten as far as I am concerned, and I wish that you would not bring it up anymore," Miriam said tersely.

"All right, Miriam. I was only teasing, I suppose you're more comfortable with the farmer boys whom you find at church."

"Melody, could we change the subject? Tell me about your wedding plans," Miriam said unable to keep the irritation out of her voice.

"Since the church is not real large, we will only be able to have close friends and relatives at the wedding so I plan for the reception to be at the Williams Opera House, allowing for several hundred to be invited. Walter is planning on bringing a small orchestra to play for the wedding, reception and wedding dance. You know that he directs the orchestra at our church there in Boston, don't you?"

"You said in your letter that he directed the music; I did not realize that meant an orchestra. I am sure that it is beautiful music. I love hearing the violin playing the old hymns. Do you suppose they had violins in King David's time, because he played stringed instruments," Miriam said trying to make conversation.

"Was he before or after King Edward? Somehow I don't remember when he reigned," Walter asked naively.

Melody looked provoked, "He was in the Bible, Walter. He was not a king of England."

Looking embarrassed for a brief moment, Walter regained his composure and asked, "Would you ladies excuse me? I think I would like to visit with your father and become better acquainted." With that comment, he stepped briskly out of the room.

"Sometimes Walter is so ignorant of the Bible. He says he has gone to church for years, however he must not have learned much because almost anything I ask him about, he doesn't have a clue what I am talking about."

"Then why are you marrying him, Melody?"

"Because we have so much in common. We both love music and singing and he agrees with me on Woman's Suffrage. He wants me to vote and even to have a singing career along with him."

"Have you asked God for His approval?" Miriam asked quietly.

"Well, no, I guess that I haven't. It just seems so right and Walter treats me like a lady at all times. I just know God would think it was all right. Walter said he will always go to church with me and he has started reading the Bible with me some. Isn't that enough?"

"No, it isn't Melody. The Bible says not to be unequally yoked with unbelievers."

"You don't have to preach at me, Miriam. Walter may become a Christian any day, just like Mother and Father did later in life. Please don't ruin my engagement party with your little sermons, Miriam. I know what the Bible says just as well as you do," Melody said as she stood up as if encouraging Miriam to leave.

Miriam took the hint, "I must be leaving, Melody. Timothy, Mother and Father and I will be here tomorrow night. And you know that I will be praying for you," Miriam reached over and hugged Melody who stiffened as if to brush her off.

"I'll call Jackson to take you home. I hope our next meeting will be more pleasant," she stated, more as a demand than a request.

All the way home, Miriam didn't say a word. Jackson said, "I see that Walter fellow affected you the same way as he did me. Can't see what Melody sees in him. He is such a stuffed shirt with his high and mighty ways. He needs to be brought down a notch or two."

"It isn't Walter so much as it is Melody, that bothers me Jackson. She has changed and she doesn't want me to ruin her party or wedding plans. I don't know what do to, I am so worried for her."

"I know you are a praying lady. Why don't you ask God what to do? He knows."

"Do you know God, Jackson? Are you ready to meet him should you die tonight? All these years that you have driven me in the carriage, I have never asked you," she asked seriously. "You are such a special friend that I want to know you will be in heaven when I get there."

"You can rest your little heart about that, Miss Jensen. The good Lord and I are best friends. His Son died for my sins and I believed that years ago," Jackson stated firmly.

"I am so thankful, Jackson. You pray for Melody and Walter also that God will stop this wedding before it happens." Miriam said as Jackson helped her from the carriage.

"You can be sure that I will. I pray for that girl every day.

Always have since she was little. She is a stubborn young woman."

Miriam had no heart in dressing for the Saturday supper so she decided to dress for Timothy's benefit and not Melody and Walter. She dressed in the black wool/silk with the white collar and cuffs. Calling to Anna, she said, "Would you help me put my hair into a French braid and hold it with these black combs? With my new crystal earrings that should complete my outfit."

"You look stunning, Miriam; just as beautiful as Melody in her expensive dresses. Timothy's blue eyes will shine with the joy of escorting you to the supper."

True to his word, Timothy arrived early so Aaron could help him into their carriage. Miriam greeted him, "Timothy, you look handsome with the white shirt and tie and your suit jacket." She noticed that his sometimes-unruly hair was held in place with some kind of hair oil.

"You look wonderful yourself. Even Melody should see the difference because your love for God makes you look happy all over," Timothy contended.

"Oh, Timothy, you are so flattering, however I like it," Miriam responded happily.

Timothy was in fine form all evening. When introduced to Walter, he grabbed his hand and gave it a real farmer's squeeze. "Ouch, you're hurting my fingers," Walter said as he pulled them away and carefully wiggled them to see if they could still move.

Moving to the table, Timothy held himself up with one crutch to help Miriam into her chair like a gentleman and sat beside her. Melody and Walter were seated across from them. As the food was being served by Annabel and Jackson, Timothy asked, "Walter, do you have a relative named Lambert Van Squoit?"

Nervously digging his finger under his shirt collar, he answered, "Yes, that is my uncle. Do you know him?"

"No, I just saw his name in the paper." Timothy answered.

"Did that paper happen to be the Kansas City Star?" Walter anxiously.

"Yes, then you are familiar with the story?"

"I do not wish to talk about it. Can we visit on some other topic? I am finding Beloit most delightful. There is so much culture here. Melody and I are planning on taking in the program at the Opera House tomorrow night. Will you be attending?"

"We have no plans to attend. Saturday evening on the farm is usually busy as we are preparing our livestock and family for the Lord's day."

"Oh, of course. We will see you in church Sunday. Melody has asked me to sing a solo and she will accompany me."

The rest of the evening caused Timothy to become even more suspicious of why Walter did not want any of the Cramton family knowing the contents of the story in the *Kansas City Star*. As Miriam and her parents were standing at the door preparing to leave, Walter cornered Timothy in the parlor. "Don't you breathe a word about that story about my uncle to the Cramton family. It would ruin everything in my relationship with Melody. Don't you dare tell her or her parents or you will have to answer to me. Do you get the message, Mr. Larsen?" Walter threatened.

"No, Walter, I can not promise you. If you really love Melody, you will tell her yourself before someone else tells her. I am not the only one in Beloit who reads the *Kansas City Star* and others will recognize that name. It is a name that people will remember. I've always felt that honesty and truthfulness were the best policy. As it says in the Bible, 'your sins will find you out,'" Timothy said as he limped over to join Miriam at the door.

"Good night, Mr. Van Squoit and Miss Cramton. May

God teach you His lessons," Timothy called as they went out the door.

"Well said, Timothy. I couldn't have worded it any better myself," Aaron said admiringly, once they were in the carriage.

Riding home under a beautiful full moon, Miriam asked, "Timothy, what did Walter ask privately before we left?"

"He wanted me to promise not to tell what was in that newspaper article that had his uncle's name in it. I told him that I could not promise, however I did tell him he should tell Melody before someone else did."

"Are you going to tell me what it said?" Miriam asked

"No, not now. I want to give Walter time to tell Melody and her parents. If he doesn't tell them before they go back to Boston, that will show me that I need to share it. I feel there are more details than were told in the newspaper and Walter knows them. Until then we need to pray that the truth will come out before it is too late," Timothy said firmly.

CHAPTER FIFTEEN

PARTING OF THE WAYS

AT BREAKFAST, Miriam stated, "I'm not looking forward to church this morning."

"Why is that, Miriam?" Lydia asked in concern. "I thought you always looked forward to church."

"You know with Melody and Walter performing it probably will be the talk of the town the next week. Our people are not used to Walter's type of singing."

"You might be surprised, Walter may sing something we all appreciate," Anna commented dubiously.

"That would be very much of a surprise, Anna, however, I hope you are correct."

Just as Miriam predicted, Walter sang an opera style rendition of *Love Divine, All Love Excelling,* with Melody accompanying him on the organ. Timothy, who was sitting behind the Jensen family, leaned up and whispered to Miriam during Walter's song and said, "Can you understand a word he is singing?" Miriam shook her head, "No." Lydia looked at her with a questioning look. Miriam could tell that she was not impressed with the singing either.

Melody and Walter sat together behind her parents and whispered during most of the sermon. People near them nudged each other and nodded towards the couple who was disturbing the whole congregation. It was obvious they were not listening to the sermon.

Following the closing song, Timothy made his way to Walter's side. Walter was expecting to be complimented for his fine singing; instead Timothy whispered, "Walter, have you told Melody yet?"

Walter drew himself up indignantly, straightened his tie, and whispered back, "No I have not, and I don't intend to tell her. And if you know what is good for you, you will not tell her either." With those strong words, he took Melody by the arm and marched her out of the church—leaving friends waiting to talk with her.

Miriam heard her say in a flustered way, "Walter, why are we leaving so fast? I have not seen my friends for months. Can't we stay and talk a few minutes?"

"No, I want to call the train station to change our tickets to leave tomorrow." The door closed behind them and the congregation looked puzzled. Miriam moved over to Mary Cramton's wheel chair and asked, "How are things going in your relationship with Melody and Walter, Mrs. Cramton?"

"It has not been a happy visit, Miriam. Walter has been so irritable and will give Melody almost no time alone with us. Did you hear what he said when they went out the door?"

"Yes, he said something about getting their tickets changed so they could leave tomorrow," Miriam answered.

"I wonder why he has suddenly decided to not stay the rest of the week. He asked us to make reservations at the Anderson house for the week. Something must have happened to upset him. He seems to be aggravated at Timothy for some reason. Do you know why?" Mary asked anxiously.

"Here comes Timothy now, Mrs. Cramton. Maybe he will tell you why Walter is so unhappy with him. He won't tell me yet what was in an article he read in the *Kansas City Star*."

215

Reaching for Timothy's hand, Mary said, "Timothy, do you know something about Walter that Thomas and I should know? He seems very agitated and anxious to get back to Boston as soon as possible. Could you tell us why he is upset?"

"Yes, I can Mrs. Cramton, however I need to talk to you and Mr. Cramton alone. Could you come to the Jensen home this afternoon? I was hoping that Walter would tell you and Melody what I read in the paper, however he said that he did not plan to say anything."

"Yes, Thomas and I can come this afternoon. I think that Melody and Walter plan to visit some of her friends from the Opera House theater group," Mary answered with certainty.

The Jensens had just finished eating dinner when they saw Jackson driving in with Thomas and Mary in the carriage. "They didn't waste anytime, did they?" Miriam said.

Lydia told Anna to take the younger girls for a walk while she and Aaron met with the Cramtons, Timothy, and Miriam. Seated together in the parlor, everyone was tense as Timothy pulled out three newspaper clippings. "These were in some copies of the *Kansas City Star* that I read while I was housebound with my leg. At the time, I thought the name and the story was a little unusual, although I did not know Walter's name until Miriam told me. Here is what the first one says: "Police record—Lambert Van Squoit of Kansas City, confidence chap, bound over in the sum of $1,000 to the Circuit Court. Lou Nichols (colored) streetwalker, in lockup; Chas. Harris, 'vag.' in lockup; Joel Hyett, drunk and indecent exposure, in lockup." Timothy looked up to get their reaction.

Another article said: "Alleged Confidence Operation—A Lambert Van Squoit was arrested yesterday morning upon the complaint of the firm of F. W. Jansen and Son and was arraigned before Squire Rodolt on the charge of obtaining money by means of a confidence game. It is alleged that the parties represented that they were agents of a new type of an automobile and made a trade with the firm by which they obtained a draft for $1000. Messrs. Jansen, after the trade, ascertained that they had been imposed upon and caused the arrest. The examination was postponed until the 14th and the prisoner was required to give bonds in the sum of $1000 for his appearance at that time, in default of which he was committed to jail."

"Would someone explain to me what a confidence operation is?" Lydia asked.

"That is where someone promises something in exchange for an investment of money and then doesn't produce it. Some people call it swindling. Usually those who are doing this have no intention of returning the money or producing a product," Thomas responded.

"Do you want to hear the next article from the paper?" Timothy asked.

"Yes, we might as well hear the rest of it," Mary sighed.

This one says, "The Charges against Mr. Van Squoit stand. He and several members of his family have been bilking others out of large sums of money with their false stories of a new automobile. People in Kansas are warned to watch out for such men and their requests for money."

"So that's why Walter was talking to me so earnestly about investing in their new automobile experiment. Since I had been wanting to purchase an automobile, I was very interested in his stories of this impressive experiment. I had been planning to give him a large sum of money before he left. He even has Melody convinced that they have a wonderful new invention," Thomas said excitedly. "How are we going to show her that it is all a confidence game? If I had given him the money he probably would have skipped town and left her to find her own way back to Boston."

"Do you think that she will believe you when you tell her, Mr. Cramton? Knowing Melody like I do, she may be more willing to believe Walter," Miriam stated.

Thomas thought a moment and asked, "Could I take those articles, Timothy and show them to her? This Mr. Van Squoit is even more deceptive than we imagined. Pray that it isn't too late to stop the marriage."

After Mary and Thomas left, Miriam and Timothy were sitting in the porch swing enjoying the warm afternoon. "What do you guess will happen when Mr. and Mrs. Cramton confront Melody and Walter?"

"My guess is that Walter will deny the whole story and Melody will believe him. Didn't someone say that love is blind?" Timothy said with a smile at Miriam.

"Yes, they did and you need glasses," Miriam chuckled.

Later in the afternoon, Emma called, "Here comes Melody driving the carriage by herself and looking really angry."

Miriam went to the door to find Melody rushing up the steps like an angry hen. "You and Timothy are trying to ruin my wedding plans. I thought you were my friend and now you tell all those lies about Walter and his family."

"Wait just a minute, Melody. Timothy just read what was in the paper. We did not make it up," she reasoned.

Timothy came up behind Miriam standing at the door, "That's correct, Miss Cramton. I asked Walter to tell you and your parents what was in the articles; he refused so I knew that I had to tell them. A true friend is honest even if they know it will hurt. We wanted you to know the truth before you married Walter."

"I don't want to hear it. If Walter said the stories are false, I believe him. We will still be getting married. Walter has already told me that his father is giving us for a wedding present a new Cadillac convertible like the one Andy Manifold purchased. He is having it delivered to Beloit in time for our wedding."

"Why doesn't he give you one of the cars he is inventing if those stories about Walter's uncle were false as he says?" Timothy asked.

"I believe Walter, and he told me after we met Mr. Manifold driving away from church in his Cadillac that his father was getting one just like it for us," Miriam answered haughtily.

"Then all the horses in town will have to miss your wedding because they go wild everytime Mr. Manifold takes his car downtown. It is so noisy that he has caused several run-aways. His wife said that from now on he has to let people know when he is taking it out," Timothy laughed.

Ignoring Timothy's joke, Melody said, "Another thing, Miriam, I am taking back my request for you to stand up with me. You don't approve of Walter nor our marriage so I don't want you to be my maid of honor."

"That is all right with me, Melody, because I was going to decline anyway. I can't condone your marriage to someone who is a non-Christian. If I stood up with you it would show that I was approving," Miriam reminded gently.

"Walter and I are leaving tomorrow morning on the first train. He is so upset with everyone in this town, that it will be difficult to convince him to have the wedding here."

"Are you still bringing an orchestra to play at the wedding?"

"Walter said that he would bring a string ensemble for the wedding and have the Manifold band play for the wedding dance. After hearing them perform at the Opera House, he didn't think we needed to bring a full orchestra because the Manifold band plays his quality of music," she stated with a sniff.

Melody left with less anger than when she arrived, although she was still determined to do things her way.

"What do you think will happen to Melody and Walter?" Timothy asked Miriam as she sat in the porch swing again with him.

"I think as long as Walter provides her with a rich living and they have success with their music, they will be quite happy, however if trouble comes or Walter isn't able to provide the lifestyle that Miriam is accustomed to living, I don't know if she will stay with him for long."

"I guess time will tell. Who knows, maybe our prayers for them will be answered and they both will decide to obey God."

"That is entirely possible, however remember you told me that the husband is to be the leader in the family. How can Walter lead regarding things of God when he doesn't even know Him personally?" Miriam asked seriously.

"I agree that it is doubtful, although we should continue to pray for them."

Aaron came out onto the porch and sat on the wicker chair nearby. "Timothy, when did you say that Dr. Blackwood would be removing your bandages?"

"The end of the month. It will be a relief to not have those boards along my leg and be able to bend it again. He said that it will be stiff and that I will have to exercise it for a few weeks to get the normal action back. My prayer is that I will be able to do the farm work as I did," he answered, looking fondly at Miriam.

"I've been reading in the Kansas City Star that Buffalo Bill's Wild West Show will be in Omaha next month. I thought we could celebrate your release from your bandages by taking you and the family on the train to see it. It should be something, with 16 trainloads of animals and people presenting our historical frontier life. They say that Annie Oakley with her trick shooting will be there."

"That sounds like something I would enjoy. I don't know how strong my leg will be, so I may be walking with a cane."

"I've been praying that God would heal it completely and that you will be able to walk normally," Miriam said.

"Even if I don't, I know God has taught me so much from this time of inactivity, and that He will give me the strength to accomplish what He wants in the years ahead."

"Would your parents and your brothers and sisters like to

go with us to Omaha, Timothy? They are welcome to join us," Aaron asked.

"I will ask them, however they are just starting to prepare the ground for the spring crop and without my help, they don't have time to get away now. Within a few weeks, I hope to be back helping them."

The next week was busy for Miriam. She delivered a baby for a family in town and received a call from a farm family. The farmer said, "My wife is asking for Miss Jensen to come right away. We live by the Paul Larsen farm." Hanging up the receiver, Miriam said, "Mother, the Smith family, that lives out near the Larsen farm, want me to come this afternoon to deliver their baby."

"Have you looked at those dark clouds, Miriam? I don't know about you going far alone," Lydia reasoned.

"Ginger doesn't spook in storms. Besides I will be near the Larsen farm should I have any trouble," Miriam reminded her.

"Why don't you call Martha Larsen and tell her that you will be coming out their way, and that you will call her when you arrive. I would feel better if they knew you were coming."

Miriam brightened, "That is a good idea, Mother."

Miriam rang central, "Give me the Paul Larsen home, Maggie."

Martha answered and after hearing of Miriam's trip said, "I will tell Timothy and we will be praying for you. The storm looks like it might arrive before dark."

"You know that storms normally bring babies," Miriam laughed.

While Miriam was harnessing Ginger to the buggy, Anna came out to the barn, "would you like for me to go with you, Miriam?"

"I would love for you to go with me, Anna, however I may

be gone for two or three days since this is Mrs. Smith's first baby. Mother needs you here to help put in the early garden. I don't think I will have any trouble. If I do get caught in the storm, I can always go the Larsen farm which is closer."

Miriam started out of town and noticed that the clouds were becoming darker and the wind was picking up. "Giddy-up, Ginger. We want to get to the Smiths before this storm hits."

Ginger seemed to sense that there was a real need to hurry. She ran with great speed and Miriam pulled her cloak around her as a bolt of lightening shot across the sky. Soon large drops of rain began to fall and the wind roared around them. The dark clouds made it seem almost like night. "Hurry, Ginger, Hurry," she called shaking the reins.

The lightening streaked all around them. The wind was tossing the buggy around more with each gust. "Oh, it is raining so hard I can hardly see the road. Lord, help me find the right road."

Not knowing if it was the right road, Miriam turned Ginger onto the first road past the Larsen's lane. By then, the rain was coming in torrents. The buggy was sliding all over the road. Ginger tried to keep going, even though she was frightened by the sharp bolts of lightening. Miriam felt the buggy tipping over, she slapped the reins and called over the roar of the wind, "Pull, Ginger, pull."

Before she knew what was happening, the buggy tipped over on it side, spilling Miriam out in the mud. Struggling to get to her feet, she felt all over the harness trying to unfasten it so that Ginger could get loose. "If I can just get you loose, Ginger, I can ride you on to the Smiths."

At last, Ginger was loose and Miriam, soaked to the skin, pulled herself onto her back. "Go, Ginger, find the Smith's house, I can't see anything in this rain," Miriam coaxed.

Praying all the way that God would protect her and guide Ginger to the Smith's farm, Miriam hung on tightly. Ginger seemed to know right where to go as she kept plodding along in the mud without hesitation. After what seemed like hours, Miriam saw a light in the distance.

"There is a light, Ginger." *Thank you, God, for guiding us to a house.* Sliding off Ginger, Miriam held up the hem of her long muddy skirt and made her way to the house. It was not until she was almost at the door that she realized she was at the Larsen home and not the Smith farm. Knocking weakly, she was surprised that the door opened so quickly.

"Oh! They did find you, Miriam." Martha said as she pulled Miriam inside.

"Who found me? Ginger brought me here in answer to my prayer."

"You mean Paul and Daniel don't know that you are here? Jonathan, run out immediately and catch your father and brother before they leave on a wild goose chase. Tell them she is here."

Miriam could not help laughing inspite of her miserable wet clothes and shivering with the cold. "So, I am a wild goose?"

"Not really, Miriam. However, if they had gone looking for you while you were right here, they would have felt it was a wild goose chase. They still have the evening chores to do."

Esther ran into the parlor where Timothy had his head bowed, praying fervently for Miriam. "Timothy she is here. Ginger brought her to our house."

"Oh thank you, God, for bringing her here," Timothy finished his prayer. "Hand me my crutches, I must see for myself that she is all right."

Miriam heard the thump-thump of his crutches. "Oh, Timothy must not see me like this. I know I look like I have rolled in the mud."

"Just why shouldn't I see you? You look wonderful because you are alive and safe. I have prayed constantly for you since you called Ma. Pa had come in from the storm and reported that it was not fit for man or beast out there, so I was very anxious for you. I will go back to my reading so you can get out of those wet clothes before you catch a cold."

"Would you like for Esther to call your folks, Miriam? I suppose we should call the Smiths to tell them that it will be a few hours before you can arrive. If they think the baby cannot wait to arrive, Paul could take me over to stay with her until you can clean up and eat. You are in no shape to deliver any baby in the condition you are in right now."

"That is right, Martha. You are so thoughtful. Yes, do call and see how far apart her pains are by now. Since this is her first, it may be hours yet."

Esther brought in the large galvanized tub and set it behind the cookstove and filled it with hot water from the stove. "Now, I will hold up a blanket so you can remove those muddy clothes and hop into this tub."

"I suppose you will also scrub the mud out of my hair?" Miriam laughed.

"I will do that if you want me to do it."

"No, if you will hold the blanket until I get bathed, that would be most helpful."

Martha came near and laid some clothes on a chair. "Here are some of Esther's clothes that you can wear until we get yours washed. You are just a few inches taller so they should fit you."

"I smell something good cooking. I did not realize how hungry I had become," Miriam said as she scrubbed.

"It is vegetable beef stew that Mama makes so good. I made the cornbread to go with it," Esther said.

Miriam had bathed and dressed before Paul, Daniel and Jonathan came in from the barn. "Our girl is found! Thank God," Paul said joyfully when he saw Miriam.

"Yes, God led Ginger to bring me here because I had no idea where I was. I told her to take me to the Smiths, however this is the place she remembered from our visit earlier," Miriam answered. "What about the buggy? It is somewhere on the road turned over on its side. I had a terrible time in the wind and rain untangling Ginger's harness. She was so patient waiting until I got her loose and then let me drag myself upon her back."

"It was a very bad storm. I had just come in to tell the family to head for the cellar when Timothy told me that you were out in the storm. I tried calling the Smiths to see if you had arrived and by some miracle the telephone worked, so they could tell me that you had not arrived yet."

"Thank you all for praying and thank God for moving the tornado clouds on east away from us."

Timothy had come in from the parlor. "Why are you all standing around asking Miriam questions? Can't you see she needs to eat to gain back her strength from her ordeal?"

"Yes, big brother, we will serve it immediately," Esther said with a finger poke to his ribs.

Martha and Esther soon had the soup ladled into bowls with fresh cornbread and homemade butter. "This tastes so good. I was about starved from getting so cold."

"Talking about cold, would you like a little kerosene on a lump of sugar to keep you from catching cold from being soaked to the skin?" Martha asked.

"Yes, I would. My mother uses it often. What am I going to do with those muddy clothes? I don't have any dry clothes to change to at the Smiths."

"Don't worry about the clothes. Esther and I will wash them tomorrow. She can loan you another outfit to take with you to the Smiths. I forgot to tell you that Mr. Smith said that her pains were still 10 minutes apart."

"I think I had better get over there. Mrs. Smith may need some encouragement that Mr. Smith won't be able to give her," Miriam said.

"I can take you anytime, Miriam," Paul Larsen said.

225

"Before you leave, Miriam, I would like to talk to you alone a minute," Timothy said as he stood up from the table. Miriam followed him into the parlor while Paul went for the buggy.

"Miriam, I did not realize how much I loved you until I thought of you out in the storm all alone. I wanted to be there to protect you. Would you come back here as soon as you finish taking care of Mrs. Smith? There are some things we need to talk about," Timothy said seriously.

"Yes, I will be back, Timothy, however it may be two or three days. Babies have their own time schedules and if Mrs. Smith has no family to care for her, I may have to stay for a few days. I promise to come back before going home," Miriam answered with a gentle smile. Her heart was beating faster at the thought of what Timothy would be sharing with her.

Seeing her muddy clothes soaking in the tub as she was leaving, Miriam said to Martha, "I hate leaving this mess for you and Esther."

"Don't worry your head about them. We are all so happy you are all right and were not hurt when the buggy tipped over," Martha answered lovingly.

On the trip to the Smith farm, Mr. Larsen commented, "You would never have guessed that we had just had a terrible storm. Look, the moon is almost to break through the clouds and the wind has stilled to almost a whisper."

"Must have been like the time our Lord stilled the storm while the disciples were in the boat. They were almost shocked that the wind and waves obeyed Him."

"I want to thank you for being so willing to go look for me in the storm," Miriam stated.

"If we had not agreed to go, Timothy would have figured out some way to go. It was all Daniel and I could do to convince him to stay in the house. If he had gone, he could have re-injured that leg just when it is almost healed," Paul responded.

"Oh no! I did not know that he was trying to go look for me. No wonder you were so glad when I arrived. I didn't think about him risking his own health to look for me."

"He thinks a lot of you, Miriam. We all do, so take good care of yourself when you are out alone like that. Don't take any unnecessary chances," Paul cautioned. "Here we are at the Smith farm. Do you want me to come see if they need anything before I leave you?"

"Yes, that would be a good idea. I may need Martha to help me." Miriam knocked and Mr. Smith opened the door looking very agitated.

"My wife is having a terrible time. I am so glad that you have arrived. She is right in there," he said pointing to a side room.

Miriam lay down her change of clothes and after washing her hands carefully in the wash-pan, she went to check on Mrs. Smith. "Mrs. Smith, I am Miriam Jensen. How long have you been having labor pains?"

"I think two days, I've lost track of time."

After checking the position of the baby, Miriam hurried back to the kitchen. "Mr. Larsen, would you go for Martha; I need her help. In addition, would you call Dr. Blackwood. She should have had the baby by now. I miss Mrs. Polinsky so much at times like this."

Going back to Mrs. Smith's bedside, Miriam said, "Mrs. Smith, I think your baby is in breech position. I asked Mr. Larsen to bring his wife over to help me and he is also to call Dr. Blackwood to come as soon as he can. I would like to pray with you that God will guide me in delivering this baby."

"Yes, do pray. I've been praying constantly that God would get me through this."

Miriam prayed and worked trying to turn the baby. How long she worked, she had no idea, although she was conscious of Martha's arrival. At last, the baby was born, however his color was very blue. "Here, Martha, see if you can get him to breathe.

Mrs. Polinsky told me not to cut the cord until the baby took his first breath. After you remove the mucus from his mouth, splash cold water and then hot water on his chest and slap his seat lightly. If that does not work, put him in cold and then warm water up to his neck. If necessary, we may have to use artificial respiration."

Working feverishly, Martha tried to get the little boy to breathe. "It's no use, Miriam. Nothing has worked," Martha whispered sadly.

Mrs. Smith groaned weakly, "How is my baby?"

"I am afraid that he has gone to heaven to be with Jesus, Mrs. Smith. We have tried everything to get him to breathe."

Mrs. Smith started sobbing quietly, "My baby, my baby."

"I feel terrible also, Mrs. Smith. Remember that God promises to never leave us nor forsake us. He is right here with you, Mrs. Smith," Miriam said in a tearful voice.

Martha and Miriam were cleaning up after dressing the little boy in a tiny gown and lying him at the foot of the bed. They had just finished cleaning up when Dr. Blackwood came in to see if they needed help. He checked the baby over and said, "This baby was dead before you delivered him. There was nothing you could have done to have saved his life."

Mr. Smith had followed Dr. Blackwood into the room. "If you had been here Doc, this wouldn't have happened."

"No, Sam. Life and death are in God's hands. We do our best knowing that God decides when any of us live or die. These women did the best that they could."

"Yes, Samuel. I thought that something was wrong yesterday when I did not feel any movement. I didn't want to admit that he might be dead so I didn't say anything."

Mr. Smith stomped out of the room without a word. "He had his heart set on a boy to work with him on the farm. It will take him a long time to recover from this," Mrs. Smith said.

Miriam was crying quietly, "I'm so sorry, Mrs. Smith. Mrs.

Polinsky told me there would be times that no matter what I did, I could not save the life of a baby."

"I am not blaming you, Miss Jensen. You have done a good job and I appreciate the help and comfort you have been to me."

"Will you need me to stay to help you for a few days?" Miriam asked.

"Could you stay until tomorrow afternoon when my kinfolks will come? We will have to have some kind of funeral for little Joseph."

"Paul could make a little pine box for your baby's casket, Mrs. Smith. Samuel is too dismayed to make it."

Miriam stayed until Mrs. Smith's parents arrived. She found that they loved the Lord and were able to comfort the Smiths over their loss.

Paul Larsen came for her later saying, "Martha called your mother to tell her that you were staying with us tonight since the roads are still muddy."

"What about the buggy? Is it ruined? We borrowed it from Thomas Cramton so I don't want to damage it."

"Daniel and I got it back on its wheels after we fixed the one wheel. We washed most of the mud off of it. It looks shipshape to me," Paul answered.

Miriam was excited about spending the evening with the Larsen family. Smelling the good food cooking as she walked into the kitchen, she said, "I feel guilty for enjoying a meal without doing any of the cooking."

"If you feel guilty, we can put you to work, Miriam," Esther joked.

"To tell you the truth, the long sad delivery of the Smith's baby has me plum tuckered out."

"It did that to me, Miriam. The Lord has blessed us with seven healthy children, and the Smiths lose their first child. It would be awfully hard to take," Martha said.

"Yes, Martha, the good Lord has blessed us with a full

quiver of arrows," Paul said, quoting from the Psalms.

"What is a quiver, Papa? Is that kind of like shaking?" Ruth, the eight-year-old, asked.

"No, Ruth, it is a leather container for arrows," Paul said.

With all the family sitting down to eat, Miriam asked, "Are you planning to attend the Buffalo Bill's Wild West Show with us?"

"We would love to go, Miriam, however this is the busy time of the year and without Timothy, the rest of us have to take over his share of the work."

"I plan to get back in the harness as soon as possible, Pa. My bandages come off next week. I'm going to really work at getting my leg strengthened."

"I know that you will be working as soon as possible, Son. I don't want you to push yourself too hard and injure it more."

Following supper, Miriam helped Esther with the dishes while Timothy bantered with them from the table. "You girls don't know how to do dishes. Now if I were doing them, I would..."

"We will put you on dish washing just as soon as your bandages come off," Miriam joked.

"And you can clean the house after all I did to clean up your piles of books and papers," Esther retorted.

"If I have to use a cane, I may not be able to wash dishes or sweep and you will still have to take care of me."

"No, you are on your own as soon as those bandages come off. We have pampered you long enough," Esther joked.

The dishes done, Miriam sat down at the table across from Timothy. Esther pulled out a chair to join them, however Timothy said, "I need to talk to Miriam alone, Esther. Would you mind keeping the little ones busy so we can talk."

"I want to talk to Miriam also," Esther pouted.

"I will be here in the morning, Esther. We will have some special time together even if we have to put Timothy out on the porch."

"I need a big sister to talk to after listening to brothers all week," Esther said as she disappeared into the parlor.

Timothy sat looking at Miriam without a word for a few minutes. His bright blue eyes were more intense than ever. "Miriam, I was planning to wait until I got the bandages off before I started making plans for us, however after the scare the other night, I feel that now is the time to talk."

"What kind of plans do you want to make, Timothy?" Miriam asked with a slight smile.

"First off, would you consider marrying me this year?"

"You know that I will, Timothy. I have been praying for this day for a long time. How soon would you like to have our wedding?" Miriam responded joyously.

"I really wanted to have the house all ready by now and my ground worked so I would know that I will have a crop this year, however with this leg, I don't know. What do you think?" Timothy asked seriously.

"I was thinking of a September wedding in Jackson's rose garden, if that would be all right with you," Miriam answered with a smile.

"So you have been thinking. What does Jackson's rose garden have to do with a wedding? I thought we would get married at the church."

"Every since I was younger, I have loved Jackson's roses at the Cramton's house. The wonderful smells and colors make me think of heaven or the Garden of Eden. I told him that I wanted to get married there. Would you like something like that?" her eyes glistening with excitement.

"I never thought about an outdoor wedding, however that might be very nice. And September would be a good time, before wheat planting."

"Well, we are agreed on that part of the plan. Do you want to work any other plans?" Miriam asked passionately. "I have had ideas rolling around in my head for ages."

"You have made me so happy by agreeing to marry me this year. I know there are many other plans we would need to make, however you have had a trying day. Maybe the next time we eat at your house we can work on them. I had better let you get to bed," Timothy answered in genuine concern.

"I am tired, Timothy. Seeing that little Smith baby lying there so still and dead emotionally drained me," Miriam said sadly.

"Esther said that you can sleep with her tonight. She has the bed ready, so get some sleep. Good night, Miriam. I love you very much," Timothy said tenderly.

"I love you, too, Timothy," Miriam whispered in his ear as she walked off to Esther's room.

CHAPTER SIXTEEN

ENTERTAINMENT

MIRIAM CAME DOWNSTAIRS for breakfast to find Timothy beckoning her to come into the parlor. "Would you mind if I rode along with you to town this morning?" Timothy asked with a smile.

"Why would you want to go to town at this time of the morning?" Miriam asked before it dawned on her. "You want to talk to father, don't you?" she spoke quietly.

"Yes, and if he agrees, we can make our announcement to your family at noon."

At breakfast, Timothy announced, "I need to go into town for some errands; I will be home soon after dinner if that is all right with you, Papa."

"Yes, I suppose we can spare you this morning if it is important." Paul seemed to sense by Timothy's request that it was something special.

"Timothy, before we leave, I promised Esther that we could have time to visit. Give us a few minutes to talk and I will be ready to leave," Miriam requested.

Timothy and Daniel had harnessed and hitched up Ginger for Miriam and had his buggy ready to tag along behind hers. Telling Esther goodbye, she walked out so Timothy could help her into the buggy.

Driving down the rode, Miriam said, "Timothy, just think in few months will be married. Would you mind if I asked Sarah Williams to stand up with me along with Anna? I can't wait to tell her about our wedding. She has been so concerned and praying about your leg."

"Yes, go ahead and ask her after we tell your family the plans," Timothy answered joyfully. "Shall I ask my brothers to stand up with me?"

"Yes, that would be wonderful. They already seem like part of our family."

Miriam and Timothy arrived in Beloit in the middle of the morning. Timothy stopped by the shop and found Aaron alone. He waved to Miriam, who went on to the house.

"My! You seem awfully happy, Miriam. What happened at the Smith home that made you so happy?" Anna asked while Miriam helped her with the cooking.

"It wasn't what happened at the Smith home that makes me happy. The Smith's baby was born dead, which tore me up, and before that you know that I ended up in the ditch with the buggy turned over. No, that isn't what makes me happy. I want to tell you when everyone is here for dinner."

"I bet I can guess. It has something to do with Timothy," Anna surmised.

"You might be correct about that, although you will have to wait to hear the whole story. By the way, Timothy is eating dinner with us today," Miriam announced.

Lydia looked surprised, however she just smiled at Miriam as if she guessed what was coming.

Sitting around the table eating potato soup and salt pork, everyone waited expectantly for Miriam to tell them her news. "What is it, Miriam? Anna said that you had some happy news to tell us," Tabitha asked.

"I am going to let Timothy tell you our news," Miriam said happily.

"Timothy cleared his throat and announced, "Last night I asked Miriam if she would marry me and she told me 'yes' so this morning I talked to her father to ask his permission to marry his daughter and he has agreed. We wanted you all to be the first to know."

"Not only do I agree, Timothy and Miriam, I want to pray that God will bless you both as you plan your wedding and marriage. Our most heavenly Father, we thank you that Miriam and Timothy have sought Your plan for their lives and have felt Your leading them to marry. Bless them as they pursue this plan. In Your name, Amen."

"I told Timothy that I want to be married in Jackson's rose garden in September."

"Did you really tell him that?" Anna asked incredulously.

"Yes, and he likes the idea once I explained who Jackson was and where the rose garden was in town."

"We are very happy for you and Timothy," Aaron said.

"Don't you get your bandages off this week, Timothy?" Lydia asked.

"Yes, Dr. Blackwood said it would be this week," Timothy answered. "The sooner the better as far as I am concerned. Those boards have made my leg miserably sore."

Timothy got up to leave. "Miriam, could you come out for dinner with my family tomorrow so we can tell them our news together?" Timothy asked expectantly.

"Yes, I would love to drive out and spent more time with your mother and Esther working on wedding plans."

Miriam was so excited to be going back out to the Larsen farm. The next morning she asked, "Mother, is there anything you need me to do this morning? I would like to go early so I can talk to Mrs. Larsen," she asked pleasantly.

"Go ahead, I can see that you are too excited to be much help around here," Lydia laughed.

Miriam could tell that Timothy had told his mother something special was to be happening at dinner. Miriam knocked on the door and Esther opened it. "So you are our special guest! Timothy told us to prepare for a special guest, however he didn't tell us who it would be. Wanted to keep us guessing," Esther said jokingly.

Once everyone was seated, Timothy said impulsively, "I want you all to know that Mr. Jensen has consented for me to marry Miriam and she has consented to be my wife."

"We are very glad for the both of you, Miriam and Timothy. We would be proud to have you for a daughter-in-law, Miriam," Paul Larsen said.

"I feel like you are already a part of our family, Miriam. Have you decided when the wedding will take place? Have you already chosen a place?" his mother asked.

"Miriam has asked if we could be married in Jackson's rose garden," Timothy answered quickly.

"Who is Jackson and what has his rose garden got to do with your wedding?" his father asked.

"For years Miriam has been friends with Jackson, the Cramton's butler-gardener and admired his rose garden. She told him that she wanted to be married in his rose garden this fall so we thought September before wheat planting would be a good time. What do you all think of that? However, we also need to check with Mr. and Mrs. Cramton on these plans."

"I think September would be an excellent time. It is cooler and the roses are usually even more beautiful at that time of the year," Martha answered. "A garden wedding might be very nice providing it didn't rain."

"And I like the idea of having you in the family also, Miriam. We need more women around here," Esther exclaimed.

"Yes, it will be nice having some more women to keep us guys well fed," Daniel said.

"You seem to always worry about your stomach, Daniel," Timothy teased. "Just wait until you start courting. We will have to check her cooking first."

"I can do my own testing, thank you," Daniel joked back.

Later as she was leaving, Timothy came over to the buggy. "I will call you as soon as Dr. Blackwood takes off the bandages and let you know how my leg is doing."

"I'll be waiting for your call. I'm so anxious to know if it is completely healed," Miriam said anxiously.

"We have to leave that in God's hands, Miriam," Timothy said as he waved goodbye.

Miriam felt like she was floating on a cloud as she drove back to town. She was thinking, *Timothy asked me to marry him and Father gave him permission! I am so happy I could shout! Thank you, God, for giving me a wonderful man like Timothy to marry. He may not be the most handsome man in the world, however He loves you and he loves me. Thank you, thank you for being a wonderful God.*

Several days went by and Miriam received no call from Timothy. Much concerned, she asked Lydia, "Mother, don't you think he would call me as soon as the doctor took off the bandages?"

"It may be that he is having a difficult time dealing with the extent of his disability. He may not be able to walk and he doesn't have the heart to tell you. Give him time to deal with it himself. He will tell you when he is ready," Lydia said as they baked bread together.

"You mean God might not have healed it? I've begged Him to heal it completely, Mother. Surely God would want Timothy to be strong and healthy like before."

"I don't know what God's plan is for Timothy. One thing I do know is that whatever the outcome, God still loves Timothy and will use this trial to shape him to be like Christ."

"Timothy is a wonderful Christian already. Why wouldn't He just heal him?" Miriam asked sadly.

"Miriam, what Timothy needs more than anything now is

your support and encouragement," Lydia reminded.

❦ ❦ ❦

Sunday morning, Miriam couldn't wait to arrive at church. "I want to be there before Timothy arrives so I can encourage him," she said as she urged the family to hurry.

Miriam sat with her family while her eyes were on the door of the church. Just before the first song, the door opened and Timothy limped into the room, holding himself up with a cane. Tears came to her eyes before she could stop them. Looking at Timothy's bright smile convinced her that he was not discouraged, however she still couldn't keep back the tears. He led the family to sit in front of the Jensen family.

The sermon that morning was from II Corinthians about the Apostle Paul begging the Lord three times to remove the thorn in the flesh from him and the Lord told him, "My grace is sufficient for you, My strength is made perfect in weakness."

"Most gladly, therefore, will I rather glory in my infirmity, that the power of Christ may rest upon me," stated Apostle Paul.

Miriam could see that Timothy was listening intently. She couldn't believe that he actually had a smile on his face. *Lord,* she prayed, *help me not to discourage him.*

Following the last song, Timothy turned around and said, "Well, I am free at last from those bandages. Dr. Blackwood showed me some exercises to help strengthen it. He said the limp would get less, however not completely go away. I brought my own buggy this morning, so I can stay as long as I want following dinner. I still have trouble stepping up into it, although it is a lot easier than it was with those boards and bandages."

Eating dinner together, Aaron asked, "Are you ready to travel to Omaha with us, Timothy?"

"How soon are you planning to leave? Every day my leg

gets a little stronger. Another week or so should make it strong enough to keep up with you."

"I will hold your hand, Timothy, to help you walk," Elizabeth piped up from across the table.

"Thank you, Elizabeth. I will probably need your help."

Miriam and Timothy moved out to the porch swing after the dishes were cleared from the table. Rocking back and forth enjoying the smells of spring, they sat in silence for a few minutes. "Miriam, are you disappointed that my leg isn't completely back to normal?"

"Yes, I have to be honest about that. I was so sure that God would completely heal it."

"I am thankful that I can walk, even if it is with a limp. Would it bother or embarrass you if I am never able to walk without a limp?"

"No, of course not, Timothy. I told you before that the accident did not change my love for you."

"Dr. Blackwood is confident that the limp will become less and I may have to use a cane some of the time. However, let's talk about something else. I want to start making plans for us. What would you think of asking your father and my father to teach us about marriage? I know that Rev. Stanwick could teach us Biblical principles also. Would you be willing to do that?" Timothy asked.

"I doubt if Father would do anything like that, although we can ask him."

"Why don't you stay here and I will go ask him right now," Timothy said as he limped into the house.

He was back in a few minutes with a huge smile, "Guess what he said?"

"He said that he was a blacksmith, not a marriage counselor," Miriam guessed.

"Sort of like that, he hesitated a little. He said he would do some studying and see what he could share. He seemed hon-

239

ored that we would ask."

"Now, who is going to ask your father if he will teach us?"

"I will ask him this evening, and maybe you could join us for dinner next Sunday so Pa could share his thoughts on marriage," Timothy said quietly.

"That would be enjoyable, but how would I get home? Should I drive Ginger out after church?"

"No, we can ask Esther to ride back with us to town as our chaperone. She would love the chance to get out of the house and not have to cook."

Miriam looked forward to the time with the Larsen family. They seemed as close to her as her own family. Following dinner, Paul asked Miriam and Timothy to come into the parlor away from the rest of the family. Miriam loved listening to Paul share about marriage. "Most of what I know about marriage has been learned from the good Book. God knew what He was doing when he planned for marriage."

On the way home, Miriam said, "Your father is a good teacher."

"I know, I have been listening to him for twenty-two years," Timothy answered.

"I can tell you all about marriage," Esther joked. "No, I mean I can tell you about Timothy. He snores and leaves his dirty socks in the middle of the floor."

"Esther, you need to leave some surprises for Miriam," Timothy chuckled and poked Esther gently with the whip.

Helping Miriam down from the buggy, Timothy asked, "Do you think your father would be ready to share with us next Sunday? Do you want me to come for dinner?"

"You know you are always welcome to come for dinner anytime. I will tell him that you are planning on him sharing next Sunday. I think that will be all right."

Monday morning, Miriam asked, "Can you spare me this morning? I would like to visit with Sarah and tell her about our wedding. I would like to have her be a bridesmaid along with Anna."

"If you can help me do the washing, Anna and Jesse can hang it up. After that you may go visit Sarah."

Sarah was out working in the garden when Miriam pulled up in the buggy. Little Charles was watching from his baby carriage. "Hello, Miriam, you arrived in time to join me for a cup of tea. My back is wearing out from this hoeing."

"I have some exciting news to tell you."

"I would guess that it has something to do with Timothy Larsen. Am I correct?"

"Yes, we have set the first of September for our wedding and I came to ask if you would be my bridesmaid. My sister Anna will be maid of honor so I would like for you to be in the wedding also."

"I would love that, however I don't have anything to wear. I can't get into the dresses I wore before we were married."

"Do you sew your own clothes? If you do, we will watch for some sales at the Blue Store in town. I saw in last week's Gazette that they had some black brocade dress goods with satin finish for 29 cents a yard. It had been 45 cents. Maybe they have some other colors. I really don't want black. What would you think of turquoise brocade?"

"We don't have any extra money to buy dress goods. Maybe our hens will start laying so I could sell eggs to pay for it."

"I have some extra money, so I will buy it. And if you need help sewing, I can come out and help you."

"You will be busy sewing your own dress and for your sisters."

"I want Mother to make my dress. She does beautiful work and they have patterns in the women's magazines. I probably will help Anna make the dress for her and my other sisters."

"How is Timothy's leg? Didn't you say that he was to get the bandages off last week?"

"Yes, he did get them off and he has a bad limp. However,

with a cane he moves quite well. He wasn't as disappointed as I was when God didn't heal it completely."

"Will this keep him from doing the farm work?" Sarah asked in concern.

"Dr. Blackwood gave him exercises to do which are supposed to strengthen it. Timothy doesn't think it will slow him down much. He is planning on going to Buffalo Bill's Wild West Show in Omaha next week with us."

"Oh, I've read that it is an exciting show. My parents took me to it when I younger. I would appreciate it more now. He is quite the performer after being a Pony Express rider and buffalo hunter. His show probably has added lots of excitement since I saw it."

The following Sunday, Timothy was walking even better. After church, they were walking to the carriages and Timothy said, "See I can jump into the buggy almost as fast as I did before. I'll race you home," he called to Aaron.

"What will the neighbors think if you come racing into our yard?" Aaron called back.

"They will think that I am hungry for Miriam's good cooking 'cause that is true," Timothy called as he raced away.

After enjoying dinner together, Aaron said, "I wish to talk to Miriam and Timothy alone, so the rest of you find something to do in the parlor."

"I was a little surprised that Timothy asked me to teach you about marriage, although I am honored. The book of Genesis came to mind as I prayed about what to share. You can see from the minute God created the animals and then Adam that He planned to create Eve because He said, 'it is not good for man to live alone and that a man should leave Father and Mother and be joined to his wife and they should become one flesh.' Don't you think that it is wonderful that God planned for marriage right from the start before they disobeyed God and sinned?

"You know I never really thought about God creating

marriage right from the start of His creating the world. He is a wonderful God," Timothy said in awe.

"Another thing that I saw was that because Adam and Eve sinned and ate of the fruit of the tree that God had forbidden them to eat, His punishment was thorns and thistles and hard work for the man and that the woman would have pain in child birth and that her husband would rule over her. And death would come to all mankind."

"Do you think that if Adam and Eve had not sinned, there would have not been pain or death?" Miriam asked.

"All I know is that after they listened to Satan, their wonderful life in the Garden of Eden was gone. God later blessed them with children and their son, Seth, was the line into which Christ was born."

"You mean that with all the pain and hard work in life, God still blesses those people who believe in Him and are obedient to Him."

"Yes, in the book of Corinthians, in the New Testament, He tells the husband to love his wife as Christ loves the church and gave Himself for it. In addition, he tells the wife to reverence her husband. That is one area that I can honestly say your mother has done exceptionally. She always respects me even though sometimes she does not always agree with me."

"Thank you for sharing that with us, Mr. Jensen."

"Could I pray with you that God would bless your marriage?" Aaron asked.

"Yes, we would like you to ask God's blessing on our marriage," Timothy answered. "My leg is getting stronger each day, Mr. Jensen. If you are ready to leave for Omaha, I am willing to give it a try."

"Would next Thursday work for you? I think if we go in the middle of the week, the crowd might be smaller and it would be easier for all of us to move around," Aaron answered.

"What time would you wish to leave? I can come anytime

since Father is still asking me to take it easy."

"We should leave on the eight o'clock train. Can you make it that early?"

"I will be there with bells on," Timothy laughed.

"We don't need bells on the horses in the summer time."

Thursday morning brought a lot of scurried activity as the Jensen family prepared to leave for Omaha. "I'm packing a big lunch so we can eat on the train and not have to pay for expensive food until we arrive," Lydia said. "Elizabeth, be sure to wear your bonnet and the rest of you take your parasols as we will be out in the sun for several hours."

"I am so glad that Timothy will be going with us. He is so much fun," Elizabeth said while jumping up and down with excitement.

"Remember that Timothy still has to use his cane so he may not be able to hold your hand," Miriam reminded.

"I know, I can hang on to the other hand."

"Doesn't Miriam get to walk with him?" Emma asked. "After all she is the one who is marrying him."

"She can walk on the other side. I need to take care of Timothy. He is my friend," Elizabeth insisted.

The town was quiet as the family loaded into the carriage for the ride to the depot. They could hear the train whistle in the distance as it chugged into town.

Timothy was waiting inside watching for them. Running to his side, Elizabeth grabbed his hand and said, "I am going to hang on to you, Timothy, so you won't get lost or hurt." Timothy looked down at her and smiled.

"I appreciate your good care, Elizabeth. I don't get that kind of care at home."

The depot was filling up fast as many other families from Beloit were taking the train to Omaha. "There seem to be others who had the same idea of going in the middle of the week," Aaron commented.

"Isn't it something that Buffalo Bill Cody lived in Kansas as a boy? His father died when he was twelve and he was hauling mail for the Pony Express by the time he was fourteen. They each traveled 75-100 miles a day as they took the mail from St. Joseph, Missouri to Sacramento, California," Lydia added.

"How did he get the name of Buffalo Bill, Mr. Jensen?" Timothy asked.

"He was hired to kill buffalo for the workmen on the Kansas Pacific Railroad and they said that he killed 4,000 buffalo in seventeen months."

"I can't wait to see his show. Papa, does Annie Oakley shoot real bullets? I saw in the paper that she could shoot a playing card thrown into the air a dozen times before it hit the ground," Elizabeth asked.

"Yes, I expect that she uses real bullets. You can't do much shooting without real bullets."

Arriving in Omaha about noon, the family found a carriage to ride to the fair grounds for the show. All around town, they saw signs saying, "**Hon. W. F. Cody and Dr. A.W. Carver Rocky Mountain Prairie Exhibit.**"

"They said in the paper that Buffalo Bill has taken his show all over the world. He spent a year in Europe. He has hired many Indians to join his show because people want to see real Indians. Chief Sitting Bull has been with him for a number of years. When his show was on Staten Island, New York, in 1885, Thomas Edison came to watch them perform under the arc lights that he had invented. He has become a long-time friend of Bill's," Aaron reported.

"Look at all the Indians and tepees, Timothy!" Elizabeth said as she held tightly to his hand.

"It looks like he has brought half a town here with all the tents, performers and animals," Aaron said.

The show started with a parade of all the cowboys, Indians, cattle, buffalo and elk, and the Deadwood Stagecoach.

"There is Chief Sitting Bull sitting so majestically on his horse. It must be difficult always being on show just because you are an Indian," Miriam exclaimed.

Tiny Annie Oakley did her rifle-shooting exhibition. "No wonder she has won honors all over the world. She can even shoot behind her back and hit a small target. They say she learned to shoot so well because as a young girl, she had to provide food for her family," Aaron explained.

Elizabeth was especially impressed with Annie Oakley. "Look how little she is. She is not even as tall as Emma is. I like her 'cause she's not afraid of nothin'. I'd like to shoot like she does."

"Sh-h-h, Elizabeth, we can't hear what they are saying about Miss Oakley," Miriam admonished.

Next came a roaring battle between the Indians and the cowboys. The crowd was standing up to catch a better glimpse of all that was transpiring in the arena. Miriam looked over to where Elizabeth had been sitting beside Timothy. "Where is Elizabeth? She was here a minute ago."

"Oh no! I didn't notice that she wasn't here. She had quit hanging onto my hand while Annie Oakley was shooting and I became so enthralled with the battle in the arena that I didn't notice she was gone," Timothy said with alarm.

Miriam leaned over to her father. "Elizabeth is gone. She was here a few minutes ago while Annie Oakley was shooting, however Timothy didn't see her leave."

"You all stay right here so you don't get lost in the crowd. I will do some looking around for her."

Timothy grabbed his arm as he was leaving. "She seemed to be awfully fascinated with Miss Oakley. You might check her tent."

"I'll go there first," Aaron said hurriedly.

"How will Aaron be able to find her in this crowd? She could be most anywhere. I think we need to ask God to guide him to her. Timothy would you lead us in prayer?"

"That I will, Mrs. Jensen. I feel it was my fault that she left. In all the excitement of the show, I forgot that she didn't have hold of my hand. So let's pray. Lord, you know where little Elizabeth is, protect her and help Mr. Jensen to find her quickly. Amen."

"Someone might kidnap her and we would never see her again," Jesse said sadly.

"I am going to see if I can see anything from the top of the bleachers," Anna said as she climbed to the top.

"We may be here a long time. With this many people it will be difficult to find a little girl," Lydia said wearily as the late afternoon sun beat down on them.

"I want my little sister," Tabitha began to cry.

"Hush, Tabitha, God will lead your father to her."

The crowd was beginning to thin out so they could see some of the tents and performers around the tents. "What time does our train leave, Mrs. Jensen?" Timothy asked.

"I think it leaves at five o'clock," Lydia answered.

Pulling out his pocket watch, Timothy opened it. "We still have thirty minutes to make it to the depot," he announced.

"I think I see Father's head coming through the crowd," Anna called from the top of the bleachers.

"Can you see if he has Elizabeth?"

"No, I can see Father and he seems to be talking to someone. Maybe it is Elizabeth," Anna called as she came down the steps hurriedly.

"Look! There is Father with Elizabeth and she is talking a mile-a-minute," Miriam commented. "Thank you, God, for leading Father to her."

"Guess who I saw?" Elizabeth called the minute she saw them. "I talked with Annie. She told me she started shooting when she was my age. She let me look at her guns and took me to see Buffalo Bill and Sitting Bull. Sitting Bull gave me some eagle feathers like in his hat."

"It's not a hat, Elizabeth. It is an Indian headdress."

"Shall we all take a minute to thank God that Elizabeth was safe?" Aaron said as he led them in prayer. "Now, we need to run to catch a carriage to the depot or we will have to wait another hour for the next train. Can you keep up with us, Timothy? I will carry Elizabeth."

"You lead the way. I will keep up the best I can," Timothy called.

They arrived just as the last carriage was ready to leave the fair grounds. "Wait up for us," Aaron called as the driver prepared to drive away.

"We only have a few minutes to make it to the train, so make it quick."

They made it to the train a minute or two before it was ready to pull out. "Timothy, you look worn out. Are you going to be able to drive home tonight?" Lydia asked in concern.

"Maybe if I sleep a little on the way back to Beloit, I will regain my strength. I didn't realize how weak my leg was until I tried to hurry. It still has a lot to gain before it's back to normal strength." With that he put his head back and fell asleep.

CHAPTER SEVENTEEN

MELODY'S GREAT SHOW

APRIL AND MAY found Miriam and Timothy unusually busy. Timothy was doing more of the lighter farm work as his leg strengthened. Miriam was busy sewing linens for the home that Timothy and she would be setting up in September.

One noontime in mid May, Aaron brought the mail from the post office. "Here is a perfumed letter addressed to Mr. and Mrs. Aaron Jensen and family. Must be from Melody."

"Open it, Father. This should prove to be a very interesting letter after what she told Timothy and me before she left," Miriam commented.

Aaron opened the letter and began to read to the family seated around the dinner table. In a very formal and proper voice, he read: "Miss Melody Cramton, daughter of Mr. and Mrs. Thomas Cramton and Mr. Walter Van Squoit III, son of Mr. and Mrs. Walter Van Squoit II invite you to the reception of their wedding, Saturday, June 6, 1904 at 4 o'clock at the Williams Opera House. A wedding supper and dance to follow. RSVP."

"So she really is going to get married in Beloit," Miriam

said in surprise. "I thought by the way she acted when she left, she might get married in Boston just to show all of us that she couldn't stand the interference in her plans."

"It really didn't say she would get married in Beloit. It said that the reception, supper and wedding dance would be in Beloit. She may get married before she comes," Lydia mentioned cautiously.

"Wherever the wedding is to be, we know that we are not invited. We are not cultured enough for her to invite," Anna said sarcastically.

"I will be visiting with Mary this afternoon. I can ask her about the wedding plans. She may need some help," Lydia said.

Lydia left the girls doing the dishes and took Miriam's buggy to visit Mary. "I'll have Annabel bring us a cup of tea. I need someone to talk to about this wedding," Mary said as soon as Lydia arrived.

"Where are Walter and Melody getting married? Our invitation said that we were invited to the reception, supper and wedding dance."

"They are getting married in our church. However, she has invited just her new friends from the Boston, New England Conservatory of Music and kinfolk living in and near Kansas City. She had all the invitations already addressed so that I couldn't change anything. I guess she does not trust me after I refused to invite half the town for the engagement party. I saw that she didn't invite you. I am truly sorry," Mary said sadly, her face downcast.

"Don't be sorry, Mary. This wedding is not the happy occasion we would desire it to be. However, for your and Thomas's sake, we do plan to come to the reception," Lydia smiled cheerfully.

"I do appreciate that because I know you will be praying. Do bring Timothy if he does not come with his parents. I noticed that she included them in her list for the reception."

"We have been praying constantly for Melody. We are afraid she may be marrying him, thinking that she will change him. That is very doubtful and she will reap the consequences of disobeying God," Lydia shared gently.

"I know, Lydia. However, there is one happy spot with our children and that is seeing Miriam and Timothy planning their wedding with God's guidance. Miriam has been almost like a daughter to me since she has been in our home so often. I can look forward to Miriam's wedding, even though I have no joy in Melody's wedding. It seems more like a funeral," Mary said tearfully, the ache in her heart obvious.

"Oh, Mary," Lydia said as she walked over to give her a hug. "God began a good work in Melody when she accepted Him as Savior six years ago, and He will continue to work. However, she may have some hard lessons before she is willing to listen to Him."

Lydia reported all that she had heard from Mary at the supper table. "Mary is struggling so with this wedding. Both she and Thomas have no joy in giving their daughter to someone like Walter. She told me that she was thrilled to see you and Timothy planning your wedding, Miriam. Timothy is such a strong follower of God that others in the community see that in him and in you. You have brought us joy in your obedience," Lydia finished with a hint of tears in her voice.

"Do you suppose that Melody would have made different choices if her parents had come to know Christ before she was born, Mother? They had to make up for so many years of teaching her the pleasures of money and entertainment," Miriam asked.

"Probably it would have made a difference. Only God knows the answer to that," Lydia answered.

"I am so thankful that you and Father had accepted Christ before I was born," Miriam said pleasantly.

"Yes, we are both thankful that someone shared Christ with us when we were younger," Aaron said gratefully.

"Since we are going to Melody's reception, are we making new dresses to wear?" Miriam asked.

"No, we all have dresses that will work just fine. We will have plenty of sewing to do for all of your sisters this summer with your wedding coming in September," Lydia smiled fondly at her oldest daughter.

Aaron was reading the *Beloit Gazette* following supper. "Listen, I found something interesting from our state capitol in Topeka, 'The state superintendent, Nelson, stood up for reading the Bible in the public school. He said every attempt to weaken the religious influence in the school, endangers the welfare of the individual pupil and the usefulness of the school. Every attempt to drive the Bible out of the school is an attack upon the civil righteousness and social progress,'" Aaron quoted. "Maybe if Melody had heard more of the Bible in her younger years in school, she wouldn't be so rebellious now."

"Father, she did accept Christ when she was thirteen and her parents started teaching her the Bible and her studies at home," Miriam countered.

"I know that, however she had already set a pattern of getting around her parents' orders and was not willing to change that selfish independence," Aaron reminded.

"Yes, she has always wanted the center of attention. She told Timothy and me that Walter's father would be giving them a car just like the one Andy Manifold purchased. And they are having it shipped to Beloit on the train."

"That 1903 Cadillac with the one-cylinder motor makes so much noise that people are calling the Manifold home to ask if the automobile is going to be out. If it was, they wouldn't take their horses out on the streets. All we need is another one of those noisy contraptions," Aaron spouted indignantly.

"What I am wondering, is why are they having it brought on the train to Beloit? They won't be living here. They will just have to pay for shipping it back to Boston," Anna said in astonishment.

"Melody wants everyone to know that she is marrying into money," Lydia said sadly. "She hasn't learned yet that money will not bring happiness."

"I think Mrs. Cramton could use more than our prayers. I would like to spend some time with her tomorrow," Miriam said thoughtfully.

"I know that she would appreciate that, Miriam. You might be able to present some ideas to make the whole ordeal more acceptable for Thomas and Mary."

"That is my prayer. I may also visit Sarah after I leave the Cramton home. I've found several samples of piece goods that I would like to show her."

Mary was thrilled when Annabel opened the door at Miriam's knock, "Oh, Miriam, I am so glad you have come. I've been beside myself with all there is to do for the reception. Melody sent out 300 invitations and she wants there to be enough food for people to stay for the dance."

"There is no way that you will know how many will stay after the reception," Miriam stated, while pondering a way to help.

"No, probably not, since she didn't put RSVP for the dance. I regret all those years before Thomas and I became Christians, that I taught her that putting on a big show would win friends. The kind of friends who come for a good time at your expense, will not be there when you have trouble. I found that out years ago when I had my accident. Melody may think she has friends in Boston. However if she and Walter lose their money or health, they will drop them for someone who can entertain them."

"Mrs. Cramton, I would encourage you to keep the reception very simple. Put out finger food which people can serve themselves. They don't need a full course hot meal."

"Melody has requested fresh fruit and melons which are very difficult to find this early in the summer."

"Be honest with her and tell her what you are going to do. She will be so busy with the wedding plans that she may not mind the change. Are you having anything to do with the wedding preparations?" Miriam asked.

"Not really, except for paying the bills. They are bringing their preacher from Boston, Bishop Cantaway, as well as the string ensemble for the wedding music. She told me in her last letter, 'I will take care of the wedding, Mother, and you take care of the reception.' She has contacted the Manifold band for the dance in the evening."

"I suppose you know that Walter's father is giving them as a wedding gift, a car just like Andy Manifold's Cadillac. She made sure that Timothy and I knew that before she left town."

"Yes, she told us what she would like as a wedding gift. However, by the time we pay for all the expensive wedding clothes, the reception and dance, there won't be much left for a wedding gift. She is having us pay for all the clothes for her attendants and for the string ensemble along with all the other wedding costs. It is going to run into thousands of dollars and we haven't even seen the bill for her wedding dress. We suggested that she have a very simple wedding with close friends and what money she saved we would give as a wedding gift. However, she would not hear of doing anything like that. It looks like she wants to show the whole town that she has married into money. That is what makes me so sad," Mary said dejectedly.

"I understand, Mrs. Cramton. You have tried to undo the mistaken training of her early years, during which she learned to love money and the friends it would bring her. That must be what the Apostle Paul meant in I Timothy six about the love of money being the root of all evil."

"Miriam, do you think there is any hope of Melody coming back to obeying God, or of Walter becoming a Christian?"

"That is a difficult question, Mrs. Cramton. We know that nothing is impossible with God. However, He never forces people to change. They have to decide they want to change before He can work. We can pray they will be miserable until they do want to obey God. We could pray for that because we know that if they don't, they will reap the consequences of their disobedience," Miriam said gently.

"Oh, I hope they will obey the Lord. I lay awake at night thinking how miserable Melody will be once she realizes how much she has rebelled against God. I blame myself for not teaching her better."

"You tried, Mrs. Cramton, and Melody made her own choices to not heed your teaching. Oh! It is almost four o'clock. I need to drive out to Sarah William's farm to work on plans for my wedding. Is there anything else that I could help you with for the reception?" Miriam said.

"You have been most helpful, Miriam. Tell me about your wedding. When and where are you getting married?" Mary asked excitedly.

"I forgot in all the excitement of Melody's wedding that I needed to check with you about our wedding plans. Ever since I started coming to your home, I have loved your rose garden and have told Jackson several times that I wanted to get married in his rose garden. Timothy likes the idea also, and we have chosen early September for the wedding. Would it be acceptable with you, if we had the wedding in the garden?" Miriam asked breathlessly.

"I would be honored to have the wedding here. Timothy is a wonderful godly young man and your example to Melody has been exemplary. Timothy's response to his accident is incredible. I remember how angry I was following my accident. I wasn't a Christian, and I blamed God for causing it to happen," Mary said unhappily.

"You don't feel that way now, do you?" Miriam asked.

"No, I see now that God used the accident to bring me to Himself. If your mother had not started coming to visit me when I was so angry at not being able to walk, I might still be a recluse shutting myself off from everyone. Her patience in telling me about Christ and teaching me from the Bible helped me see that God really did love me. All that I needed to do was to believe in Him and He would give me eternal life. I can see now that He had a plan all along to bring me into right relationship with Him."

"I am so glad for you, Mrs. Cramton. You have been an encouraging friend to Mother. Sometimes six daughters gets her down. I really must go," Miriam said as she looked at the grandfather clock in the hall.

"Would you pray with me before you leave that something good would come from this wedding?" Mary asked joylessly.

"I would love to pray with you, Mrs. Cramton. What seems impossible to us, doesn't mean that God is limited."

Following the prayer, Miriam let herself out the door. Leaning back inside she called, "Telephone me if there is anything else I can help you with, Mrs. Cramton."

"Thank you, Miriam. You already have been a tremendous help," Mary assured her.

Driving out to Sarah's home, gave Miriam time to reflect on all that Mary said. *Lord, you have taught Mrs. Cramton so much about Yourself. Now please work on Melody and Walter. Guide my time with Sarah that I can be an encouragement to her,* she prayed.

Sarah was excited to see Miriam. "Have you seen today's copy of the *Gazette*, Miriam? Your picture is in the paper," she commented.

"Whatever would my picture be doing in the paper?" Miriam asked in surprise.

"Remember that contest they were having to get subscriptions for the *Gazette*? The editors were offering to give away a piano to the woman who received the most votes. You're one of the top four women whom people voted for with their new subscriptions."

"Now I remember that Timothy and his brothers said something about seeing if they couldn't help me win. I thought they were joking. Hope they didn't end up having to purchase 10 subscriptions for the *Gazette* just to get my name near the top," Miriam said laughing.

"Now that you are getting married and having a house of your own, you will need a piano. I've never learned to play. Now I wish someone had taught me to play. Then I could sing songs with little Charles."

Sarah and Miriam discussed the dress goods for Sarah's dress in Miriam's wedding. "Oh, look at the time! I really should be going. Timothy said that he might come in for a visit tonight."

"Miriam do you have a counterpane for your bed? I would like to knit one for you, if you don't have one already," Sarah asked.

"No, I don't have a counterpane. Although, I have made several crazy quilts from flour sacks. A counterpane would look so nice on top."

Sarah nodded and then switched subjects. "By the way, how is Timothy's leg healing?"

"Since we returned from Omaha, he said that it has grown stronger. He is doing some work on our house this week. He wants me to come out with his mother to look at it so that she can help me decide what to do about curtains. His mother is good at wallpapering, so I can pick out paper at the Emmert Drug Store."

"Oh, I almost forgot about another item in the paper. It was the announcement that Melody Cramton and Walter Van Squoit were getting married next month. Isn't she a friend of yours?"

"Yes, we were very good friends at one time. However, she is not comfortable around me now that she has chosen to marry a man who is not a Christian. She even retracted her request that I be her maid of honor after Timothy told her parents about an article he saw in the *Kansas City Star* involving Walter's uncle."

"It must make you sick at heart to see a friend disobeying God," Sarah responded sadly.

"Yes, it is discouraging to see her throw away everything that she believed in earlier. Another problem that Walter may not know about Melody is that she is not a homemaker. She has done almost no cooking or cleaning in her life. Unless he provides a maid, they may starve," Miriam said emphatically,

"Do you suppose Melody would contact you, should she have trouble later on in her marriage? And would you be willing to help her, knowing that she had jumped from the frying pan into the fire by her own wrong choices?"

"Of course I would do what I could. Meanwhile keep praying with me that she will see marrying Walter is a terrible mistake," Miriam said.

"You mean you think there is still a possibility that she could come to her senses?" Sarah asked in surprise.

"A slim possibility, although as I told her mother, nothing is impossible with God. I really must be going or I will miss supper and not be ready when Timothy comes this evening," Miriam said hurriedly.

Driving home in the evening cool, Miriam enjoyed the scolding call of the blue jays and the warble of the meadowlark. She couldn't keep from praising the Lord. *Thank you, Lord for Your beautiful spring times. It is just like You created it all over again as the little flowers come sprouting out of the ground. In addition, You even created some with wonderful smell like the lilacs. I want a whole row of them around Timothy's and my house. Thank you Lord for bringing Timothy into my life.*

Supper was ready when Miriam arrived home. "It must be nice to gallivant all afternoon while we slave away at the stove," Anna teased.

"I suppose I did enjoy the time with Mrs. Cramton,

although it is discouraging to see she can't enjoy Melody's wedding. She said it was more like a funeral for her. Later, Sarah and I had a wonderful visit."

"Did she say anything about your picture in the paper?" Emma asked. "Papa showed it to me when he came home with the paper. You might win the piano after all. Can I come out to visit you and play your piano?"

"I probably will not win it. Although if I do, you can come out anytime," Miriam answered with a smile.

Miriam was sitting in the porch swing after helping with the dishes. Timothy rode up on his horse. "Well, how is my beautiful princess this evening?" he called as he swung off his horse and tied him to the hitching post.

"Fine, thank you, prince charming," Miriam teased back.

Sitting down beside her in the swing, Timothy said, "You would be proud of all that I accomplished on the house today. I plastered an upstairs room which the former owners had left unfinished."

"What will we be using that room for since we have one bedroom downstairs, don't we?" Miriam asked.

"Well, we might need it for company staying overnight, or we might need it for future children, or right now for storage of extra clothes and household stuff. Why don't you come out tomorrow so you can help decide how we will build the new porch? I tore off the tiny old porch so I can build on a full-length one with a porch swing to relax after a hard day at work."

The telephone rang, jarring the family out of a relaxing evening. Lydia answered, "Yes, she is here." Calling to Miriam, Lydia said, "I think it is a farmer wanting you to deliver a baby. I can barely hear him. It sounded like he said his name was Thompson." With that, she handed the receiver to Miriam.

""Where did you say that you live, Mr. Thompson? I am not familiar with your farm," Miriam asked.

Timothy came up behind her and said, "I know where

they live, tell him that I will lead you out there as I go home."

"Timothy Larsen says he knows where you live. I will come as soon as I can pack some clothes and get my horse harnessed and hitched up," Miriam answered.

Hanging up the receiver, Miriam said, "How far do the Thompsons live from your farm, Timothy? I've never heard of that name before."

"I have, Miriam," Aaron stated. "Mr. Thompson has come into the smithy for repairs. He is somewhat of a surly man with a chip on his shoulder. I think they have several children since he usually brings one or two sons with him."

"Do you think that Miriam is safe around this man, Mr. Jensen?" Timothy asked in concern.

"I don't think there is a problem with that. It is his family that he treats so gruffly. The one time he brought his wife with him, he ordered her around like a servant. She seemed so dejected and sad. You will have a ministry with that family, Miriam."

"Would you all pray with me before I leave?" Miriam asked seriously.

After the prayer, Aaron said, "I'll go get Ginger hitched to the buggy. Do you want to go with me, Timothy? That way we men could visit a little without the women."

"We let you visit, Father," Miriam responded back, laughing. "You just have to wait your turn."

It was dark by the time Miriam and Timothy left Beloit. Timothy rode beside the buggy telling Miriam where to turn. "They live several miles off the main road. Their little farm is rather rough and hilly. Mr. Thompson doesn't seem to know much about farming," Timothy instructed.

Arriving at the Thompson farm, Miriam could see a tiny light in a window. Two scrawny barking dogs met them. Mr. Thompson opened the door and yelled, "Aw, shut up, you mutts. Let the lady in the house."

Timothy got off his horse and helped Miriam down and

walked her to the door. "Mr. Thompson, I am Timothy Larsen and this is Miriam Jensen, whom I plan to marry this fall. Since I was in town and on my way home, I showed her the way out here," Timothy announced.

"Yeah, I know where your old man lives. You live about a mile from here if you go the way the crow flies. Pleased to meet you," he said as he grabbed for Timothy's hand. Looking at Miriam, he said, "The wife is in that back bedroom. Better get in there right away. She isn't doing too well."

Timothy asked, "Do you want me to put Miss Jensen's horse in the barn or will you take care of her?"

"Here, I'll get the lantern and show you where to put her. O tarnation, this fool lantern is out of kerosene. I thought I told you kids to fill the lanterns. Ted run and get the kerosene," he yelled.

"Yes, Pa, I'm a goin'," the young boy of about ten years said as he ran out the back door and came back with an old can.

After putting Ginger in the barn, Timothy came back to the house to tell Miriam goodbye. "If you need anything, telephone me. Ma can come if you need a woman to help."

Miriam hated to have Timothy leave. However, she knew she had to depend on God for wisdom and strength as she hurried back to Mrs. Thompson. Around midnight, a little girl was born. Miriam went to find Mr. Thompson and found him asleep at the table. "Mr. Thompson, you have a baby daughter. However, your wife isn't doing well. Could you telephone Dr. Blackwood? I need his help."

"What in tarnation is wrong with her? She has had babies before," Mr. Thompson said in exasperation.

"I don't know for sure what is wrong with your wife, so I really would like for you to call Dr. Blackwood."

"All right, I will call him. However, I ain't got no money to pay him. Can't you take care of her good enough?"

"I've done all that I know to do. Maybe if you had some

261

white oak bark, it might help stop the bleeding," Miriam stated anxiously.

"Did you ask the wife if we had any? I don't know where she keeps nothin' in this house."

Miriam, praying for wisdom, went to ask Mrs. Thompson. "It is in the kitchen cupboard. If you look up there you might find some other herbs also."

After applying the white oak bark, Mrs. Thompson seemed to being doing better. Miriam said, "I am going to fix myself a mat here beside your bed so I can help you if you need it."

Miriam slept fitfully. Just before falling asleep she prayed, *Lord, I feel so inadequate. I don't know how to help her. Since Mr. Thompson won't call Dr. Blackwood, I have to depend totally on You to heal her.*

By morning, Mrs. Thompson was some better. "Can you stay with me for a few days, Miriam? If you don't the mister will have me out cooking and cleaning the minute you leave."

"I will be glad to stay, Mrs. Thompson. You have lost so much blood that you have no business doing any work for a week."

Miriam cooked breakfast and found there were three children. She had only seen the one son the night before. "How old are you?" she asked the timid little girl eating silently with her older brothers.

"Four," she answered so quietly Miriam almost didn't hear.

"Did you know that you have a new little sister born last night? Would you like to see her? Your mother hasn't told me her name since she isn't feeling very well. Maybe today you can help her pick out a name," Miriam said, taking the girl by the hand.

"Mama," the girl asked, "What are we going to name my little sister?"

"What would you like to name her, Ginny? You can help pick a name," Mrs. Thompson said weakly.

"I want to name her Lucinda after my friend at school," the girl answered eagerly.

"That is just what we will name her. Now go eat your breakfast."

Ginny ran to the kitchen and announced, "I named my little sister, Lucinda." Miriam followed the girl back to the kitchen.

Mr. Thompson, finishing his breakfast looked at Miriam and grumbled, "I suppose you'll have to stay a few days and cook. I can't pay you much. However, I would be much obliged if you could stay," he ended almost pleasantly.

"I can stay for a few days, although I must request that you call Dr. Blackwood to check on your wife. You could pay him with a few dozen eggs or a couple of chickens. Your wife is still not doing well and we could lose her yet," Miriam requested.

"What in tarnation do you mean by that?" he demanded, slamming his fist down on the table so hard that it made the dishes jump and the children pull back fearfully.

"I mean that she lost so much blood, she is awfully weak. Dr. Blackwood will know if there is anything more we can do."

"All right, I'll call him. What little good it will do," he said as he scraped his chair back from the table. Looking at the kids just sitting there, he yelled, "Don't just sit there, get out and do the milking and take care of the chickens. Ginny, you help Miss Jensen with the dishes."

Miriam was relieved after Mr. Thompson had made the call to Dr. Blackwood and gone outside. His angry outbursts set her nerves on edge. She and little Ginny had an enjoyable time doing the dishes and cleaning up the kitchen after she took oatmeal broth to Mrs. Thompson. "Ginny is here to see her little sister again," Miriam said while sitting Ginny on the edge of the bed.

Mrs. Thompson opened her eyes wearily, "I think I am feeling a little stronger, thanks to you, Miriam."

"Here is something for you to drink, Mrs. Thompson. It

263

will help you regain your strength. Can I help you sit up in bed so you can nurse the baby?"

"Yes, would you bring a pillow because my arms are so weak," Mrs. Thompson asked.

"I convinced your husband to call Dr. Blackwood. He should be able to help you since I have done all that I know to do. I keep praying that God will heal you."

"Oh, do you know God? I've always wanted to go to church, but the mister will have nothin' to do with church and preachers. Says they aren't much better than doctors cause all they want is money. Could you tell me how I can be right with God. I am afraid to die," Mrs. Thompson said mournfully.

"Mrs. Thompson, all you need to do to be right with God is to believe that Jesus died for your sins and accept Him as your Savior. He told us that if we believed in Him, He would give us eternal life," Miriam answered gently.

"I do believe that He died for my sins. Would you pray for me now?"

"Yes, I will. Would you like to pray also? Remember you are His child now and He is your Heavenly Father, who will never leave you. You can come to Him anytime," Miriam said.

Following the prayer, Mrs. Thompson's dejected look went away. Miriam put little Lucinda in the cradle beside the bed and helped Mrs. Thompson back down onto the pillow. She was asleep even before Miriam was out of the room. "Come, Ginny, why don't you help me start dinner," Miriam said as she took Ginny by the hand.

Dr. Blackwood arrived by mid-morning with Mr. Thompson right at his heels. "Good morning, Miss Jensen. How's things going with Mrs. Thompson?"

"I think she is doing better, Dr. Blackwood. I used the white oak bark for her last night as that was all I knew to do. Would you see if there is anything more that should be done. She lost a lot of blood."

After checking Mrs. Thompson, Dr. Blackwood patted Miriam on the arm, "You did the right thing, young lady." Looking at Mr. Thompson, he said loudly, "If she can have complete bed rest for a week, there is a good chance she will recover. However, getting up too soon could kill her," he said with a wink at Miriam.

"I suppose you want to be paid, Doc? Would a couple of dozen eggs do?" Mr. Thompson said gruffly when Dr. Blackwood came outside.

"Yes, my good man. The wife was just begging me this morning to see if I could find a few eggs when I was out making house calls today. She will be grateful for these."

Miriam cooked, cleaned house and read the Scriptures to Mrs. Thompson each day. The family didn't have much in variety of food, although there were plenty of chickens and eggs. So she made up a large batch of chicken and noodles. "These taste so good, Miss Jensen," the oldest boy commented as he shoveled in huge mouthfuls.

Towards the end of the week, the color was beginning to return to Mrs. Thompson's cheeks. "You are looking real chipper this morning, Mrs. Thompson. Do you want to try sitting up in the rocking chair for a short spell?" Miriam asked cheerfully.

"Yes, I feel much stronger, thanks to your good food and care. If you would like to go home tomorrow, I - I - think it would be all right," she said hesitantly.

"You still are awfully weak. Why don't I stay until Saturday morning. I have a wedding reception to attend Saturday afternoon, so I would like to be home by noon."

Miriam did stay until late Saturday morning and could see that Mrs. Thompson was getting around much better. "I have bread baked, the washing done and a big pot of beans cooking. Do you think you can take care of things now, Mrs. Thompson?"

"Yes, I think with Ginny's help, I can manage. Thank you

for staying and for all you have taught me," Mrs. Thompson answered gratefully.

Leaving the Thompson farm, Miriam noticed how dilapidated the buildings were on the farm. *It isn't anything like the Larsen's farm. No wonder they are so discouraged. They are barely growing enough to keep food on the table. Thank you, Lord, for allowing me to share about You with Mrs. Thompson.*

The birds were singing and the lilacs and red bud trees were blooming so Miriam kept thinking. *What a beautiful day Melody has for her wedding. I wonder if she has even stopped to thank you for that, Lord?*

The minute she walked in the door at home, Tabitha squealed, "You won! Miriam, you won!"

"I won what, Tabitha?"

"You won the piano. The lady from the newspaper telephoned Mama and told her that you got the most votes for the piano," she crowed again, clapping her hands.

Miriam pulled out a chair and sat down quickly. "I can't believe it. Now Timothy and I have our very own piano! Our very first piece of furniture for our new home. I can't wait to tell him. Mother, have you heard from him? Is he coming to the reception with his family or is he going with us?"

"I have not heard from him since you left, so I assume he is coming with his family," Lydia said.

"I saw Melody and Walter's car come into town. They drove it by the smithy on their way to the Cramton home. I wonder who will drive Melody to the wedding. I don't suppose that Thomas has even driven a contraption like that. They say that the first time Andy Manifold drove his car, he ended up in a cornfield. It has a tiller and levers and pedals. By the time his friend got it stopped they were headed right for a telephone pole," Aaron reported.

After a bath and dinner, Miriam began to relax from her strenuous week. "I sure have no get-up-and-go after cooking

*Melody and Walter Van Squoit's wedding and 1903 Cadillac
in front of the early Beloit Christian church.*

and cleaning all week."

"Why don't you go rest for awhile. We will call you in time to dress for the reception," Lydia said.

It seemed to Miriam that she had just gotten to sleep when Anna was shaking her, "Wake up, Miriam. It's time to dress for the big occasion. I pressed your black silk while you were sleeping."

"Oh thank you, Anna. I don't know what I would do without you."

"I won't be your maid after you get married so I guess you will learn to do without me," Anna teased. "I even got out all of your clothes and your new hat."

Miriam worked extra hard to look her best. Her new black gloves with the black straw hat adorned with white flowers and feathers set off her outfit exceptionally well. Going out to the kitchen where her father was chomping at the bit to leave, Miriam asked, "How do I look, Father?"

"Pretty enough to be the bride. You will turn all eyes away from Melody today."

"Father, you flatter so much. You know that Melody will be the star today."

Lydia came out of the bedroom. "Miriam, since you are dressed, would you please fix Elizabeth's hair? I need to finish Emma and Tabitha's hair and bows."

"How soon should I bring the carriage, Lydia?" Aaron asked patiently.

"We are almost ready, Aaron. By the time you get the horses harnessed and hitched, we will be out there."

"By the way, what are we giving Melody and Walter for a wedding present, Mother?" Miriam asked.

"I ordered a large family Bible with their name engraved in gold on the cover."

"Are you sure that is a good idea, Lydia?" Aaron asked as he was heading out the door.

"You mean about giving them a Bible?"

"No, I mean about putting their names in gold. Their chances of staying together are so slim. What would they do with the Bible if they divorce?"

"Oh Aaron, let's not think about that. We will continue to pray that Walter becomes a Christian and Melody decides to be obedient to God."

The Jensen family arrived at the William's Opera House as Melody and Walter drove up in their new Cadillac. Melody waved excitedly at them, while all around them, horses were rearing or trying to run away from the noisy car. Walter expertly drove it to the front of the opera house and shut it off. He came to the back of the car and opened the door to help Melody out as a true gentleman.

"He does look handsome with that goatee and mustache, doesn't he, Miriam?" Anna whispered.

"Yes, I suppose. However looks aren't everything," Miriam reminded.

Melody stood beside the car a few minutes, "Look at that dress, Mother! Have you ever seen a brilliant blue silk wedding dress in Beloit before? With that gold silk jacket, she certainly will be the talk of the town. I bet Mr. and Mrs. Cramton will be paying for that dress for months."

Without another notice to the Jensen family, Melody grabbed Walter's arm and walked inside the opera house. Following them, Miriam was surprised at how different the opera house looked. New electric lights, new velvet curtains and matching wall paper. An elaborately decorated cake was prepared for cutting by Melody and Walter. Together, they cut the cake and sipped wine from the same crystal goblet. Melody gave Walter a little wave and swishing her full ruffled skirt, rushed off to visit with one friend after another. She would hug this one and move on chattering all the time.

"She acts like this party was just for her. She didn't even take Walter along to introduce him," Miriam commented.

The Larsen family came in and Timothy joined Miriam just as Melody hurried past them. She looked their way without a word and started talking excitedly with the first person she found. "She acts like those little banty chickens we have out at the farm, chattering and racing all over the place. She certainly isn't very friendly with you, her best friend. And there is Walter, standing all alone. Maybe we should go rescue him, Miriam. We could tell him that the string ensemble he brought from Boston does play wonderful music. They play almost as well as you and your father do on the violins," Timothy smiled fondly at Miriam.

"Oh, Timothy, they are much more talented than I will ever be on the violin."

Walking over to Walter, Timothy said, "Good evening, Walter. That sure is a high-falutin' music group that you brought from Boston. I reckon that every one is enjoying it."

"Well, thank you, Timothy. Will you be staying for the dance? The Manifold band will be playing some of the time."

"We plan to stay for the dinner, however we won't be staying for the dance. My family needs to get home so we can prepare for church tomorrow."

"Oh, tomorrow is Sunday, isn't it? I had forgotten with all that is going on around here. I have to get the car to the depot tomorrow so they can ship it back to Boston and Melody and I can leave on our wedding trip to the Niagara Falls. We will be gone for two weeks."

"It must be nice to be able to take off work that long. On the farm, we can't be gone for two weeks at this time of year," Timothy replied.

"At the Conservatory, they don't do much during the summer. I will be teaching voice in the fall. In addition, my church has allowed me two weeks off for the wedding. After you and Miriam get married, why don't you visit us? We could show you the sights around Boston. Don't suppose a farm boy like you has ever seen the big city."

"I have been to Kansas City and Wichita. However, I never really had a desire for the big city. I feel closer to God's creation out there on the farm."

"Well, nice seeing you again. I must go find Melody," Walter said impatiently.

Timothy chuckled, "Well, that ended the conversation. One mention of God and he changes the subject."

"I pray that Melody will read the Bible we gave them and maybe share some with Walter. We can continue to pray that they will build their marriage with God as the center."

"You are right, Miriam. However, I must admit I don't have much faith that Walter will change. He is too determined to live for money and culture."

Miriam and Timothy found Aaron and Lydia visiting with Mary, Thomas and Thomas's mother. "Hello, Mrs. Cramton," Miriam said. "How are things going for you this evening?"

The older Mrs. Cramton answered in her usual form, "I think it utterly ridiculous that my granddaughter would waste so much money on an outrageous dress like that and on top of that have the nerve to have a dance. If I had had a chance to talk to her, I would have told her a few things."

Mary Cramton said, "Really, Mother Cramton, Melody's original idea was much more ridiculous. Miriam's idea of keeping things simple has really helped." Looking at Miriam she asked, "You will stay for the supper, won't you?"

"Yes, although not for the dance."

"I wish that Melody had not insisted on the dance. However, by the time we heard about it, there was nothing we could do."

"Are you paying for their wedding trip along with all of the reception and wedding?" the older Mrs. Cramton asked.

"No, his father is footing the bill for the trip."

"I don't suppose we will see much of Melody and Walter once

271

they get settled in Boston," Miriam commented thoughtfully.

"Melody told me that as far as she was concerned, she had no reason to come back to Beloit. If we wanted to see them, we could come to Boston. Since it is so difficult for me to travel, that means we probably won't see them more than once a year," Mary answered.

Miriam leaned over to Thomas' mother, "Mrs. Cramton, I would like for you to meet Timothy Larsen, my fiancé. We will be getting married in September. I want you to come to our wedding. It will be in your son's rose garden."

"Is this young man of yours a Christian, Miriam?" Rose Cramton asked.

"O yes, Mrs. Cramton. He loves the Lord and we have prayed about our marriage for a long time," Miriam assured her.

"Then I would be honored to come to your wedding. I remember your visit in my home in Kansas City and how you tried to keep that granddaughter of mine on the straight and narrow. However, she would have none of it. I'm going to have to spend more time on my knees for that young lady, I can see that," she responded sharply.

Chapter Eighteen

Summer Excitement

LIFE SETTLED back to normal after the excitement of Melody's wedding. Miriam said to her mother one morning, "I am grateful for Mr. and Mrs. Cramton's sake that Melody and Walter are not living in town. There was enough gossip about Melody's high-falutin' Boston husband without them living in town."

"I agree, Miriam. Mary and Thomas were miserable all through the reception. They are praying that the marriage will last past the first year. Knowing Melody, most anything could happen," Lydia agreed.

A week after the wedding, Timothy told Miriam, "You won't see much of me for the next few weeks. It is corn-planting time so all of us men will be in the field. Ma can help you paper the living room and kitchen at our house if you are ready for that. She said that she could spare a few days before she gets into the busy gardening and canning time."

Miriam agreed, so she and Martha spent several days wall papering which gave the rooms a new airy look. "The dainty pink flowered paper makes the room look like spring," Miriam exclaimed when they had finished. "Mrs. Larsen, since you have helped me with wall papering, could I help you when the threshing crew comes?"

273

"You are welcome to come anytime, Miriam, and we can use your expert help baking pies. Esther would appreciate your company and I know that Timothy wouldn't mind a bit having you visit," she answered with a smile.

"I need to learn more about farming and harvest time. Will you call me when the crew is due at your farm?" she requested.

"Either Esther or I will call you a day or so before they arrive. The wheat is already in the shocks so by next week it should be dried enough for threshing," Martha assured as they parted and Miriam drove back to town. As she was driving along she noticed the wild plum and elder berry bushes were blooming. *I must remember where they are so we pick them for jelly and jam,* she reminded herself.

A few days later, Miriam was busy sewing her wedding dress when Martha called on the telephone. "The crew is due to come Wednesday morning early. If you can be here by eight o'clock you can help with the pie baking."

"I will be there before eight," Miriam answered. "I don't want to miss out on anything."

Hanging up the receiver, Miriam said excitedly, "Now, I will have my first lesson cooking for a threshing crew. Mrs. Larsen said they would have eight or nine men and some wives, so they will need many pies."

"Yes, that will be a new experience for you. By this time next year, you will be cooking for your own threshing crew," Lydia responded.

"That means I need to learn everything that I can this year," she said anxiously.

Miriam was up at the break of dawn. Her father came out to the kitchen to find her fixing breakfast for the both of them. "My! That bacon smells good. I could not believe my nose when I smelled it cooking so early. What gets you up so early this morning?"

"I want to arrive at the Larsen farm early so I can watch

the threshing crew set up and help Mrs. Larsen with the cooking. Do you have work waiting for you at the smithy?"

"Yes, there is work left from yesterday and probably some farmer will be waiting at the door when I arrive. At this time of the year, something is always breaking and they want it fixed instantly," Aaron said laughing.

Aaron helped Miriam harness and hitch Ginger to the buggy before he left. "Can I deliver you to the smithy, Father?"

"No, the walk will do me good, and it is the time I do my best praying. You go along and enjoy your visit with the Larsen family."

There was a light fog over the valley as Miriam drove along listening to the noisy calls of blue jays and the cooing of the doves. *What a beautiful morning for threshing wheat. Help me be a good helper today, Lord,* she prayed. Arriving at the Larsen farm, Miriam was surprised to see so many men, horses and hayracks. Some men were working on the huge threshing machine/separator and others were working on the steam engine, which ran it.

As she came inside the house, she found Martha, Esther and a couple of neighbor women already baking bread and cooking a large kettle of chicken and noodles. Miriam put on her apron and joined Esther at the table working on piecrusts. "My! Am I ever glad to see you. My arm is getting tired already with rolling out these crusts and I still have four yet to go," Esther admitted eagerly as Miriam took over the rolling.

"I would like to see how the threshing machine runs, if we have a minute to go outside, Esther."

"As soon as we get these pies in the oven, we can run out and watch for few minutes. I think Mama would watch the pies for us," Esther volunteered.

The girls hurried with the pies, slicing apples and covering them with crusts until they had all seven in the oven. "Is it all right, Mama, if I take Miriam out to see what goes on with the threshing crew?"

"Yes, we can watch the pies if you are not right back," Martha said as they went out the door.

The girls walked out to where they could see the threshing machine and steam engine. "If you want to climb up in the haymow with me, we can see unusually well without having to be out in the dust and dirt," Esther said.

A bundle hauler was just coming in with his hayrack loaded with bundles of wheat. Driving up beside the threshing machine, he started pitching bundles into the machine. Another hayrack was being unloaded on the other side.

"See, the wheat is pitched into the threshing machine where it is separated from the straw which is blown into a pile. The wheat is then dumped into a wagon to be put into those bins inside the barn," Esther explained.

Paul saw the girls up in the haymow and called, "Bring the men some cool drinks, Esther." They waved back to let him know that they had heard.

Going to the well, they filled two large buckets with water and taking several tin cups, they carried the water to the men coming up on the hayracks. Timothy was one of the first to come by with his hayrack. "Thank you girls, for the drink. I was getting mighty thirsty. Would you like to ride with me on the hayrack after dinner, Miriam?"

"Yes, that would be a good way for me to learn what really goes on with a threshing crew," she replied enthusiastically.

"And a good way to get all itchy with dirt and chaff," Esther laughed.

"You sound like you have been out there many times," Miriam said.

"Yes, my brothers want me to help pitch on bundles, however it is heavy dirty work. And Papa really doesn't want me to do it. Besides Mama needs me in the kitchen. That is my kind of work," she said strongly.

In order to feed all the men at the kitchen table, Martha

had the men eat first while the women and children waited. They were devouring huge platters of chicken and noodles, mashed potatoes and gravy and fresh tomatoes.

"Give me a piece of Miss Jensen's famous apple pie," Paul Larsen called from the far side of the table.

Miriam blushed as all the men turned to look at her. "She bakes the best apple pie in the county," Timothy boasted. "I know because I've been eating them for most of a year. That is why I am marrying her this September." Miriam was even more embarrassed after the comments by Timothy, although she knew he was proud of her.

"Well, congratulations, Timothy. You have found a good woman," one of the older men said. They all nodded in agreement.

The men scraped back their chairs, reached for straw hats with, "Thank you for the good meal," coming from a few men. Timothy stayed behind to remind Miriam, "Come out when you get finished here."

"I'll be there," Miriam responded with enthusiasm.

The women and children ate, and the women all helped Martha and Esther clean up the kitchen, which was becoming very warm. "I'll be thankful to get out under your shade trees, Martha," one of the farm wives said, expressing the desire of them all.

"Now you can enjoy a ride on the hayrack, Miriam," Esther said when they had the kitchen all back in order. "Button up your sleeve cuffs and put on your bonnet so you won't have your hair full of chaff."

Miriam stood under the trees watching the men coming by with the hayracks. One man was kept busy filling the steam engine with water from the water wagon. Timothy saw her standing in the shade and drove close by, "Care to take a ride, Miss Jensen?" he said in mock formality.

"Yes, Mr. Larsen, I would enjoy a ride."

Gathering up her long skirts, Miriam took Timothy's hand

as he helped her into the hayrack seat. "See that farmer over there," Timothy said, pointing to a hayrack just coming to the threshing machine. "He is somewhat of a clown. Loves to create some excitement while we work. Most of the farmers know that Glen is quite a card, so he usually doesn't surprise them. Keep an eye on him so you won't miss the fun."

"What does he do out in the field?" Miriam asked.

"Never know what might happen, because each time he may do something different. About the time we are all hot and tired, Glen creates something to wake us up."

Miriam decided she would watch the wiry little farmer. "Look at the way he jumps around loading the wagon. He is so agile that he makes you think of a young child."

"He is full of surprises. I've seen him do a backward flip or cart wheel in the middle of the field or yard most anytime."

"Look, Timothy, his wagon is loaded and he is crawling under the bundles with the reins. What is he doing?"

"Watch closely, it will be exciting whatever he has planned," Timothy said.

Miriam saw Glen reach out his pitchfork and poke the horses in the rear causing them to take off in a dead run. Men who had not seen what he was doing, yelled "Run-a-way! Someone get a horse and catch the horses before they wreck the hayrack! They are going to get killed running into the threshing machine!" Men were running for horses while the seemingly runaway hayrack headed straight for the threshing machine. At the last minute, it swung around and Glen jumped out from under the bundles and started pitching bundles into the machine as if nothing had happened.

"Timothy, how many times does Glen do this each year?" Miriam asked incredulously.

"Oh, usually once at each farm. Although sometimes he changes the stunt so we never really know what to expect. So far, he has never damaged a hayrack or horse or other men. If it had been a real runaway, one of the men would have had to jump on a horse and catch the team before they ran into or through something. We have broken up several hayracks that way and sometimes a horse breaks a leg going through a fence, so a runaway is no laughing matter."

"Do you want me to stay on the hayrack while you load, or do you want me to help load?" Miriam asked.

"You stay there and hold the reins. The horses get kind of spooky with this kind of work and they seem to sense that no one is holding the reins while we are loading."

Miriam sat in the seat while Timothy pitched the load off into the threshing machine. She didn't like the tremendous noise of the steam engine belching smoke and the threshing machine roaring so loud she couldn't hear Timothy talk. *Lord, keep the horses calm. I don't want to have a runaway and dump Timothy off the hayrack*, she prayed quietly.

Jumping back into the seat and taking the reins, Timothy said, "Want to ride another round with me?"

"Yes, although being around those machines is frightening. I was afraid the horses would bolt," she answered nervously.

"Naw, they usually don't bolt around the machines because they know the driver is still on the rack. It's when we are off the hayrack loading that they can spook and take off. And then usually we can jump back on and grab the reins to pull them to a stop."

Miriam sat in the driver's seat, with the reins in her lap, watching Timothy load the wagon with bundles. She noticed a covey of quail come up quite close eating the wheat on the ground. A little later as another hayrack came by on its way to the threshing machine, the covey of quail burst into the air right under the noses of Timothy's team. Before Miriam could get a tight grip on the reins, they were racing full speed for the south end of the field. She pulled and pulled on the reins, yelling "Whoa, horses, whoa." It seemed like nothing would stop them.

She could hear Timothy yelling behind her, "Someone get a horse and catch that team! They are headed for the river!"

Hearing his cry about river, Miriam pulled even harder. *Lord, help me. Stop them!* she prayed. Finally, they began to slow down just as Daniel came racing up on a horse to grab the reins and turn them around right at the edge of the cliff above the river.

Timothy came limping up behind the hayrack. "Oh, Miriam, I was so afraid the team would take you right into the river," he said, panting and leaning on the wagon trying to catch his breath. The horse's sides were heaving and they were foaming and blowing from their nostrils. Miriam started to get down from the hayrack. However, she found her legs wouldn't hold her up. Timothy caught her as she started to fall.

"Timothy, I just kept praying and praying that God would help me stop them. No matter how hard I pulled on the reins, they would not stop. I was so scared." They walked over to the edge of the cliff. Miriam almost fainted. "It looks like it is twenty feet to the river from here. Oh, I could have been killed, if we had gone over the edge."

"I know, Miriam. That is why I ran so hard to try to catch the hayrack. But my lame leg just won't let me run that fast anymore. I sure didn't expect my team to spook like that, although when I saw that covey of quail burst up right under them, I knew we had a runaway starting."

Miriam's face was white as a sheet. "I'm so sorry, Timothy. I should have had a tighter hold on the reins," she said shakily.

"I think I had better take you right back to the house. You look awfully pale," Timothy said with gentle concern.

"I will be all right. Finish your loading and then you can take me back," Miriam responded bravely.

"If you are sure you are all right. I'm about finished with this load."

Miriam kept a tight hold on the reins while Timothy finished loading. She was still shaking from the frightening experience. Driving back to the farmyard, Timothy helped Miriam down. She hurried over to get him a drink. "You ran so hard, Timothy, I know that you hurt your leg," she said as she saw the pain in his eyes.

"Don't worry about me, Miriam. I'll be all right," he said as he drove on to the threshing machine.

Miriam walked slowly back to the house where Martha was visiting with the other farm wives. Martha saw Miriam's pale face. "What happened, Miriam? You look so pale," Martha asked worriedly.

"Can I talk with you alone, Mrs. Larsen?" Miriam asked with a trembling voice.

"Of course, my dear," Martha said, putting her arm around Miriam and leading her into the house where they could talk alone.

The minute they were inside, Miriam burst into tears. "I'm not fit to be Timothy's wife," she sobbed.

"Whatever are you talking about, Miriam? What happened out there to make you think such an outrageous thought? Let's go into the bedroom where we can talk without interruption. Come sit here beside me on the bed," Martha said leading her gently to the bed.

Miriam continued to cry while Martha waited for her to regain her composure. "Now why don't you tell me what happened?"

"I wanted to help Timothy, instead I let the team run away almost into the river. Timothy ran after it to catch them and I know that the run hurt his leg. I finally got them stopped at the edge of the cliff," Miriam started crying again at the thought. "Daniel came and turned them around. How can I ever be a wife for Timothy when I make mistakes like that?"

"Miriam, runaways happen many times during wheat threshing. The least possible provocation will set them off. Timothy will not blame you for it, and even if it had been your fault, that is no reason to think you are not fit to be Timothy's wife. I've done many crazy things since I have been married to Paul. However, he is very patient and helped me through them. You have just had your first lesson on being a farm wife. You have learned from the lesson and you will be an even better wife because of it," Martha assured her.

"Thank you, for helping me see that, Mrs. Larsen. I still feel bad about making Timothy run so hard on his weak leg," she said sadly.

"He will recover. It was his concern for you that caused him to run. I shudder to think what would have happened if you and Daniel had not been able to stop the team," Martha said, putting her arm around Miriam. "Now dry your tears and wash your face at the basin over there. Why don't you lie down here on my bed for awhile to recover from your scare."

"Don't you need my help taking drinks and sandwiches to the men?" Miriam asked.

"We won't have to take them for another hour or two. Esther can help me with that if you are still resting."

The rest of the threshing day went without incident. Miriam came out to find the men were getting ready to take their teams and go home. "Aren't they going to do anymore today? There are still lots of bundles in the field that I can see out the bedroom window," she asked in surprise.

"No, there is too much danger as it becomes evening. Men and horses can be injured in the coming darkness. They will be here first thing tomorrow morning," Martha answered.

"Do you want my help tomorrow?" Miriam asked.

"Why don't you just stay here tonight in Esther's room so you won't have to drive back after dark?" Martha suggested.

Timothy came into the house all covered with dirt and chaff. Hearing the end of the conversation he said strongly, "Yes, you stay, Miriam. I want to talk to you. Besides you have had enough excitement today."

Taking clean clothes, Timothy went out to join his brothers to bathe in the stock tank behind the barn. Coming back from his bath, Timothy beckoned for Miriam to join him out in the yard. "Ma told me when she brought lunch that you were blaming yourself for the runaway. I saw the covey of quail explode into the air under the horses. If you hadn't been there holding the reins, we would have lost both the team and the hayrack. I saw that you were trying to stop them and that Daniel was almost there to turn them around, so I slowed down my running. I think you did a wonderful job keeping the team from going into the river."

"Then you don't blame me for not stopping them sooner?" Miriam asked seriously.

"Miriam, you did as good as anyone could have done in a situation like that. Even if it had all been your fault, that is no reason for you to think that you are not fit to be my wife. We both will make many mistakes over the years. That won't change us from being fit to marry or being committed to stay married."

"Timothy, you are so wonderful to say that! Not all men would see it that way. When I took care of Mrs. Thompson with her new baby, I could see that he would blame her for things that were not even her fault. He even blamed her for not recovering sooner with this baby," she responded gratefully.

"My father has taught us all these years that God is in charge of everything that comes into our lives, and we need to learn lessons from each problem. Mr. Thompson doesn't understand how God works, because He doesn't know God."

"Nor does he act like he wants to know Him. Mrs. Thompson seemed afraid to tell him that she had accepted Christ," Miriam said sadly.

"Maybe after we get married, we can visit the Thompson family. He might allow us to share with the family about God."

"I know that Mrs. Thompson would love to have fellowship with other Christians," Miriam said.

"Guess what I am going to buy after I sell my share of the wheat next week," Timothy asked teasingly.

"Does it have something to do with our wedding?" Miriam asked with a smile.

"It could at that. I want to purchase your wedding ring at the Manifold Jewelry store."

"I can't wait to see it. Although, I suppose that will be at the wedding," she said excitedly.

"Yes, that will be your first look at it and then you can see it on your hand for the next 100 years," Timothy added happily.

"When do you think we should bring the piano I won out to the house? Now that the wall papering is done, the room is ready for it," Miriam asked gently.

"I am a little afraid to put anything of value out there until it gets closer to our wedding day. I will see what Father says about putting it there after we finish helping the neighbors with their threshing," Timothy promised.

"What about the other furniture that we need? Mother said that we could have her older kitchen cabinet and a small table and chairs. Are we going to purchase any new furniture?"

"We need to see what our parents have that they are not using and watch for auctions or sales. We may be able to get most of what we need without buying new," Timothy suggested.

"Mother also said that she had an extra kerosene lamp that we could have and Father is making me an ironing board," Miriam added.

"Once we get this threshing and plowing finished, we can meet with Rev. Stanwick to get his counsel on our wedding plans and on our marriage."

"Did you see in the *Gazette* that Noah and George Cline were building a steam boat for use during the Chautauqua in August? If you have any time for some relaxation, it would be fun to ride on it. They have a top deck for the Manifold band to sit and play a few numbers. Will your family be camping out at the park during the events?" Miriam asked.

"I am sure that we will be attending some of the celebration, although we won't be able to be there all ten days. I know there are some speakers and concerts Father has said he plans to attend. However, someone has to take care of the cattle and chickens during the day. Mother is usually busy canning the garden produce in August, so we really can't be gone for more than a day at a time. I will plan on taking you for a ride on the steam paddle boat," he assured her.

"I doubt if our family will be camping out overnight, although probably Emma and Jesse would like to camp out. With all the people coming in on the train, the park will be full and we would sleep better at home anyway. The man that I want to hear speak is Dr. William Spurgeon of England. I've heard so much about his newspaper writing. However, I couldn't believe that he would come to central Kansas to speak at our Chautauqua."

Miriam helped feed the threshing crew another day before leaving in the late afternoon. Timothy came to help her hitch up. "I'll see you Sunday. We will be moving to help the neighbors thresh the rest of the week. I can eat with your family Sunday, if you will have me." Timothy said with those bright blue eyes watching for Miriam's response.

"What do you mean, 'if we will have you'? You know you are almost part of the family by now. Elizabeth gets upset if you don't eat with us. She always has a story she is waiting to tell you or something to show you."

"I enjoy her also, she is a sweet little girl."

Arriving at home that evening, Miriam was met by Anna waving a letter in her hand. "You have received a letter from Mrs. Walter Van Squoit III. It is postmarked from Niagara Falls, New York."

"I can almost guess what she has written, 'I am having a wonderful time. Wish you were here,'" Miriam joked.

"You could open it and read it," Anna laughed.

"Give it here and I will read it to you. 'Dear Miriam, Walter and I are having a wonderful wedding trip. We have taken in several concerts and are planning on traveling on to New York City for a few days. I plan to attend a woman's suffrage meeting there while Walter looks into some contacts for his music. Walter is very desirous that women achieve the right to vote, so he encourages me to attend these meeting. We should be back in Boston in a week. Your friend, Mrs. Walter Van Squoit.'"

"You were correct, Miriam. Everything is wonderful, Walter is wonderful, and she is happy, happy, happy. Wonder what she will write if Walter doesn't provide her with a maid and she has to do the cooking. Maybe she will insist that Walter take her out to eat every meal," Anna responded.

"That would mean she would have to get up early to dress for eating breakfast and she couldn't sleep late every morning. No, that wouldn't work. Walter will just have to find a maid for her or he will suffer the consequences from Melody," Miriam said sarcastically.

"Now girls, Melody might surprise all of us and learn to keep house. We need to pray for them and not joke about all the problems they may have," Lydia reminded.

"You are right, Mother. I got carried away in my joking about Melody. I guess I don't have much faith that she will change after making so many wrong choices all these years. You would think by the time a woman is twenty she would be making more mature choices," Miriam commented.

"Talking about choices, Sarah Williams called and said that she wanted to see you as soon as you returned. She has made some changes in the dress she is sewing for the wedding, and wants to know what you think. Her husband can bring her by on the way to work tomorrow if you can take her home," Lydia reported.

"I'll telephone her right now. I want to talk to her anyway," Miriam responded eagerly.

Miriam was sewing on her wedding dress, when Sarah knocked on the door the next morning. Miriam greeted her, "Oh Sarah, come right in and show me what you have done with your dress."

Putting little Charles down to play with Elizabeth, Sarah pulled the dress out of her carpetbag and shook it out. "See, I took some of the apricot pieces left over and made ruffles to go down each panel of the skirt. How do you like it?"

"I love it! You are so talented. They should have you designing dresses for the big stores back East. It is prettier than the dresses they have in *Ladies Home Journal*," Miriam exclaimed.

"Thank you. I am glad you like it," Sarah responded modestly. "How are you coming on your wedding dress? Didn't you say you were making it out of cream colored silk satin?"

"Would you like to see what I have done so far? Sewing on all that lace by hand is taking so much time. Mother is making the veil for me."

"Yes, I would like to see it because you have told me enough to make me really anxious to see it," Sarah answered.

"Sarah, do you want to see how well my dress matches with yours?" Anna asked. "I've just about got it all sewn."

"Are all of you wearing different shades of apricot silk?" Sarah asked.

"Well, it looks like that since we found this wonderful sale at the New York Mercantile on dress goods. We bought all that they had and it was enough for each of the younger girls to have matching dresses," Miriam answered.

Lydia came into the room and watched for a minute, "Miriam, I was just thinking that you need to get your invitations to the wedding sent out. With all the work on the sewing, I had forgotten to mention them to you."

"Are you going to send an invitation to Mrs. Walter Van

Squoit III?" Anna asked with a laugh.

"I know one that I sure want to send and that is to Mr. Cramton's mother in Kansas City. She has been like a grandmother to me. I know she prays for me all the time," Miriam answered. "Do you think I should one to Melody, Sarah?"

"Since I don't know her, I am not a good judge of that. Although, since you have been good friends and she wanted you to come to her reception, I would say you should send one to her," Sarah answered.

"I can't imagine her coming all the way from Boston just for your wedding, Miriam," Jesse said as she listened while doing her hemming on a dress.

"I think that Sarah is right, you should send her an invitation, Miriam. That may give her an opportunity to ask you about your wedding and you can share with her how different a Christian wedding can be from the show she brought to Beloit," Lydia commented soberly.

"Then I will send one to Walter and Melody. We need to make up a list of those who need invitations."

The telephone rang and Lydia answered, "Yes, Mary, you can talk to Miriam. She is home from helping feed the threshing crew." She handed the receiver to Miriam.

"Yes, Mrs. Cramton, I can stop by today. You say that you have a surprise invitation for me? Now you are really making me curious. I will take Sarah home after dinner and will stop by soon after that, if that is acceptable with you. Thank you, good-bye."

"What do you think that Mary has in mind? She is always thinking of ways that she can help us. I wonder what it will be this time?" Lydia asked.

"I can't wait to talk to her. She sounded so excited with some plan that she has for me," Miriam answered.

After dinner, Miriam took Sarah and little Charles home and hurried back to the Cramton home. Mary was sitting at the dining room table when Jackson opened the door at Miriam's knock. "Come right over here, Miriam. This morning I came up with this most wonderful idea and I asked Thomas at dinner if it would be acceptable with him and he agreed," Mary said with a delightful smile.

"You've really got me curious, Mrs. Cramton. What do you have planned?"

"I would like for you to have your reception here at the house after your wedding in the garden. That way your guests could come in here for the cake and drinks and if they wanted, they could eat out in the garden. What do you think of that?"

"Oh, Mrs. Cramton, that would be so nice of you to provide that. However, I can't ask you to do all of my wedding. We were thinking of having everyone come to our home after the wedding or to the church. It would be asking too much for you to open up your home for everyone," Miriam said anxiously.

"Quite the contrary, Miriam. Both Thomas and I agreed that we wanted to do that for Melody's wedding. However, she was not interested in a small wedding here at home. It would be a real blessing to us if you would allow us to do this for you and Timothy," Mary assured her.

Fighting to keep back tears of joy, Miriam answered, "I would love it, Mrs. Cramton. You are such a special friend to our family."

"Then it is settled. The reception will be here and I will be talking to your mother about the plans. Annabel is also excited about the idea and wants to help me with it."

"Thank you so much, Mrs. Cramton. I must hurry home and tell mother. She was just reminding me today that I need to get the invitations for the wedding sent out. We can add this about the reception as I write. Knowing Mother, she may be over tomorrow to make the plans. She is so excited about this wedding, which is keeping us all busy along with the garden work and canning."

"Oh, Miriam, I just thought of something. What do you need in the way of furniture for your home? We have so much that we don't need, and my aunt who died last month willed me all of her furniture. Tell me what you need and I will have Thomas check to see if we have it. You are welcome to it, because we are going to have to sell it or give it away because it is taking up so much space."

"You continually surprise me, Mrs. Cramton. Didn't Melody want any of her aunt's furniture?" Miriam responded happily.

"Of course not. She said she and Walter were purchasing all their furniture in Boston and she did not want any old junk that Aunt Sofia had. So make a list of what you need and send it with your mother tomorrow."

"I can tell you right now that all we have is a piano that the *Gazette* gave me, a small table and chair and a kitchen cabinet from mother. That is all we have so far," Miriam answered.

Timothy finished up with the plowing early. The Chautauqua started in August, so while he was eating with the family following church, he said, "I am planning on next Tuesday to hear Dr. Spurgeon. If anyone cares to ride the steamboat with me, I can come early."

"I'm going with you, Timothy," Elizabeth said excitedly as she grabbed his hand.

"I will buy tickets for all of you girls to ride, if Miriam will allow all of you to come with us," he said looking mischievously at Miriam.

"Why shouldn't I allow them to come?" Miriam asked.

"Because I told my brothers and sisters that if you allowed all of your sisters to ride with us, then I would bring all of them also. I don't know if Daniel and Joseph will come. Although all the rest except for Isaac want to ride. He is too little to enjoy it."

"We will take up the whole boat with just our family," Miriam laughed. "Will your parents be coming in later or will we be substitute parents for eight all evening?"

"Pa said that they would be coming to hear Dr, Spurgeon, so we won't have them all evening."

Lydia and I will also be coming to hear Dr. Spurgeon. If he can come clear from England to take a job as editor of the Washington Post and takes the time to come to our little town, I should go hear him. I bet Thomas will be in the front row. Also I think the Manifold Band will be providing a concert that evening, so we will join you for that performance and relieve you of your large family,"Aaron said with a smile.

Tuesday afternoon, Timothy arrived in the Larsen carriage with one brother, Jonathan, and sisters, Esther and Ruth. Elizabeth was standing on the porch waiting for him to arrive. "I get to hold your hand, Timothy," she said jumping up and down excitedly. "I don't want to fall into the river."

"The last time you held my hand, Elizabeth, you got lost and scared all of us. Maybe you had better hold Miriam's hand today," Timothy reminded as he helped the girls into the carriage.

"No, I want to hold your hand," Elizabeth insisted.

Once at the dock, Timothy walked up to the booth and asked, "I want to purchase 10 tickets to ride *The Western Call.* What time will they be leaving?"

The ticket manager said, "You are the first to get tickets for this afternoon, so as soon as we get 30 or 40 more passengers, we will set off."

Miriam and Timothy herded their extended family into the boat. "Now, you hang on tight to Timothy, Elizabeth. I don't want you running around and falling off the boat," Miriam reminded strongly.

"I won't fall off the boat, there's snapping turtles in there," Elizabeth answered anxiously.

"How do you know there are snapping turtles in the

The Western Call steam paddle boat built in 1903 in Beloit.

river?" Timothy asked.

"'Cause Jonathan told me there were," Elizabeth answered emphatically.

"Jonathan, don't tell such stories unless you have seen the turtles," Timothy spoke sharply.

"Yes, Timothy, I'm sorry. I don't think there are turtles out there right now, Elizabeth," Jonathan answered meekly.

The Manifold band members climbed to their places on the top deck and started playing the marches they were famous for playing.

Miriam and Timothy were visiting, "How would you like to have this many children when we have our family?" Timothy asked happily, his big blue eyes on Miriam. No one noticed that Elizabeth had squirmed loose from Timothy's hand. There was a loud blast from the boat's whistle and a call "All Aboard" as the steam powered paddles began to turn.

"Where is Elizabeth, Timothy? She was there a minute ago. Why won't that girl stay where we put her? I don't see her anywhere down on the boat. Do you suppose she has gone up on the top deck to talk to the band members?" Miriam asked anxiously as she stood looking around the boat. "Did any of you see Elizabeth leave?" Miriam asked the others.

"I saw her over by the stairs a few minutes ago. However, I don't know where she went," Anna answered.

The boat was moving into the deeper part of the river. Suddenly someone from the upper deck screamed, "A little girl just fell overboard! Someone go after her."

Timothy and Miriam both ran to the side and saw that Elizabeth was out in the middle of the river with her dress floating up around her. "What are we going to do, Timothy? She can't swim," Miriam almost screamed.

Timothy already had his shoes off and was heading for the side of the boat. "I'm going after her. Tell them to stop until we can get her back in the boat," he called as he jumped into the water.

Everyone rushed to the side of the boat making it lean far into the water. "All of you back into your seats," the owner called. "You can tip us over and that won't help the little girl."

Miriam could see that Timothy had a hold of Elizabeth's clothes, although she was fighting to get on top of him. *Please Lord, keep her from fighting so he can bring her to safety,* she prayed.

Timothy was able to pull her close to the boat and a man reached down and pulled her out. Someone else gave Timothy a hand to pull him back into the boat.

When Miriam rushed to Elizabeth's side, she was choking, sputtering and crying all at once. Holding her tight, Miriam whispered, "You are all right, Elizabeth. Timothy pulled you out."

"I know a snapping turtle was biting me. Jonathan said they would bite off my fingers," she said spreading out her fingers to see if they were still there.

The manager of the boat said, "Looks like we better take you back to shore so you can get some dry clothes. After you have changed, come back to finish your ride."

"I guess we all will have to keep a closer watch on Elizabeth all the time. She is so curious to see everything and is never afraid to meet a stranger," Miriam said as she led Elizabeth off the boat. Timothy found his shoes and the rest followed him up the dock.

"Why did you ruin our boat ride, Elizabeth?" Tabitha asked. "Why don't you stay where you are told so we won't have to look for you all the time?"

"I thought it would be all right to go up and talk to the drummer upstairs. I told him that I wanted to learn to play a big drum like him. I didn't know the boat was ready to leave. It made me fall when I was looking over the side for turtles."

"It is not called upstairs, Elizabeth. It is the upper deck that you went to fall overboard," Emma complained.

"Let's not bother her anymore about it," Timothy reminded. "I am just thankful that I was able to save her. A little longer out there in stronger current, we might have both drowned."

CHAPTER NINETEEN

PREPARATIONS FOR THE WEDDING

Miriam HAD NO REQUESTS to deliver babies during the early part of August. "I am so glad that I've had this time to prepare for the wedding, Mother. If I'd been gone a week taking care of a new mother, I'd never have gotten everything done," she shared as they canned beans together. "Timothy told me Sunday that he would be coming in today so that Reverend Stanwick could talk to us about the wedding. He said that Reverend Stanwick would arrive at two. Do you think we'll be done with these beans by that time?"

"We're almost done. If not, Anna can help me finish them. I want you to have some canned goods for your pantry shelves."

"Timothy is going to bring a wagon so we can load up some of the furniture Mrs. Cramton is giving us. She wants us to take it all. It is enough to furnish our whole house. Her aunt must not have known that the Cramtons already had beautiful furniture and could buy anything they needed. I am very thankful for it. Father is supposed to quit work early so he can help load it and take it out to our farm. It will be fun fixing up each room just the way I want it," Miriam said joyfully.

Miriam finished hemming her wedding dress while the other girls worked on various sewing projects for the wedding. "Miriam, tell me again what I will be doing in your wedding?" Emma asked.

"You, Jesse, and Ruth Larsen will be ribbon girls and Tabitha will be flower girl and Elizabeth will be ring bearer."

"Are you sure that Elizabeth won't lose the ring or get so busy talking to everyone that she will forget to bring it at the right time?" Jesse asked.

"No one knows what Elizabeth will do, sometimes I think not even Elizabeth knows. But she should be able to hold the ring pillow for a few minutes. By the way, where is she now?" Miriam asked.

"She is sitting out in the porch swing. She said she couldn't help me clean our room," Tabitha answered.

Miriam found her on the porch swing. "I am waiting for Timothy," she informed Miriam. Soon he came driving in with the wagon. She ran out to meet him. Grabbing his hand, she pulled him around behind the house before Miriam could even greet him. She followed, to find Elizabeth showing him her collection of butterflies. "Look, Timothy, this one is my favorite. Her name is Samantha and this one is Polly," she said pointing to a large yellow and black one.

"They are very pretty, Elizabeth, but right now I need to talk to your sister before Reverend Stanwick arrives. Be a good girl and don't bother us while we talk to the preacher. We will be doing some serious talking. Do you think that you can do that?" Timothy said, looking down at her pleasantly.

"If you'll take me for a ride on the wagon, I might be able to be quiet," she smiled innocently.

"Now, Elizabeth, you shouldn't bother Timothy like that. We will be loading furniture and you would get in the way," Miriam interrupted.

"Oh, I think we could arrange for her to play in the house

296

with Seth Cramton. She wouldn't be in the way there," Timothy volunteered. "Yes, Elizabeth, you can ride in the wagon after we finish talking to Reverend Stanwick."

"Oh! Goody, goody," Elizabeth squealed as she ran to tell her mother and sisters."

"You spoil her, Timothy. She thinks she can talk you into doing anything," Miriam complained.

"I don't think she'll be any problem as long as she's in the house playing with Seth."

"You don't know Elizabeth very well, if you think that. However, maybe this time she will behave herself."

Walking back to the porch swing, Timothy said, "why don't we pray together before Reverend Stanwick arrives."

"Yes, I want God's leading in our wedding; that it will be a picture of Christ as the center of our marriage."

Following their prayer together, Miriam asked, "Do you want to take the furniture out to our house tonight?"

Before Timothy could answer, Reverend Stanwick drove up in his buggy and walked onto the porch with Miriam and Timothy. "Good afternoon, my young friends. Are we going to do our planning out here in the wonderful fresh air?"

"Yes, if that is agreeable with you. Take that seat there and we will sit here on the swing," Timothy responded, pointing to a wicker chair.

"I'm honored that you have chosen to get some counseling before your wedding. My greatest joy next to seeing someone accept Christ as Savior, is marrying a couple who know Christ and want to be obedient to Him," Reverend Stanwick said as he seated his six-foot frame in the chair.

"We want to make Christ the center of our marriage. Can you teach us how to do that?" Timothy asked.

"From all I know about the both of you, I imagine that you are already doing much of what I will recommend. Although, I shall give you some suggestions. First off, start the day with Bible reading together and praying for God's guidance. Also make it your priority to be with God's people regularly for worship."

"Yes, we have been reading the Bible some together and praying. Can you help us plan our wedding so it shows others that we want Christ to be center of our home?" Timothy asked seriously.

"I can bring that out in my short sermon during the wedding and you could say a few words about that yourself, Timothy." Reverend Stanwick nodded his head, shaking his heavy beard.

"I don't know if I am much of a talker up in front of everyone. I'll have to pray about that."

"Also, the songs that you choose can portray Christ and His love for His bride the church since Saint Paul told us men to love our wives as Christ loved the church."

"You have given us several possibilities, Reverend Stanwick. We'll need time to think and pray about this," Timothy said pensively.

"By the way, when and where is the wedding?"

"I forgot that we hadn't told you that the wedding will be the first Saturday in September at Thomas and Mary Cramton's rose garden at two o'clock," Timothy answered.

"As long as it is not raining, I see no problem with that. Do you have a place chosen in case of rain? You know that it does rain in Kansas at this time of year," Reverend Stanwick reminded.

"I think that the Cramton's would allow us to have the wedding in their home if it is raining," Miriam answered.

"Do you plan for the rehearsal to be in the evening before or that morning?" Reverend Stanwick asked.

"We would like to have it in the evening, because my family will have chores to do in the morning. It will hurry us to arrive before two o'clock," Timothy answered quickly.

"Well, it looks like you have done a good job planning. Do you have any more questions for me?"

"Would you pray for God's blessing on our wedding and marriage before you leave, Reverend Stanwick?" Timothy requested.

"I would be glad to do that. Most heavenly Father, we know that from the beginning You have planned for marriage where a man is to leave his father and mother and cleave to his wife and the two shall become one flesh. Now bless Timothy and Miriam as they finalize the plans for their wedding and may it be a picture of Christ's love for the church, His bride. In the name of our Lord and Savior, Jesus Christ, Amen."

"Thank you, Reverend. I forgot to ask you if you wanted us to have the rehearsal at the Cramton garden or at the church?" Miriam asked.

"If the wedding is to be at the Cramton's garden, then the rehearsal should be there also. And I love the great outdoors."

Reverend Stanwick shook hands with both of them. "Call me if you have more questions about the wedding service or need advice for your marriage."

As Reverend Stanwick drove away, Miriam said wistfully, "Timothy, I would like for you to share at the wedding why we want Christ to be the center of our marriage."

"If that will make you happy, I will see what God would have me say. I also have a request for the wedding. I would like your father to play his violin for the wedding. Being outdoors we won't have any other music unless we invite the Manifold band to play."

"I don't think we need the band. They probably do not know any hymns for weddings. I think probably Father would play some hymns."

Aaron came home early as they had requested, "Are we ready to go load furniture? If so I'll go hitch up the Smith's wagon. Going now should give us time to deliver it and unload before dark."

Elizabeth came running from behind the house, "I get to go with Timothy and Miriam," she said excitedly.

Aaron looked surprised at Timothy and Miriam. "Did you tell her that she could come along?"

"Timothy told me I could go, didn't you, Timothy?" Elizabeth asked quickly.

"Yes, I told her if she didn't disturb us while we were talking to Reverend Stanwick, that she could go with us and play with Seth while we loaded furniture."

"All right, Elizabeth, climb up with Miriam and Timothy and see to it that you behave yourself," Aaron cautioned.

"Before we leave, Mr. Jensen, could I ask a special request for our wedding?"

"Yes, Timothy, what is it?" Aaron responded warmly.

"Miriam and I would like for you to play hymns on your violin for our wedding."

"If you choose songs that I know, I might be willing to consider it. Although you must realize that I have never played for a wedding. One that I know that might be appropriate is, *Now Thank We All Our God.* You remember the words say, 'Who, from our mother's arms, Hath blest us on our way with countless gifts of love, And still is ours today.'"

"That would be a good one. Please play that one. Wish we had someone to sing the words," Timothy said quietly.

"Also, Timothy, you could sing. You have a good voice," Aaron reminded.

"I couldn't sing alone. Maybe Daniel would sing with me. I will ask him tonight," he pondered.

"That would be perfect, Timothy. Now that we have our music decided, let's go get our furniture," Miriam said joyfully.

They drove the two wagons to a door in the Cramton's stable. Jackson saw them and came to help, "Let me call Matthew to help. He is young and strong," Jackson said.

Miriam couldn't believe her eyes at seeing the furniture. It was like new. "Look at that beautiful oak dining table and chairs with a matching sideboard, and a china cabinet with diamond glass panes and plate racks. Here is even a heavy crocheted wool rug."

"Here is a box that says, 'china for six,'" Timothy said. "Does she want you to take that also?"

"Mrs. Cramton told me to take anything that we could use. She will give the rest of it away as they don't need it. Let me see the china. Oh, it has a gold edge so they are very expensive. Isn't it wonderful that God has answered our prayer for furniture?" Miriam exclaimed.

"Here is a brass bed in perfect condition with metal wire springs and a hair-filled mattress. That is an expensive set. There is a matching dressing table and wash stand."

"Look at the oak writing desk, just the thing I need for my Bible study and bookkeeping. In addition, there are matching bookshelves. This amount of furniture will about fill up our house," Timothy exclaimed.

Following loading both wagons completely full, Miriam said, "I am going inside to thank Mrs. Cramton for all of this wonderful furniture."

"Why don't you stay and visit with her about the wedding details while we take this out to the farm. My brothers can help unload it. Maybe Jackson could take you and Elizabeth home," Timothy said, looking at Jackson.

"You know that I will take you home anytime, Miss Jensen. Just call me when you are ready to head home," the old man answered pleasantly as he headed back to his roses.

"You mean you don't want me to go along and tell you where to set everything?" Miriam asked anxiously.

"You could go, although aren't there things you need to confer with Mrs. Cramton? You can come out anytime this week and pick up Esther to help you move the furniture to wherever your heart desires," Timothy said with a smile.

"I guess that will be all right if you will be very careful with the china cabinet and the china. I wouldn't want it broken before we even get to use it," Miriam said.

"We will handle them just like they were fresh eggs," Timothy assured.

"Come along, Timothy. Don't let my daughter make you promise anything impossible to fulfill. We want to get this unloaded so I can get back before suppertime," Aaron laughed.

Miriam stayed and visited with Mary, "Have you heard anything from Melody, Mrs. Cramton?" she asked in concern.

"Just a brief letter about their wedding trip. She wants us to believe that she is truly happy. And probably she is as long as she doesn't have to settle down and be a keeper of a home. She learned early from me about entertaining and she loves it. Staying home to cook and clean was never something that she was happy doing. She did enjoy cooking with you and your sisters. However, not here at home."

"Mrs. Cramton, we both know that Melody will have difficulties in the years ahead. That may be the way that God brings her back to obeying Him," Miriam reminded.

"I hope you are correct, Miriam. Now, to change the subject, is there something we need to talk about for the wedding?"

"Yes, Timothy and I have decided that we need to feed supper to our out-of-town guests and we plan to do that at our home."

"Wouldn't it be easier for everyone to stay right here following the reception and eat rather than have everyone drive over there? We would be all set up," Mary encouraged.

"Mother said that you had insisted on providing everything for the reception so we can't ask you to provide your

302

home for the supper. You have done too much already," Miriam persisted.

"Nonsense. I love doing this for you," Mary answered.

"It will mainly be my kinfolk from Kansas City who would stay to eat supper. Timothy said that most of his kinfolk live close to Beloit, so they wouldn't stay for supper," Miriam answered gently.

"All right, if you insist, although I love doing it. You can see where Melody learned her love of entertaining. There is one thing about the reception that I forgot to ask you about. What kinds of wedding cake do you and Timothy want?

"Yes, I was thinking we were going to provide that so I forgot to tell you. Timothy has requested the dark rich fruitcake that has been a tradition in his family for weddings. I can ask his mother for the recipe. I know that it has lots of raisins, eggs and brandy. His mother said that for some weddings, they would cut small wedges of the cake and pack them in dainty white boxes for the guests to take home."

"Please bring the recipe at the earliest possible moment so Annabel can have it made and curing. Fruitcake is always better if it is cured."

"Oh! Look at what time it is. I should get Elizabeth home before Mr. Cramton comes home for supper. Thank you so much, Mrs. Cramton, for all that lovely furniture. It is nicer than anything that Timothy and I could have purchased. We had been praying that God would help us find some used furniture and He did," Miriam said, giving Mary a hug.

"I am so glad that you could use it, Miriam. Since Melody didn't want any of it, I was going to have to sell it or give it away. Melody said that she and Walter would purchase their furniture in Boston," Mary sniffed sadly.

"Do you know where Seth and Elizabeth are playing? I haven't heard them since we have been talking," Miriam asked.

"They are probably playing in the garden. See if Jackson

has seen them," Mary suggested.

Miriam hurried out the door to look for the children. Seeing Jackson trimming roses, she called, "Jackson, have you seen Seth and Elizabeth? Mrs. Cramton said they had been playing out here."

"They were here for awhile, although I haven't seen them for thirty minutes or more. I didn't notice that they were gone. Maybe they are playing out in the woods by the lane."

"I'll go look in that cave Melody and I used to play in when we were girls," Miriam said as she gathered up her skirt for a fast walk down to the woods. The weeds around the woods were so tall that it was difficult to see anything. So she carefully made her way through the weeds and walked under the trees to the cave. *They are not here. Where could they be? Lord, help me find them. Knowing Elizabeth, she probably insisted that Seth go somewhere with her,* Miriam thought as she made her way back through the tall weeds.

Arriving back to the garden, Miriam asked, "Jackson, could you take me down the road in the buggy to see if we can find them? I've looked everywhere around here. Mrs. Cramton will become worried if we don't find them soon," Miriam said anxiously.

Jackson came quickly with the buggy and helped Miriam up, "They may have gone downtown. I wasn't paying much attention. However, it seems like I remember Elizabeth saying something about ice cream. I figured she meant that Annabel was giving them some."

Miriam watched both sides of the street as they drove along looking for some sign of Elizabeth and Seth. "Do you see any sign of them, Jackson? Surely they couldn't have gone very far in thirty minutes."

"That little sister of yours moves mighty fast. I saw her dragging Seth all around the yard this afternoon and he couldn't get lose from her hold," Jackson said laughing.

They were almost to the Ice Cream Palace when Miriam

spotted Elizabeth pulling Seth along. He didn't seem willing to go with her so she was not allowing him to let go of her hand.

"Let me off here, Jackson, I see them. Looks like Elizabeth is responsible for the whole plan," Miriam said, as she stepped down from the buggy.

"Don't be too hard on her, Miss Jensen. They are safe and we found them quickly."

Walking up behind them, Miriam could hear Elizabeth telling Seth, "Just come in with me and I will get you ice cream too. I have a nickel."

"Let's go back home, 'Lizbeth. Papa won't like it that I came downtown. He spanked me the last time I left without asking Mama," Seth said almost in tears.

"Where did you get a nickel, Miss Jensen?" Miriam asked as she caught up with them.

"You scared me, Miriam! Seth and I are going to get some ice cream. Aren't we Seth?" Elizabeth asked innocently.

"No, my Papa will spank me if I don't get home right away," Seth replied and reached for Miriam's hand for support.

Taking Elizabeth by the hand, Miriam said determinedly, "You are coming home right now, Elizabeth Jean."

"I didn't get my ice cream," Elizabeth sobbed.

"We are taking Seth home right now before his mother worries about him. Then Jackson is taking you and me home right after that," Miriam insisted.

Elizabeth buried her head in her hands and cried, "I want some ice cream."

At the Cramton home, Jackson got down from the buggy and without a word, marched Seth into the house. Coming right back, he climbed into the seat and drove off.

"I don't want to go home," Elizabeth said bursting into tears again.

"You are going home, Elizabeth," Miriam said firmly.

Arriving at home, Miriam took Elizabeth by the hand and

headed for the house just as Aaron came driving into the yard with the farm wagon. Elizabeth took one look at her father, jerked loose from Miriam's hand and ran to climb upon the seat, "Please don't spank me, Papa," she sobbed.

"What are you talking about, Elizabeth?" Aaron asked, looking at Miriam for an answer.

"She can tell you, Papa," Miriam said. Jackson drove off shaking his head.

Aaron lifted Elizabeth off the wagon and started for the house, "You and I need to have a talk, young lady." Walking into the house and seeing that supper was waiting on the table he said, "Elizabeth and I need to have a talk before we come to supper." With that comment, he walked into the bedroom and closed the door.

"What happened, Miriam?" Lydia asked after the door was closed.

"She took Seth and walked downtown. He kept begging to come back. However, she wouldn't let him. She said that she had a nickel for ice-cream."

A much-subdued Elizabeth came out to supper. "Let's ask the blessing for our meal," Aaron said as he sat Elizabeth on her chair and sat beside her.

The week before the wedding, Miriam said, "Esther and I have the house all arranged, Mother. The wedding dresses are all finished, so all we have to do is fix food for the supper after the wedding. I am going to bake up extra bread and pies."

"Did I tell you that Aunt Mable and Uncle Charles and the girls are coming for the wedding? They telephoned today so I told them they were staying with us. Aaron's grandmother and aunt will be coming from Minneapolis, but they made reservations at the Anderson house."

Timothy arrived that evening for a short visit. "I was visiting with our new neighbor today and he said that his wife's baby was due soon. He wondered who he should call when the time arrived. I hope that it was all right that I told him to call you," Timothy asked in question.

"Timothy, I don't know if I can go. What if they call before the wedding? You should have told him to call Dr. Blackwood," Miriam said apprehensively.

"You know the way babies are. That baby may not arrive for another week or two. I don't think you have any need to worry."

"I hope you are right, because the last minute details take so much time. Mother can't do all the cooking for the supper and still prepare for company."

"Let's not worry about it. I came here to read some Scripture with you and pray before heading home. I plan to pick up our cook stove and chimney pipe tomorrow so that I can get it all set up."

"Do you also want to pick up the piano that I won? It is still at the store waiting for us to pick it up," Miriam reminded.

"Yes, I think it would be safe at the house now with only three days until the wedding. Daniel can stay at the house until we get back from our little trip."

"With all your farm work now, you still plan to take a trip? I really appreciate you for doing that. Where are we going?" Miriam questioned.

"It is a surprise. I don't want to take any chances of my mischievous friends finding us," Timothy said mysteriously. "Let's read the story of Ruth and Boaz from the Bible. It is a wonderful description of Christ-like love."

"I love the book of Ruth also, Timothy." They read and prayed together. Timothy got up to leave saying, "I need to get home so I can get an early start to finish everything at the house tomorrow. I will see you Friday at the rehearsal."

Sometime in the middle of the night, the telephone rang. Aaron stumbled out to answer it. "Yes, this is the Jensen home. Yes, Miriam Jensen lives here. You say that Timothy Larsen told you to call her when your wife was ready to have her baby. Wait just a minute while I call her."

Going to wake Miriam he whispered, "Miriam, Timothy's neighbor just called to see if you could come deliver their baby. Shall I tell them to call Dr. Blackwood?"

"No, Father, I have time to go out to deliver it. Tell him I will be out as soon as I get dressed and get Ginger harnessed up."

"I am taking you out, Miriam. I don't like for you to be out alone at night."

"Father, I don't want to make you to miss your sleep. I have driven Ginger after dark before."

"I insist. This may be the last time I get to take you for a ride before you become Timothy's bride. Besides, it is a beautiful moonlight night," Aaron responded.

Once they were out on the road, Miriam said, "Father, I really appreciate all that you have done to protect me. Timothy appreciates it also."

"God made fathers responsible for protecting and caring for their families."

"I know that. However, you do so much more. I am thankful that God put me in our family and that you are my father," Miriam said gratefully.

"I know that Timothy will be your protector also, Miriam. He already is watching over you in so many ways. God has prepared a mighty good husband for you."

"I know, Father, and I am so thankful that God kept me from getting involved with Marshall Thompkins."

"This is such a beautiful night that I hate for our little journey to end, although here we are at the Russell farm. I see that they have a light burning. I'll wait until you are inside so if there is anything you need, come back out and get me."

Miriam gathered up her skirts and made her way to the door. Mr. Russell answered her knock. "Come in Miss Jensen. My wife says the baby is coming right away. I hated to call you at this time of night. However, she insisted. Call me if I can bring anything for you."

After checking Mrs. Russell, Miriam came to the door and asked, "Would you tell my father to go on home. I think I won't need Dr. Blackwood's help. Could you find me some green soap so I can do a thorough job of washing up? I see that you already have the water heated. That helps so much."

Going back to Mrs. Russell, Miriam asked, "Is this your first baby, Mrs. Russell?"

"No, we have a little girl two years old."

"Did you have any trouble with her birth?"

"No, not much. Although it was a long trying session. I was with labor pains for two days."

"It won't be that long this time. You were correct in saying that the baby is arriving soon."

Within a couple of hours, a baby boy was born. "You have a little boy, Mr. Russell," Miriam called to him, as he was sitting out in the kitchen. "Would you like to come bathe and dress him while I finish helping your wife?"

"Sure thing, a little boy! Just think of that. I'm glad they both are all right. When you finish, Miss Jensen, there is an extra bed where you can rest. Timothy told me that your wedding was Saturday so I know that you need the rest. My mother-in-law will be coming tomorrow so I can take you home after breakfast."

"I would be most grateful since we have cooking to do tomorrow. I told Timothy that he should have recommended Dr. Blackwood for you to call."

"My wife wanted a midwife. She doesn't want a doctor delivering her babies. Thank you for being willing to come," he spoke sincerely.

Miriam was asleep the minute she fell into bed after taking care of Mrs. Russell. She was still sleeping when she thought she heard a baby crying. Getting up and dressing, she noticed that it was late in morning. "Oh, I should have been out there cooking breakfast." She hurried with her dressing and opened the door to find Mr. Russell cooking oatmeal for a little girl at the table. "I am so sorry for not waking up. What can I do to help?"

"I knew you were tired and my ma taught me to cook. Set yourself down and have a bowl of oatmeal with us. Agatha heard the baby crying, so I took the little one to her and he is having his breakfast. She seems to be feeling much better than she did when Samantha was born."

Mrs. Russell's mother arrived soon after breakfast. "Are you ready to leave for home, Miss Jensen? Here is a ham for your services. It might be something you can use for your wedding supper," Mr. Russell said.

Arriving at home, Miriam found her mother and sisters cooking. "I guess you don't need my help."

"No, if you want to rest this morning, that will be all right with us," Lydia said.

"I think I will go see if Mrs. Cramton needs any help with the reception and go out to talk to Sarah. I forgot to tell her that she will have to stand in for me during the rehearsal," Miriam said joyfully.

At the Cramton home, Miriam walked out to look at the rose garden. Roses of every color were in bloom. Reds, pinks, yellows of every hue, some climbing and others were surrounding the garden. And the wonderful perfume of their smell greeted her. Seeing Jackson still pruning and watering, Miriam sat down to watch a few minutes. "Jackson, you have done a marvelous job. It looks and smells just like heaven out here."

"I didn't know there was going to be roses in heaven. They have thorns and weren't thorns punishment for Adam and Eve's sin?" Jackson asked half in jest.

"You have stumped me there, Jackson. Maybe there will be thornless roses in heaven. You will be at the wedding and reception, won't you? I forgot to send you an invitation. However, I want you sitting right here with everyone else."

"I ain't got a suit. All I have is some overalls," he mumbled.

"You come in your overalls. Maybe Mr. Cramton could loan you a white shirt and jacket. I will ask Mrs. Cramton when I go inside. Just make sure that you are here."

"Can I come to the rehearsal? Usually that is more entertaining," Jackson said with a laugh.

"You are welcome to come to the rehearsal tomorrow evening. We might even have you be a flower girl," Miriam joked.

"I've never been to a wedding before, so this will be real special. Annabel and I can't wait for the excitement to begin."

Miriam knocked lightly on the door and stuck her head in and called, "Is the reception hostess accepting callers today?"

"She certainly is, and you are just the lady that I needed to talk to about some of the plans. Annabel thinks we should have orange flavored punch. However, I think we should have strawberry. What is your choice?"

"I guess my choice is strawberry. I really am not particular. What have you done to this room? Isn't that a new chandelier? And you've added new mirrors haven't you? And all these potted plants, where did you get them?"

"I have been wanting a new chandelier since Seth threw his ball and broke part of the old one. Jackson grew the potted plants for me, and Thomas thought we needed more mirrors. He likes mirrors. Your wedding just speeded up plans we already had," Mary said excitedly. "I am getting more excited every day. Would you like for me to serve some refreshments following the rehearsal?"

"You have already done so much, Mrs. Cramton. I thought we would just have everyone come over to our house for some tea and cookies."

"I would enjoy visiting with everyone. You are all friends. I don't know Sarah or Timothy's brothers very well so please come here. I won't want to miss any of the celebration."

"Certainly, we will come for light refreshments tomorrow evening. Promise me that you won't go to a lot of time and expense," Miriam reminded.

"I'll let Annabel decide what we should serve. It will be a surprise."

"I need to go see how Sarah is coming with her plans for the wedding. She was looking for someone to take care of little Charles for the day so she would have time to dress. If I hurry I can visit her and be back for dinner. Thank you for everything, Mrs. Cramton."

Driving out to Sarah's farm, Miriam looked up at the big fluffy clouds. *Thank you, God for such a beautiful day. I could just sing with happiness. You have blessed me super abundantly. Even the sunflowers and goldenrod look happy today.* Turning into Sarah's drive, Miriam saw her out in the yard with little Charles. "Sarah I'm back from being a midwife. Do you have a minute to talk? There is something I forgot to ask you about the wedding," Miriam called as she stepped down from the buggy.

"You mean there is something we haven't gotten done? Seems like there are a million and one details to putting together a wedding."

"This is fairly simple. I read in the *Ladies Home Journal* that it is not good for the bride to participate in the rehearsal. She is just supposed to watch. I want you to stand in my place."

"You mean I have to be both bride and brides maid? Won't that be a little confusing?" Sarah laughed.

"I just want to do everything right. Also, bring your husband tomorrow night. Mrs. Cramton is going to serve refreshments after the rehearsal."

Friday morning, the whole Jensen family was scurrying around like little mice. "We must get all the washing done and the house cleaned before noon because your Aunt Mable and Uncle Charles are arriving on the train," Lydia reminded the girls after breakfast. "I will cook the dinner while Miriam and Anna work on the washing. Jesse and Emma, I need you both to sweep and dust. Tabitha and Elizabeth, you can wash and put away the breakfast dishes and set the table for an extra four arriving for dinner."

Miriam and Anna already had water heating in the copper boiler to start the wash out in the lean-to. "I wish Jesse wasn't busy, she could run the wringer to speed up the washing," Anna said.

"As soon as I get the white clothes boiled, I will run the wringer while you rinse. This new soap that Mrs. Smith made sure cleans better than the batch we made. I am going to get her recipe and make some for Timothy and me. It makes washing go faster."

Miriam and Anna were hanging the last load on the clotheslines as Aaron came driving in with the carriage bringing Uncle Charles, Aunt Martha, and their two girls. The girls waved and hurried to greet them. "Oh, it is so good to see you, Miriam. Coming for your wedding has been a highlight of our summer plans," Aunt Mable said as she gave Miriam a hug.

Elizabeth came running out the door and asked, "Which one of you is Elizabeth?"

Her eighteen-year-old cousin smiled and said, "I am Elizabeth."

Little Elizabeth took her cousin by the hand, "Then you are going to sit with me for dinner. We two Elizabeths need to stick together," she announced while pulling Elizabeth into the house.

Anna called laughingly after them, "Watch out, Elizabeth, of anything my little sister might suggest."

Once they had greeted everyone, Lydia said, "The food is ready. We really need to eat before it gets cold."

"Let's thank our Lord for the food," Aaron said.

"The rehearsal is this evening, Martha. You and your family are welcome to come and watch, or you can stay here to rest from your trip," Lydia announced.

"I think we would prefer to rest. Leave the supper dishes for us so that we can be useful," her sister responded.

Miriam visited awhile in the parlor with her aunt and uncle, although all the noise was disturbing her. "I think I will take a walk, Mother. I need some time alone to think." She started for the door after getting her parasol.

Suzanne, her oldest cousin, followed her to the door. "Would you mind if I came along? There is something serious I need to share with you," she said quietly.

"No, if you don't mind taking a long walk. Get your parasol and come along."

Walking down the lane together, Suzanne said, "It seems like years since we talked. The last time your family was in Kansas City, you were there such a short time we didn't have any time alone. I have some serious questions about marriage. You wrote that you and Timothy wanted to make Christ the center of your home. How do you find a husband like Timothy? Some of the young men in our church seem so a - well - picayune, if you know what I mean. They only seem interested in themselves and getting rich. From what you have written about Timothy, he doesn't seem to be that way."

"Why don't you come to the rehearsal tonight and meet Timothy. You are correct, he is not that way. He and I have been praying ever since we were young, that God would find a strong Christian for us to marry. Our fathers both saw that we had that goal and agreed for us to court. Keep praying, Suzanne, and don't let Satan tempt you into something less than someone who loves God. I almost fell for Satan's trap with a handsome new attorney in town. He was exciting and cultured. However, not a Christian, although he came to church. God opened my eyes before I made a terrible mistake and missed the one God had prepared for me," Miriam confided hesitantly.

"Please continue to pray for me, Miriam, that I won't get ahead of God. I know that it would be better to never marry than to be disobedient to Him."

"You are so right, Suzanne. And God does not say that everyone should marry. Saint Paul said if we are content to be single then we should stay that way, so that we have more time for the Lord's work," Miriam said seriously.

By the time the girls returned from their walk, supper was being prepared. "Miriam, Timothy telephoned to say that Reverend Stanwick would like to talk to the both of you before the rest of us arrived for rehearsal. Timothy said he would come by to pick you and your father up right after supper. He said something about needing to practice singing with the violin before anyone else heard him," Lydia reported cheerfully.

It was a beautiful Indian summer evening with just a breath of wind. Miriam and Suzanne waited on the porch swing for Timothy to come. Elizabeth came out and stood in front of Miriam. "Why can't I go early, too? I am in the wedding."

"No, Elizabeth, you need to stay here and take care of your cousin, Elizabeth, so she won't be lonesome while we are gone. You can bring her to rehearsal if she would like to come."

Aaron came out as Timothy pulled in the drive. Looking back into the house he said, "I will come back for you and the girls, Lydia, as soon as we finish practicing our music." To Timothy he called, "I will take my own rig so that I can come back for Lydia and the girls." He walked to the barn carrying his violin case.

"My father has never played for a wedding before so he is doing this as a special favor for Timothy. He seems so proud to have a son-in-law like Timothy," Miriam said to Suzanne.

Timothy came to help the girls into the buggy. "Timothy, this is my cousin, Suzanne Watson. She is praying that God will

315

bring a God-fearing husband into her life," Miriam said with a little chuckle.

"Pleased to meet you, Miss Watson. Inspite of Miriam's teasing, I assume you are serious in your request," Timothy responded congenially.

"Yes, I am very serious about it. I have seen too many of my friends having their marriage fail after only a few years. I know that God has something better."

Reverend Stanwick was sitting in the rose garden visiting with Jackson when Timothy and Miriam arrived with Suzanne. "Well, are you both ready for the big step?"

"Yes, we are," they both answered at once.

Miriam introduced Suzanne to Jackson. "This man grew these beautiful roses. Maybe he can tell you some of his secrets for growing them so large while we talk to Reverend Stanwick," she said.

Aaron went over to a corner of the garden and started practicing on his violin. Timothy and Miriam sat in front of Reverend Stanwick. "I need to check with you on the final details before the rest arrive, and to pray together." They discussed with him the order of the service and the additions they had added like Timothy and Daniel's duet. "Do you have a particular scripture that you would like me to read?"

"Yes, please read I Corinthians thirteen, the love chapter. We want that to be true of our marriage," Timothy answered immediately.

"That is a wonderful chapter. Marriages would last a lifetime if people applied even half of those attributes of love," Reverend Stanwick answered emphatically with his beard jumping.

"If you have no more questions for us, Reverend Stanwick, I would like to practice with my future father-in-law on our song," Timothy said.

"Go right ahead. Jackson and I have not finished our con-

316

versation about growing roses."

Miriam took Suzanne over to meet Thomas and Mary who were sitting near the house thoroughly enjoy the whole proceedings. "Mr. and Mrs. Cramton, this is my cousin, Suzanne Watson, from Kansas City. I asked her to come to rehearsal so she could meet Timothy."

"Yes, I am so eager to learn about a Christian marriage," Suzanne answered wistfully.

Soon the Larsen family arrived and Aaron returned with Lydia and the girls. Everyone was in a jovial mood. Miriam sat with Jackson while Sarah stood in her place as bride. Before the rehearsal started, little Elizabeth came up to Timothy and reached for his hand. "Timothy, will you still come to see me after you marry Miriam? I will miss you so much. Will you come see me?" she asked sadly.

Timothy stooped down beside her and gave her a hug. "Elizabeth, we will probably be at your home almost as much as we are now. If your mother will have us, we will eat with you every Sunday and you can come out to visit us anytime. You could even stay overnight, if your sister approves."

"Oh, goody, goody. I will go tell my butterflies that you will be back," Elizabeth said as she skipped away.

Aaron was so nervous starting his music that he squawked and squeaked through a few notes. Although once he relaxed, it was beautiful in the evening air. Timothy and Daniel sang through one verse of, *Now Thank We all Our God* and Timothy gave a brief version of his talk.

They were ready to practice the part where Elizabeth hands the ring to the best man. "No! I am not going to give it to you," she told Daniel who reached for it. Everyone started laughing much to her enjoyment.

Aaron came over and whispered to her. "Now, do that part of the ceremony again, Reverend." This time Elizabeth handed the make-believe ring to Daniel.

Reverend Stanwick said, "Let's end this rehearsal with prayer. Lord, we thank you that Timothy and Miriam have chosen to be obedient to you and enter into Christian marriage. May they be blessed by their obedience. In the name of Jesus. Amen."

Thomas called to everyone after the rehearsal, "You are all invited inside for some refreshments."

Miriam walked into the house with Suzanne and Timothy. "Look at all this food, Timothy! I told Mrs. Cramton not to go to a lot of work. She has enough food here for fifty people." Turning to Mary who was sitting in her chair near the table, she said, "Mrs. Cramton, you didn't listen to me. I told you not to make anything fancy. This is a banquet."

"Yes, these are some wonderful fixins' you and Mr. Cramton have provided," Timothy said as he popped a stuffed olive in his mouth.

"I had Annabel make some Marlborough sherbet because I love it. With all the fruit juices, it tastes good on a late summer evening," Mary said with her face glowing. "I told you that I loved to entertain and I am so happy for you and Timothy. I haven't been this happy since Thomas accepted Christ."

It was almost nine o'clock before anyone started to leave. "We really must get these girls to bed, Aaron, or I will never be able to get them out of bed tomorrow."

"Yes, we must be going. Reverend Stanwick, Thomas, and I were having such a good visit. Seems like we are too busy other times for a good long visit."

Timothy was visiting with Sarah William's husband like he was an old friend. Going out the door together, Miriam said, "Sarah it looks like our husbands enjoy being together also. I am thankful for that. You will have to come out and visit us next week after we arrive home from our trip."

Suzanne rode home with Miriam and Timothy. "It is so peaceful and relaxing out here away from the city noise. I hope that sometime I can live in a small town like this. I remember how you thought this would be a very dull place, Miriam. And just think what has happened since that time. If you had not moved here, you would have never met Timothy."

"I didn't know that you used to think that Beloit was such a dull, small town, Miriam. What changed your mind?"

"You mean who changed it? It was Melody. Anna and I started visiting with her and from that time on, life became almost too exciting. I think we had the guardian angels awfully busy during those first years here. Someday I will have to tell you some of the escapades Melody thought up and I went along with to try to talk some sense into her."

"Is this Melody coming to the wedding tomorrow?" Suzanne asked.

"We sent her and her new husband an invitation, even though they live in Boston. I don't expect them to come. As I said, I never know what to expect from Melody. She constantly surprises me."

Helping the girls down from the buggy, Timothy said, "Get a good night's sleep, Miriam. We have a busy day tomorrow."

"I will try, Timothy. However I am so wound up now that I may not sleep a wink. Good night and you get some rest also."

Suzanne asked Miriam as Timothy drove away, "I noticed that Timothy has a slight limp. Was he born with that problem?"

"No, it just happened this winter when he broke his leg. It is a long story, although the result is our wedding. It brought us closer together through some difficult circumstances. God taught us many lessons through that time," Miriam answered fervently.

Martha helped Lydia prepare beds so that soon everyone was in bed. Miriam lay in bed beside Anna after they had prayed together. Her thoughts were racing down so many roads. "I am never going to get to sleep," she was thinking. Anna noticed that she was still awake.

"Do you want to talk, Miriam. Can't you sleep?"

"I can't seem to go to sleep. Just think, tomorrow afternoon I will be Mrs. Timothy Larsen!"

"I will miss our nightly talks and prayers together. However, I am so glad that you are marrying Timothy. Pray that I will have a husband like that should the Lord want me to get married."

"I have prayed for all of you since I realized what an important decision marriage is to God. I am thankful that Father helped me find Timothy."

CHAPTER TWENTY

THE WEDDING

EARLY SATURDAY MORNING, Miriam thought she was dreaming. "It's raining!" she exclaimed as she jumped out of bed to look out the window.

Anna rolled over and moaned, "What are you doing up so early? You woke me up from a lovely dream."

"I heard it raining. It can't rain on our wedding day! I am going to ask the Lord to roll the clouds away like the song we have been singing in church, 'It's Just Like His Great Love. It's just like Jesus to roll the clouds away. It's just like Jesus to keep us day by day.'"

"Would you mind doing your praying somewhere else and let me go back to sleep?" Anna asked groggily.

Miriam knew she couldn't go back to sleep so she dressed and slipped quietly into the parlor and lit a lamp. She opened her Bible to Psalms, which had always been a comfort to her. *Heavenly Father, I need some encouragement today. You know that I don't want rain today. However, if that is Your plan for our special day, help me to accept it.* Reading through Psalms 136 she thought, *You said, Lord, that Your mercy endures forever and that you alone can do great wonders. So I know that you can make the rain stop.*

She was continuing to read when Lydia came to start

breakfast. Coming to the door, she said, "Couldn't you sleep, honey? I know that it will be an exhilarating day for you."

"The rain woke me up. I have asked God to roll the clouds away. However, this time alone has been good for me. I needed to talk to the Lord," Miriam said seriously.

"Would you like to help me with breakfast? Slices of that ham that the Russell family gave you for delivering their baby would taste good. Is Anna awake, we could use her help now."

"Well, I woke her up complaining about the rain. I think she fell back to sleep. I will go call her."

The rest of the family began wandering in for breakfast. Aunt Martha said, "That is a wonderful smell to wake up anyone. I love the smell of ham."

"I received the ham as payment for delivering the Russell's baby this week," Miriam said.

"You must be very busy, if you are delivering babies two days before your wedding."

"Usually I am not that busy. There are other women who deliver babies. However, Timothy had told his new neighbor that I delivered babies, so they called me."

Everyone seated themselves around the table for breakfast. Aaron said, "Let's pray. Lord, we ask your special blessing on Miriam and Timothy today that their wedding will go well and that You would bless their marriage. Thank You for this food and the hands that provided it, Amen."

Immediately after the breakfast, little Elizabeth asked, "Can I put on my wedding dress now? I like to swirl around with all those ruffles."

"No, Elizabeth, we have to curl your hair this morning after we give you an egg shampoo to help it to curl. We will also eat dinner before you can put on your dress," Lydia answered.

"Mother, would you want me to help with fixing Tabitha's and Emma's hair?" Miriam asked.

"That would help. Anna could you press all the dresses

322

while Miriam is busy with the girl's hair. The flat iron is heating on the stove."

"Suzanne, Elizabeth, and I can do the dishes, Lydia," Martha suggested.

"That would be most helpful if you would."

"I think the best thing for us men, Charles, is to find something to do outdoors. The rain seems almost stopped and I need to curry the horses and get the carriage cleaned up for this afternoon," Aaron said.

"Lead on and I will follow," Charles answered his favorite brother-in-law.

The telephone rang in the middle of the morning. Lydia answered. "Yes, Mary, we will need to make two trips to deliver everyone to the wedding. You say that you are sending Jackson to pick up Miriam and her sisters. That would be wonderful. What time will he be coming? All right, they will be ready at 1:30. Thank you so much."

Hanging up the receiver, Lydia said, "Jackson insisted on coming to pick you and your sisters up for the wedding in the Cramton's new carriage. He wouldn't allow Matthew to come."

"You should see their new carriage, Mother, it is beautiful with fringe all around the top. With those beautiful black horses, it is a carriage fit for a queen. You will be queen today, Miriam," Anna said.

"Is there anything I can do to prepare dinner, Lydia?" Martha asked.

"Yes, we are going to slice those fresh tomatoes, cut up the roast beef from yesterday and have slices of the bread Miriam baked. That should be sufficient since Mary will probably have another banquet prepared for the reception."

Aaron came into the house before noon and announced, "You may not have noticed that the sun is shining and the grass is drying out. It is going to be a wonderful Indian summer day after all."

"Thank you, Lord!" Miriam exclaimed with joy. She sat down with the family to eat dinner. "I am not hungry. I think I would rather start getting dressed. It is going to take extra time to fix my hair."

"I will help you, Miriam, as soon as I finish with my dinner," Anna said.

"Take your time, I need to pack some clothes for our trip."

"Where are you going, Miry?" little Elizabeth asked.

"It is a secret, and not for little girls with big ears," Aaron chuckled.

"I am going to ask Timothy if I can go," Elizabeth responded.

"No, Elizabeth, you can not go. This trip is just for Miriam and Timothy," Aaron stated strongly.

Elizabeth began to pucker up, "I want to go with them. Timothy is my friend."

"Elizabeth, I think you and I need to have a little talk," Aaron said, while taking her by the hand to the bedroom.

"Don't spank me, Papa," she cried.

"I am not going to spank you. We just need to talk," he said closing the door behind them.

"Do you suppose that she will do her part in the wedding as she is supposed to do?" Anna questioned.

"After your father has finished talking to her, she should be obedient," Lydia said quietly. "At least I hope she doesn't create a scene during the wedding."

With Anna's help, Miriam started dressing, starting with the white cotton drawers embroidered with her maiden initials, then her chemise, next the corset which Anna laced for her and two petticoats. "Now I am ready to put on the wedding dress that took so long to make and press. I am afraid that I will wrinkle it before the wedding," Miriam said anxiously.

"You could stand up except for the ride to the Cramton home," Anna suggested.

"Well, help me finish my hairdo and put on the veil. For something old, I have grandmother's handkerchief. For something new, my dress. And for something borrowed… what can I use for that?" Miriam asked.

"You can borrow my hair combs, if you return them. And for something blue, you already have blue knitted trim on one petticoat," Anna laughed.

"Before I put on my new white patent leather shoes, I should put a silver coin inside. Hope that doesn't make them any tighter than they are already."

"Here is your parasol. You look wonderful. However don't look in the mirror, just take my word for it. You aren't supposed to see yourself before the wedding and neither is Timothy," Anna reminded.

"You better hurry and put on your own dress, Anna. Jackson will be here right on the dot of 1:30, and I do need to arrive before the Larsen family does, so I can wait inside the house."

Miriam stood in the kitchen while her sisters finished dressing and came out with their matching apricot dresses. "Now, Elizabeth, when you arrive, sit down with Anna and do not be running around. After the wedding and reception, you can change your clothes because this dress is not to be worn chasing Seth around the garden," Lydia warned sternly.

"Seth won't be running around the garden today, Mama. He knows his father would spank him for doing that," Elizabeth responded quickly.

"Here is Jackson. Come look at this rig, Charles," Aaron called from the porch. "I will help you girls into the carriage." To Jackson he said, "You really look dressed up today, Jackson. That black jacket and white shirt look all-fired spiffy with your overalls."

"Thank you, Mr. Jensen. These girls look like a whole garden of apricot roses with a white lily in the middle. Are we ready to leave?" he asked as he shook the reins on the high stepping black geldings.

"I truly feel like a queen today, Jackson, in this beautiful carriage with you as driver," Miriam exclaimed.

"You are the queen for today, Miss Jensen, and you look like one. Now where do you want me to stop the carriage?" Jackson asked.

"Let me off at the front door so I can wait inside. Anna and the girls can wait in the garden until the rest of the family arrives."

"You would think this was Miz Cramton's wedding the way she is all fussed up about it. She had Annabel cooking all week, although Annabel loves doing it for you. I've cleaned the front steps at least ten times just to make sure there isn't one speck of dirt," Jackson chuckled.

"I've made so much extra work for all of you," Miriam said anxiously.

"Now, don't you worry your head about that. No, not one little bit. We all are lovin' every minute of it."

Miriam was surprised to see new potted roses all around the front door of the Cramton house. Jackson helped her down from the carriage while Anna held up the hem of her dress to keep it from getting dirty. Thomas opened the door before she could knock, "Come right in beautiful bride. Mary is waiting in the parlor for you," he said with a deep bow.

"Mr. Cramton, you are making me feel like a queen also. Jackson told me I was queen for the day."

"Well, you are in our eyes also. We all rejoice with you and pray for God's blessing on your marriage," Thomas assured.

"Miriam, you made that dress! I can't believe you sewed it all. It is more beautiful than the $500 one that Melody purchased in Boston. I don't know why she chose brilliant blue. It may be in style in Boston. However I love your creamy white silk dress, it's so much more exquisite," Mary flattered. "Here is your wedding bouquet, I had it made up from some of the roses Jackson raised. I thought the peach colored roses with baby's breath would look wonderful with your dress."

"Thank you, Mrs. Cramton, you are so thoughtful. Before I forget, where could I change clothes after the reception? I need to put my valise there so Timothy and I can leave from here for our trip."

"You may use Melody's room. Just leave your wedding dress there and I will take care of it for you. Your mother probably doesn't have a good place to store it anyway."

"Are you coming out to the garden during the wedding, Mrs. Cramton?" Miriam asked.

"No, it is so difficult to move my wheel chair over the lawn. I can see well from here and with the windows open, I can hear everything of the service. That way I will be ready for those who come inside for the reception. Look, here come Timothy and Daniel in the buggy. Doesn't Timothy look handsome in his black suit? He must have put some bear grease on his hair, it isn't blowing like it usually does."

"Yes, he does look handsome. His family is coming next in the carriage. There's Grandmother Glendinning and Aunt Jesse in the next buggy. Everyone is coming at once," Miriam said excitedly.

"Your parents are pulling in now. Doesn't your mother look pretty in that pale peach silk and the matching hat?"

"My heart is pounding, what if I faint before I get out there?" Miriam said breathlessly.

"Take some deep breaths and I will pray that you can relax," Mary answered.

The grandfather clock struck two as Aaron came to the door to escort Miriam to stand beside Timothy under the rose arbor. They waited until Tabitha and Emma tossed rose petals along the path to the arbor. Anna and Sarah stood on one side and Daniel and Joseph stood up with Timothy. Elizabeth walked alone with the ring pillow in her hands, swishing her ruffled skirt from side to side. "Are you ready, Miriam?" Aaron asked a little nervously.

"Yes, Father, I am ready," she said as she looked at Timothy whose blue eyes were shinning as he waited for her with a big smile. "I am not going to faint after all," she said in relief.

They had just gotten up to the rose arbor when there was a slight disturbance behind them. Some people were whispering. Miriam wanted to look, she wondered, *Who would cause a stir like that?* She kept her eyes on Timothy, who could see what had happened. He didn't seem concerned so she relaxed.

Aaron picked up his violin and after a scratchy start played, *Love Divine, All Loves Excelling,* in a clear melodious sound. Everyone quieted down and sat in awe at the quality of his playing. Reverend Stanwick, standing in front of Timothy and Miriam, said, "Brethren, we are gathered together on this special occasion to witness the vows of Timothy Larsen and Miriam Jensen. Let's first of all ask God to bless this special occasion."

Following the prayer, he continued, "Since God has fore-ordained marriage at the creation of the world by saying that a man must leave father and mother, cleave to his wife, and the two become one flesh, Timothy and Miriam have chosen today as their wedding day. They asked me to share with you their desire to make Christ the center of their home. The Scripture they have chosen for today is I Corinthians 13. 'Though I speak with the tongues of man and of angels and have not love, I am become as sounding brass or a tinkling cymbal … Love suffers long, and is kind; love envieth not; love vaunteth not itself, is not puffed up. Does not behave itself unseemly. Seeketh not its own, is not easily provoked, thinketh no evil, rejoiceth not in iniquity, but rejoices in the truth; bears all things, believes all things, hopes all things, endures all things … And now abideth faith, hope, love these three; but the greatest of these is love.'

Timothy will now share with you a few words about their desire to be obedient to God," Reverend Stanwick continued. "Turn around so that the congregation can see your face."

"Friends and kinfolk, I am not much at talking in front of people, but ever since I was young I've prayed that God would give me a wife who loved God and was obedient to Him. He answered that prayer by bringing Miriam into my life and her father has allowed me to court her these last few months. We ask that you all pray that God will bless our marriage and that we will be obedient to him. Thank you," Timothy said quietly.

"Now we will be favored with a song, *Now Thank We All Our God*, by Timothy and his brother Daniel," Reverend Stanwick announced. Aaron accompanied them with the violin. Hearing Timothy sing gave Miriam goosebumps. She was thinking, *He sings with such assurance of God's love and ours.*

Reverend Stanwick said, "Now we will have the giving of the ring." Daniel reached for the ring on the pillow in Elizabeth's hand. She started to jerk it away with a whispered, "No!" She then stopped and glanced up at Timothy, who shook his head. Sheepishly she handed the pillow to Daniel. Miriam could see her standing there with pouting lips. *She doesn't want me to take Timothy away from her. She still isn't convinced that she will see us almost as often.*

Daniel handed the ring to Reverend Stanwick. "See the perfect circle of the ring, it is a symbol of perfect love which continues forever and ever. Timothy, take this ring, place it on the finger of Miriam, and repeat after me. With this ring, I thee wed…"

Miriam loved the feel of the ring on her hand and thought, *This is a symbol of our marriage and I will wear it proudly.*

Aaron played another hymn, *O Perfect Love*, with the same sweet quality.

"Let us pray," Rev Stanwick announced. "Heavenly Father, we ask that You bless this marriage with Your love as

Miriam and Timothy seek to be obedient to you. We ask this in the name of Your Son, Jesus Christ, Amen," To Miriam and Timothy he said, "Turn around and face the congregation. Now, may I present to you, Mr. and Mrs. Timothy Larsen. What God has joined together let no man put asunder."

Timothy took Miriam's hand and walked back through the congregation toward the house. Two occupants of the last row almost exploded out of their seats as Melody and Walter came toward them. Melody hugged Miriam saying, "Miriam, that was a wonderful wedding service. We almost didn't come. However, at the last minute, I decided that we should be here so we threw our clothes in the valise and took the last evening train out of Boston. We've been traveling all night. Almost missed the wedding because we couldn't get a carriage to take us from the depot," she said irritably.

"Yes, she was as mad as a March hare before we found a ride," Walter added indignantly.

Melody, dressed in a very expensive, although rumpled dress, walked along beside Miriam. "What made you decide to have your wedding here, Miriam?"

"Ever since I first came here to visit you, I have admired the roses that Jackson raised. I told him a year or more ago that I would like to get married in the garden. That was even before Timothy started courting me. Your mother was so excited about us having the wedding here that she insisted on having the reception at the house. She would have done the same for you, Melody."

"I couldn't allow her to do it because I was afraid that she would try to prevent me from marrying Walter."

"How are you enjoying housework and cooking now, Mrs. Van Squoit?" Timothy asked from the other side of Miriam.

"I can't say that I like housework, so Walter found a maid for me the first week. I am much too busy to be stuck at home all day with mundane things like cooking and cleaning. We women in suffrage must get the word out for our cause. We hope to be voting by the next election," Melody answered arrogantly. Looking up suddenly at the other guests, Melody asked, "Isn't that your great grandmother Glendinning, Miriam?"

"Yes, it is. I didn't know that you knew her."

"Don't you remember that I took the train to Minneapolis and visited with her about Woman's suffrage before I went to Boston? I must visit with her about all the progress we are making." Melody left them with Walter, who was walking behind them.

"Walter, how is married life treating you?" Timothy asked.

"We were eating out every meal until I found a maid who could cook. Melody doesn't seem to be able to cook anything. Said she forgot everything she had ever known about it," he grumbled.

"Come on inside, Walter, and meet the rest of our families and friends. Looks like Melody will be awhile visiting with Miriam's great grandmother," Timothy invited.

Walking into the dining room, Walter gasped, "What a spread they have for you! They didn't provide that much for their own daughter."

Miriam whispered to Walter, "I told Mrs. Cramton not to do all this; she insisted because she loves to entertain, she said. She also said that's where Melody learned her love for entertaining."

"Does she ever! She uses up half my paycheck entertaining every week," Walter complained.

Mary spotted Melody and Walter and rolled her wheel chair over to where Walter was talking to Miriam and Timothy. "I didn't know you were coming, Walter. Will you be staying the night here?"

"Melody hasn't said what our plans will be. All I know is that we will be leaving tomorrow afternoon," Walter answered rather brusquely.

Mary said to Timothy and Miriam, "You need to come cut the wedding cake. The silver knife is there beside it. We are all

Miriam and Timothy's wedding at the Cramton home.
(Known as Bartleson house in Beloit, built in the 1890's.)

waiting for you to feed Timothy the first piece, Miriam."

Miriam picked up the knife and with Timothy's hand around hers, they cut a small piece. "Now feed it to him, Miriam. Then he can feed a piece to you," Mary instructed.

Timothy took Miriam around the room to meet his aunts and uncles and she introduced him to her great grandmother who was still talking to Melody. "Grandmother, this is my husband, Timothy Larsen. Thank you for coming to the wedding."

"It wore me out, although Jesse got me a good room in the hotel."

Suzanne came over to Timothy and Miriam, "That was a beautiful wedding. It showed how important Christ is in your marriage. Are you going to throw your bouquet so we unmarried ladies can catch it? I don't really believe that proves we will be the next one married, although it is fun."

"Yes, I can throw it from the top of the stairs." She was lifting her skirt and carefully walking up the stairs when Thomas spotted her and called, "Watch out girls, the new Mrs. Larsen is going to throw her bouquet. See if you can catch it."

Anna was visiting with her cousins when the bouquet dropped almost into her hands. "I caught it without even trying!" she exclaimed.

Elizabeth came shyly over to Timothy and reached for his hand. "Can I go with you and Miry on your trip?" she whispered.

Timothy stooped down so that he could hear above the noise in the crowded room, "What did you say, Elizabeth?"

"I asked if I could go with you and Miry on your trip tonight." she asked so sweetly.

"I am sorry, Elizabeth, this trip is just for Miriam and me. However, one of these days we will take you on a trip with us. Do you think you could wait until then?" Timothy asked pleasantly.

"Maybe I could, but I want to go this time," Elizabeth said sadly.

Timothy looked at the clock and said to Miriam, who came to stand beside him, "It is almost five o'clock. Why don't you change to your traveling clothes and Daniel will take us to the train depot. The train leaves at six."

Elizabeth listened to all of the conversation and without a word to anyone, disappeared into the kitchen where she had put her clothes for after the wedding.

Miriam saw her leave and thought she might have gone to talk to Annabel.

Miriam motioned to Anna to come help her with the wedding dress. "Timothy wants to be leaving soon for the depot. I need help taking this off."

"Do you know when you will return, Miriam?"

"No, however Timothy said we would be gone only a few days. He has farm work to do as soon as we return. If anyone calls for help with babies, send them to Dr. Blackwood. I haven't asked Timothy how soon he wants me to be available for midwife work again."

Miriam, dressed in her black silk and black hat, stood waiting for Timothy at the door. Melody saw her and came over to whisper, "You might like to know that I have been going to a little church on Sunday evenings. They have some good Bible preaching that I miss. Don't give up praying for Walter, he may decide to go with me some Sunday night."

Grabbing her by the arm, Miriam said, "Melody, why don't you stay here with your parents tonight and rebuild a good relationship. They are still hurting from the way you handled the wedding."

"I'll think about it, Miriam. Oh, there is Timothy. He looks like he is ready to leave. Thank you for inviting me to the wedding. I am glad I came."

Miriam gave her mother and father a hug. "Thank you for all you did for all this to happen today." Going to Mary Cramton, she said, "Mrs. Cramton, thank you so much. You have made me feel like a queen today. I hope you have enjoyed it as much as I have. I will visit you after we return from our trip and do a more thorough job of thanking you."

"You have thanked me sufficiently. It was my pleasure. We will take care of your wedding gifts until you return. There is no use of your mother taking them over there. Or did you want Martha Larsen to take them to your home?"

"Just keep them here. That will give us an excuse to visit you very soon. Oh, before I forget. I suggested to Melody that they stay here tonight. She said that she would think about it," Miriam spoke quietly to Mary.

Miriam saw Rose Cramton sitting over in the corner. "Timothy, I must speak to Mrs. Cramton, before I leave. I need to tell her that our prayers for Melody are being answered." She hurried to speak to Thomas's mother who was visiting with some of Timothy's kinfolk.

"Mrs. Cramton, I wanted you to know before I left that Melody told me a minute ago that she is going to a little church Sunday evenings that teaches good Bible lessons. She told me to continue to pray for Walter."

"Thank you, my dear, for taking time from your special night to tell me. Now, go with your husband and my prayers go with you," she spoke earnestly.

Daniel was waiting in the buggy for Miriam and Timothy. "Look at the old shoes they tied to the back, and Miriam, get prepared for the rice to be thrown. I see people out there holding bags of rice," Timothy whispered to her.

Running through the rice shower and calls of, "May you have lots of prosperity and good," Timothy helped Miriam into the buggy, and waving to everyone, they took off at a fast pace into the late evening shadows.

Pulling into the depot, Daniel stopped and helped Miriam down while Timothy brought the valise. Out from under a blanket in the back, hopped Elizabeth. "Please let me go with you, Timothy," she begged.

"Elizabeth Jean, Father will spank you when he finds out that you have come without his permission. You get right back in that buggy with Daniel and stay with Mother and Father. Do you hear me?" Miriam said firmly.

"Yes, Miry. Why can't I go with Timothy?" she sobbed.

Timothy took her by the hand and whispered. "Tonight you get to ride in the buggy with Daniel, my brother. He is almost as good as me. You can show him your butterflies until I get back. Would that be alright?"

"I guess so," she sniffed and put her hand in Daniel's big hand allowing him to put her back in the buggy.

"Sometimes my little sister can be awfully stubborn. Father had told her this morning that she could not go with us."

"She is so sweet that is it hard to turn her down. We will have to have her visit as soon as we return," Timothy said gently.

The train was almost ready to leave, so Miriam and Timothy found seats in the back. "I am so tired, Timothy, I think I would fall asleep immediately, if I wasn't so excited from the wedding. Just think of all the work we did preparing for our wedding and it is all over in a few short hours."

"Put your head on my shoulder and rest. It will take several hours for us to arrive in Wichita," Timothy said as he took her small hand in his work hardened hand. "I want you to know how much I love you and how much I thank God for you," Timothy whispered in her ear, although they were the only passengers in the back of the car.

Laying her head on his shoulder, Miriam snuggled up to her new husband. "I love you too, Timothy. God has truly blessed us by answering our prayer for a Christian helpmeet."

"Let's just rest for awhile and reflect on this magnificent day." He tipped up her head and gave her a long, gentle kiss. "That is your first kiss, Mrs. Larsen. How does it feel?"

"It feels wonderful, Mr. Larsen," she whispered. "It was

worth all the waiting while we courted. Isn't God's plan wonderful?"

"That kiss is just the beginning of what you will receive in the years to come. I want you to be the happiest wife in the world," Timothy promised as he wrapped his arms tenderly around her. "We both have learned that God's plans are always magnificent, Miriam, because He created us and knows exactly what we need. We can trust Him with every area of our lives. Even the accident with my leg worked out for good and your runaway with the horses taught us both something of God's protection. God planned for married love. I know, because He put so much about it His Word. We can read Song of Solomon together while on our wedding trip. Yes, Mrs. Larsen, I am looking forward to a hundred years of living with you."

— *The End* —

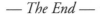

Coming next in the Miriam Series:
Miriam and Timothy Face Life

AUTHOR'S NOTES

Courtship of Miriam has a setting in Beloit, Kansas 1900-1905. The history part of the book is as true as I could find from research. Much of the information was found in the *Beloit Gazette* 1903 issues as well as from the Mitchell County Museum. Carlton and Gladys graciously looked for pictures and information on events and buildings in Beloit during the early 1900s. Peg Luke provided the picture of the paddle wheel steam boat.

Marla Jean Davis, of Abilene's *Shooting Star Enterprises*, provided information on the clothing worn during the 1900s. Marla Jean designs vintage clothing. Carol Bloom of Lawrence provided her knowledge of cloth and her special *No Idle Hands* book for a resource.

A biography of Buffalo Bill Cody provided the information on his Wild West show appearing in Omaha.

The information on Woman's Suffrage came from my husband's great grandmother's copies of *The Woman's Column* as well as information from an encyclopedia. Janet Glendinning

Adee's diary also provided additional information on women gaining the right to vote.

Information on famous people appearing at the Beloit Chautauqua came from the *Beloit Gazette*. Booker T. Washington was another famous person who spoke there.

Courtship in 1903 may sound like something impossible for today, but many families across the United States are going back to courtship for their children to prepare them for marriage. They find that it promotes long-term marriages and is well accepted by their teenagers who have been taught the advantages of courtship and met their future spouses in this method.

As I learned from a book called, *From the Front Porch To the Back Seat,* dating was not the accepted policy in United States until cars became more prevalent. I have recently heard tapes and read books from several teenagers who highly recommend courtship as a wonderful policy freeing them from being pushed into dating. In the resource list, I have included several books and tapes that are available, should you desire more information on the topic of courtship.

RESOURCES

Books by Castleberry Farms Press of P. O. Box 337, Poplar, Wisconsin 54864 or from most any Christian bookstore. Their books include: *The Courtship of Sarah McLean*; *Waiting for Her Isaac,* and *The Courtship of Jeff McLean.*

Tapes and Books by Norm Wakefield whose two daughters met their husbands through courtship, can be ordered from: Elijah Ministries, 17911 Bushard St., stw. 13, Fountain Valley, California 92708 or e-mail him at **elijahmin@earthlink.net** or go to his website:

> **http//home.earthlink.net/~elijahmin/**

Their tapes include:
> *A Marriage Arranged in Heaven*
> *Robert and Alyssa Welch's Testimony*
> *Preparing Your Teen for Life*

Josh Harris' tape and book, *I Kissed Dating Goodbye,* can be ordered from Nobel Publishing Company, P O Box 2250, Gresham, Oregon 97030. Telephone orders: 800-225-5259.

Family Ministries, PO Box 1412, Fair Oaks, CA 95628. Credit card orders: 800-545-1729.

Preparing Your Children For Courtship and Marriage: from Toddlers to Teens by Reb Bradley. 6 tapes and syllabus $32.

Dating: Is It Worth the Risk? booklet $5.

Her Hand in Marriage by Douglas Wilson for parents. $5.

The Author:

This is Donna Adee's second historical novel. She has written many stories about life on their farm in central Kansas, some of which have been published in farm magazines. She has also written biographical sketches for magazines such as *Mature Living* and *Parenting Treasures*.

Her first book, *God's Special Child, Lessons from Nathan and Other Children With Special Needs* is the story of their son, Nathan, who was born with Prader Willi Syndrome. This book has been an encouragement to parents whose children have many types of special needs. *Miriam's Dilemma* was the first title in the Miriam Series.

Donna and her husband, Ellis, are parents of two other children, Chris and Eric, and have four grandchildren.

Cover Illustrator:

Ann Gower lives with her husband, Dan, and niece, Lindsey, on a farm near Tonganoxie, KS. Ann has done wildlife pictures for the Denver National History Museum and pastels for the director of the Denver Zoo. Her carefully researched historical mural covers a wall in the Tongonoxie city library.

Chapter Illustrator:

Julia Bland of Lincoln, Kansas, has had a lifetime hobby of drawing and painting. She works mostly in pen and ink, water colors and oils. She is a member of the Kansas Academy of Oil Painters and her work is found in homes and businesses in the Lincoln area.

Julia is a pastor's wife, the mother of six children and she is the grandmother of fifteen.

She is the author and illustrator of several books of sermons for children, which are a resource for pastors and teachers in religious education. Julia and her husband, John, continue to serve churches in Barnard and Ashgrove, Kansas.